FROZEN Barriers

Sara Shirley

Cover Design by Renee Ericson, RE Creatives

Formatting by Jovana Shirley, Unforeseen Editing, www.unforeseenediting.com

Editing by Paige Maroney Smith

DEDICATION

For my husband RLP

You told me to write.....
.....I hope I made you proud

Fran.
Thank you
for all the love
and support.
love
Sara

CONTENTS

PROLOGUE

Emily

2001

It was time for my skating club's annual showcase. I had just celebrated my eleventh birthday the week before, and Mother insisted we not have a huge party for fear that my showcase outfit might not fit. Instead, I was forced to listen to my parents, Victoria and Charles Cameron, argue over ridiculous nonsense that I couldn't understand at such a young age. My mother, the always-perfect image in the public eye, was nothing more than a closet Cruella Deville. She saw I was visibly affected by the argument and assured me that my father was just trying to make her understand what was best for his family. I shook my head as though I didn't understand completely, and in all honesty, I didn't. Why couldn't I have a normal birthday party like every other kid my age? While everyone else at my private school had their own fair share of family issues, at least their parents didn't have issues celebrating birthdays. Most of my friends at school stopped inviting me to their own birthday parties simply because Mother said it was not a healthy environment for an upcoming star figure skater to be involved in. At eleven, who was I to say otherwise? She was my mother; I assumed she knew what she was doing. Man, was I ever wrong! It was times like this that I wished they would have had another child, so I would at least have had someone else around to endure some of the constant alone time.

The showcase dress rehearsal always fell on a Friday afternoon. Mother would have me released early from school because she said dress rehearsal or not I was still going to spend the extra time getting hair and makeup done just in case something didn't look right with one of the four group outfits I was forced to wear. Heaven forbid I looked like an eleven-year-old instead of some freak show from those pageants on television. She constantly told me, "Appearances, Emily— always remember you must not embarrass the family." *Thank you, Mother. I'll try not to forget the oversized mansion you and Daddy reside in on the cul-de-sac in Andover, Massachusetts.* I was but a mere doll Mother played dress up with all to keep face and make sure everyone else in the skating club knew she had money and prestige and some of the other girls' families in my group did not.

Yes, even at eleven, I realized my life was going to be lonely and controlled, or rather, dictated, until I was actually able to make my own decisions as an adult.

Once my mother carefully placed all my skating outfits, skates, and grooming kits into the Mercedes, we were ready to go to rehearsal. Mid March in New England was never a pretty time of year. Snow started melting, leaving a muddy mess around every corner. Puddles formed, and the ugly brown snow that looked pretty in December was showing again. I somehow always related the layers of snow to my mother. No matter how many fresh coats of snow we received over the winter, if you kept peeling back each layer, the first layer was still the ugliest. Yeah, that was my mother. Fresh and pristine on the outside, but inside, she was still hideous.

At the rink, I was usually always quite happy. This was the only time I was able to socialize with girls my own age, and they had shared the same interest as me, skating. I had a few girls whom I actually considered close friends, even if they were only friends at the rink. Lily, Suzanne, and Morgan were my only chance each week to have a normal life of an eleven-year-old, even if it was just for the times we were training at the rink.

Mother dropped me off with my skate bag and told me to go inside while she brought in the remainder of my gear to the dressing room. I laughed as I walked into the rink. *Dressing room?* Clearly, she was delusional. Figure skaters didn't get *dressing rooms* at rinks; we got the stinky sweat-smelling hockey locker room still reeking from the stick practice that cleared out five minutes before we set up shop. I hated those hockey players. They always smelled, and they looked like mini transformers in their padding, waddling around like they owned the place. They ruined the ice every time we had skate practice after them because the Zamboni could never grind down their divots enough, and we'd catch toe picks and edges on all the holes in the ice. If I even so much as hit one of those holes and fell, Mother made sure I knew what was at stake. "Appearances, Emily." I swear, if I was ever admitted into a loony bin, it was because I just kept saying "appearances" over and over again.

Just as I was about to round the corner to go into the *dressing room* to change into my skates, a hockey player came barreling around the blind corner, knocking me on my rear. As I gathered my thoughts and glanced up, I scowled at the boy who looked no more than thirteen and stared at me with his mouth gaped open and his hair all disheveled from his hockey helmet.

He reached out his gloved hand to me and said, "Sorry, Barbie, didn't see you. Here, let me help you up."

I looked at his outstretched, wet gloved hand and back to his smirking face and said, "Eww, get your smelly glove away from me. I can help myself up, you jerk! My mother is going to be livid if you messed up my hair and dress." I quickly stood and inspected my first costume, and it looked okay. As I felt around my hair, nothing appeared out of place, so I glanced back over at the overstuffed Michelin kid seething as I remembered his comment just a moment before. "Where do you get off calling me Barbie? Who do you think you are?!"

His smile quickly turned into shock. "I …uhh…sorry. I really didn't see you."

"Whatever!" I stormed my way back into the locker room and started to get ready for the longest weekend of the skating season, not giving a second glance to the boy who almost ruined my appearance.

JEREMY

2001

My mom rushed home from her part-time job to ensure I was able to make it to hockey practice at the Valley Forum just south of the New Hampshire border. We lived over the border in a small Boston suburb called Tewksbury. On a good day without traffic, it was about a half-hour drive, which meant Mom had to leave her job early on Fridays since my little sister, Courtney, needed to be picked up from school, too. My older brother, Josh, at sixteen, was considered more responsible and was allowed to take the bus home alone or go to his friend's house after school.

My father, Travis Page, worked long, hard hours at a chemical distribution company in an industrial park. The pay was just enough to ensure we had a roof over our heads and a happy family environment to come home to. My mom, Grace, worked at the local grocery store bakery in order to pay for my hockey training. I could have chosen a less pricey sport, but once Dad gave me my first pair of skates and stick for my ninth birthday, I knew hockey was the sport for me.

Four years later, I was still going strong and moving up each year with my youth hockey team. I always guaranteed this was the right decision when I had my entire family cheering me on in the bleachers at all my games. Dad may have shown up late, but he was always there hitting me hard on my shoulder pads after every game saying, "Hell of a game, Jeremy! You keep getting better every fuckin' game!" Yeah, that was my dad, the proud one, with a mouth like a sailor. I think he showed everyone at work my hockey stat cards at least fifteen times each year when they came out.

Practice was finished, and a tournament was scheduled against another youth hockey team in the area. I was just about to start removing my gear in the locker room when I realized I'd left my stick in the player booth by the ice. I quickly turned around and sprinted back out to the ice area. It was not easy trying to speed walk in hockey skates and full gear. I was pretty tall for my age, but I still resembled that kid from the movie *A Christmas Story.*

As I turned the square corner to the hallway, my chest face planted right into this skinny blonde girl who dropped to the wet cushioned floor like a sack of potatoes. *Shit!* She quickly glanced up at me, and I immediately went speechless. She had the most amazing blue eyes I'd ever seen. She could seriously have passed as a cross between Princess Barbie and Cinderella with that sparkly fru fru dress and makeup thing she had going on. She couldn't have been more than ten, and yet, looked like a teenager with all that makeup. And, no, I had a little sister, so clearly I'd been forced to suffer through some Barbie playtime. That was the only reason I knew what Barbie looked like. I had a hockey image to maintain. If the guys at school found out I was forced to have Barbie playtime with Courtney on weekends, I would have never heard the end of it.

I quickly realized this girl was staring up at me scowling, no, seething at me. I reached out my gloved hand and said, "Sorry, Barbie, didn't see you. Here, let me help you up."

Her little nose squinted up, and she shook her head, swiftly standing on her own and boldly stating, "Eww, get your smelly glove away from me. I can help myself up, you jerk! My mother is going to be livid if you messed up my hair and dress!" Well, that was about right. I must have bumped into the Ice Queen instead of Princess Barbie. She briefly inspected her costume and hair and turned back to me. "Where do you get off calling me Barbie? Who do you think you are?!" I was completely speechless. I apologized nicely and offered to help, and yet, she was still mad at me for bumping into her. Was it really that bad? She didn't look hurt. No sooner did I apologize again, did she storm off shouting, "Whatever!"

I turned and continued walking back to grab my stick, almost getting run over myself this time by an older woman dressed in a business suit and moving with determination. Her arms were full of costumes, and she was wheeling in a suitcase. She offered no apology or acknowledgement of her little bump into me. If I had to take one guess, I could probably guess whose mom that was.

I grabbed my stick and hurried back to the locker room to change. After packing up my gear, I made my way out through the rink area to the front doors. On the way, I saw what could only be described as a guy's worst nightmare. Hundreds of girls of all ages dressed in sparkly spandex and God-awful glittery, sequined costumes screeching and crying. I tried to maneuver my way through all the girls waiting to take the ice, but most of them just rolled their eyes at me and started whispering. Once I saw Suzanne Dunn, I couldn't make my way to the exit fast enough. Suzanne and I attended Tewksbury Middle School together, and she was the craziest chick I knew. It also didn't help that she was smitten with my older brother.

Once he went off to high school, she thought if she made friends with me, she would be able to hang out with me to get to him. Little did Suzanne know, my brother, Josh, thought she was certifiably nuts!

"Hey, Jeremy!" Suzanne said.

"Shit," I mumble. "Hey, Sue. How are you?"

"Good, is your brother here?" I literally laughed. She looked at the smirk on my face, and you would have thought by the way she looked at me that I just told the teacher she cheated on her math exam, which technically she did last week, but I wasn't going to get involved.

"No, he's over at his friend's house tonight," I responded and slowly tried to move away from her when I saw out of the corner of my eye that blonde beauty with hypnotizing eyes making her way onto the ice. Suzanne turned to another girl and started talking to her, pointing to the girl on the ice. She must have known her if they were in the same skating club, but I was going to try to avoid any further conversations with her if I could.

I continued walking alongside the rink walls, noticing the perfectly put together woman who knocked into me before watching the girl on the ice. She was either her mom or coach; that was for sure. Either way, she looked like she meant business. Most skating moms sat and talked in the bleachers while their daughters trained on the ice. Not this woman, something told me she was different than the rest of them. I kept walking farther away, still studying the girl on the ice as the music flowed over the speakers and she effortlessly floated across the ice. She glided over to the end of the rink where I was walking, noting me watching her. She must have lost her train of thought, because at that moment, she caught an edge and slid right into the boards. Definitely embarrassed, she got up, brushed off the ice shavings, and skated away. The music stopped, and then I heard from the players' bench. "Emily Beth Cameron!! What was that?! Do you have any idea how careless that fall was?!"

Emily. My Barbie had a name. She spun around, and I saw genuine fear in her eyes. All the moms behind me started whispering, and I glanced over at Suzanne, who for the first time since I met her, did not say a word, but stared at Emily with sadness written all over her face. *What the hell?!* This was just figure skating, right? Hockey was full of fights, yelling, and sticks to the face. This was figure skating. It was supposed to be fun and happy, full of flair and beauty. What I was witnessing was clearly not that.

My mom appeared from the outside doors, and I started walking away, but briefly glanced back. Suzanne gave me a wave goodbye, and then Emily took her place at the end of the ice nearest me as her mom screamed, "Again, Emily!"

Emily turned and faced the glass, looking at me as I smiled at her. Immediately, she rolled her eyes, and our connection was gone. Her hand came up and visibly wiped away a stray tear from her eye. She shook her head as if clearing her thoughts, and then she struck a starting pose, letting out a long breath and planting a huge fake smile across her face as the music started and Gwen Stefani's voice singing "Just a Girl" echoed through the arena. Just like that, she turned and skated away.

It was then I heard my mom by my side ask, "Jeremy, do you know that girl?"

"No, Mom, not really, we kind of just bumped into each other earlier." I laughed a little.

"Poor girl looks years beyond her actual age. It's a shame." I saw my mom watching her skate across the ice some more and realized she noticed the difference between Emily and me. Emily was forced to skate, and I skated because I loved the game. In my game, it was as though she was in the penalty box and never coming out.

CHAPTER one

2013

My earliest memory in life involves figure skating. Every memory since is only of figure skating. I wake up, train, and sleep. I believe I might actually be permitted to eat and shower somewhere in there, too. I have no other friends outside of the rink walls, and I'm not allowed. For over fifteen years, this has been my life. This was never my choice; it was what Mother told me to do growing up. I'm apparently never going to be allowed anything else until the day I retire. Ha! That's not going to happen. She'll never allow me to retire from this life. Some days I wish for that one fall that ends my career altogether, so my life can finally change. Then, what happens with my life? I haven't lived a normal life growing up. I don't have friends to support me, and it's not as though I'm hiring material for a job. I mean, seriously, I may have a college degree, which I'm pretty sure my father bought off because I spent the majority of my college years competing for the coveted gold medal. I live this nightmare every single day.

I thought on my eighteenth birthday that I would have the final say and be able to move on from the competitions and from the daily trips to the rink for training with my overpriced coach. I wanted to begin living my life; I'd already lost my childhood and teenage years to my mother's insane addiction to my skating career. Eighteen came and went, and I thought I had a chance when I graduated from high school and cornered my parents in Daddy's office, explaining how I wanted to learn what it was like to be in the real world and see what other options I had outside of the skating world.

My father sat there silent, sitting is his oversized chair, staring at me without any emotion. His eyes turned to my mother, who looked right back at me and said without waver, "Emily, your father and I have spent a fortune on your skating career, in which you have made a name for yourself on the national level. How would it look if you were to just walk away now? You have to consider how this affects your family name. It's not a wise decision when there is so much more for you to accomplish, or should we remind you how you failed to make it on the podium to get to the World Championships last year?"

There it was. Me against the world. I was never going to win, for fear my parents' precious name would be tarnished by my sudden retirement in order to live my own life. Heaven forbid I ruin their appearances by moving on in the world.

Since I didn't make it to the World Championships that year, my mother felt I needed to have a better path. That better path involved me enrolling in college in Boston, which I never saw a classroom, and then losing my only friends I had at my old rink. I had a new coach, Suzy Stacy, a former coach to Olympic medalist Nancy Kerrigan. My mother wanted to spare no expense. Being a medalist and on an Olympic team meant more to her than it did to me.

I had hoped my training would slow down, as I grew older, when in fact, it has become just the opposite. I make the drive into Boston four days a week for hours of training sessions with Suzy. Then, in between that, I have ballet, strength, and yoga classes amidst a strict diet plan and regular visits to the salon and spa. All of this just to keep my mother happy. At least at night, once I've made it home from unbearable traffic for an hour on Route 93, I can still relax in my room, open my e-reader, or turn on the television or radio and escape before I fall asleep.

The only day of the week where I find inner peace and happiness now is when I drive here to my old rink and have early morning ice time all to myself. My mother isn't here to critique my skating, and with solitude and my iPod blasting through my little Bose speakers, I just skate and feel the music. Sometimes I run laps around the rink. Other times, I choreograph my own routine and just free skate. There are no judges or appearances; it's just me. It also keeps my mother happy, as she finds no problem paying the rental fee for my own ice time. She said, and I quote, "How wonderful, dear. You'll be able to work on all the errors you made with Suzy during the week." Yeah, that's my mother. Thanks for the support!

On occasion, I see my friend Milton walking around the old Valley Forum. He's worked here since I was a kid. He usually keeps to himself while working on the daily repairs around the rink. Sometimes, when I get here, he'll still be on the Zamboni making sure I have a fresh coat of smooth ice. By the time I lace up my skates today, he's just about finished, and I tell him good morning. It's nice to have someone to talk to who won't judge me for what I've become. Hell, it's nice to have someone just to talk to.

JEREMY

I skate around the rink, warming up my legs and burning off the low-lying fog that is usually present on the ice surface early in the morning. The blades on my skates grind into the fresh coat of ice, allowing me to hear the crunching sound as I round each corner of the rink. I set up a net on the far end of the ice and drop about twenty pucks at the blue line near center ice. One by one, I slash my stick against the puck and aim for the net. They all go in, of course, it's always easier to score that goal when a goalie isn't standing in front of the net. After hitting the last puck, I hug the end of my stick between my Incredible Hulk sized gloves and sigh. This is my alone time. I have about twenty minutes each morning of free ice time, thanks to my buddy Dave who manages the front office and helps in the pro shop. He and I have been hockey buddies since middle school, so he lets me blow off some steam before all the Pee Wee League kids come in for practice.

Since my hockey days at Boston University, I've been actively trying to get drafted by the NHL. I've made a little progress, playing for the Manchester Monarchs just north of here in Manchester, New Hampshire. They are part of the American Hockey League and affiliated with the LA Kings. I'm not gonna lie; I would love to have been chosen on the Providence Bruins team, as they are an affiliate of the Boston Bruins, but beggars can't be choosers, and right now, I'm just glad I'm skating anywhere in the league.

I have never turned a blind eye toward where I came from. This rink, this is where my heart is and always will be. It's my sanctuary away from the team, the contracts, fans, booze, and well, eager women. It's crazy that even Minor League hockey players seem to be something of value to the opposite sex. It's here where I began my hockey career, moving from Squirt League to Pee Wee before starting high school hockey for Tewksbury. I managed a nice hockey scholarship to Boston University after being captain my junior and senior years and was named All-State Hockey Player my senior year.

On one of my days off from team practice and regular season games, I skate with the kids. It's funny how they all look at me as though I'm the rock star of hockey because they come up to see me play in Manchester sometimes. I've been out of college now for three years and haven't moved up in the hockey league since. It has always been my dream to make it big time, but if I'm dealt the cards I'm given, and this is the life I'm meant to live, then I'm not going to complain, because at the end of the day, I still have my family, friends, and in about fifteen minutes, a whole lot of smiling faces.

My mom, Grace, the eternal optimist, still believes I am meant to coach and stay in the area and to find the love of my life, settle down, and raise a beautiful family. I laugh at her ideas and often tell her that perhaps she has me confused with my sister Courtney. She's constantly seeking out the love of her life just so she can settle down. With my schedule and coaching, I'm lucky if I have time during the season to even sleep. I've dated a number of girls since college; however, I believe it was my college girlfriend Becca who said it best when she dumped me.

I still remember the day after my last game at Boston University my junior year. This was my last chance to get drafted by the NHL. Becca was with me and a number of others in my dorm, waiting through each of the picks to see if my name was called. I had secured plenty of records at BU, and my junior year was the best by far. Coach kept telling me I had a great shot, and he'd be surprised if I wasn't picked that year.

Team after team went up to the podium, but none of them called my name. Once the last team, and my last hope, walked up and off the stage, my NHL chances flashed before my eyes. Becca stayed by my side the previous two years and said she would stick by me no matter what because she loved me, and her feelings would never change. I thought I loved her too, but I was clearly thinking with my other head. She was my first sexual encounter, and although I wasn't her first, she at least made hockey off-season manageable.

It wasn't until I came out of my non-NHL draft haze that I realized she had disappeared. I went back to my bedroom and found her sitting at my desk playing with my iPod. She heard me come in and looked up at me when I shut the door. Quickly standing, she walked over to me. Placing her hand on my chest, she asked me to have a seat and that what she had to say wasn't going to be easy, but it needed to be said.

"Jeremy, we need to break up." Okay, I thought, that just came out of left field, but before I could interject, she continued, "I think you and I are moving in all the wrong directions. I mean, it's been fun the past two years standing by you as the captain of the hockey team, but it's clear you aren't going to have a future in the NHL, and unfortunately, I just can't sit around and wait for you to make it big time."

I thought, What the fuck?! Is she for real right now? I stood up and demanded, "What do you mean you can't sit around and wait? I thought you said you loved me and that your feelings would never change?"

It was at her response that I realized women are out for one thing and one thing only. Are you ready? Here's her response. "Oh, Jeremy, I never loved you. I just told you that in the hopes you would someday make it to the NHL, and you would marry me and support me while I looked good at your side. I mean, I heard all the talk about you being the next big thing in the NHL, but after today's draft, well, I can't just sit around anymore. I need to find someone who can give me what I want, and you aren't it anymore."

Deep Breaths. In and out. Fuck being calm! "Get out! Get the fuck out! Don't you ever think about seeking me out in the future when your plan goes to shit. You just totally summed up what you were to me all these years, a bad lay and even shittier girlfriend."

She walked out of my room and out of my life. Good riddance! She may have been a nice body with long blonde hair and a nice rack, but in all honesty, she wasn't ever wife material. And after that moment, I didn't think anyone would ever be.

My phone started ringing in my pocket, and I pulled it out to see my parents on the caller ID. I answered, knowing full well why they were calling. But after listening to

Becca's nonsense the past half an hour, I needed to talk to the people that really loved me for me.

I heard Dad on the other end of the line. "I saw the draft on TV, Son. Sorry, kid, I know what hockey means to you. But at the end of the day, you know you will still walk away from all of this with a great degree in Business Management. With that backbone, you will have an endless amount of opportunities if hockey isn't in the cards for you professionally."

"Thanks, Dad. I know I just have to keep working hard this next year and see what happens in the future."

My mom piped in and tried to change my train of thought, "Jeremy, be happy with the life you choose. It may not be what you dreamed of at the moment, but you can always change. Be happy with a life you can change to your needs. If you were contracted into the NHL and you weren't happy with that, how long do you think you would have had to be unhappy for?"

Shit, Mom had a point. I'd always wanted the big NHL contract, but it wasn't something I could try on for size, and if I didn't like it, return it for a refund. No. NHL meant contracts that have a legal binding over your head and your life. If I didn't like what was going on, I couldn't legally just walk away. It's funny how one minute my life was depending on one thing, but in the next, I had all the support in the world from my family telling me maybe this was a blessing in disguise.

That was four years ago, and all these years later, I look back and laugh. I'm happy with what I do, and I'm living my life without regret. I check the clock and realize the kids will be in the locker room soon, so I better go gear up. As I make my way back to the locker room, I turn the corner and nearly run right into a petite little blonde wearing a spandex skating outfit and leggings over her skirt. She's got her earplugs in and must not have heard me coming. I wonder what she's doing here so early. They have another rink on the other side of the building, but typically figure skaters aren't here this early in the morning. I stand off to the side and allow her to go by toward the exit. When I glance at her again, she's already well past me as she walks out the front door. Funny, that almost looks like Emily Cameron. No, it can't be. I haven't seen her since that night back in high school. I'm quickly brought out of my trance by a bunch of screaming eleven-year-olds in the locker room. I chuckle and walk toward the sounds, thinking, *Yeah, this is my happiness. These kids are my heart and soul, and no NHL contract would have ever brought me that.*

CHAPTER
two

Emily

2005

High school was always a difficult time for me. I hardly spent time amongst the other students in my grade at Andover High School. Most of the time, I ended up having to make up classes because I was out so much for training and competitions. It was no wonder after my freshman year of getting almost all incompletes in my classes that my parents were forced to home school me with a tutor. Apparently, no amount of bargaining with the school principal would allow student athletes any special benefits.

My tutor worked odd hours just so my parents could ensure my training never suffered. Imagine. My education took a backseat to my skating. I really couldn't make this shit up as the years progressed. I could hardly contain my anticipation for the day I turned eighteen. I was sure at that moment I would break free of the prison sentence I seemed to be serving all those years.

It was also even more troublesome when I began developing and maturing into my adult body. My mother would get upset at the fact that she couldn't control my little growth spurt. My breasts came in, hips turned out, and I grew to an above average height of five-foot-seven. In the skating world, this was the worst possible scenario. Jumps became even more of a challenge. The taller I became, the harder it was to judge my landings.

Mother was less than impressed. She insisted on extended training sessions to ensure I was on the right path to success. More coaching sessions were involved and increased gym time to make sure the Cameron *image* stayed intact. She never wanted to have me put forth any bad image that would come back negative to my father's business.

I rarely had time to socialize with my friends that I grew up with at the rink. Up until high school, I trained with my only three friends at the Valley Forum. Suzanne, Lily and Morgan were my link to the outside world and gossip. Being tutored at the house never allowed me to have any friends like the normal kids that were my age. I was at least allowed a computer, which kept me in touch with my girls by email and MySpace. I never had much time for phone calls, but I was able to drop them texts here and there just to see how things were going when I wasn't around the rink.

Suzanne seemed to be the most assertive of the three; she was slightly older than me and went to Tewksbury High School. Being seventeen, she was just finishing up her senior year. After free skate one day, I was packing up my gear when she approached me. Suzanne was preparing for her senior prom and had come up to me in the locker room to ask me if I wanted to head out for a bit to shop around for her prom dress and maybe grab some lunch. I'd never been approached much about spending time away from the rink with friends. To say I was stunned would have been an understatement.

I went to find my mother outside, and she wasn't immediately convinced I should go; however, once Suzanne was at my side trying to get my mother to agree, she finally conceded. Clearly, my mother knew she had an audience and didn't want rumors to spread about her inability to allow her only daughter to enjoy herself once in a while. My mother took my bag from my shoulder and leaned in to give me one of her fake hugs, only to quickly whisper into my ear, "Do not disappoint me, Emily." *Well, yes, Mother, that's exactly my goal in life. To spend a few hours outside of your grasp only to attempt to maliciously scar the family name.* She really did think so little of me as a human, let alone her own flesh and blood.

After Mother left, Suzanne dragged me by my arm to her car. I'd never been more excited and scared to have "girl" time in my life. I wasn't exactly sure how to just be normal since I'd never had an opportunity to have a social life. Suzanne, on the other hand, was a social butterfly.

Once we were in the car, I asked her where we were headed to find her prom dress. She turned down her radio and said that we were going to a small dress shop in Tewksbury. I found a bold curiosity, and asked, "Who are you going to prom with?" I was almost certain she was about to burst out of her skin she was so excited.

"His name is Josh Page. He's a few years older than me, but we have been dating for about a year now."

I was unaware of dating or boys in general. Yeah, we had a few guys who were in the skating club, but none of them were exactly looking for a *female* to date, if you catch my drift. This was a whole new territory for me, and my mother had never been forthcoming on dating advice, so I decided to approach the subject with Suzanne without making me appear too eager or ill-informed.

"Are you planning on having sex with him after prom?" She began laughing hysterically at me. I knew I should have curled into a ball and just kept quiet.

"Oh my gosh, Emily! I'm not a virgin. Josh and I have certainly had sex long before this."

"Really?" I said, more of a question than a statement.

"Yeah, hold on. Are you saying you haven't had sex yet?" Wait. No. Now, I want to crawl into a hole and never come out!

Suzanne turned her head to look at me and said, "Oh, Emily, don't worry. I'm sure you and your boyfriend will get there soon. I was fifteen when I first had sex." My gaping mouth must have been quite the image.

"Suzanne, I don't have a boyfriend. I've never even been on a date or kissed a boy."

It was then that I think Suzanne may have finally realized the error of her assumption and just how inexperienced I really was. "Emily, how have you never been kissed yet? I mean, look at you! You are stunning, and you have boobs that I would kill to have. You are every guy's wet dream!"

I knew I might regret it, but I wasn't going to learn *anything* from my mother, so it was either ask Suzanne or Google it later. "What's a wet dream?"

Suzanne quickly responded, "Oh my God! You are too funny!! Clearly, you haven't had Sex Ed at school, or your mother hasn't given you all the details needed yet, so I'm going to help you out with a little Sex Ed 101."

JEREMY

2005

I had just finished hockey practice when my brother came to pick me up at the rink. Josh had gotten fitted for his tux for his second prom. I still couldn't believe the idiot fell for that smitten kitten Suzanne. Nice girl, but those two together scream trouble. I already had my measurements for prom ready to go. With my senior hockey season over, I was still trying to stay conditioned for when I began college hockey in the fall with BU, so prom was the last thing on my mind. I probably wouldn't have even been going if it hadn't been for Josh. He said if he had to endure all the pain associated with being a college freshman at a high school prom, then I was going to have to suffer, too.

I didn't have much time for girls in high school, but that didn't stop any of them from hounding me to take them to the fuckin' event. They wouldn't relent until I finally picked one to go with. Suzanne was spending an afternoon at the house with Josh when she cornered me and said if I didn't choose a prom date soon, she was going to pick one for me. I laughed in her face, except for the fact she was dead serious. Once I stopped laughing at her, Josh looked at me and then back at Suzanne and shook his head.

Suzanne picked up her phone, and I heard her say, "Hey, Morgan! Just wondering if you are busy May 15th? ...No, you say?...How about you join me at my prom?...No, I know you don't swing that way, girl! I meant, tag along with me, but be Josh's brother's date... I don't know, 6'1", 210 pounds, brown hair, decent... No, you don't have to sleep with him, unless you want to... Okay, yeah, sounds good. Later." She hung up and stared at me with evident anger showing over my face.

"What the fuck was that?" I screamed.

"Jeremy!" I heard my mom scold from the kitchen. "What have I told you about your language? Just because your father can't control his profanities is no reason for you to follow in his footsteps."

"Sorry, Mom," I cowardly said.

"Suzanne, how could you possibly set me up with someone I've never met?"

"Oh, c'mon, Jeremy. You know Morgan. She's at the rink with me all the time," Suzanne said nonchalantly.

I tried to think of all the girls I'd seen with Suzanne at the rink. I never usually paid much attention to any of them, simply because they brought nothing but drama. There was one girl I remembered from years ago and thought maybe it was her, so I asked, "She's not the one whose mom always yells at her when she's on the ice, is it?" Suzanne gave me a look and a smirk like she knew exactly who I was talking about.

"That's Emily, but unless you want your ass handed to you on a platter, you'll steer clear of her. Her mother is the devil incarnate! I've been trying to get that poor girl to hang out with us for years, but her mother won't allow her out, for whatever reason. It's as though until she's an Olympic medalist she'll never let her have any fun, so she trains and competes. That's it. Rumor is, she's changing skating clubs soon too, because to have Olympic backing, you've got to have a big name club attached to your name."

"Is she really that good?" I asked, not sure why.

"She's the shit, but she never seems to love the fun in all of it like Morgan, Lily and I do," Suzanne said with a look of curiosity as she bounced her head between Josh and me.

"Okay, so clearly, we've sidetracked here to talking about this Emily, who the fu...heck is Morgan?" I summoned.

"Don't worry. You can meet her after I go pick out my dress next weekend. Josh and I are going to grab some lunch afterwards."

"Fine, but if you set me up with some bimbo who will not shut up all night, I will make sure my mom and dad know what you and Josh are up to in the hot tub out back at night. They wouldn't want their little Courtney walking outside to a sex session on full display, now would they?"

Josh stood right up and hugged Suzanne into his side. "Don't get your panties in a ruffle, Jeremy. You know once I'm done at the police academy, I'm out of here anyway."

My brother was about to complete the police academy in New Braintree and would soon be the newest patrolman on the Massachusetts State Police force, which meant he'd be moving out of the house just about the same time I would be trekking off to start my freshman year at Boston University. College life was not for him. As much as my parents would have loved for him to finish his education, his heart was only interested in going into the police force.

I was sitting in Josh's car, heading to lunch to meet Morgan, my set-up date for the prom, and feeling nothing but dread. Was it wrong to not want to attend your own prom?

Josh glanced over at me and punched my shoulder. "Hey, stop sulking! If Suzanne is friends with her, she'll be fine. Plus, it's not like you have to date her or anything. She'll probably spend most of the night with Suzanne anyway, so I guess you can dance with me." Josh winked at me and chuckled.

"Fuck off, asshole!" I spouted at him.

We pulled up to Margaritas, a local Mexican restaurant. "Guess we beat the girls," Josh said. "I'm going in and grabbing a table and let Sue know to meet us inside."

"Fine," I said, making my way toward the front door.

Once we were seated, it was about twenty minutes before Suzanne walked in with a cute little blonde chick with an incredible rack and small frame for her height. If this was Morgan, I had zero complaints, and would even hug Suzanne for the set up. Once the blonde looked over to us after stopping her conversation with Suzanne, raising her sunglasses on top of her head, her eyes met mine.

"Fuck me," I whispered. Josh took it upon himself to jab me in the side, clearly hearing my murmured words.

Suzanne came over to the table and sat down after giving Josh a little more than affectionate kiss in public. She looked at me as I gestured with my eyes to perhaps introduce me to the girl she set me up to take to prom.

"Oh!" she said. "Let me introduce you guys. Josh, Jeremy, this is Emily. She skates with me at the rink." *Hold the phone! Did she just say 'Emily'? Where the fuck was Morgan?* Not that I was complaining, because seriously, this girl was smokin' hot, but didn't Suzanne just say a few weeks ago how much baggage she had going on with her life?

"Hi, it's nice to meet you. Suzanne has been talking about this prom all afternoon. You guys must be excited to be going," Emily said, trying to avoid eye contact with me by glancing down to her lap as she turned a sweet shade of red.

"Emily, you might know Jeremy. He skates at the Valley Forum sometimes. Not so much anymore, now that he's out of the Pee Wee League, but he grew up there basically with all of us," Suzanne declared.

Emily peered up at me and quickly said, "I'm not sure I remember seeing you, but it's very possible I might have run into you in passing."

"Barbie." It slipped out of my mouth before I knew I said it out loud. Shit! Emily gave me a look of not only confusion but also recognition, but at least she couldn't place where she'd heard that before.

The waitress came over with chips and salsa and took our drink and food order. Emily ordered a side salad with no dressing. All three of us looked at her as if she had three heads, maybe because we all ordered enough food to feed a small city and this girl ordered a side salad and water. I mean, I got the need to stay in shape, but Emily clearly didn't need to watch her figure. She was maybe 110 pounds soaking wet. It was at this moment I was staring at her body, and most notably her C-cups, that she caught me gawking. Her mouth dropped open, and her teeth pulled at her lower lip. I swear my cock sprung to life. I needed a distraction and fast, so I said to Suzanne, "I thought you were supposed to be bringing Morgan with you?"

Shifting in her seat, Emily looked at Suzanne and asked, "Was Morgan supposed to come here, too?"

Suzanne answered, "Well, see, I set her up to go to prom with Jeremy because he didn't want to go, and Josh didn't want to not have a wingman all night. But, I never mentioned to her about the lunch, and then when I saw you at the rink, I asked you to tag along instead."

Emily looked taken aback. "So, you didn't really need my help today dress shopping? You were supposed to bring Morgan instead for your double date?"

Suzanne appeared as though she just ripped the poor girl's heart out. "Oh, Emily, no! Morgan already had her dress from her own prom at her high school, and she couldn't care less about Jeremy. She's just going with us so the dicks don't outnumber the cupcakes."

Emily appeared utterly confused, so I piped in, "What she means is Morgan and I don't even know each other. Suzanne just doesn't want to be outnumbered by the guys all night. Isn't that right, Sue?" Suzanne nodded and smiled at Emily, and things seemed to be cool again with the group.

Josh and Suzanne were feeding each other some of their lunch while Emily kept picking at her salad until she finally said, "Suzanne, I really think I ought to get going. My mother is going to be upset if I'm not back soon to take care of my class work."

Not ready to leave, Suzanne responded, "It's still early, Em. What's another half an hour? It will only take us ten minutes to get you home." Emily scratched her head, visibly despondent for some reason. I'd seen her mom at work years ago, so I had an idea why she wanted to get home, and yet I couldn't fathom living with such an overbearing parent.

Without thinking, I spoke up, "I can take you home if you want." Emily looked up, and I saw both relief and fear in her eyes. "I can take Josh's car, and Suzanne can take him home when they're ready."

Suzanne looked thrilled I suggested such a thing. "That would be great, Jeremy. If Emily really needs to leave then that will work out perfectly. Are you sure you don't want to stay, Em? I mean, if not, it was really fun this afternoon. It's just too bad we don't get to hang outside the rink more often. And, I still need to teach you more about wet dreams." My soda went spewing all over the table as I had a choking fit. Josh patted me on the back, trying to help me out.

"I told you she didn't have a filter," he said. "On that note, Emily, the ride back to your house still stands if you want to go."

Emily stood and thanked Suzanne for a great time. She was about to give her some money for lunch, but I quickly grabbed her hand from her purse, and her eyes shot up to mine.

"I've got this, Barbie." I threw a twenty onto the table and waved bye to the other two as I escorted Emily out to Josh's car.

In my brother's old Honda Accord, Emily buckled in and advised me where she lived in Andover. I started toward her house, and she cleared her throat, a sign she was uncomfortable sitting in the car with me.

"Why do you keep calling me Barbie?" she asked quietly. I chuckled to myself because she clearly had no idea who I was.

"I must have really made quite the impression on you if you don't remember me." She shook her head as she stared at me in utter confusion. "About four years ago, you were coming in for a dress rehearsal or something, and you were dressed in some crazy frilly getup with sparkles and nonsense. I was just finishing hockey practice at the Forum when you came out of nowhere, and I ran right into you, knocking you on your ass. I called you 'Barbie,' and when I bent over to try to help you up, you were so pissed you stormed off. I remember watching your practice session with my mom afterwards and thinking with your costume, makeup and hair, even at such a young age, you reminded me of a Princess Barbie doll. It kind of stuck, I guess."

She chuckled, and I felt as though I had butterflies in my stomach. *What the hell was wrong with me?* Girls never had that effect on me. Somehow this chick had worked her way around my finger, because I was pretty sure if she said jump, I'd ask how high.

"Oh my gosh! That was you? I was so mad at you for knocking me over that day," she said. We were maybe five minutes from Emily's house when she quickly suggested, "Perhaps you ought to drop me off at the end of the driveway."

"Emily, I can drive you up to your door, a few more feet won't run the gas tank dry."

"No, it's not that. It's just I was supposed to be out with Suzanne, and it might upset my mother if I show up with you," she timidly said.

I understood then. I remembered how her mom was and agreed, even though I wanted her to speak up and fight for once instead of getting trampled again. "Fine, but on one condition."

"What's that?" she questioned hesitantly.

"If I drop you off out here, you have to at least take my number and call me when you get home."

"Are you serious? You want me to call you when I get home when you are dropping me off at the end of my driveway?"

"Yeah, you can never be too careful. Plus, if you went missing between here and there, that will all be on me, and I don't really want to be the one who lost Emily Cameron."

She chuckled softly and glanced up at me shyly. "Give me your number, but you are totally being ridiculous and stop it with the Barbie name. I'm not eleven anymore."

"No, Emily, you are definitely not eleven anymore." With that slip of the tongue, I caught a slight blush creep across her cheeks as she looked away. *Why the hell was I flirting so much with her?* Clearing her throat, she pointed out that her parents' house was coming up just ahead. Pulling up to the end of her driveway, I parked outside of a large gate. "Look, if I can't see the house from here, how am I really supposed to know you got home okay?"

"Jeremy, really, it's right there. Nothing is going to happen, but for the sake of making you happy, I'll call you the minute I get inside."

With that, I gave her my cell number as she plugged it into her phone. Emily grabbed her bag and moved to open the door, but turned around to face me before leaving. "It was nice meeting you, Jeremy. I really appreciate the drive home and thanks for lunch."

"It was nice to meet you under different circumstances, Emily. I know Suzanne can be a bit much at times, but hopefully, we can all hang out again sometime soon."

She opened the passenger door and stepped out of the car, leaning over before shutting the door and giving me a nice view of her great rack. I chuckled to myself because she clearly had no idea she was flashing me.

"I hope so, too. It was fun to be away from the rink for a while with new people." She shut the door and quickly stepped through the gates and down the dimly lit driveway.

I wondered if she'd actually make good on my request for a phone call, so I waited it out for a few minutes. I mean, how long did it take for someone to walk the length of a driveway? If this were my house, I'd already be calling her. Clearly, we came from two completely different lifestyles, but somehow I had a feeling she was not all that happy living in hers.

About ten minutes later, my phone lit up next to me. Seriously, any longer and the neighborhood watch women would have been calling the police because I was sitting in my brother's old Accord on the street.

"Hey, Barbie."

"Stop calling me that! How did you know it was me calling?" she said quietly.

"Um, well, let's see. The only person I've been waiting for a call from is you and considering I no longer see you walking down your driveway, I'd assume it was either you calling or my brother looking for his car. But, my brother comes up on my caller ID as "Shithead," so it had to be you."

She chuckled. "You are a strange one, Jeremy Page. Did you really wait out there this entire time?"

"I'm a man of my word. If anything were to happen to you on my watch, I'd be devastated. I'm glad you made it home all right, though. Call me if you are ever at the rink again. Maybe I can show you some new moves."

"Only if you wear one of my frilly outfits and a whole lot of spandex," she retorted with a flirty attitude in her voice,

"I look forward to your call, Emily. I'll see you around."

"Sure, Jeremy. Thanks again for the ride. Bye."

With that, she hung up, and the line went dead. I turned on the engine and started to drive off when my brother called me.

"Dude, where the hell is my car? I've been waiting at Mom and Dad's for thirty minutes now, and Courtney is driving me nuts with the Spice Girls movie!"

I knew exactly what movie Josh was talking about, and Courtney had it playing all day and night, but so long as I had my earplugs in at the house, it wasn't so bad.

"I just left Emily's house, and I'm on my way home now."

"Please tell me you didn't do anything in my car, Jeremy," Josh said with a hint of curiosity.

"Dude, the girl is hot, but seriously, unless global warming occurs anytime soon, that's one ice princess who will never give me the time of day, let alone use your backseat for a make-out session." Although, in the back of my mind, she really was fun to be around and I would have liked to see what made her tick inside. Something told me there was more to her than what was on the surface. Hopefully, she'd call me, and I could make good on that deal. I could do more than make her blush if she caught me wearing anything in spandex.

CHAPTER Three

2013

It is my day off from training and the rink. I've made plans at the spa for a mani-pedi and then I'm heading over to the gym for a quick Barre and yoga class. At least I'll be able to take away a little bit of stress while I'm there. In a couple of months, my training will be probably every day, as my mother will require me to prepare for the US Nationals. Everything will be riding on my placing, considering this year's competition will be held in Boston. Mother says Daddy has donated a lot of money toward the advertising for his company and how it would look good for the family if I were to medal in my hometown. No pressure on my shoulders at all. A part of me would like to just stick it to them and not place in the top ten. That would really piss them off to no end. But, at the end of the day, who am I kidding? I'll end up making them happy, even if it means I'm not.

I'm wrapping up at the day spa and trying to keep my nails from hitting against anything when I hear someone shout my name. "Oh my gosh, Emily Cameron! Is that you?" I turn my head in that direction only to see Suzanne walking toward me. I smile politely, as it's been at least eight years since I've seen her. As she approaches me, she hurriedly strides up looking me over. "It is you! It's been so long. I can't believe how good you look! What on Earth are you doing up here?" She was always one for being overly dramatic.

"Hi, Suzanne. It's nice to see you, too. I was just in the area, so I drove up to see about getting a mani-pedi." I wave my nails at her. "It's my only day off for a while, so I needed some time to de-stress."

"Oh! That's right. You're still competing. I thought I read somewhere you were a top contender for this year's Nationals, right?!"

I sigh because this is all anyone knows or asks about me. Never does anyone ask me what I want to do or like to do besides the skating career. "Yeah, I'm still skating. You know my mother. She'll never let me do what I want, so I'm still training like crazy and competing at least five months out of the year."

She must sense my sadness because she immediately slaps her hand on my shoulder and looks me in the eyes. "Well, we need to totally catch up. I was about to go grab a quick bite and drink across the street. Come join me. I'm not taking no for an answer."

As she's grabbing my hand to drag me out the doors, she's chatting on the phone with someone, but as I look at the time on my phone, I realize there is no way I'm making it to my gym class on time. So much for my day off.

Suzanne and I walk across the parking lot to the Ninety-Nine restaurant. As we walk inside, Suzanne drops her phone back into her bag. We walk past the hostess station and down the back to a table where two guys are sitting with another girl. The girl looks up and smiles at Suzanne before bringing her into a huge hug. Suzanne whispers something into her ear before leaning over to one of the guys whose back is toward me. I wonder if I'm crashing this lunch, but she did say she wanted to catch up, so I'm pretty sure she thinks her friends won't mind me being here with them.

Once Suzanne turns back to me and waves me over, the guy she was talking to gets up and faces me. It's when I meet his eyes that I realize they are the only eyes that have ever had an effect on me. Those eyes that caused my heart to flutter and my hands to sweat from being so close so long ago. He moves over to me, allowing Suzanne to move into the booth and me to sit next to her.

As I make a move to slide in next to her, he leans down to my ear and whispers, "Hi, Barbie. You never called me back about showing you my moves." A ripple of something goes down my spine as I look up to him with my mouth hanging wide open in shock.

He's no longer that high school senior; he's a tall, lean mass of pure sex on a stick, and if I thought he was hot back then, it's going to be torture trying to get through lunch with him sitting beside me. At least this time around I have my own car to get me home.

JEREMY

We are all sitting in the booth at the Ninety-Nine waiting for Suzanne to come back from getting her phone fixed at the mall. Josh's shift ended, and he drove up to meet us. My sister Courtney is still good friends with Suzanne, and as odd as it is, Suzanne is a great addition to our little circle. She and Josh broke up a long time ago, but Courtney always saw her as the sister she never had, and well, they stuck like glue, and Josh just had to get used to it.

It isn't often that all of us have days and time off to meet up, so this is one of those gatherings that feels like a reunion. Courtney's phone starts ringing, and she begins chatting with someone, giving me a look and an evil grin. When she hangs up, she quickly starts giggling. Sometimes it's hard to forget my little sister is a junior in college and no longer a kid.

"What's so funny?" I'm intrigued at who might have been on the phone with her.

"You'll see. According to Sue, someone else will be joining us for lunch," Courtney says before a huge grin spreads across her face.

Aww, shit! Who the fuck did she run into at the mall, and why did she think it would be a good idea to bring them to have lunch with us?

Josh pipes up and asks, "Did she tell you who it is?" Courtney sucks on her straw and just nods her head up and down. "Do we know this person?" More nodding up and down. Courtney jumps out of the booth as she sees Suzanne walk in and gives her a squeal and hug. They start giggling, and Courtney looks over Suzanne's shoulder.

I have a feeling the other person is standing behind me, so I can't see. However, Josh is staring over his shoulder, and his jaw drops. "Holy shit," he whispers.

Suzanne leans down and whispers into my ear, "I seem to have stumbled upon someone at the mall who I believe you may have some unfinished business with." *Oh, for the love of God. Who the fuck did she find over there?* I stand, thinking I'm about to pummel someone, and then I see her eyes staring back at me. Fuck me. I just ran into her at the Forum a short time ago, but she walked by me. Now, she's staring at me, and it's like she's back in the car with me all over again, just eight years later and completely grown up. She's still got that killer body and insane rack.

I'm about to have a little fun with her, and I bet I can make her squirm in her seat a bit. As she's scooting into the booth next to Sue, I lean down and gently graze her ear, whispering, "Hey, Barbie. You never called me back about showing you my moves." She quietly gasps, turns her head slightly toward me, and just as I expected, her face blushes. I laugh to myself and sit down next to her, pushing in so close that my leg touches hers. She pulls back slightly, although she thinks I don't notice her nervousness. As she tries to slide farther away, I'm drawn into her low-cut top, and she smells like coconuts or something tropical. Motherfuck! I'm going to need to readjust myself a few times before this lunch is over.

Suzanne starts the introductions. "Emily, you remember Josh and Jeremy, but I don't believe you've met Courtney. Courtney is their little sister. She and I never could quite separated each other after this douche nozzle and I split up." At that remark, Josh growls deeply while bringing his beer up to his lips.

Emily shifts slightly, but speaks up, "Hi, Courtney. It's a pleasure meeting you. Yes, I remember Josh and Jeremy. It's been a while, but you guys haven't changed that much."

I laugh at that statement. Obviously, she didn't believe that because she completely ignored me at the rink a little while ago. Emily must notice my attention to her statement, as she turns her head toward me and cocks her eyes as if asking me, *What the fuck is your problem?*

Oh yeah, time for the games to begin. I bow my head, so only she can hear me. "Barbie, obviously, we all can't look the same after eight years or else you wouldn't have completely ignored my presence at the Forum just a few weeks ago. But, hey, we all can't be as *perfect* as you." Somehow, I think I may have sounded more annoyed than I wanted because she seriously looks wounded by my words and on the brink of tears. Shit. Her mouth drops open, and she turns her body away from me so all her attention is back on the rest of the group. Courtney, however, blatantly kicks my shin under the table, letting me know she heard my statement, and I guess it *didn't* come out as I intended it to.

"So, Emily," Suzanne says, "what have you been doing all this time since you left the Forum club? I don't usually see you on Facebook much since I graduated from college."

"My mother had me transfer to Boston Skating Club, and I attended Boston University for a while to major in geography, not that it did any good, though, since I've only been allowed to skate competitively for the last five years. I probably would have been able to stay in touch more had it not been for training and school."

Josh leans up on the table. "Funny you and little brother over here never ran into each other. He was apparently some hot shot on campus while he played hockey at BU."

"I never spent a lot of time on campus while I was there. I did a lot of my courses online because of my training schedule. Most of my competitions were during the school year, so I was either on the road or at the skating club until the season ended," Emily explains with sadness in her voice.

"Wow, you must be really good then if you travel that much for competitions. What's the one place you've been to that you've absolutely loved?" Courtney's eyes light up. "I love traveling. I just don't have the money to go very far, but someday."

"Well, I love the traveling aspect of competing, which is why I majored in geography at BU. I love history, environments, and cultures, but I never really got to experience much of that while away. Probably the most visually stunning city I've been to is Paris," Emily says with more enthusiasm.

"Don't let her fool you, Court. Emily here is the shit when it comes to skating! She ditched my skating club back in high school because she was that good. Isn't that right, Em? In fact, she's going to be one of the top contenders for the National Championship in Boston this year." Suzanne is so excited she's jumping in her seat.

Not trying to be mean, but more inquisitive, I ask, "I'm surprised you're still skating after all this time. I mean, for a figure skater, you're what twenty-two now? You must be starting to think of what you want to do once your competing days are over."

Again, Courtney kicks my shin under the table. *What the fuck?* I scowl at her as she gives me a stern eye. What did I say?

Emily looks at me, clearly taking my statement the wrong way. "Jeremy, I know I won't physically be able to compete much longer, and although it's not my first love, I really have no choice in the matter. As for what I plan to do after I am done, I'm not sure. I've never had that option to think about. *My life.* I've always had dreams of what my life would have been if not for skating or my parents, but I've never had that choice. So, if you want to sit here and try to make it sound as though I'm washed up at twenty-two and have no future path, go ahead. I don't see you with the big NHL contract, so that evidently means your big BU hockey player status didn't get you very far if you're still here and skating at the Forum."

Ouch. This one has fire underneath her façade.

"Oh my God!" Josh leans up to signal Emily for a high five. "That was fuckin' awesome, girl! I don't know where you just pulled that from, but damn, you just put Jeremy back in his rightful spot!" Everyone starts laughing, including me, because I'm truly happy where I am and contract or no contract, this is my life, and I'm still having fun. But, when I see Emily sitting there no longer chuckling, I know I fucked up.

Of course, at that moment, the waitress steps in and asks the girls what they'd like to drink. I'm more than shocked when Emily orders herself a Shipyard Pumpkinhead beer with a rim job. I glance at her, completely engrossed in her boldness, when the most amazing words come out of her mouth. "I don't know about you, Jeremy, but I just love licking off those rim jobs!" Time for me to readjust my cock again, thanks in part to my naughty little ice princess sitting next to me.

CHAPTER
four

Emily

Who does he think he is? He has no idea what my life is like, and to make it sound as though I'm some perfect little snotty brat with nothing but a face and bank account? True, my parents have funded my skating career; however, I've managed to do a few shows and won competitions that have allowed me to earn my own money. It hurts that he actually sees through my worst fear. What will I do when I can no longer compete? What happens when the endorsements are no longer there and the next generation of skaters is on the cusp of hitting it big? I honestly have no idea. I never wanted to continue with this lifestyle after high school, but once I managed to advance to the senior level, my parents wouldn't hear of me quitting. All they kept talking about was winning and making the family proud.

I must have been lost in my own mind, as I'm brought out of my thoughts by snapping fingers in front of my face. "Hello, Earth to Emily. Your rim job just arrived," Suzanne jokes.

"Oh, sorry. I didn't mean to zone out," I respond quietly.

I glance back over toward Jeremy who now has his phone out tapping on his screen and sipping his beer. I must have offended him or something because he's no longer even paying attention to the group. Fine, he wants to ignore me. I'll get his attention. Gathering up all my courage to act sexy in front of people I barely know, I pick up my Pumpkinhead beer and more than eagerly start licking off the cinnamon sugar rim with my tongue, moaning as if it's the best thing I've ever tasted. I can see out of the corner of my eye Sue, Josh and Courtney all chuckling at my apparent sexual bravado. I then look up to my right to see Jeremy's eyes bugging out of his head, his mouth hanging open, and his hand slightly tugging at his shorts. I stop my licking while staring him straight in the eyes, and because I can't hold it in any longer, I begin laughing hysterically.

Suzanne wraps her arm around my shoulders and exclaims, "Oh my God! You little vixen! I see I taught you well back in high school!"

"Hey, Jeremy. When is your next practice?" Courtney asks. *Practice?* I thought he was just skating around at the Forum.

"The team starts back up next week, but we've got meetings all this week, so I've got to work on some conditioning skills before then," he says, lowering his phone into his jeans pocket.

"Are you going to get us tickets again this year? You know Dad is your biggest fan, and he loves seeing you skate," Courtney says as she picks at the label on her beer bottle.

"Yeah, don't forget about your brother over here either, or the next time you drive down Route 93 you are getting pulled over," Josh says teasingly since he knows I drive that route all the time to get to the rink. Most of the time, he's covering the Boston area with his cruiser, but he'll swing up to the Andover sector on occasion.

"I'll see what I can do for you guys," Jeremy says.

Evidently, I missed something here. Why would they need tickets for games if he's only at the Forum? Sue must have sensed my confusion. "He's been playing for the Manchester Monarchs for a while," Suzanne states quietly into my ear.

Shit, really? Of course, this big cocky ass plays for a minor league hockey team. Me and my big mouth just made me the laughing stock of this table. They all probably think I'm completely full of myself. I honestly should have never agreed to come over here with Suzanne. Jeremy must have somehow heard Suzanne, because the minute she goes back to talking to Courtney, he leans his face my way and gives me a look and a smug smile that says, *Who's the ass now?*

I shake my head and look up from my beer as my eyes start to mist. "I'm sorry. I didn't think…I really ought to…Can I squeeze by you? I need to use the restroom." Jeremy moves out of the way, giving me a questioning look, but there is no way I'm making eye contact with anyone at the table now.

"Em, are you ok?" I hear Suzanne ask, but before I know it, I'm already in the ladies' room locked inside the stall. Why do I even try to be in social situations? I was never able to have normal friends to hang out with and talk to my entire childhood. Now, look at me. I'm so socially awkward that I've become a sniffling mess because I tried to be funny and fit in. I've completely embarrassed myself and now I've got to figure out some kind of excuse to get out of here as soon as possible.

After about five minutes, I make my way out of the bathroom doors only to walk right into a tall wall of a muscular man. His arms wrap around my elbows, and I look up into the same big, brown eyes that I was running away from to begin with. I step away quickly, trying to make my way back to the table and then the hell out of here.

"Emily, stop," Jeremy says firmly. I turn around and look to the floor since I've managed to not only insult him, but also embarrass myself. "You all right? You took off really quickly from the table. I thought maybe that rim job didn't exactly agree with you." Jeremy laughs as he crosses his arms and leans back against the hallway wall. "Tell me something. Did you run off because you can't handle your booze, or because you tried to have a comeback line and instead made your face look like Christian Grey's red room of pain?"

"How do you…"

"Seriously, I have a twenty-one-year-old sister, and have you met Sue? I know all about those books you girls are reading these days," he replies. *Of course, he does.* He's quick to respond to my inquisition. "Now, how does someone like you know about the red room of pain?" Okay, we need to seriously get off the topic of the only form of romance in my life, not that BDSM screams romance, but a girl can dream. Now's not the time to admit to him that I occasionally dabble in erotic romance novels.

"Listen, Jeremy. I'm sorry for being so quick to judge you back there, but you have to understand, I'm not like the rest of you. I'm not used to being in social situations a lot where the television cameras aren't involved, and even then, everything I am supposed to say is scripted. I should really get going. If you don't mind, I'm just going to settle the bill with Suzanne and head out, but it was nice to see you again."

JEREMY

Why am I so completely wrapped up in this shy little skater chick? One minute she's licking cinnamon sugar off the rim of her beer causing more than just a stirring in my pants and the next she's embarrassed to the hilt because she wasn't aware of my hockey career. She might have gotten away once eight years ago, but I'll be damned if she thinks she's spending the next eight stuck in the same secluded life I know she's living. I'm not sure why she's staked her claim on me; it's not like either of us has a shitload of time to spend together. I might have knocked her on her ass years ago, but every time I see this girl, she knocks the words right out of my mouth.

I push off the wall and make my way back to the table, only to see Emily isn't there. "Where did Emily go?" I ask everyone.

Suzanne looks up at me. "She said she had a yoga class or something to get to. I gave her my cell number, and she said she'd give me a call to get together soon." Bullshit. She's running again. You don't go to yoga after drinking a beer. I make my way to the front doors to see if I can catch her before she leaves, and I hear Courtney ask everyone where the hell I am going off to in a hurry. I'll have to explain this one to her later. Hopefully, she won't say much to Mom. She's already wondering when either of her two oldest boys is going to finally settle down and have grandkids for her.

If she hears I've been running after a girl I've basically met twice in my life, she'll be planning my wedding before the end of the night.

Fuck it!

Once I'm outside, I see her across the parking lot looking for her keys inside her purse. I start sprinting across the lot before she's just about to unlock the doors. "Emily!" I shout. She turns and sees me running toward her, and her face shoots up in shock. I make it to her car, putting one finger up as I'm leaning over onto my knees and trying to catch my breath. Seriously, I better start hitting up the gym a lot more in the next week. Spending my summer at the beach only doing twelve-ounce curls was not a wise idea.

"Jeremy?" she questions as she plays with her car keys in her hand.

"Hang on two seconds…" I raise my hand with one finger pointing up.

"Aren't you supposed to be in good shape to play hockey?" I hear her ask just in front of me.

"Yeah, well, when you have the summers off and your friends want to do nothing but sit on the beach, drink beer, and play golf, you tend to lose interest in going to the gym." I laugh, simply because she's probably in better shape than me right now. Coach is clearly going to kick my ass when I report to training camp next week.

Emily leans against her car as I start to stand back up. "You don't seem to be in so much of a rush to get to that yoga class anymore."

I see her eyes stalling and searching for a reason in her head. "What are you talking about? I really am heading to a class."

I call her bluff. "Emily, you're heading to a yoga class just the same as you were planning on calling Suzanne to meet up again."

"What do you want from me, Jeremy? I don't fit in with you guys or anyone for that matter."

"Excuses, excuses! Stop pushing people away because you think you don't fit in. You did the same thing to me eight years ago. You know how long I waited for your call that never came? I even tried calling you a couple times after that to see if you were going to the rink. You never answered."

"Jeremy, it's not that I didn't want to hang out with you. I did actually think you were funny, but you just don't understand how my parents dictated my life back then. My God, they still do!"

"Emily, listen to me. I may not know you all that well, but I can see underneath all the fake smiles and frilly costumes there is a funny, beautiful person just waiting to live her life. What's holding you back?"

She pushes off her car to face me. "I don't know what you want from me, Jeremy. I can't even offer anyone a normal friendship. I have one day off a week, and this isn't even the busy time of year for me."

Something inside me keeps telling me to fight for this girl. "Quit. Just say the hell with it! Do what makes you happy for once. From the first time

I knocked you on your ass when you were eleven at the Forum, I knew you didn't belong in that life."

"You don't even know me, Jeremy! Shit! I don't even know me," Emily exclaims.

"Emily, I want to get to know you, but you keep pushing me away. There's a group of people back in that restaurant who have zero judgment on anyone. Come back inside for a while and just hang out, relax and have a few laughs. I promise you've got nothing to be embarrassed about. Plus, you owe me for standing me up back in high school," I point out.

"I didn't stand you up. It's not like you asked me out on a date," Emily barely whispers as she goes thumbing through her bag. Little does she know I heard her. She doesn't expect me to wrap my arms around her waist and start spinning her around in the air. Emily lets out a huge gasp as I lift her. "Would you put me down, you big ape! People are staring!"

I slowly lower her to the ground, not letting my arms leave her waist. As her feet hit the ground, she has the largest *real* smile plastered on her face and the sweetest of giggles coming from her mouth. She finally realizes how close she is to me and tries to back away. Nope, I'm not letting that happen.

"See, I knew you could really smile and let loose. Now, what if I were to ask you out on a date? Would you go out with me?" It's a long shot I know, but something is telling me I need to get to know this girl better.

"Jeremy, you know I can't..."

I stop her before she says another word. My hands quickly come up to grab her face as her hands grip my wrists. She briefly looks into my eyes right before my lips crash into hers. I feel her go limp in my hands as her hands fall and grasp the sides of my T-shirt. She lets out just the slightest moan before I pull my lips from hers. Holy shit, why did I just do that? She's going to absolutely freak the fuck out now.

Leaning my forehead against hers, I whisper, "Emily, please, just one date. I don't even care if it's a date. Just spend some time with me." Pulling away to look her straight in the eyes, I continue pleading my case. "If you want, we can even hang out with Suzanne or Josh. I mean, I realize that's always awkward since they are no longer dating, but they are still good friends. Please?" Emily looks like she's about to pass out and goes to lean against her car again. Her hand comes up to touch her lips, and she's not looking at anything but my eyes. "Em? What is it?" Oh, shit. I never even thought of this before I kissed her. "Oh, shit, Emily. I'm so sorry. Shit, you've already got a boyfriend, don't you?! I've totally just screwed this up, didn't I? Please tell me I'm not a complete idiot for doing that."

She drops her fingers from her lips. "Jeremy, really, you think I've got a boyfriend? I have one day off a week to do my own thing."

Sara Shirley

I give her a questioning look. "So, if that's not it, then what was with the look of absolute terror on your face a moment ago?"

She sighs as if what she's about to tell me is something that will give me the same expression. "Jeremy." She sighs again. "I've never been kissed before."

Upon hearing those words, my eyes almost fall out of my head as I run my hands through my hair and start pacing in front of her. "You can't be fuckin' serious! How is that even possible? Never? Like as in I'm the first?! But, you're gorgeous and sexy as hell. How…really…and I just did that…aww fuck." Now, I'm pacing faster and running my hands over my face in frustration, trying to think of some way to fix this.

"Was I really that bad at kissing?" she asks softly.

I already basically screwed this up big time and now she thinks she's a bad kisser. I need to make this right and erase what might have been the worst first kiss in history. "Hey, Emily. Can you shut your eyes for a second?" She gives me a suspicious look and then a slight smirk on her face like she knows what I'm about to do, but she plays along anyway. She stands straighter, shuts her eyes, shakes her long blonde hair out away from her face, and tilts up her chin. "Oh, you think you know me, now do you?" I question, teasing her. She just stands there giggling under her breath and trying not to laugh, but I catch her peeking out of one closed eye. "No cheating!" I scold, and with that, she goes back to being serious.

I slowly make my way in front of her and wrap one arm around her waist and my other hand behind her head in her hair. I lower my mouth just enough to graze the skin on her lips. I lick my lips before I connect with hers, turning my head slightly and pushing my tongue along her lips. Urging her mouth open, I sense her unease at not knowing what to do, so I take control and slowly slip my tongue in and tangle it with hers. Within seconds, her hands are on my triceps, gripping tightly as her body goes limp in my arms. I gently push her back, so she's leaning against the side of her car, and my hips slide up against her body. Before I know it, her tongue is dancing around with mine, and she's fucking annihilated any other girl I've kissed before her. I take a slight nip of her bottom lip, and she flinches. *Shit, I got carried away.* She moves away and goes to rub her hand against her lip, but before she can get her hand there, I slide my thumb across her bottom lip and place a simple kiss there. "Does that help erase the worst first kiss of all time, or do I need to try again?"

Snapping out of her daze, she looks up at me, mouth agape and asks, "Huh?"

I laugh softly. "I'll take that as a yes." Oh, fuck yeah, that's definitely a yes in both of our books.

CHAPTER
five

The minute his lips leave mine I lose a sense of wholeness I never thought I could feel. I mean, I don't have anything to compare it to in the past, but seriously, Jeremy just basically turned his shock and awe kiss into dust. It was so sensual and calming that it almost felt as though I was floating in warmth and never wanting to be put down. I'm not even sure if I did anything right. Up until now, I've only managed to learn what I know from books and YouTube. Obviously, Jeremy has had so many more opportunities with other women, but if that's the case, why is he still standing here with me in this parking lot giving me my first kiss? I know I should find out the answer, but honestly, I'm scared shitless right now.

This is really the first time anyone has paid any attention to me when it doesn't involve my skating. Jeremy asked me to go out on a date with him and to hang out with the rest of the group some more. I don't think he really understands when I say I don't have time, plus my parents would probably go over the deep end thinking he doesn't fit the family image. He may have a hockey career, but even with that, they won't ever consider him suitable since he doesn't come from money and isn't making six figures at a Boston law firm.

Even without the status under his belt, my parents wouldn't allow it. They'd claim he'd be a distraction from my training, and training is exactly what I'll be doing day in and day out in another week. Sure, I've been stepping up my preparation over the summer, but September is rapidly approaching, and the coaches will be requiring my diligence to perfection. I'll be doing more triple loops and laybacks to make my head spin permanently on my shoulders. I'm expected to be on the podium in Boston come January at Nationals. If I'm not there and on my way to the Olympics, my parents will certainly remind me of my embarrassment to the family.

I'm lost in my thoughts when I see Jeremy saying something in front of me. "Huh?" is all I can muster.

He steps back and looks at me with the biggest shit-eating grin on his face, as if I'm the only thing that matters right now, and I'm the one who put that smile there. Me? Who am I? Why is this guy who I've only basically met a few times, seeing me for who I really am and cracking through my façade I've built over the last twenty years?

Jeremy goes to grab my hand to bring me back into the restaurant, but I don't move. "Em? C'mon. I thought you were going to give it another go and just hang out with us? Plus, we need to discuss the details of this date." *I can't do this. It's never going to work. Not with him, not his family or Suzanne.*

"Jeremy, I can't do this." My voice comes out softer than I expected. I know I'm hurting him and everyone else again, but this is for the best, whether he knows it now or figures it out when I stop answering his phone calls again.

"What do you mean you can't do this? You can't go back into the restaurant, or you can't actually stand up and move forward with your life enough to actually go out with me just once?" His voice contains pain and anger.

"I mean, us, them…I just can't, Jeremy. Today was fun, and that kiss was something I'll never forget. In a couple of weeks, you'll be back to your hockey, and I'll be training even more than I am now. By then, everyone in there will forget they even saw me again," I say firmly, pointing to the restaurant. "You'll forget about me, too. This is why I don't get close or open up to anyone because the look on your face right now makes me realize I've hurt you. If I never let anyone into my awful lonely world, then nobody ever gets hurt." Turning back to my car door to leave, I lift my head and see Jeremy running his hands through his hair as though he's frustrated. "It was good seeing you again, Jeremy. I wish you the best of luck with the Monarchs, and please tell everyone inside that it was good to see them again, too." I slowly open my car door to get in and leave, but a hand on my elbow stops me.

"Em, don't go like this. Tell me that kiss didn't mean something to you. Tell me you didn't feel the same thing I did while I had you in my arms. Give me one good reason why I shouldn't pursue this with us?"

"Jeremy, I can't hurt you, and I won't. That kiss will be imbedded in my mind forever, but we both know it won't work out with us." I move to sit in my driver's seat, reaching for the door. Jeremy appears and hovers over my doorframe.

"I'm not letting you go again for another eight years. Get that through your head. I know deep down you don't mean what you say, so I will be calling you, and we will have that date eventually. Admit it. You need someone fighting on your side for once, and that person is going to be me."

The door shuts to my Audi A4, and I let out a gigantic sigh, resting my head against the headrest and closing my eyes. I start up the engine and lean over to fasten my seatbelt as the voices of Lady Antebellum echo through the speakers and the chorus of "Just a Kiss" seeps into my head. I can't help but think how ironic, and yet, amusing today has been. Never in my wildest dreams did I think I would have my first kiss when I woke up this morning. I also never thought I would be running into the one guy who could actually penetrate the thick layers surrounding my heart. A slight giggle escapes my mouth.

How in the hell did Jeremy Page just work his way back into my life and basically uproot it in less than two hours? One minute I'm running from him and the next he has his arms wrapped around me with his lips locked on mine. I have absolutely nothing to compare it to, and I can only hope I wasn't bad because all I could think about after his lips left mine was that I wanted them back on me. Yeah, okay, so I know I'm being greedy, needy, whatever, but seriously, he just screams hunk, and regardless of my current status in life and non-existent love life, I have needs. It definitely doesn't hurt that he basically fought me tooth and nail against me telling him I couldn't possibly handle anything like this with him.

As I'm pulling out of the parking lot, my phone ringing brings me out of my crazy thoughts of Jeremy. I look at the screen and read "Unknown Caller." It could be just about anyone on my mother's long list of contacts wanting to set up another interview. Usually, she schedules these herself, because she wants to ensure she's there to control the questions and answers. She's the freakin' puppet master, and I'm the doll attached to the strings.

I slide my finger across the screen and quickly answer the phone. "Emily Cameron."

"So, you do still have the same phone number," a familiar male voice says through the phone. I glance back down at it, questioning how it's even possible.

"How?" I ask with a little more authority.

A slow chuckle comes over the line, and I'm really trying really hard to figure out how he has my number. "Seriously, Em, you have no idea, do you?"

"Jeremy? How did you get my number?" I wonder because if he's had my number this entire time, why has he never called me?

"Well, if you weren't so worried about getting away from me at lunch, you might have seen me scrolling through my phone looking for a contact. You forget many years ago I made sure that when I dropped a girl off she called me when she got home. After she called me, that number stayed in my contact list because she promised me she'd call me later."

"You saved my phone number for all these years?? Are you kidding me?! Better yet, why are you just calling me now?" He had my number and never called. Not that it would have mattered. My parents would have shipped me right off to an entirely different state if anyone even attempted to interfere with their grand plan of what my career entailed.

"I did call, a couple of times. You just never answered, and I never left a voicemail. But, enough about the past, the way I see it you now have my number, and I'll be expecting a phone call from you soon, when you are ready to make good on that deal."

"Jeremy, I don't have a lot of spare time. I just hope you won't be disappointed again..."

"Emily! No excuses this time around. I'll be in touch, and we'll go from there, okay?"

"Yeah, okay." I sigh. How is this ever going to work?

"Oh, and Emily...the next time I see you, you can bet your sweet ass I'm claiming your lips again!" He must have heard me gasp loudly because he let out deep laugh through the phone. Little did he know, his voice was causing all kinds of tingles throughout my body. Things I've never felt before. He wanted to kiss me again, but why? "I'll call you later. Have a good night, Emily."

"You too, Jeremy. Talk to you soon." With that, we both end the phone call.

I pull up into the driveway to my parents' house. My only saving grace is that I no longer live under the same roof as them, although they still basically control my career and market me like I'm a fine wine when it comes to all the publicity stints I'm forced to do. When I was eighteen and trying to rebel against the sad state of my life, the only reprieve I was granted was some added space by them allowing me to move into the guest apartment above the three-car garage. I had my own space, which allowed me to come and go as I pleased, even though it was only to school and the rink all through college. Now that I've graduated and am basically concentrating only on skating, my apartment is like my sanctuary.

I park my car in the garage and make my way up the back stairwell to unlock the door. I step inside, flicking on the kitchen area lights. Although it's relatively small, I find solace in what is normally a chaotic life. When I stand in my kitchen area, I can see my entire studio apartment. With strategically placed furniture, I've managed to separate my bedroom, kitchen and living room quite nicely. Tossing my keys and bag onto the kitchen table, I slip off my flip- flops that are still slippery from my earlier pedicure. Grabbing a bottle of water from the fridge, I turn to flip on my television mounted above the fireplace. I'm scrolling through the channel guides and stop as I notice there's another *Friends* mini-marathon on.

I can sit here all day and lose myself in this show, imagining my life in the big city and having close friends who make me feel more like family than mine ever will. Somehow I manage to catch the episode where Ross and Rachel have their first kiss. I still love this episode, especially when the Central Perk doors fly open and Ross steps in from the rain, grabbing

Rachel's face with both of his hands and bringing his lips to hers. No matter how many times I watch it, I still love it.

Touching my fingers to my lips, I think of the feelings I experienced a short time ago when Jeremy allowed me to have my first real kiss. Does he really think a date with me will go well? I can't understand his persistence. I mean, I can certainly try to make time for him on my days off, but what happens when I'm traveling for five months straight for competitions? My parents will hate him immediately and consider him a distraction or not the type of person I should be seen with in public. It's always about appearances with them. Training comes first, always. I'll end up having to ignore his phone calls from here forward, and after a while, he'll probably understand and just stop calling again. But, why do I feel as though I'm already hurting him again before this even starts? One kiss and I'm already losing focus. I'm so confused and screwed!

I stand up, stretching my arms above my head before bending over to link my hands around my ankles to stretch out. Thinking a long, hot shower will get my mind off today's events, I start walking into the bathroom set off from the sitting area. Turning on the shower, I begin to strip down as the room begins to fill with steam from the hot water. I swipe the condensation off the mirror and glance at the reflection staring back at me. I've certainly changed a little over the years. I'm at least four inches taller than the average skater out there, and my body is not built like the stick figures I see getting ready to take my place once I'm no longer able to compete. I'm not saying I'm any more talented than them, but with age comes maturity, and I've clearly grown into my mature body at twenty-two.

Releasing my bra hook and tossing my lace thong into the hamper, I climb into the shower. Relishing in the scalding water, I bring my face under the hot spray and run my hands through my long blonde hair. Letting out a long sigh from sheer relaxation, I close my eyes and see Jeremy's face as he fills my thoughts and warms my body even more. I envision him trailing his hands on more than just my face and hips as he runs them over my bare chest and in between my legs and whispers dirty thoughts into my ear. In that instant, I see his shirt pulled off over his head and his pants quickly unzipping to expose his arousal that's evident through his tight boxer briefs. *Hey, this is my erotic dream. He will not have on tighty whities. Hell no! I don't care how good Jamie Dornan looks in those Calvin Klein ads. So, boxer briefs it is!* As I am dreaming, his boxer briefs…oh, yes, I glide my fingers just above the inside fold of the elastic band, slowly tugging down to reveal his throbbing…*Ding!…Ding!…What the hell?!* My eyes shoot open as I try to slow my pulse…*Ding!*…Turning off the water, I open the shower door, grab my towel and wrap it around my body, squeezing the water out of my hair as I make my way into the other room. *Ding!* I look around and pick up my phone from the coffee table. Two missed calls and two new texts. How long was I in the shower?

Glancing down, I pull up the icons. I open the missed text messages and read the first one.

Hey Emily! It's Sue. Hope u don't mind but I got your # from Jeremy. How does he have your # anyway? He told me to stay in touch with u, something about he'd never kiss & tell. IDK?! It was gr8 seeing u today, we ought to catch up more when you have a little xtra time. Call me.

Apparently, Jeremy is now going to make sure I have Suzanne to keep an eye on me as well. At least he didn't say anything to her about the kiss in the parking lot. I know for a fact if she finds out, she'll take it upon herself to know every single detail. Most of the stuff I've learned about sex and human anatomy I give credit to Suzanne after our afternoon shopping for her prom dress.

I save Suzanne's phone number into my contacts just in case and move onto the next text.

I see you are already avoiding my phone calls. Don't worry. I'm not giving up just yet.

Listen to "I Won't Give Up." Know u are worth it. Goodnight, Emily. Don't wait too long to start living your dreams. Someday they might actually come true.

I return to my bedroom as I pull up YouTube to search for the song he mentioned. I lie down on my large comfy comforter, hugging my pillows as I stare at the sheer fabric draped over the top beams of my four-poster bed. I hear Jason Mraz's lyrics pour out of him and into my soul. This hockey player, who throws punches during games and is the epitome of rough and tough, references a song about not giving up on "us," and even if I need my space, he'll be there when I figure it all out. I'm not even sure how or why a stray tear falls down the side of my cheek. In twenty-two years, my parents have never given me one ounce of love or support for what I might want to do in my life. Then, there's Jeremy, who I've been around for all of about four hours, and he's somehow connected with me more in that short time, and it honestly scares the shit out of me. I don't even think; I just roll over, grab my phone, and start typing.

I'm not sure when and I'm not sure how you managed to actually see "me," but I don't wanna be someone who walks away so easily. Give me time to think, and I'll make time for "us" and that date. You have my word this time. Night, Jeremy.

I jump off my bed and walk to my French doors, grabbing both handles and opening them into the room. Walking outside onto my small balcony, I sit under the starry sky and lie back in the chaise lounge. I shut my eyes slowly and see his big, brown eyes staring back at me. I'm not sure how my life just got even more complicated than it was yesterday, but maybe it's time for me to really consider my future. What if this is my last chance at the Olympics? I know this isn't forever. I've just got to figure out how my parents will handle that revelation. Jeremy might be willing to fight for me to go one direction in life, but I know for a fact, my parents will be fighting for me to go in another direction.

JEREMY

As I'm finally sitting in my apartment living room after getting all my hockey gear for the new season ready to go, "Sail" pumps through my stereo system, mentally preparing me for what hopefully will be another successful season with the Monarchs. The bass gets my blood pumping. In not so many words, I have to wonder if not being drafted into the NHL is a blessing in disguise since I'm still living in the area near my family and friends instead of moving all over the place. With the Monarchs, the pay isn't nearly as good; however, the number of games is significantly less and that still allows me to spend time helping out with the kids in Pee Wee hockey at my old rink. During the regular season, I'll typically swing by and help out my old coaches, and the kids think it's great.

Just as I'm packing everything into my hockey bag, my phone starts ringing. I glance at the screen, and see it's Dave. He and I go way back to Pee Wee hockey at the Forum. It's funny in so many ways because he never really left the rink and is currently the front office manager at the Forum and sometimes fills in at the pro shop. He's one of my best friends, and if he's calling, he must either be in the area and wants to grab a drink or is looking for me to play a little one-on-one at the rink.

I slide my finger across the screen. "Hey, what's goin' on?" I ask, walking toward the kitchen to grab a beer.

"Hey, asshole! Where the fuck have you been all day? I tried calling earlier and got sent right to voicemail," Dave states, as if I should answer every time he calls.

"Yeah, sorry, I was out with Court, Josh, Suzanne …and uh…Emily Cameron," After that name leaves my mouth, I wait for it.

"Shut the fuck up! The Emily Cameron?! As in the one from the Forum back in high school?"

"The one and only. Sue ran into her at the mall and took her hostage for lunch at the Nines."

"And?"

"And what?" I ask, knowing exactly why Dave is pressing the issue. He and Josh are the only two people who know how long I waited for that girl to call me back in high school. The call that never came.

"Dude, don't hold out on the details. I know how you were the summer after we graduated from high school. It's like that phone was connected to your hip permanently. Emily Cameron is the one girl you couldn't smooth talk into going out with you. So…?"

I know if I don't give him any details he'll never leave this alone, whatever *this is* with Emily. Sighing, I say, "We all had lunch. I may have said something rude, and she took off running again. I stopped her in the parking lot. We talked, and …we might have kissed." And, I wait for it again.

"I'm coming over. Get the beer pong table ready! You're spilling the details."

Shit! I'm totally fucked now. Dave knows he kicks my ass in beer pong every time, which means he'll get the entire story from start to finish.

Pulling out the table from the storage closet, I make more noise than necessary, because the scratching of claws against the hardwood floors seems to follow me back toward the kitchen. I put down the table and turn around to see my four-legged roommate, Aspen. He's my three-year-old Bernese Mountain dog and the best company when I need someone to listen to, even when he doesn't understand the words coming out of my mouth.

"Hey, boy! C'mere. Do you want a treat before all the chaos starts in the house?" *Woof.* Aspen sits his butt on the floor, keeping his body perfectly still, well, everything is still except for his tail going a mile a minute. Reaching into the jar on the kitchen counter, I grab a biscuit and toss it to him. Leaping up, he grabs it and darts off back to my bedroom where his bed is setup. He'll probably stretch his neck out to see what's going on in the house in a little bit, but other than that, he's the mellowest dog I've seen. I sometimes envy his life.

Fifteen minutes later, Dave walks through my door with a thirty pack of Bud Light in one hand and a bag of red Solo cups in the other. I give him a questioning glare as to why a thirty pack.

He starts placing the beers inside the fridge and looks at me. "Had to get thirty just in case one game isn't enough for the whole story…and I will get the *whole* story." He points a finger at me while cracking open the first beer and half-filling the Solo cups. "House rules, for every shot I make, you have to answer one of my questions. For every one of the shots you hit, I'll give you fifteen minutes of free ice time at the Forum," he says as he finishes pouring the beer into the plastic cups on the table.

"Well, it's a good thing I live here because I have a feeling I might be drinking most of those beers and not getting any ice time." I laugh.

"Okay, let's get this game started." Dave rolls the ping-pong ball around in his hand, blowing on it while giving me a stare. Basically, he is silently saying I'm fucked! He lines up behind the board, staring at the triangle of cups at the other end. He lets the ball sail out of his hand, and it floats down, ringing the top of one of the cups before falling into the beer.

"Shit! All right, let me have it."

"How did you end up kissing Emily Cameron and still manage to keep your balls in tact?" Dave asks as he leans against the kitchen counter.

"It kind of just happened, and she actually wanted me to kiss her, I think. Her body was telling me she did, anyway. I mean, I've kissed plenty of girls before, but none of them hold a candle to Emily. I don't know what it is about her. I'm still trying to figure it out," I explain as I chug back my first pong cup and set it to the side.

"Wait. So, the ice queen of Andover wanted *you* to kiss *her?* Sorry, man, but I just can't see it. That girl had you by the balls after graduation, and you were only waiting on her phone call. What the fuck are you gonna do now that you've kissed her?" Dave pushes off the counter and heads to grab the ping-pong ball off the table.

"Hey! I believe that is a second question, and you haven't hit that shot yet," I point out as he sets up his angle behind the table.

"That's how you're gonna play." Dave sighs and tosses the ball across the table, sinking another one. "Now, answer."

I shake my head, thinking seriously he must practice playing this all day long because there is no way he can sink balls every shot. Ha! Well, not only is he "King of the Pong Table," he's also a charmer of the female species. I swear he goes to my hockey games more for the girls than to watch me play.

"I'm waiting, dude," Dave says, chucking back a cup of beer.

"When did I make a shot?"

"You didn't, but I was getting thirsty just standing here."

"Fine, so back to your interrogation. I'm not sure what I'm going to do about Emily. I mean, I told her she wasn't getting away without a fight this time around, but she's still scared. I think it's more to do with her parents than her, but she won't come out and say it to my face. I had Sue text Emily to make her think she's reaching out as a friend, and I tried calling her before, but it went to voicemail."

"Let me guess. You didn't leave a message, again."

"Well, no, I sent her a text instead."

"Has she texted you back?" I cross my arms over my chest, leaning up against the back of my sofa and giving Dave a taunted look while nodding toward the beer pong table. "Really? Fine." He sunk it again.

Shaking my head at his talent, I respond, "No, she hasn't replied yet."

"Dude, I get it, really I do. I mean, I've seen her pictures and she's gorgeous, but is that something you want to try to finagle with all you've got going on during the hockey season?" I stand there staring and silent after his questions. Dave huffs and turns to the counter, grabbing all the ping-pong balls, and one after another, he sinks the rest into the cups. Serious talent that goes unnoticed. "There, happy now? Game over. I win. Now, talk."

Just as I'm about to speak up about how I have no idea how I would anticipate ever having a possible relationship with Emily, my phone whistles at me from the coffee table in the living room. I walk over and pick it up, unlocking the incoming text. A smile forms across my face as I see her words written plain as day on my phone.

I'll make time for us.

Dave comes over with two cups in his hand. "What? Dude, you lost. Drink up. I'll even help you out."

"You're too kind, but back to your last question. I have no idea how anything with Emily will work, but if she's willing to try, then in my book, we're good. And, she's already responded to my earlier text. So far, that's more progress than I had eight years ago."

"Well, I hope it works out for you, because if you go into that funk like you did before, you're going to get kicked off the Monarchs team, and if that happens, it will really put a damper on my sex life."

"So glad to know you openly admit to using my hockey career to benefit your sex life," I chide, knowing that Dave hangs out with me after games just to hit on girls at the pubs.

After sucking back the rest of the beer pong cups, I put away the table and grab another beer from the fridge and sit back in the living room with Dave. Turning on the television, I quickly flip to the local sports channel to watch the chatter about this year's NHL season. It hurts that my time to get brought up to the majors slips further away each year, but I'm still skating, and that's all that matters. After today, another part of me thinks had I not been here, and instead playing in the majors, my arms would have never been wrapped around Emily, and I would have never been able to give her the first kiss of her life. Letting out a long exhale, I grab my beer and bring it to my lips as I flop back in the chair and throw my feet up on the coffee table.

I see Dave glancing my way from the other end of the sofa. "Aww, shit, man. I know that look. I swear to you. If you do this again, I will beat your head in with that hockey stick."

"I know she's worth it. I don't know why, but I have a feeling."

"You have a 'feeling.' Fuck, we're going to need more beer, and clearly, I'm staying over, so I better go put my bags in the spare bedroom."

"Your bags?! As in plural? How long are you staying?"

"Well, let's see. The last time it took you three months. I hope this time it won't be that long of a recovery period," Dave states as he walks back down the hall to the spare room. I hear some rustling and then a squeaky toy. *Woof woof.* He must have found Aspen. The toy flies down the hall, landing directly on my head just as Aspen searches around the room for it.

"What the hell was that for?"

"If you think that hurt, what do you think that hockey stick will feel like? Keep that in mind before you fall all over Emily Cameron again. You feel me? 'Cuz that hockey stick won't hurt nearly as much as your heart will if you get too close. You don't exactly have the best track record with chicks. Need I remind you of Becca? I'm just glad after that whole incident you didn't consider any steady relationships after that."

I sit, silently taking in all that he has said and gently rubbing Aspen's floppy ears as his tongue dangles out of his mouth. It scares me to think I never considered serious relationships after Becca simply because I never had time. I'd have random hook-ups after games and go back to the chick's place, but they were always too easy, too much like Becca. In it for the status only, they would go back to their girlfriends and tell them they screwed a hockey player. At least I didn't have to use more than one hand to count how many girls I'd been with. With Emily, I've already tainted her. After finding out she'd never been kissed until today, I've had my mind made up since she challenged me at lunch and then licked that sugar rim off her glass that I'm fighting for her, whether I get hurt again or not. I'm not backing away, even if it burns me again.

Looking up from Aspen's soft eyes, I say to Dave, "If I'm going to go through hell and back again, at least it's going to be her I'm doing it for. Call me crazy, but I'm going all in on this one. I just hope luck is on my side."

"You'll have no problem getting to hell; you've seen her mother. That's not going to be easy to get through, but for some reason, I think you'll handle her better than anyone. She's totally not going to be into you for a status fuck, but if you are going to go to battle for a girl, at least it's one as smoking hot as Emily. Best of luck, man. You're gonna need it, but I'll have your back if you need me."

"Thanks. Somehow I have a feeling I may just need you for support in the not so distant future."

"Whatever you need, man. Now, enough of this relationship sappy shit. Let's find me some hot chicks on TV wearing little to no clothing, preferably with large tits."

"Here, take the remote. Find whatever you want. I'm heading to bed. I've got a long day tomorrow. Just, please, whatever you do, *do not* whack off on my sofa!"

"Hey, I only did that once, and it's not my fault you happened to walk in on me at the wrong time!"

"Really? You brought back one of the strippers from Promiscuous to give you a private show in my living room, and that's called the 'wrong time'?"

"Dude, she was willing to do it for free. Who was I to say no?!"

"Oh my God, how are you even my best friend? I'm going to bed. C'mon, Aspen. Leave Uncle Dave to himself, so he can have his *alone time.*"

"Damn straight. Hey, Jeremy…good talk."

"Thanks, man."

CHAPTER
six

The following morning I wake up to the sound of my alarm clock going off before the sun peeks above the horizon. Stretching my arms up over my head, I roll my legs out from under my nice warm goose down comforter and trudge my way into the kitchen. Turning on the coffee maker, I turn to get dressed for practice while the machine warms up. Coffee is my lifeline these days. Waking up at five in the morning to make it to Boston for practice four days in a row is starting to wear on me, so I can't function without my liquid caffeine.

I throw on my warm-up pants and lycra top before stepping back into the kitchen to pull my travel mug down from the black open-faced cabinets above the stove. I push the *Brew* button and then proceed to brush my teeth and fix my rat's nest I called hair last night before going to sleep. I smell the faint aroma coming into the bathroom of the freshly brewed coffee and already my eyes are widening.

I shove my gear into my bag, toss my phone into my purse, throw on my sneakers, and lastly, take a quick mental check that I have everything before heading out the door. I swing my bag over my shoulder, while grabbing the coffee mug and car keys in one hand and a granola bar in the other. Making my way down the stairs, I pop my trunk to my Audi and toss in my bags. Getting into the car, I hit the button for the garage doors to open as I slowly start to back out. As I'm about to drive off, I see my mother opening the front door to the main house, waving me over. *Sigh.* Petulant woman. She can't even walk over to my car. I drive the short distance to the house and roll down the passenger window to see what on Earth she wants now.

"Good morning, Emily. I trust you know that today during practice with Suzy that a group of photographers from the *Boston Globe* will be by to ask you a few questions about the upcoming season and the Nationals."

I glance at her like she has three heads, and then it dawns on me that I never checked my emails from her yesterday. Every week on my day off she sends me my schedule. It normally stays the same; however, I never gave it a second thought, and with a major season quickly approaching, I should have remembered.

"I'll take that as a no, Emily? We've got too much at stake this year for you not to take this seriously. I spend all day ensuring your schedule properly consists of adequate training as well as significant PR coverage. Your father donates enough to make sure you are seen and reported as being the next top contender for a gold medal. Remember that you not only have to represent Cameron and Dean, LLC, but also this country."

Rubbing my face with my hands, I look up to see my mother staring at me with her calculated thoughts before placing her hand inside the door and grabbing the fluted glass filled with orange juice from the foyer table. *Nice try, Mother. We all know you slipped an added substance in there.* Manipulative bitch!

Just as she's closing the front door, I hit the button to roll up the window. I hear my phone chime in my purse, as I'm about to throw the car in drive. Who the hell is texting me at 5:30 in the morning? It's probably my mother requesting I bring home more wine for her to go comatose on during dinner. I'm pretty sure once I moved out of the main house, Mother and Daddy stopped speaking and now basically remain married simply for the social status and image of the perfect family in the skating world. How did I get so lucky?!

As I look at the screen, the name that appears completely takes me by surprise.

> *Heading up 93 toward Manchester. If you're up, know I am thinking about you. No, I'm not a sappy wuss, but a song was just on the radio and it made me think of you.*

I realize I'm driving on the same highway, just in the opposite direction. I see what's left of the stars in the sky as the sun begins to sneak over the horizon. Turning on my Bluetooth, I say "Jeremy" loudly as my phone registers my voice over the speaker. I hear it ringing, ringing, ringing. *Come on. Answer.* I know he has his phone on, or has he already made it to wherever he's going?

"Hey, there." A deep voice fills the air in my car.

"Hey, good morning. What was the song?"

A slight chuckle comes over the speaker. "Oh, just a song by The Fray. It was stupid, really."

"Oh-Kay," I slowly draw out. I'll remind myself to look up their songs later since he doesn't want to talk about it. "So, what are you doing up so early?"

"I'm heading up to Manchester to get started on my conditioning skills because someone told me yesterday that I'm supposed to be in shape. Wonder who that could have been?" I start giggling in the car. "Now, there's a sound I can never get tired of hearing, although I am a little shocked."

"Shocked? Why are you shocked?" Did he not want me to call him back? Maybe he's had time to think about the whole situation with all of us being friends and realizes it is a bad idea. I'm still not convinced this is a good decision, but I called him, so I've already started this potential train wreck.

"Well, you see the last time you said you'd call was eight years ago. When you texted me last night and said you'd be in touch, I thought for sure I'd be waiting another eight years. But, Em, I'm happy you called. It's nice to hear your voice on what could only be described as the most boring drive north ever."

"Jeremy, I really am sorry I never called you. I just never knew it would hurt you more than me staying friends and then disappointing you down the road. I hope you understand it was just easier not to have me in your life then. The same can be said now, but I'm willing to try because you asked me to."

"No, Em, I'm sorry. That's never going to happen." *What the hell?* Is he attempting to give me a headache this morning? First, he says he's willing to fight for me, then he's thinking about me and waiting for my call, and I actually tell him I'm willing to try to see if this can be real. Now, he's telling me no. I'm totally confused, and I guess I'll just let him be and maybe he'll call me at some point. No, hell no!

"You know what, Jeremy? I was willing to give you a shot, and now you're telling me no? At what point did I misconstrue your words between yesterday and this morning? You did say you wanted a *date*. Tell me, dammit, because I'm confused as all hell right now." I'm not sure at what point that boldness in me all goes to shit, because the next thing I hear is him laughing hysterically. "What the hell are you laughing at, you ass?"

"Em, I'm laughing because you clearly took my words out of context. When I said no, I meant it was not easier for me to not have you in my life then. It's certainly never going to be easier now if you did the same thing. So, no, it's never going to happen. I said you're worth fighting for, and I'm damn well planning on doing that, and you aren't going anywhere. Got it?" Sighing with embarrassment, I reply, "Oh…umm… yeah, I got it."

"So, are you off to training in Boston?" he asks as I hear him shuffling something on his end of the line.

"Yeah, I've got a four-hour session with my coach, and someone is coming over to the rink for an interview. I guess my mother sent me the information yesterday, but I never checked my email, so she was less than happy with me this morning before leaving. I'm sure I'll hear all about it when I get home."

"I've got a few things going on this afternoon, but if you want some company, just let me know. Sue mentioned she was possibly hanging out with Courtney later, too. I'm sure given how quickly you needed to get to *yoga* yesterday, Sue would want to catch up further, and just so you know, I didn't mention the kiss, but I think she suspects something."

"Jeremy why would she *suspect* something?" I grumble over the speakers.

"Oh, I don't know. I might have mentioned something about me not kissing and telling, and then I might have told my friend Dave, who has a very big mouth and is close with Sue, so umm…yeah…tonight…"

"Jeremy!" I scold.

"…I'll consider that a definite maybe on meeting up tonight…"

"Jeremy! I could kill you right now."

"…Oh, would you look at that…Gotta go, Em. I'm at the rink…Hey, great talk…Call you later…"

"Jer-"

The sound of a dial tone is the only thing I hear. Oh my God. I want to kill him for saying anything. A first kiss is one thing when it's private, but it's another thing to have him tell his closest friend and insinuate it to Sue. I feel sick, but now is not a good time to be sick to my stomach. I nibble my granola bar and sip away at my coffee to hopefully calm my anxiety before I arrive at the rink.

One day. It took only one day for someone to completely uproot my structured life, and I have no idea if this is good or bad. All I know is the sun is rising, and the sky has turned a bright red. Now, I'm no sailor, but I believe the old saying is "Red sky in morning, sailor take warning." Well, ahoy, Captain! I read you loud and clear. My day is about to go bad quickly; I just know it.

JEREMY

Quickly hanging up from my morning phone call with Emily, I can't help but notice the smile plastered across my face in my rearview mirror. She's trying, and that's all I can ask for right now. No one has ever pushed her to break out of her shell. Calling me and hanging out with us is probably the first real shot she's had at friendship outside of the skating community. I'm proud of her for taking that step, but a part of me keeps saying she's going to break my heart one way or another. *She's worth the fight.* I keep telling myself this mantra over and over. Please don't let me be wrong again.

I wasn't lying when I told Emily that I was at the arena. Although it was fun teasing her about Sue having an idea that something happened with us.

The truth is she's only just slightly suspicious. Knowing Sue, she'll push me until I tell her the entire story. I can't say I'm going to lie, but she'll be one more person working on my side to help push through Emily's nearly impenetrable walls that she guards. Once those start to crumble, I may just have my chance at what I lost all those years ago.

Pulling up in the arena parking lot, I get out of my F150 Platinum pickup and grab my bag from the bed. As I approach the back entrance, I pull out my security badge and enter the building to the ice level and head back toward the locker room to change into my practice gear. Halfway there, I run into a couple of teammates that I haven't seen since last season with the Monarchs. We might be teammates, but I try not to get too attached to many of them. Some of them get brought up to the next level of the league, and there are others that get traded. Either way, for me, once they are gone, I already know they won't be staying in touch. So, for the few that do actually come back the following season, it's a miracle. Right now, there are five of us that are still contracted from last season. Bryce and Dylan are nice enough friends, and we've been known to hit up the town after a few games, but outside of that, I'm really at a place in my life where I'd rather just relax at home. I may be twenty-five, but years of playing hockey and road trips tend to take a toll on one's body. Broken noses and groin pulls are all fun and games until you've had enough of them to know when it's time to call it a career.

"Hey, man, how was the off season?" Bryce asks.

Looking up and dropping my bag onto the floor, I say, "Summer was good. I spent some time working with the kids in the summer program again at the local rink. It didn't pay much, but it was fun, and that's all that matters."

"That's cool. Are you still hitting that brunette you met after our last home game in the spring?" Dylan asks while giving me a slight punch to the shoulder before winking at me.

Ugh. Avery. Pretty girl but absolutely dumb as rocks, and although she was a sure thing since she was at least five tequila shots deep by the time we left the local pub, she was in no way, shape, or form someone I wanted to bring home to Mom. The fact that Dylan is asking me now after all this time leads me to believe he's either still interested or has already hit that after me and doesn't want to burn any bridges before the season starts. Yeah, he's the team man-whore and proud of it.

Bursting out a loud laugh, I say to him, "D, she was a stage nine clinger, one I blame on the amount of alcohol consumed that night. Otherwise, there would have been no chance of my dick ever finding itself inside that abyss of a pussy." As mean as that may sound, the Monarchs finished the season on a very good note, and we were all out living it up a little too hard. Avery was a mistake I can honestly blame on too many shots of Patron and a rather lengthy dry spell from sex in my life. The only things I was thankful for were she never tried to get in touch with me afterward and I at least remembered to use a condom. Something tells me that girl has been around the block a few times from the stories I hear in the locker room.

Dylan laughs after some time, and then as we start walking back toward the locker room, he turns and says, "Dude, you were so fucked up that night I'm just shocked your dick actually worked long enough to make its way into that cum dumpster."

"You know what? There are so many things wrong with that image I'm just glad I can't remember much of that night, but the unfortunate part of it is that I can confirm she is not worth the effort."

After changing into some basic hockey gear in the locker room, the three of us make our way out to the ice and quickly open up with some laps around the rink. Even after the last month or so hanging out at the Forum with the kids during summer camp, nothing compares to the feeling of just getting into the full swing of the season.

CHAPTER
seven

Emily

Practice at the rink is anything but exciting today. Suzy has me work on some standard runs and different edges going into jumps as we start to test out some new choreography for the upcoming season's programs. Many times I wish I could hear the music and feel it to the point that the movements come to me naturally. However that may be, it's not the case. Each movement is calculated. Every edge, spin and jump placed specifically in order to provide me the best chance at receiving the perfect score. I laugh at that perfect score because it will never happen. Not even on a perfect performance. I can go out there and skate my heart out and never falter, but the judges always find something. That *something* will be the first thing my mother will point out immediately after the competition. *Emily, it appears there might have been some minor flaws in your performance today.* Regardless if I place first, that is not what's important in Mother's eyes. Need I remind you of her alter ego, Cruella Deville? Better yet, I believe she's now morphing into Maleficent as she gets older. Somehow I think she senses my strong disapproval toward this skating career she so kindly forced me into all those years ago.

After four hours of grueling practice, my love for *Les Miserables* has now taken a turn for the worse. I know by the end of this season I will hate hearing what has long been my most favorite musical. To keep the audience entertained, my coach and choreographer feel it is important to choose music that has a significant impact on the past year in the entertainment world. *Damn you, Anne Hathaway!* Never again will your Oscar winning performance bring me happiness. It's all been tainted after this skating season.

After pulling into my garage, I grab all my gear out of my trunk and lay everything onto the floor to dry. Quickly taking the stairs and opening my door to my refuge, I kick off my pink sneakers and connect my iPhone to the charger before flipping on the surround sound for music to fill the walls of my place. A new song starts, and I'm immediately transported into a whole new place. I grab a bottle of water from my fridge and start moving my hips in the living room as ZZ Ward's voice beats against the walls. Then, the bounce and finger snaps join in, as I'm lost in my own world and happy.

Laughing at myself, I remember my phone has been off since I went into practice. I hit the *Power* button as I pass it heading back toward the French doors to let some air into my room. There will only be a few more nice days for me to enjoy what's left of summer. A slight sea breeze begins making its way through the air, and a chill runs up my back as a cloud passes overhead. I really need to escape to a warmer climate one day. I have to laugh at that, but sure, I can certainly dream.

I'm taken away from my mental images of tropical paradises when I hear my phone ding, alerting me I have a text message. I pick up the phone off the table and see the number "2" hovering over the message icon on my phone, indicating two texts. I open the first one from Sue.

> *Hey! Taking Courtney out for a couple of drinks tonight for her birthday. Just us 3. Thinking the martini bar Eavesdrop @ 7p. It's a funky little place but they make great drinks. Would like to catch up some more if you are around. Text me back if you are in.*

What harm will it do to have a drink or two and reconnect with Sue and get to know Courtney some more? I did tell Jeremy I would at least try. I really didn't leave on such good terms the other day when I stormed out of lunch because of Jeremy. I might as well have a little bit of fun tonight. I don't have to be at the gym until three tomorrow, and that's only for strength and ballet for three hours. How bad can it be? I quickly respond.

> *Absolutely! I'll meet you there at 7. It will be good to catch up some more.*

Within a few seconds, I hear my phone and see Sue has already responded.

> *OMG! You are really coming out ?!?! Yay! You totally just made my day, girl!!*

What a nut that one is! I made her day. Seriously, Sue needs to make more friends if I'm the one handing out the happy cards. I remember that I still have one incoming text from Jeremy to read. Tapping my inbox, I read his words displayed across the screen.

> *Working on getting back into shape so I can catch you faster the next time you run =) I'm still waiting to hear about that "date." Courtney says she asked Sue to let you know about Eavesdrop @ 7 for her bday tonight. Hope you go for girls' night out, but know Courtney might poke you to talk. She likes to play matchmaker for my brother and me. Beware JK - TTYL*

He's relentless about this "date." Perhaps if I play hard to get he'll just forget. No, he won't. I laugh out loud. Who am I kidding?

I'm not sure I'm ready to start talking about what happened with Jeremy a couple of days ago, so I'm hoping Sue just wants to concentrate on Courtney's birthday tonight instead. I've got a few hours before I need to leave, so I quickly check my emails just in case my mother has scheduled anything further this week for me. Nothing appears to have changed since she ever so kindly reminded me of my lack of attention to my schedule this morning. With that in mind, I shut off my tablet and head into the shower and change for our girls' night out. It's funny how my life seems to have changed in just a couple of days. I glance up at myself in the mirror and chuckle. I'm genuinely happy for the first time in my life.

Pulling up to Eavesdrop, I park my car to the side of the lounge and inspect myself in the mirror. I've gone a little over the top for just a night out with Suzanne and Courtney, but it's not overboard. I'm wearing my skinny jeans and off the shoulder blouse with my platform heels, which may I add, are a total bitch to drive in. It took all of about five seconds before I kicked them off and drove barefoot. I'm more suited for wearing my Chuck Taylors or flip-flops.

Slipping my heels back on, I make my way inside the lounge. Its soft lighting and varying color pattern immediately make my eyes pop open wide. Along the outside walls is one large, cushioned seat with throw pillows and small tables set in front. In the center of the room are randomly colored round and square cube seats and overly large velvet chairs. It's almost as if I followed Alice into the rabbit hole and made my way into Wonderland.

Out of the corner of my eye, I spot Sue waving her arms at me, and I make my way over to them. I give her a quick hug and head over to greet Courtney the same, but she jumps up and bounces toward me, hugging me tightly to a point that I almost can't breathe. She grins as she backs away and more than excitably says, "I can't believe you came out. Thank you so much! We are going to have such a great time! They make excellent martinis here, and the bartenders are not too bad to look at."

Glancing over toward the bar, I see two tall guys in their mid-twenties with their sleeves rolled up to their elbows, shaking cocktails while their muscles move with the drinks. My mouth begins to water, but I'm not sure it's for the drinks.

"Uh-oh, I think Emily just caught on to our little secret." I hear Sue tell Courtney just loud enough for me to hear.

Quickly coming back to reality, I plank my ass in one of the oversized velvet chairs, and my ass feels like a million bucks in this chair. After plenty of crashes on jumps today at the rink, this extra padding under my ass is heaven at the moment. Snapping out of my daze, I remember it's Courtney's birthday. "Oh, Courtney, Happy Birthday!" Handing her a small gift bag, I say, "It's nothing much, but I hope you like it."

Taking the tissue paper out of the bag, Courtney pulls out the vanilla scented bath scrub and loofa set. "Oh my gosh, Emily, it's perfect! I love everything vanilla. How did you know?"

I shrug. "Lucky guess, really."

"Okay, let's get this party started! We need to get some drinks and snacks ordered. Now, Emily, I'm not sure if you've been here before, but they have the best finger foods that go with their drinks. But, since we are here for Court's birthday, may I suggest we all start off with the birthday cake martini? They are absolutely amazing!"

Courtney chimes in, "Sure, I'm game for whatever comes my way, but I've got to be slightly good. I've got classes in the morning."

"Oh, pish-posh. Skip them. The photos will still be there when you get back to the next class!" Sue scoffs.

Photography must be a passion of Courtney's if she's taking classes. "Where are you taking photography classes?" I ask.

"I'm enrolled in the community college trying to get my foot in the door for a magazine or travel company. I absolutely love portraits and landscapes. I've put in a few hours here and there doing baby photos and such to pay for tuition and supplies. Still living with my parents helps too since it allows me to seek out as many opportunities in the field and not burden them financially. I'm just hoping to get picked up full-time once I graduate in May next year."

"You must really have a talent. You'll have to show me some of your work sometime." *Whoa, where did that come from? Did I just suggest I'll be hanging out with her again? Oh, Emily, you must be coming down with something. This is so not like you.*

I'm removed from my inner dialogue when the hot bartender saunters over to see what he can get us to drink. Sue tosses her hair over her shoulder and glances up at him, batting her eyes. "Hey, Sean. Can we get three birthday cake martinis 'cuz it's Courtney's birthday and an order of the fried dough dippers, stuffed strawberries, and mini lemon blueberry cheesecakes?"

"Suzanne, are you sure that's not too much food?" I ask.

"Nah. Plus, knowing Sean, he'll hook us up with something else."

"How do you know him?" I ask, thinking perhaps they used to date.

"I teach his current girlfriend how to *dance*," she says suggestively.

"Oh! So, you teach dance now? That's great! I mean, I remember how good you were with ballet and choreography years ago. It was only fitting you would make that a career."

Courtney lets out a snort. "Oh, that's not the type of dancing she's talking about. Is it Suzanne?"

Kicking Courtney's leg slightly, she returns her glance my way and says, "What Courtney here is trying to say is that I teach pole fitness classes along with other standard dance styles."

"Pole fitness, as in *stripper* moves? Wait. That's like the new thing, right? So, you teach that?" Why am I so intrigued by this? You'd think I'd be horrified to find out my old friend is now teaching other women how to gyrate and be seductive on a pole.

"It's actually quite fun. Most girls leave my studio with more bruises and aching muscles because it's hard work. I usually have at least two bachelorette parties a week in the summer. You ought to come by sometime, and I'll teach you some moves," Sue says enthusiastically.

I'm immediately rescued from having to answer that question when the bartender brings us our drinks. When he hands off the first martini to Courtney, she begins squealing as he reveals a candle in the middle of her drink held up by a huge dollop of whipped cream and jimmies. Suzanne and I grab our drinks, and she begins to toast. "To Courtney! Happy Birthday. May you have a great year filled with good times and lots of sex!" Groan. I'm clearly still the virgin of the group. Clinking our glasses together, I bring the sweet concoction to my lips and glance at Sue as she gives me a wink before sipping her own drink. Yeah, she knows I'm a virgin, but something tells me she's about to start asking some questions.

"So, Emily, Jeremy seemed to be a little less of an ass after he ran after you at lunch. Any idea why that would be?" Suzanne continues to hold my stare, hoping I'll cave. Continuing to gulp back my drink, I hope by the time I'm done she'll have moved on to another topic with Courtney.

I finish my drink in record time, and the girls keep their eyes on me. "Damn, Emily!" Courtney exclaims. "I thought I could pound down the liquor."

Eyeing the bartender, I catch his attention and tip my empty glass around in the air, hoping he takes my hint that I need to keep these coming. I see him nod and begin to make another cocktail to help with my liquid courage. I hear Suzanne clear her throat. Glancing up, I still see her eyes fixed on me as if to say *I'm still waiting for an answer*. Shit! I'm not getting out of this.

Sigh. Here goes nothing.

"Jeremy tracked me down in the parking lot, and we had a little talk. It seemed we might have gotten off on the wrong foot the other day. We're good, we kissed, and he wants me to go out on a date with him."

Wait for it. It's coming.

In perfect unison, the two girls in front of me jump out of their chairs and immediately saddle up alongside me on a stool. "You did what?" Sue shouts.

"You are talking about my brother, Mr. Moody, right?"

Ah! Here's my drink. I thank the bartender again, and Suzanne orders herself another round as well. I continue to tell the girls how Jeremy and I may have had a few misunderstandings and how he returned the second kiss with such passion and intensity before asking me to go out with him. I left out the fact that he texted and called me this morning. The less they know the better. I haven't even talked to Jeremy to see where he stands at the moment. After this morning's conversation and how it ended, I can't be too sure he is still adamant about this so-called *date*.

More questions ensue after that, and I feel as though I'm in the speed round of *Jeopardy*. Before I know it, I've consumed four martinis and only picked at some of the fruit on top of the mini cheesecakes, and I can't understand what is coming out of my mouth. I see Courtney talking on the phone, but for the life of me, I can't make out anything she's saying. Things start to blur, and I begin to stand, but Suzanne grabs my wrists and we both thud down and start giggling after losing our balance. As I'm in a conversation about pole dancing with Suzanne, her eyes drift away from mine and over my shoulder. Her face turns up into a wicked smile, and she points before shouting, "You! How could you not tell me about you two?!"

What the hell? As I attempt to stand up on my wobbly legs, I giggle. *Why are my legs like rubber?* I turn, and my eyes run up the length of the guy standing in front of me, meeting his intoxicating big brown eyes. "Oh, shit," I whisper. That's when I feel as though I'm falling, and the last thing I remember are two warm, strong arms wrapped around my body.

JEREMY

I leave the rink early in the afternoon and am thoroughly exhausted. It's one thing to skate around with the kids in the summer camp at the Forum, but when you are up against guys on your own team, it's a whole other form of workout. My legs ache, and I'm pretty sure I'll have bruises in a few places tomorrow morning if I don't ice down my shoulders tonight. The ride back to my place is painful, and I know my arms are junk after I try to pull all my gear from the back of my truck. It was apparent how out of shape I was when I tried to catch my breath with Emily. I don't even know how that girl does it, but just the thought of her brings a smile to my face.

The last thing I wanted was to come home to Dave at my place, but clearly he wasn't kidding when he said he was planning on staying a while.

It comes as quite the shock when I walk in with all my gear and find him in my kitchen in nothing but his boxer briefs, chugging back a beer and scratching his balls. How he hasn't found the right girl after all these years isn't such a mystery.

"Are you planning on getting dressed today, or are you just planning on showing me your junk until you leave?" Smirking back at me with the beer at his lips, he grabs a hold of his cock and squeezes tight. "I'll take that as a no."

After showering and making some burgers on the grill, I grab a beer from the fridge and sit down in the living room to watch some TV. Dave is right behind me, plopping his ass in the chair next to me. After taking a bite out of his burger, he mumbles, "How was practice today?" Glancing from the TV over to him, wiping the burger juices from my mouth, I say, "Decent. It was good to see a few of the guys again and really toss the puck around, but I know I'm out of shape, and I'll be hurting in the morning." Dave nods back at me as if understanding. He never had any interest in having hockey as a career, but he still loves the sport and is probably one of my biggest supporters. He may be a total ass sometimes, but I'll never not want him as my best friend.

After finishing dinner, Dave and I sit back in the living room and play with Aspen as my phone begins ringing. Looking at the caller ID, I see it's Courtney. *Why would she be calling me?* I know she was heading out for birthday drinks tonight at Eavesdrop with Sue and Emily. When I called Courtney on the way home from Manchester to tell her Happy Birthday, she was ecstatic that Emily was going to join her. Courtney isn't hard to please, but she also has a soft heart, which she wears on her sleeve. Hopefully, Emily didn't cancel at the last minute, and that's why she's calling me.

Pulling the phone up to my ear, I say, "Hey, Court, everything all right?" I hear music in the background and what sounds like Sue and Emily talking about stripping and something about hooking up with the bartender. What the fuck?

Courtney answers, "Jeremy, I have no idea who else to call. Sue and Emily are trashed, and they shouldn't drive, but I don't have my car here to bring them home. Sue picked me up, and now I don't know what to do." What the hell? Sue was supposed to be watching out for her.

Dave gives me a questioning look as I respond, "Court, hang tight. Dave and I will be there in a little bit, okay?"

I hear Sue in the background slurring, "Courtney, is that Jeremy? Aww, Jeremy and Emily sitting in a tree k-I-s-s-I-n-g."

Shit.

"Okay, thanks, Jeremy. Sorry to bug you. I just didn't know what else to do."

"It's fine, Courtney. You did right by calling. I'll be there soon. Bye." I hang up.

Dave glances over after pulling a toy out of Aspen's mouth. "What's going on?" he asks, eyeing me curiously.

"Emily and Sue are toasted, and we're needed pronto."

Dave and I hop into my truck and make the fifteen-minute drive to Eavesdrop. We quickly head inside since it sounded as though the girls were already tanked before we left. Nothing, and I mean nothing, could have prepared us for what we walk in on in the lounge. The first person I make eye contact with is Sue, and her eyes shoot wide open. "You! How could you not tell me about you two?!" she shouts. Holy shit, she's now drawing attention to herself, and how much did she drink? Sue can usually hold her liquor, but I've never seen her this drunk, except for perhaps one of my birthday parties at my parents' house when she was singing something from *Mary Poppins* or some shit like that.

It's now apparent that Sue must have poked Emily enough to get the details out of her about our little interlude the other day. So much for just coming to give the girls a ride home. Rubbing my hands over my face, I glance up to see Emily trying to stand and turn around. I hear Dave hiss next to me, whispering, "Holy shit, Emily got hot, dude!" I growl, not even sure why, but I see Emily eyeing me up and down. Damn, she's smokin' tonight and those heels. Shit, my dick stirs in my pants just thinking about them wrapped around me. *Get your head off sex, asshole. You're here to help the girls.* At that moment, I notice her legs wobbling, and she starts to tilt over. I immediately rush over to her and wrap my arms around her before she hits the floor. I make my way to the chair and rest her on my lap with her passed out head in my neck.

"Jesus, how much did she have to drink?" I ask the girls.

Sue hiccups before saying, "I don't know, maybe one more martini than I did. I lost count at four." I glance over at Courtney, looking for a more sober explanation.

She catches my silent question and chimes in, "I have no idea, Jeremy. I thought she was okay, but she didn't really eat very much except some fruit. I'm really sorry. I didn't know."

"It's fine, Court. Can you just get me a bottled water from the bar? Dave, I need you to take my truck and make sure the girls get home." Shit, I don't even know if Emily still lives at the same house in Andover. I've somehow got to get her sober enough to talk to me, and that's when I notice the clear plastic on her wristlet. "Dave, I need you to see if Emily has an address on her ID on the side of the wristlet."

Sue's got her head lying on Dave's shoulder. He pulls out an ID from her clutch and hands it over for me to see the address. It's the same one as when I dropped her off years ago. Shit. I really hope Emily wakes up well before getting home to avoid having to try to explain this to her mom. If she's still as awful as she was years ago, she'll never allow Emily out again.

Shifting in my seat, I rub Emily's back, and she moans just slightly and reaches out to wrap her limp arms around my waist. I bring my lips down to her ear as I continue to rub her back. "Shh, I'm gonna get you home." I kiss her forehead and then glance up to see three pairs of eyes glaring into me. "What?" I ask as if I don't know why they are all staring at me. I've never been one for showing affection in public, let alone around my family or friends. There is just something about Emily that is special, and I can't quite figure out why she brings out a caring side of me. Something tells me I need to find out.

Courtney hands me the bottled water and Emily's purse and car keys, which Dave must have found in it. Glancing up at Courtney, I ask, "Quite the night out, huh? Are you all right to drive Sue's car home?"

She nods back at me. "Yeah, I'm good. I only had two drinks 'cuz I've got classes in the morning. Will you call me and let me know how Emily is when you get her home?" I sense the concern in her voice, but that's how Courtney is. She doesn't have to know the person more than a couple of minutes before she starts caring about them.

"Yeah, no problem, Court. I'll see you this weekend at Sunday dinner." I start to stand and gently drop Emily's legs to the ground, hoping she'll stand willingly. No such luck. I pull her up to my side by the waist and give Courtney a kiss on the cheek before starting to make my way out of the lounge. Looking back at the girls, I ask if the tab was settled as Sue nods her head with the bottle of water to her mouth. I'll just assume that's a yes. I give Dave a look that says I mean business when I hand him my keys to my truck. "Do not, and I mean do not, mess with my truck." I trust Dave, but he's still Dave, and he'll be fine so long as he has Sue in the truck with him. It's when he's alone with his thoughts that I begin to panic.

It is much easier to get Emily to her car once I pick her up outside of the lounge. It would have been too much of a scene had I carried her out in my arms, so I did my best to get her legs to move with me. Hitting the *Alert* button on her key fob, I find her car easily. As I lower her into the passenger seat, she starts to stir just slightly. Her big blue eyes peer up at me, "Jeremy?"

Pushing some stray hair away from her face, I lean down toward her. "Hey, Em. How are you feeling?" She leans over the edge of the car and throws up all over the ground.

At the same time, Dave walks over and sees the situation unfolding before walking away, holding up his hands and saying, "Call me if you need me to come pick up your ass. I'm out of here." Big help he is.

Grabbing the water from my back pocket, I kneel down to Emily's level and unscrew the bottle cap, handing it to her. "Em, you need to drink some of this. Are you okay for a while, so I can try to drive you home?"

Nodding, she looks up at me with soft eyes. "Yeah, I'm fine. You remember where I live, right?"

"Same house in Andover, right?" I ask as if I didn't already know.

"Yeah, just when you get there, pull into the garage on the far right of the driveway. My place is over the garage," she says as she starts to pass out again. Clicking her into the seatbelt, I shut the door and walk around to the driver's side and hop in. After adjusting the seat and turning on the car, I pull out of the parking lot. Her iPod begins playing, and the song that comes on surprises me a bit, considering these are songs she chose herself. Another version of "House of the Rising Sun" fills the car. I would have taken her for more of a current pop or show tune chick, but never classic rock.

I glance down at the iPod screen to see the song is from the *Sons of Anarchy* soundtrack. *Oh, please, don't tell me she's a Charlie Hunnam fan and only watches that show for a sighting of his naked ass.* Scrolling through her menus of music, I see she has all the *Sons of Anarchy* seasons' soundtracks and more hard and classic rock, very little pop, and only one Broadway musical called *Once*. Not a bad selection, chickie. She never ceases to surprise me.

Pulling up on her street, I turn down the radio and try to wake her just to make sure I brought her to the right place. "Em, hey, we're home," I softly say as her eyes open slowly. "Hmm?" she questions.

"We're at your house. Can you tell me where you want me to park the car?" I whisper into her ear as she leans against the car door.

"The large garage over there. Just hit the button above the visor, and the door will open to pull in."

Pulling down the driveway, I spot the garage and drive up slowly and hit the button. As the door finally slides all the way up, I pull in and kill the engine. Glancing over, I see Emily's eyes have shut again. I quietly get out of the car and go around to get her out. She's basically dead to the world. I grab all her belongings and pull her up in my arms, shutting the car door behind me. Looking around, I notice a stairwell at the back of the garage and head up, assuming that must be where she lives. Once at the top of the stairs, I set her feet down and pull her key chain out of my pocket. There are only a few keys, and on the second one, I manage to unlock and open the door.

As I feel around the inside wall for a light switch, I find one and flick it on. I pick up Emily and set her on one of the round kitchen table chairs before turning toward her cabinets and looking for a glass to get her some water. Locating them almost immediately, I fill the glass and place it onto the table in front of her. Her head rests on her arm as she keeps slipping in and out on me.

"Emily, can you try drinking some more water, please?" Her eyes open to meet mine as she grabs the glass and slowly takes small sips. Suddenly, her hand flies up to her mouth, and I watch her gag. "Em, are you okay?" Running for what I can only assume is the bathroom, she disappears and I immediately hear her throwing up in the toilet. I walk in her direction and stand in the doorway, not sure if she wants me to help or not. I grab a washcloth from the towel rack and run it under cold water. Once I'm near her, I run the cold towel over her neck and rub her back. Once she's done expelling all the liquor it appears she consumed tonight, she stands and makes her way to the sink. Grabbing the mouthwash, she swishes it around her mouth before spitting it out into the sink. She turns around to face me, and her eyes meet mine. "You feeling better, Em? Can I help you or get you anything?"

She doesn't respond, not even a word, as I continue to stare at her, looking for any kind of answer. What happens next is probably the last thing I would have expected from her. Tears well in her eyes as her entire face bunches up, and she lets go of all her emotions. Shit.

"Hey, hey, hey, what's with the tears? Why are you crying?" I ask as my thumbs run under her eyes to wipe away the tears.

In between sobs, she says, "I ruined the whole night. I was so nervous about hanging out with Sue and Courtney. Then, I went and ruined her birthday, and you had to come to help me. I'm so embarrassed and sorry. I ruined your night, too. Didn't I?"

"Hey, listen. You probably won't remember this conversation in the morning, but I can certainly tell you that you didn't ruin my night or the girls' night either. I'm happy to help you. If you ever need help, you can call me anytime. I'd rather know you're safe than not." More tears start falling, and she reaches out to hug me. I circle my arms around her and rub her back, trying to soothe her. I start to make my way out to the living room, but she grabs my hand, stopping me. "Jeremy, please don't leave."

"I'm just going to the kitchen to grab some water for you, and I've got to check on everyone else." She follows me into the kitchen and grabs the water from the table, taking small sips again. I grab my phone and send Dave and Court a text.

> *Emily isn't doing well. Not leaving her alone. I'll call you in the morning. Everyone else get home ok?*

Ding. Damn, that was fast. I see from the icon that it's from Dave.

Everyone is home. Sue is still with me, but don't get pissed. She's sleeping on your sofa. Be careful with Emily. TTYL

Why do I not want to know exactly why Sue is on my sofa? Dave can be quite the playboy sometimes, but I don't think he would cross that line with her, or maybe he would. I'll address that later. Right now, I've more pressing matters, like the girl across the room from me who just asked me to stay with her. Her eyes are glued to me right now, and I know I need to tread lightly.

"Okay, Em. Let's get you to bed, so you can sleep this off."

She stands and walks backward toward her four-poster bed while giving me a seductive eye. *I will not take advantage of her; she's drunk, and she'll never remember a minute of this.* I need to keep telling myself that. Before I can repeat it, she slowly removes her top, revealing a lace bra and then kicks off her heels.

"Em, what are you doing?" As she finally bumps into the bed, she makes a move to remove her bra, and that's when I move swiftly across the room and engulf her with my arms. "Not like this, Em. You will regret doing anything right now when I know you won't remember this in the morning. You're so much more than that to me. Okay? But, trust me when I say, it is taking a lot of effort to keep my hands off of you right now."

Reaching up, she wraps her arms around my neck and brings her lips up to within an inch of my face. She looks into my eyes and slowly places her lips unto mine and then pulls away. "Thank you," she says.

I hold her close to me and look her in the eyes. "I told you before, and I'll tell you again, Emily, you're totally worth fighting for." Reaching behind her, I pull her fluffy comforter back, lift her up and tuck her back in. "I'll be sleeping on the sofa if you need me at all." She nods and yawns as I reach over to grab one of her extra pillows and the throw blanket from the bottom of the bed. Before I even make it to the sofa, she's already asleep.

I strip off my T-shirt and unbuckle my belt, kicking off my sneakers by the heels and tossing my jeans onto the other chair before curling up on the sofa. Before I slip off to sleep, the last things I think of are how on Earth am I sleeping in Emily's house and please don't let her mom catch me in here, because I'm quite fond of my balls, and I'd like to keep them attached to my body.

CHAPTER
eight

Emily

As the sun screams its ugly head into my room, my head feels as though a jackhammer is going off in it. Holy shit. How much did I drink last night? Rolling over to face away from the demon light, I see my heels kicked off randomly onto the floor and my shirt thrown next to them. What. The. Hell? Pulling up the sheet, I notice I'm wearing only my bra, and my jeans are still safely attached to my legs. How did I get home last night? Why can't I remember anything after seeing Jeremy at Eavesdrop? Oh. My. God. Please don't tell me last night really happened. I hear movement from my bathroom. No. No. No! Now I feel as though I'm going to vomit, and there's only one place for me to go running. Aww, shit!

Throwing back the blankets and rushing toward the door, I have no idea who or what's on the other side, and right now, I don't even care that I see guys' clothes thrown over my sofa. As I open the bathroom door with one hand and cover my mouth with the other, the last person I think about seeing is Jeremy. He's standing there dripping wet from a shower and completely naked. My eyes shoot from the floor up to his face as he senses me coming in and removes the towel from drying his hair. I zone my eyes away from his penis and six pack abs. I rush for the toilet to expel the remaining demons in my stomach. As I continue to dry heave, I see Jeremy swiftly wrap the towel around his waist and rush to my side.

Chuckling a bit, he says, "It's not every day a girl sees me naked and throws up afterwards. Way to make a guy feel good about himself."

I glance up at him to see he's smiling and still rubbing my back. "Can you get me some water from the fridge, please?" Shaking his head, he stands and walks out of the bathroom. While he's gone, I can't help but picture him as I just saw him standing there dripping wet with it all hanging out. I'm no prude. I've seen my fair share of photos from various book blog sites on Facebook and videos, but to see it all for real the first time, I'm in shock.

Jeremy comes back into the bathroom with a bottled water and hands it to me as I sit up and lean my back against the wall. It's at that moment I realize I'm still in my lace bra, and he can basically see everything. I make to cover myself with my free arm, and he crouches down to my eye level.

As if sensing my nervousness, he says, "We didn't do anything last night, in case you were worrying about that. I'm going to get dressed and then make some toast for you. And, we'll talk, okay?" I nod back at him, and he smiles and walks back into the other room. I finish my water, throw on my pajamas that I had hanging on my bathroom door before brushing my teeth and fixing my hair. I don't look good, but it's better than nothing.

Making my way toward the kitchen area, I see Jeremy standing there, fully clothed, and making coffee and buttering the toast. He's moving around my kitchen as though he's lived here for years. It's kind of nice, but I'm still nervous about actually having a guy here in my place. It's all new, and I don't know how to act. Clearly, I'm not off to a good start after my showing last night.

"You need to eat this. How do you take your coffee?" He asks, handing me a plate of toast.

"Cream and one Equal, thanks," I say. He makes his way over to the fridge and glances around in there before grabbing the carton of creamer and turning back to me, giving me a look. "This is not cream. There is no such thing as fat-free cream," he says with a straight face. "Hey! It's cream, and it all tastes the same once you put it in the coffee anyway. I can't have fatty foods," I say more sternly than I should have, considering my head is pounding again.

As I'm rubbing my temples with my fingers, I see Jeremy make his way into my bathroom again, coming back shortly afterwards with a bottle of Advil. "Here, take these and eat the toast. You'll feel better."

Popping the painkillers and eating a few bites of the toast, I notice Jeremy making his way back over to the kitchen table. When he sits down in front of me, I sigh, as I know I have to ask, "Okay, tell me. How bad was I last night?"

Letting out a full-belly laugh, he responds, "Well, let's see. First, you consumed what I can only assume was a total of four martinis. You were talking to Sue about pole dancing when Court called me for help. Once I arrived, the minute you stood up, you passed out and then threw up in the parking lot before I drove your car home. Once I got you here, you proceeded to try to seduce me and kiss me before I told you I wasn't going to allow myself to be the guy who took advantage of you in that state when I knew you wouldn't remember any of it. I slept on the sofa, and then, well, you basically saw the goods this morning, and now here we are. That about sums it all up."

Shit, I really made quite the impression with everyone last night.

"Can you please give me Courtney's number? I need to seriously apologize not only to her, but also Sue. I can't believe I let myself act that way. I was so nervous, and I don't know what I was thinking. Then, trying to come on to you, I'm so sorry. This is such a disaster." I flush in embarrassment and drop my face into my hands. I mumble into my hands, "If you drove me home, where is your truck?" All I need is for my mother to see someone else's vehicle in the driveway, and she'll be over here knocking down my door.

"My friend Dave came with me to Eavesdrop last night, because as it turned out, Sue also needed a ride home. Courtney took Suzanne's car back to her house, and Dave took my truck and Suzanne back to my place. He's been kind of staying there a couple of days for some reason or another. I don't even want to think of what he and Sue got up to after I left with you. Dave may be my best friend, but he's definitely more of a one-night stand kind of guy," he says as he stands to put his coffee cup into the dishwasher. I look up at him, thinking at least I'm not the only one out of control, but I feel I owe him more than just a thank you.

"I can't really thank you enough for what you did for me. I'm just glad Courtney made the call because I don't know how I would have made it home. I hate that I was even in that state to begin with. I hardly drink, so having more than two drinks was not a good idea. I must owe someone some money since I can't remember paying the bill."

He stares back at me as he leans against my counter. "The bill has been taken care of. Don't worry about it." Glancing down at his watch, he checks the time. "I've got to actually call Dave soon to see if he can come pick me up. I've got a meeting with the Monarchs this afternoon."

I check the time on my phone on the table in front of me, seeing it's already ten, and remembering I've got ballet and strength training later. "Shit! I've got to get ready, too. Thank goodness I'm not skating this afternoon. I'd probably be sick all over the ice."

JEREMY

It's clear that Emily has never been hungover before. I'm glad that I stayed the night with her. Somehow I don't think she would have been able to handle waking up alone and feeling the way she does without thinking a million other thoughts. I just really didn't think she'd see my naked body and then throw up afterwards. No, I wasn't expecting that. I have feelings too, and it wasn't even cold after I got out of the shower. I'm not huge, but I can still hit the right spot when it counts. I can't say that the minute Emily walked in and saw me I didn't think about pushing her up against the bathroom wall, unclasping her bra, freeing those lace bound breasts of hers, and forcing myself to have her right then and there. Oh, I did, but the vomiting put a wrench in that thought.

She feels a lot better since she has showered, so I check in with Dave, but whenever she walks by me in the kitchen and the smell of vanilla hits me, it is me that is feeling light-headed. The fifth time I ring Dave with no answer, I go to find Emily, who is down in the garage loading up her car with her bag for this afternoon.

I find her just as she is closing her trunk, and she looks up at me, as she must have heard me coming down the stairs. She looks stunning in her dance clothes with her hair pulled back into a ponytail. "Did you get a hold of Dave?" she asks.

"No, I'm not sure why he's not answering his phone, but I really do need to get back to my place to get to work," I say with a slight hesitation in my voice. "You think you might be able to drop me off on your way out? I'm still in Tewksbury, so it won't be too far." I'm afraid of what she'll think once I show her where I live, but she might understand, considering the kind of apartment she lives in.

"Yeah, sure, it's the least I can do since you helped me this morning and last night. Let me just head back upstairs and grab the rest of my stuff, and we'll leave," she says as she runs up the flight of stairs. Shortly after that, I hear the sounds of a locking door upstairs and garage doors opening behind me. Once she comes into view, she gives me a look and then tosses her keys at me. Sweet, a girl that has no problem letting me drive. I give her a glance as if asking if she is sure. She shrugs her shoulders and says, "It's just easier for you to drive the car to your house instead of giving me turn-by-turn directions." She does have a point, but at least this way I can have the next few minutes in the car trying to get this girl to go out with me for dinner this weekend.

Both of us get into the Audi, and I start up the engine, proceeding to pull out of the garage and down around the driveway. It's not as though I'm complaining or even want to ask, but I feel as though I ought to. "How is it I never had the pleasure of running into your parents at all while I was here last night?" I look over and see Emily scrolling through her phone before she glances up at me to respond.

"Daddy mostly stays in Boston these days or is out of town, and then Mother, well, she's got the entire house to herself, and outside of polishing off multiple cocktails before noon, her only other chore in a day is to make a few phone calls for my *benefit* and let me know when and where I need to be. I hope you didn't expect me to sugar coat any of that." She chuckles while turning on the radio. "I try to avoid them at all costs these days. Once I finished college, I moved into the garage because I couldn't take a lot of the madness in the house."

"Not to sound mean or anything, but what's keeping you holed up still at your parents' house?" I ask, even though I really have no right. She stares out the window, scanning the passing houses and pushing a stray piece of hair behind her ear. God, she's gorgeous. She really has no idea how much natural beauty she possesses.

She sighs and turns to me. "Some things are still beyond my control. Everyday I try to be a little stronger than the last in the hope that one day my life won't involve training, competitions, and my parents hounding me about success and making the family look good. I've only ever been a marketing tool for Daddy's company, and well, you know how my mother is. I just want to wake up and have it all gone, but then I think to myself, what the hell do I do afterwards? I'm afraid when it's all over and I'm finally able to walk away, I'll have nowhere or no one to walk toward." She turns her head and begins sniffling and wiping her eyes with the backs of her hands.

I am really at a loss for words, because in some ways, I can say the same for me. Granted, I still coach the kids during the summer, but what happens to me when that contract doesn't come, or I get traded? I've been lucky so far, but the AHL is a business, and they can drop you whenever they feel like it. An injury can put you out for life, and then what? How do you move on when the only thing you know, you can no longer do?

Gazing over at Emily, I grab her hand in mine and begin rubbing her knuckles. Her soft eyes meet mine, and she smiles slightly, but it becomes genuinely larger when I bring her hand up to my mouth and kiss it. Pulling the car over to the side of the street and turning it off, I move to face her and reach out to rub the side of her face. "If and when you're able to walk away, you can always walk toward me. Got it?"

Tears form in her eyes again, and she nods back at me. "Is this where you live?" she asks, facing the house we're parked in front of.

Looking at the old cape-styled home with red shutters on the front windows and then over to where my truck is parked in the driveway in front of the huge garage, I begin laughing. "Funny thing. You're not the only one who still lives with their parents," I say, thinking she's probably wondering how much of a mamma's boy I really am.

In all reality, after college when the AHL finally picked me up off an amateur tryout agreement and then signed me to a one-year contract, I didn't know if it would last. Renting or buying wasn't really a feasible option for me, so with the money I earned from some of my first contract, I renovated the entire top level of the garage into a two-bedroom apartment. It also helps when I go on the road with the Monarchs to know that my parents will take care of Aspen for me. Road trips aren't long, but it's long enough that he needs taking care of. Either way I love coming home to this place. It's always been filled with loving people and great memories.

Emily turns back at me and laughs. "Oh my gosh! I think you and I might have more in common than we think! Do you have time to show me your place? I mean, you don't have to, but I see Sue's car is still parked up there, and I need to apologize for last night anyway. I mean, that is still the same car she had years ago, right?"

Wait. Why is Sue's car still parked in the driveway? Maybe Dave didn't take her home, or Courtney came here after leaving Eavesdrop. Dave did say she was asleep on my sofa last night, and he didn't answer his phone at all this morning. Something isn't adding up. Now, I need to find out what the hell happened last night. Grabbing the keys and going to open the door, I nod to Emily to come along. This may be a bad idea. All I need to add to this morning is my mom to come out the front door before I make it safely into my place.

Emily keeps up with my pace, and once we get to the stairs, I urge her up in front of me as I place my hand on the small of her back. I unlock the door and open it, letting Emily walk in first. Immediately upon entering, she turns around, pulling her hands up to her face, muttering something along the lines of, "Oh my gosh! Oh my gosh! Please tell me I am not seeing what I think that is."

Pulling her into my chest and rubbing her back, I scan my living room, and my eyes fall upon what can only be described as a conjoined pile of naked flesh surrounded by most likely my entire liquor cabinet. Leaving Emily facing away from the sight, I walk over to lay my hands on the back of my sofa, looking at the two sleepyheads that are starting to stir on the floor. Oh, hell no! This is going to be fun. With all my might, I suck in my breath and scream, "Cock-a-Doodle-Doo!"

Dave shoots straight up, while his partner in crime comes into view and raises her arm to block the bright light. He rubs his hands over his head and then stares up at me, clearly hungover. "Fuck, dude, what are you yelling for?" He still hasn't processed the fact that his dick is hanging out or that Emily is in the room, so I help him out a bit.

"Well, let's see. It could be because I tried calling five times earlier, and you didn't answer, probably because you drank my entire stash of Patron. It could be because Emily just walked in to see your twig and berries hanging out on my living room floor, or it could be because I told you to take Suzanne home, not back to my place and screw her on my floor." At my last statement, his eyes go wide, and he looks down next to him to see Sue's eyes bugging out of her head just as wide as his. Well, I guess neither of these two expected to be hooking up with each other last night. Sue shoots up off the floor, grabs a blanket from the couch, and runs down the hall to the bathroom. I turn to Emily. "Emily, can you maybe just go try to talk to her? She might feel better having it come from you." She nods my way and makes her way down the hall toward the bathroom.

In the meantime, I have Dave to deal with. "Dude, can you perhaps put some pants or something over yourself? I mean, really, Emily already threw up after seeing my junk this morning. I'm shocked she didn't toss her cookies after seeing all this, too," I say, making my way to the fridge to grab some water. As I glance back over to him, he slowly gets off the floor, grabs his boxers and tugs them on. Leaning on my counter with my arms out in front of me, I take the water bottle up to my mouth, chugging back the cold fluid before asking him, "Do I even want to ask what happened last night?"

Sighing, Dave looks down the hall and back to me. "I remember leaving Eavesdrop, and the minute Sue got in the truck, she had her tongue in my ear and rubbing her hands over my dick. Shit, you know me. I'm not one to say no. She said she wanted me to make her scream and her toes curl anyway I knew how. The next thing I knew she called Courtney and started giggling, so I grabbed her phone and told Courtney to just come back here. When we got here, I told Courtney I was going to let Sue sleep on your sofa. That part of my text wasn't a lie. Then, Sue found your Patron, and we started playing *Truth or Dare*. Bad choice, I know! After, I think, my sixth shot, I might have started thinking more with my dick than my head. Sorry, dude, but not really. I mean, Sue *is* crazy, but she's hot."

I honestly can't help but laugh because I don't think Dave understands the level of crazy he just got himself into. Back in middle school, he knew how nuts this girl was, but he always had a weak spot if she showed him even the slightest bit of attention.

Two loud shrieks followed by laughter from down the hall break my train of thought. Dave and I run to where the boisterous sounds are coming from. Stopping in the doorway, I see one of the funniest sights ever. Emily is sprawled out on the floor of my bedroom as Aspen huddles over her body, licking her face and jumping back to grab his stuffed duck from the floor, trying to get her to tug it away from him. I whistle to get his attention, and he leaves Emily's side long enough for her to stand up and adjust her clothes. I glance at her, taking in her smile and asking if she's all right.

She walks over to me and kneels down to Aspen, rubbing behind his ears and saying in her lovey dovey talk, "Of course, I'm all right, but who is this big ball of fur that just gave me the best kisses in the world?" Best kisses? Really?! I don't think so.

I lean into her as she stands back up and pull her toward my chest. "Perhaps you don't remember *the* kiss I gave you a few days ago? But, if that wasn't up to your standards, I can certainly up my game." With that statement, I slide my mouth down her neck as I feel her shiver and the slightest of moans comes from her mouth. The clearing of Dave's throat behind us reminds me that we are not alone. Turning to him, I give him a glare that asks, *What the fuck?*

"Not to interrupt, considering I'm already on the shit list, but where is Sue?" he asks. Emily slides out from under my grasp to face Dave. She walks over to him, reaching out her hand. "You must be Dave. I don't know if you know me, but I'm Emily. I want to thank you for helping last night in our drunken state at the bar; however, Sue may not be entirely sure of what happened. If you so much as hurt her, I will have no problem shoving your nuts up your ass." She starts to make her way back toward the bathroom, where I assume Sue is hiding out, and says "Jeremy, just out of curiosity, since I don't have too much to compare them to, but from what I saw this morning, shouldn't his be just as big as yours? It wasn't that cold in the living room, was it?" With that, she smirks, and I see Dave's face scowl at her insinuation.

"Dude!" Dave shouts.

Now, I'm full on laughing hysterically. "Seriously, that one's got a naughty side to her, and I'm just starting to see how playful she can be. Don't you even say anything about her."

Dave puts his hand on my shoulder. "No way, man. I couldn't care less about her small dick comment. What I want to know is how the fuck did she see your dick, and what did you really do last night?"

CHAPTER
nine

As I knock on the bathroom door before I step in, my hands are still shaking from my little bravado show I just put on in front of Dave and Jeremy. I've never done or said anything like that before, since I have always been in the public eye and worried about how it would affect my family image. I have to say, to let go for once felt incredible.

I walk in to find Sue, still curled up on the bathroom floor with her knees pulled tightly to her chest. With tears rolling down her face, she raises her bloodshot eyes to me. In my heart, I know I need to be here for her, but the clock on the wall keeps reminding me that I'm going to have to act fast if I'm to make it to my training session on time. I know that if I'm even just one minute late, my phone will ring off the hook, and my mother will not relent until she determines where I am and why I'm not one hundred percent focused on the goal at hand. Unfortunately, what she doesn't know is that goal has only ever been hers and never mine. Medals and trophies, all that means nothing when your career is over. It's friendships and love that hold the key to happiness and help fulfill your dreams.

Pulling up a seat next to Sue, I drape one arm over her shoulder and try to comfort her. She hasn't said much to me about what happened last night, other than the obvious. Earlier, I went in search for her clothes from last night, but never found them, as I was attacked by one of the largest, most loving dogs I've ever met. As I continue to rub my hands over her arms to ease her, I try to get some details about last night, but I feel as though I really need to apologize for my own actions first.

"Sue, please tell me what I can do to help. I can't help but feel as though I'm partly to blame for this."

Her eyes shoot up and stare right at me. Wiping her hands over her face, she sniffles back, "Why would you even think me sleeping with Dave is partly your fault?"

Looking back at her with sad eyes, I reply, "Well, if I hadn't been so nervous about hanging out with you and Courtney, I never would have had so much to drink, and you probably would have been in the right frame of mind to drive home alone. Because of me, Dave had to take you home, and well, we both know what happened after that."

Sue's tears have stopped, and she wraps the bathroom towel around her tighter as she says, "I'm the one who led him on and basically told him to ravage me last night. Don't get me wrong. Dave is a hot fuck and has the body of a god, but he's been a playboy since I met him in middle school. We've been playing this game for years. I'm crying because I never actually realized that I had feelings for him, and I know he'll never feel the same way toward me."

I hug her tightly, and we stand to face each other. "So, you forgive me for being an out of control drunk last night who made you sleep with Dave?"

Chuckling, she waves her hand in the air. "Yeah, we're good. It was fun, just us three. I think we probably need to make it up to Courtney, though. Poor thing didn't realize we were going to need a rescue team. Which, by the way, you need to tell me all about this thing with you and Jeremy." Turning on the faucet, she starts running water over her face and then takes some toothpaste from her finger and starts cleaning her teeth.

While she's brushing and spitting, I may as well tell her my story about the past twelve hours. Once the water is turned off and she stares at me because I've not only informed her of the kiss the other day, but also my liquid courage and throwing up after seeing Jeremy naked, she laughs at me as if it happens to her all the time. A knock comes from the door, and I turn to open it slightly after Sue gives me the okay.

Jeremy sticks his head in. "Everything good in here?" I nod back at him as he looks at both of us, clearly thinking he's not going to have to deal with girl problems as long as Sue is laughing.

"Yeah, we'll be out in a minute, but can you try to find Sue's clothes for her?"

He nods back at me as he starts to close the door, but comes back in before it shuts and whispers into my ear, "After you're done in here, meet me in my room. I want to ask you something, okay?" I stare up at his big brown eyes and shake my head.

After he shuts the door behind him, Sue grabs my shoulders and turns me to face her. "Do you even realize how bad that boy has it for you? I've known him basically my whole life, and he's never acted like he does when he's around you." I stare back at her with a confused look.

"You're crazy. He barely even knows me. He keeps insisting on me going out with him, but I just don't know if that's such a good idea."

"Why wouldn't you go out with him?"

How do I explain to her that there are so many reasons why I can't see a relationship with him, let alone anyone else in my near future? Until a few days ago, I had absolutely no experience dealing with guys. Now, here I am seeing Jeremy wet and naked this morning, and what do I end up doing? I throw up. I guess in some ways I do kind of owe him. Spending one night out with him won't be so bad.

"I'm not even sure if he's interested, but if he asks, I guess it wouldn't be so bad to get to know him better," I tell Sue as I lean against the door, playing with the ends of my hair.

"Well, what are you doing still standing in here with me? Get your ass out of here and go talk to him," she presses.

"Are you sure you're all right?" I ask, knowing that I'll stay with her before heading to see Jeremy if she asks.

"I'm fine. I've got to go have words with that asshat in the other room anyway. I need to clear up a few fuzzy details about last night and head out. Call me later and let me know how things turn out with Jeremy, okay?"

After confirming I'll be in touch with her later, I make my way down the hall to Jeremy's room. Opening the door further, I see him grabbing his hockey gear and throwing it into a bag almost as big as me. Once I walk through the door, I turn slowly and shut it behind me. Trying to find my inner strength, I start making my way over to where he is now standing staring at me. He must have sensed something was up when I shut the door and didn't say anything. Honestly, I have no idea what I want to say or even what he wants to talk to me about, but I'm here now, and I can't turn back. "What did you want to ask me?" I ask, just above a whisper.

I see him toss the items he has in his hands into the bag on the floor as he goes to sit at the end of his bed. He slowly pats the space next to him, telling me to come sit. I give him an odd look, and he says, "I'm not going to bite. Just come sit, please." Slowly, I walk over and sit next to him. As he scoots a little closer, his hand comes up to grab my chin, so I have to look him in the eyes. "Do you have any idea how beautiful you are? You don't, do you? I know this is all new for you, and I'll be as patient as you need me to be. But, you do owe me a date, so before you try to talk your way out of it, I'm going to tell you right now, our first date is going to happen. I know you felt a connection when we kissed the other day. Just live in the moment and let your heart tell you what to do before your mind starts working out a different answer."

Out of his entire statement, the only thing that registers in my head is he thinks I'm beautiful. Even after last night and this morning, he still wants to go on a date with me, and I know I have no reason to say no. However, I feel like being a tease, so I play with him a little.

Standing and moving in front of him, I slide between his legs, placing my hands on his shoulders. "Now, just because I've seen you naked doesn't mean I'm obligated to go out with you." Slowly moving my nervous hands down to his chest, I lean into his ear and whisper, "It just means I have to do something in return for you." I feel his heart start to race under my hand, and I know I'm doing something right. "So, Jeremy, besides going on a date with you, what do you want?"

I'm pretty certain he can hear my heart racing if he wants to. I'm not even sure where this whole new version of sexy Emily has come from, but she has made herself known, and I'm kind of digging her. It's a new kind of rush I haven't felt in a very long time, if ever.

Jeremy brings his hands up to my hips just over my yoga pants and picks me up and tosses me back onto his bed as he leans over me. "I said I'd be patient, but I'm not made of steel when you say things like that," he says with a stern face, rubbing his hand down my thigh as he continues to say, "There are so many things running through my mind right now, but I'm not sure you are ready for what they are." I'm not sure I'm prepared for any of those things either, but I won't lie and say I'm not attracted to Jeremy. I'm just nervous I'm not as experienced. Everything will be a new endeavor for me. There is only so much you can learn on the Internet.

I'm taken away from my thoughts when I feel Jeremy slide his hand under my yoga top as his thumb rubs the skin just above my hip. I can do this. Can't I? For some reason, the more he touches me, the harder it is for me to resist reaching out and touching him. Why am I mentally holding back? I have a gorgeous guy in front of me who's into me, making my heart race, and I need to let go and free my inhibitions.

His eyes are still locked with mine when he whispers, "Stop thinking in that head of yours. You asked what you could do for me, so I'm telling you. You're going on a date with me Friday night."

I nod my head and say, "Yes, I'll go out with you, although we really have done this all backward. Haven't we? We kissed. I saw you naked and now we go on a date. I really thought those items would be in a different order. Since we're here now, maybe we could do some other things backward." *Seriously, where did my inner sex kitten come from? I'm starting to like her!*

The look on Jeremy's face is probably that of utter shock. He glances over at his clock and then back to me. "Fuck it! I'll be a little late. When you have requests like that, I'll be more than happy to adhere to them. So, what were you thinking?"

Shit! He wants me to tell him what I want us to do. I have things in my mind, but I'm not sure how to physically word them. I know we're not ready to take this that far, but a little fun won't hurt. I decide showing him may be a better plan of attack instead of trying to be all seductive vocally. Slowly lowering my hands to the hem of my top, I cross my arms and lift my shirt over my head, never losing eye contact with Jeremy as I toss itonto the floor. His eyes go wide, and his hands go to reach my neck as he brings his lips down over mine. I can feel his desire for me with every swipe of his tongue.

His hands roam from my neck down toward my breasts. I look at him and can tell he's making sure I'm all right with what he's doing. Nodding my approval, he pulls back from me, removing his shirt as well. His firm abs and toned arms are on full display again in front of me, except this time I'm reaching out to touch him, pulling him so his body is flush with mine. Tingling sensations shoot throughout my body in response to our closeness. Reaching for his hand, I slowly bring it up to touch my breast, and he lets out a hiss as he begins kissing my neck. As he gently massages and rubs my nipple, I hear him say, "Emily, you're driving me absolutely insane. You're sexy as hell, and you're going to have to tell me when to stop because I'm about to lose control around you." When I feel his erection rubbing up against my leg, I know this is real and it feels incredible.

A moan escapes my mouth, and without thinking, I arch my back into his still kneading hands. His lips crash into mine, and I run my hand down his back and over his jean-covered ass. Pushing his leg between my thighs, I open my legs to let him in. The more he kisses my lips, along with the feeling of his chest rubbing across my nipples, the more I get aroused. Wetness floods through my core, and I'm not sure what or how I'm going to get the release I need.

Jeremy looks at me and says, "Tell me what you need, Emily."

I slowly move my hand to rub the front of his jeans, and I see his eyes roll toward the back of his head as I hear him groan. *I know this is right. I know I can say this to him.* "Make me come, Jeremy. I need you."

"Emily, I'll make you come any day of the week. Just tell me how you want it. I don't want to push you too far," he says while his face is nestled in my collarbone, slowly placing kisses toward my breasts.

I need to be bold and carefree, but I know in most sexual areas, I have absolutely no experience. Doing the only thing that's familiar to me, I reach up for Jeremy's hand and keep my eyes locked on his. I slowly bring his hand down toward the throbbing between my legs. His eyes widen as I slip his hand underneath my pants and allow his fingers to feel where I need him right now. He looks into my eyes, searching for any kind of hesitation. He must think I'm made of glass or something because the look he's giving me tells me he's more worried than I am. Pushing my pelvis up further, I force his hand deeper into my heated wetness. The hesitation that was in his eyes has now been replaced with unbridled desire.

"Emily, you have no idea how beautiful you are. Please, just let me know if I go too far, okay?" he whispers as his hand starts stroking my arousal over my clit. Immediately, I feel a sensation spread all over my lower body, and my eyes close at the sudden onset of desire for more connection.

Shamelessly, I reach out and start unbuttoning his jeans, pushing down the zipper and reaching in to return the pleasure he's giving me. The moment I find it and begin stroking my hand over his hard length of soft skin, his index finger delves deep inside me, igniting my whole body on fire. His lips crush mine, probably to muffle the moans that continue to grow louder. "What are you doing to me? If you keep touching me like that, I'm not gonna be able to give you my full attention where you need it," he says in between breaths.

"It's only fair, right?" I whimper as my breaths become strained. *Oh my God.* "Don't say you don't like it," I taunt him as beads of sweat form on his forehead. *Just a little higher.* "Am I doing this right?" *That's the spot, right there.*

I continue my torturous pace, stroking his cock in my hand as his fingers work their way feverishly inside me. His cock throbs as pre-cum begins to trickle from his tip at the same time I feel pressure and tingling surmount in my core. He emits a moan, and I know he must be close, too.

"Emily, don't stop. Shit, that feels incredible. Come with me, babe." As I look up into his eyes, my hand strokes faster as his fingers move frantically. Then, his finger juts up and hits the spot that sends me spiraling out of my body. My hand stills on his dick.

"Oh my God, Jeremy!" I shakily scream.

I see his eyes squeeze shut as I move up and down his length again and warm cum drenches my hand. With his eyes barely open, he moans, "Fuck, Emily!"

As we both come down from our high, the realization sets in of what we just did. Everything we've done so far has been so backward, but it feels so right, so familiar. It's as though we've been together for years.

As his lips start placing soft kisses along my neck, our moods shift. Softly laughing, I say, "Perhaps we could try for that dinner date now. I'll promise not to drink martinis if you promise to keep your clothes on, so we might actually have a normal conversation. Deal?"

Lifting his head, he answers, "I'm pretty sure that can be arranged. As much as I want to stay here with you in my bed all day, we both have to get to work now."

I look at the clock, realizing I should have left about a half hour ago. "Shit!" I shout. Just as I'm about to get moving, Jeremy's door swings open and Dave storms in. My eyes go wide in horror as I remember I'm naked from the waist up, and my hand is still inside Jeremy's underwear. Jeremy immediately grabs his comforter up over the side of me while lowering himself to block Dave's view of my chest.

"Fuck, Dave! Ever hear of knocking?" Jeremy scolds. Nestling my body into his, I try shielding whatever is about to go on between the two of them, and the last thing I expect to feel is safe and protected while I'm wrapped in his arms.

JEREMY

Since Emily left my place the other day, I've been on cloud nine. Everyone seems to think I've lost my shit because I haven't been this happy in a long time. After Dave walked in on us, we had a little talk about his night with Sue. Turns out those two love to hate each other, but unmistakably are meant to be together. That's apparent from his nonstop talking about the occurrences of their drunken night.

I've been to practice at the rink the past two days and just finished getting all my contract paperwork in order for the Monarchs. The few of us that are returning this year are signed in for our contracts for the upcoming season. The new guys are talented, decent players. This happens every year, though, being with the AHL. All of us understand we can be called up at any point, just like that. Chances are, most of these guys will start out here, but will be moved over the course of the season. I've been lucky enough to stay where I am for the past couple of years. Somehow I know it won't stay this way for long.

Emily has also been busy with her training. I've managed to sneak a few texts and phone calls to her, but we really haven't had time to spend together. After she and I were wrapped up in my sheets the other day, I really had a hard time letting her go. A part of me knew that our time together would be short-lived because of our schedules, but I told her in the beginning she was worth fighting for, and I damn well meant it.

Courtney had apparently dropped the ball to my mom about Emily, too. Just yesterday, after a pretty lengthy day of training camp at the rink, she cornered me in the driveway before I could get to the door. I love my mom, but I've avoided bringing women home for this exact reason. She jumps at the first chance she knows I'm involved with a girl. Since even before that bitch Becca stormed out of my life, I'd never brought anyone back to meet my parents. I want to find the right person who likes me for me. When Mom confronted me, she knew I'd cave and talk to her. It could have been the plate of freshly baked oatmeal raisin cookies she taunted me with, too. *What? I'm easy to please, and cookies are my weakness.* My mom's cookies are the best, and she knows they're her best bargaining tool.

We were sitting in my kitchen with Aspen while I disclosed that Courtney did in fact harbor some information from her. I was forced to explain that the girl who snuck into my life was none other than Emily Cameron. My mom could not forget that name even if she tried. After that day at the rink and then my infamous summer after high school graduation, my mom understood how much Emily meant to me. She also realized that Emily had the power to break me again if this didn't work out.

I devoured the entire plate of cookies while watching my mom listen to me explain everything that happened since seeing Emily at the restaurant. I even confessed Emily's playful side from the other day. Mom knows I'm no virgin, and she's also not one to pass judgment.

Her only response to my confession was, "Sweetie, I know you will understand when I say this, that I have your best interest at heart. I know how much you care for Emily, I do, but remember her lifestyle is much different than yours now. I just don't want to see you get hurt all over again, but if you pursue her, and she makes you happy, you know your father and I will support you regardless." I knew they would be my support system if this didn't work out with Emily. She continued, "I want to finally meet the girl who captivated you so many years ago. Everyone will be here for Sunday dinner, so please be sure to invite her over. From what Courtney and Josh have already told me, I know she will fit in just fine." As she stood to leave, she turned around in the doorway. I must have been in a daze trying to process everything. Concern etched all over her face, she asked, "Jeremy, everything good at hockey today?"

"Yeah, Mom, the team is looking real good for this season," I said.

"Well, then there isn't any reason for you to have that worried look on your face, now is there? Hockey is good, and you've got a beautiful girl back in your life," she told me straight up with no bullshit. She was right, though. She always was. Hockey had always been my first love. I'd just have to figure out how to fit Emily in there, too. She could be that one missing puzzle piece that was holding me back from feeling complete, but it was still way too early to think of that.

Mom left shortly after that, and today is a new day. I'm going to keep trying to get Emily to open up to me, so I can get to know what's inside the real Emily Cameron. As I'm flopped down on my bed, staring up at my ceiling, I can still smell Emily's vanilla body wash lingering around me. Thoughts of her lying here almost completely naked, gazing up at me with those big blue eyes and her long blonde hair spread out under her consume me. I feel my cock stir as more thoughts invade of how warm her pussy writhed against my hand and her own hand jerking me off. God, this girl is driving me insane, and it's only been a week since we reunited. Pulling myself off the bed and stripping off my clothes, I make my way to take a shower.

Turning on the water, I wait for the steam to envelope the room before I hop in. Leaning my hands against the tiles in front of me, I shut my eyes and let the water saturate my head and face. A vision of Emily's smile enters my mind, and I feel my cock harden. Reaching down, I start stroking myself until I'm completely hard. I have the image of her beautiful body lying under me in my bed. Imagining I'm inside her thrusting hard, I quicken my pace as her words to me the other day infiltrate my mind. "Jeremy, make me come." Squinting my eyes shut tight, I grip my cock tighter and feel the warm fluids start spurting out of me. *Fuck me!* My free hand slams against the wall as my release shatters every muscle inside my body. Opening my eyes, I realize I'd much rather have had Emily's hand wrapped around my shaft than my own. What is this girl doing to me? I need to stay focused. Hockey needs to be my priority. I've just got to figure out how to balance both. I can do this, right? No problem. I don't want to go through the same shit I did with Becca. I honestly don't need that type of relationship again. I can only hope Emily will be worth it in the end.

After showering, I make my way into the kitchen to boot up my laptop and make myself some dinner. The surround sound is blasting some Flo Rida song, and I can't help but start whistling along. I finish putting together a turkey sandwich with stuffing, cranberry sauce and lettuce. The hockey season will be in full swing in just a couple of weeks, so I need to make sure I start eating healthy again, which also means spending more time working out at the gym. Leaning over the counter while taking a bite of my sandwich, I start reading through my emails. Plenty of junk, as usual, but also emails regarding promotional events I am required to attend for the Monarchs. One in particular is in another week. It's the annual team tailgate party. All the guys will be there as well as many of the season ticket holders. It's a good time for the most part. The AHL doesn't have a huge following, but many of the season ticket holders have the same view about hockey as I do. They just love the game.

Scanning the web some more after jotting down the hockey schedule for the next month, I start searching out places to take Emily Friday night for our first official date. The weather is still supposed to be decent for New England standards. The middle of September can be tricky around here, but the forecast for tomorrow is still calling for clear skies and an evening temperature of around sixty-five degrees. Tapping my fingers on the keys, trying to figure out the best place to take her, I finally plan the perfect evening. Pulling up the website on my laptop, I get the information I need and grab my phone to make the call. She's going to love it.

CHAPTER
ten

Emily

It's been three days since I last saw Jeremy, and it's not as though I have had much of a choice. Neither one of us has had any spare time in our schedules since I left his place after our intense bedroom escapade the other day. I spent much of the beginning of the week holed up in my apartment trying to find the exact music to fit my mood this season. It took several hours of searching, but I found it, and it will be a program I can let emotions flow and immerse myself into the free skate that represents who I am. The music speaks to me, and I know it is the right choice.

My mother decided to show up in Boston yesterday to critique my progress during my all day training and choreography practice. Needless to say, she wasn't impressed; she never is. I'm only glad she doesn't make it an everyday occurrence to check on me. She's a distraction and even the coaches notice, but they never say anything because she signs their paychecks. I did a full run-through of the program just to see how it flowed with the music, and for the first time in a long time, I was happy with it. Then, I heard my mother chime in from the bleachers.

"Emily Cameron! This year is the biggest year of your career, and you are going to go on national television and perform that program? Please tell me you aren't serious." I caught all my coaches rolling their eyes, and a hint of anger began to boil within me. I've never given a shit about my mother's opinion of my skating, but I've also never said anything to make her see my displeasure. I've always put on the fake smile and just gone back out there, fixed what needed fixing and moved on. Not this time, this program was mine and I would not let her badger me about it!

Placing my hands on my hips, I came to a sudden halt in the middle of the ice and turned to face her. With every ounce of strength I could muster, I yelled, "Yes, Mother! I will be performing this program all season long, and you will not say another word about it. This is *my* program, not yours, and for once I'm happy with the outcome and how it makes *me* feel!"

The rink went dead silent as my last word echoed through the building. My coaches appeared aghast that I finally spoke up to her, or was it they thought I had lost my mind? Either way, my heart was hammering in my chest. I'd never once spoken to my mother like that, and I noticed a remorseless look in her eyes. Turning around again, I skated toward Suzy.

She gave mea look that I could tell was questioning if I were all right. Nodding back at her with a slight smile, I spun around to make my way back toward center ice.

"Let's run through it one more time, and then I'm calling it a day," I shouted, but not before glancing over to where my mother stood before, only this time she was gone.

Jeremy hasn't said anything all week to lead me to believe our date is still going to happen on Friday. We've maybe talked at most for ten minutes, simply because by the time either of us gets home, we're both completely exhausted and just want to fall asleep. I've actually had more communication with Sue and Courtney than I have Jeremy. Their schedules just seem to be more compatible with mine.

I would have thought after what happened between us earlier this week that he would have tried to make more of an effort to be in touch. He was livid with Dave after he barged in on us, but I felt protected with him. Apparently from what info I gathered from Sue, while Jeremy and I were having our *sexcapade*, her word not mine, she and Dave had a pretty heated discussion in the kitchen about their miscommunication that ultimately ended in them having sex more than once that night. I barely know Dave, but evidently, it was my day to see multiple naked guys. From what I saw of him, he certainly keeps himself in just as good of shape as Jeremy. Jeremy has the more defined "V," but Dave has more upper body muscle.

Sue carried on about how if she hadn't drunk all those martinis and then polished off the Patron with Dave, there would have been zero chance of them hooking up. I called her bluff on that one. Somehow I think those two are more attracted to each other than they let on.

Of course, I couldn't get away from her inquisitive mind before spilling the beans about what Jeremy and I did in his bedroom. There was squealing, and she was jumping up and down and clapping her hands like a rabbit on speed. Grabbing her phone, she quickly called Courtney to tell her the *news*. I could have nearly died and apparently so could Courtney, as I believe I heard her yell at Sue that she totally didn't want to know that info about her brother.

Since then, it's been Sue and Courtney calling me and asking about my so-called date. I have to keep telling them the same thing, though, that Jeremy hasn't mentioned it at all since I left his apartment. I've almost convinced myself that he has already become bored with me and realizes that "we" as a couple could never possibly work out. It's Courtney who continues to tell me that her brother isn't like that, and that if he said he

was going on a date with me, then he would for certain be going on a date with me. I kind of enjoy having Sue and Courtney to share my life stories with. I guess this is what I've been missing all these years.

Now, while back at my place, relaxing on my sofa while watching *Friends* again, I realize that tomorrow is my date with Jeremy. As I'm about to grab some sushi from the Japanese restaurant down the street, my phone rings. Looking at the screen, I see it's Jeremy. Maybe Courtney was right after all, and I should really try to think more positively about people.

"Hey, there," I say, pulling the phone up to my ear.

"Did you miss me?" Jeremy playfully teases back.

After my horrific day, I could use some fun, so I let my hair down a little. "Well, I'm not sure. Last time I checked it was my fingers that got me off." Hearing him groan on the other end of the line makes me laugh quietly.

"Emily, so help me, if you keep talking dirty to me, I will not be taking you out on a date tomorrow."

"Oh, we really are going out on a date tomorrow? I assumed since you hadn't mentioned it, that it wasn't happening, so I made other plans," I lie.

He must have taken the bait since his aggravation is evident through the phone. "Emily, why would you make other plans? I told you when you left the other day I was taking you out." I can't help but chuckle; he really is quite gullible. "You little devil, you didn't make other plans, did you?"

"No, I'm just trying to get you all riled up. Did it work?" I say as I lie back on my sofa.

"You'll pay for that one when I see you."

"So, where are you taking me?"

"It's a surprise, but I can tell you to dress nicely, but not too nice. You may need to bring a sweater, just in case, and do not eat before I pick you up. Understood?"

"So, let me get this right. You're feeding me, and I may or may not need clothing. Is this some sexual ploy of yours to steal my virginity?"

"Keep talking like that, Emily, and your virginity will be long gone after tomorrow night." I gasp in shock because I've never considered him to be that *forward*, and he did say he wouldn't push me too fast, but I did provoke him a bit. Sensing my apprehension, he says, "Emily, you know I'm just teasing you. I told you I wouldn't push you, and I won't. You're in control of everything, just like the other day. But, for now, let's just focus on our first date tomorrow, okay? I'm really glad I'm the guy who's giving you so many firsts these days."

After finalizing the details for what time he would pick me up, I make a mental note to head over to the salon tomorrow morning to get waxed, just in case his hand turns into Thing from *The Addams Family*. I'm not saying it's going to happen, but I also never expected what occurred between us the other day either. There's a level of comfort when I'm with him, which I can sense brings out a different side of me. It's foreign, but it's exhilarating. I hear him ask me a question, pulling me from my thoughts.

"I'm sorry. I didn't hear you. What did you ask?"

"I asked if you had any plans for Sunday evening?"

Thinking for a moment, I say, "Well, I have something Sunday morning, but no, nothing on Sunday evening, why?"

"My family has Sunday dinner every week, and my mother asked me to invite you over. Would you maybe want to come by? Courtney and Josh will be here, so it won't be too painful."

He seriously thinks that meeting his family would be painful. Everyone so far has been sweet and loving. Now, if I was to invite him to have dinner with my family, that would be painful, but I don't tell him that.

"Of course, I'd love to come over. I can't wait to meet your parents."

"You say that now, but my mom will probably force you to eat a ton of carbs and my dad will drop more swear words in one dinner than you've probably heard in your life."

"Sounds perfect," I say just above a whisper because it does sound perfect. It sounds like a *real* family.

JEREMY

Last night after hanging up with Emily on the phone, a strange feeling came over me. I couldn't place it, but I knew in more ways than one I missed her. I missed her smile and her laugh. I just missed the little things she has no idea she does when she's around that absolutely drive me wild.

I didn't have any practice with the team this morning, so I made my rounds around town. I managed to get a haircut, clean out the truck, and pick up the most beautiful bouquet of flowers for Emily. I said to the florist that I wanted something elegant, but simple. Once she was done mixing and matching flowers, I ended up with a large arrangement of sunflowers, calla lilies, and daisies.

It's now Friday afternoon, and I'm at my place sitting in the backyard with Dad and Josh as we toss Aspen some toys in the yard. Dad's been busy cleaning the hot tub, and Josh and I have been helping with the yard work. Apparently, Dad got wind that he is going to have a special guest at the house on Sunday afternoon, so he wants to make a good first impression. I'm not sure who's going to be more nervous, Emily or my parents. This will be a first for everyone. I've never had any girl back here, ever.

"Do you think I ought to go buy new seat cushions for the patio furniture?" Dad asks. He is trying too hard to make the house presentable.

"Dad, everything is fine. Emily won't care about any of that stuff. Trust me," I state firmly.

Josh makes his way over toward us after putting away the lawn mower. Standing next to Dad, he tells him, "You know, Dad, you never did anything like this when I brought my girlfriends around."

With a loud deep laugh that only a Page man can evoke, Dad emphasizes, "Yeah, well, none of those girls you ever brought around made it to the front page of the sports section of the *Globe*." Josh laughs because we know he's just kidding with Dad.

It's true, though. Emily made the cover of the sports section of the *Globe* this morning. I have no doubt her parents were behind the article, which sells her out as being the next favorite to win the US Figure Skating National Championship in Boston in January. It discusses her achievements since last year's World Championship, where she placed fourth, and how she has the potential to medal at the Olympic games in February.

Her picture is nothing but stunning. She's wearing long leggings that go over her boots and a tight high-necked long-sleeved top, which shows off her curves. My father bolted from the kitchen table this morning with his coffee in hand just to show the picture to my mom.

"Grace! Grace! I can't believe it. We've got a major athlete coming to the house on Sunday! Look." He shoved the paper in her hands, and she took one look at Emily's picture and then glanced up at me as I was putting my coffee cup into the dishwasher.

I'm not sure, but I could almost say I saw tears in her eyes as she whispered, "She's beautiful."

I know Mom, I know. I'm just hoping not to screw it up again.

Leaving Dad and Josh to the backyard affairs, Aspen and I return to the apartment because I have to get ready for my date. I putter around in my closet, looking for something to wear tonight as Aspen curls up on his bed on the floor in my bedroom. Standing there in front of my closet, I run my fingers over the slight stubble on my jaw.

"What should I wear, buddy?" Aspen's ears perk up. Grabbing a black button-down shirt and gray dress pants, I lay them out on the bed. I forego the tie because I know my plans for the night aren't that formal.

Checking the time, I realize that I've got about an hour before I need to leave, so I quickly hop into the shower. I skip shaving, deciding to leave a slight amount of stubble on my face, and throw some gel into my hair to tussle it a bit. I dress quickly and grab everything I need from the kitchen counter, ensuring three times that I haven't forgotten anything.

I head out to my truck, and as I'm about to shut the door, I see Mom and Dad on the front porch. Dad's arm is hung over Mom's shoulder, and Mom has her arms wrapped around his waist. She smiles as she sees me leaving and then blows me a kiss. As I pull out of the driveway, I see my dad place a kiss on her forehead as they turn around and head back inside. I absolutely love my parents. Not a day goes by that I don't envy what they have going for them. After all these years, they are still in love with each other and want nothing but happiness for Josh, Courtney, and me. I hope one day that will be me.

Pulling up outside of Emily's garage, I rub my hands together, trying to dry the nervous sweat from my palms. I know. I've already had my hands down her pants, and now I'm nervous. It's just the fact that this is the date that we should have had years ago. This is my shot to finally make Emily Cameron my girlfriend. Taking the flowers from the passenger seat, I make my way out of the truck and through the garage door that's already open. Once at her door, I knock softly, hearing movement on the other side.

"Be right there," she says. A few seconds later, the door opens, and I'm at a loss for words. Emily stands before me as she finishes placing an earring in her ear. She's wearing black leggings with brown knee-high riding boots and a low-cut white blouse underneath a blazer matched with a cheetah print scarf. Her blonde hair is all loose and curled at the ends. She's absolutely breathtaking. She normally is regardless, but tonight there just aren't words.

She gives me a questioning look as if she's wondering why I still haven't said anything, and I snap out of my daze. "What?" she asks with a slight pitch to her voice. "Am I not dressed up enough?" Really? How could she think she's not dressed up enough?

Bringing the flowers in front of me, I start making my way closer to her. When I'm right in front of her, she softly takes them in her hands as I lean down toward her ear and say, "You could be wearing a plastic poncho, and you'd still be gorgeous." I slowly place a soft kiss on her cheek before pulling away, never taking my eyes from hers.

"Are these for me?" she asks as she smiles and then glances to the flowers.

"I wasn't sure what your favorite was, so I went with a variety."

She smiles even brighter. "Well, you're in luck because gerbera daisies are my favorite!" Why doesn't that shock me? Of course, she loves daisies, simple and cheerful, not stuffy and formal like roses. She walks to the kitchen, opening a cabinet and pulling out a vase before arranging the flowers on her kitchen table. She grabs her purse from the counter and heads back my way. Placing her hand gently on my chest, she looks up at me and says, "Thank you for the flowers. They're beautiful." I'm pretty sure she can feel my heart beating through my shirt at the moment, because if I didn't already have the perfect night already planned out, I'd be content just sitting here all night with her in my arms.

"We should get going if we're going to make our reservation," I tell her, trying to get her out of the apartment before I change my mind and just strip off her clothes and our first date never happens.

"Where are we going?" she asks, while walking out the door. Placing my hand at the small of her back, I close the door behind me.

"You'll find out soon enough, but it's going to be the best first date you've ever had!" Glancing back up at me, she points out, "Well, that won't be hard. I've never gone on a date before." *Shit. I forgot she's never dated, kissed, or even been with a guy before me. I'm a total ass.*

As we make our way out through the garage, another car pulls up just as Emily presses the button to shut the door to her stall. The woman gets out of the car and begins walking toward Emily. As my eyes dart between Emily and her, I wonder how this is going to play out. Emily's body goes completely rigid. Then, the woman, whom I can now only assume is her mom, stares directly at me. Those eyes are not kind, and I know I'm not anything she wants her daughter to be involved with. She quickly snaps her head back to Emily before expressing her disapproval.

"Emily, where do you think you're going? Who is this guy?" Thinking there is no way she's about to ruin my night, I head back close to Emily, wrap my arm around her waist and reach my hand out to her mom.

"Mrs. Cameron, my name is Jeremy Page. It's nice to meet you, but if you'll excuse us, Emily and I have to be going. We have dinner reservations that we must get to." She doesn't make any effort to take my offered hand, so I pull Emily back toward my truck and open the door to allow her in. Making my way back to the driver side, I see Emily's mom still standing there, staring in disgust and anger. "Have a good evening, Mrs. Cameron, always a pleasure running into you," I say sharply before shutting my door and starting up my truck. Because I'm a complete ass sometimes, I drive over the dusty gravel driveway close enough that the plume of dust engulfs that wretched woman as I watch her in my rearview mirror. I laugh at my brazenness, but once I glance over at Emily, I realize the smile that was on her face back in her apartment has disappeared. Grabbing her hand, I bring it up to my lips, giving it a soft kiss.

"Hey, first date, remember. I will not allow you to be unhappy. It's you and me tonight."

A slight smile forms at the corners of her lips, and I know she's back from wherever her mom just sent her mind. "Let's get this date started then."

With that, I chuckle and turn on the radio as The Black Eyed Peas sing about tonight being a good night. Fuck yeah, it is!

CHAPTER
eleven

Emily

About twenty minutes later, Jeremy drives us through downtown Newburyport and heads toward a small island community called Plum Island. It's been years since I've been down this far, and with the increasing number of coastal storms the past few years, I'm surprised to see many of the houses on the island are still standing. We drive to the far end of the island near a lighthouse and boardwalk toward the ocean. I wonder why he would bring me here? After parking the truck, he reaches for a backpack from the backseat and hops out of the truck.

Once he's at my door and opens it, I question, "I thought we had dinner reservations? I didn't exactly bring beach attire."

Smirking at me, he playfully says, "Don't get your panties in a ruffle. We have a while before dinner. You just have to trust me."

"Okay, but there is no way I'm skinny dipping, and you're going to have to give me a piggy-back ride since I wasn't aware I needed flip-flops tonight," I tease back, shrugging my shoulders as I get out of the truck.

"Emily, if you ever want to hop on and ride me, you don't have to ask," he says with a huge cocky grin on his face. Opening the backpack shoulder straps for me, he helps me push my arms through and then bends over, saying, "Hop on, babe!"

Laughing at the ridiculousness of the scene, I grab onto his shoulders and pull myself on his back as he carries me down the boardwalk toward the crashing waves and blinding setting sun. Once he's at the end of the boardwalk, he lowers me to the ground while he takes off his shoes and socks, rolling up the bottom of his pants. Handing me his shoes, he motions for me to return to his back as he carries me to a secluded clearing where he lowers me to the sand. He removes the backpack from my shoulders and opens it to reveal a large blanket that he throws over the sand. Sitting on the blanket, he takes my hand to pull me in front of him to sit in between his legs.

I watch as he pushes his heels into the sand, and I concentrate on his breathing as he settles his chin on my shoulder. We watch the boats go in and out of the harbor as the waves crash and the lowering sun glistens over the water. We're quiet for a moment before he says, "You know, back when we were in high school, that night I dropped you off, I wanted to ask you to go to prom with me."

Turning my chin to look at him, I say, "You had just met me. Why would you have wanted to ask me? I thought you wanted to go with Morgan?"

Looking into my eyes, he faintly says, "I never wanted to go at all; I only went for Josh, but after spending that afternoon with you...I don't know. Something happened, but you never called, and I realized any chance I had to ask you slipped away each day that passed."

I had no idea he thought of me like that back then. Although, knowing this now, I doubt I could have changed the outcome. Chances of going to his prom would have been slim to none if my parents had any say in the matter.

I'm not sure what to say to him to change the past, so I say the only thing I can think of at the moment. "Jeremy, I'm so sorry I never called you back after that night. Honestly, I had no idea you were interested. Had I known, it still wouldn't have changed the last eight years. You still would have gone to college, and I still would have been living the *dream* my parents wanted me to."

"I guess you're right, but since I never got to dance with you at my prom, I'll ask you now." Pushing back away from me, he stands to walk in front of me and holds out his hand. "Emily Cameron, may I have this dance?"

Looking around the beach, I don't see any activity. It is the middle of September, so most of the summer crowds are gone, but there are still boats in the water. Glancing up at him, I shake my head before placing my hand in his.

"You're a strange one, Jeremy Page, but I'll dance with you; however, it doesn't appear you have any music." I see him reach into his pocket to pull out his iPhone and push some buttons. As he wraps his arm around my waist and takes my other hand in his, I stare into his chocolate eyes, and we start moving. The music begins, and my heart skips a beat. The sound of the piano starts those four simple notes, and I know the song immediately. How? There's no way he could know. Guy and Girl start singing, and my eyes glisten over with moisture. "How could you know?"

Resting his head on my forehead, he says, "A drunk hot chick left her iPod inside her car one night I drove her home, and somehow this was the only musical listed. I thought it *had* to have some meaning in your life. Emily, please tell me those are happy tears."

He did this for me. He found the one song that had the meaning of hope and connection no matter how different we are. I'm so lost for words right now, but once I speak, I'm even more speechless. "Miluju Tebe." The words flow from my lips, and Jeremy glares at me as though I'm crazy.

Right now, I think I may be. Why those words slipped from my mouth I don't know. I basically just quoted a line from the musical where Girl tells Guy "It is you I love" in her native language. I can't possibly love Jeremy, but my feelings are so strong at the moment, it's my only reasoning for saying them.

"I'm not even sure what you said, but I do have one more thing to ask before we head to dinner."

Grabbing something from his front pocket, he backs away from me and kneels down on one knee before me. My eyes shoot out of my head. He cannot be doing this. *No freakin' way!* I need to stop him, but it's too late. He's already started talking. Raising a black velvet box toward me, he slowly opens it while saying, "Emily Cameron, will you do me the honor of becoming my girlfriend and escorting me to the first home game of the hockey season?"

Opening my eyes in relief that it isn't a marriage proposal, I glance at what's inside the box. A sterling silver necklace sparkles in the sunset along with an opal birthstone, a diamond hockey stick pendant, and a round silver disc hand stamped with a number "3." I can only assume the three is his hockey number because I'm pretty sure he doesn't know my birthday is in March. Placing my fingers over the necklace, I stare at it silently for a while before I realize he's still kneeling there in the sand waiting for my answer. Oh my god. He just asked me to be his girlfriend. How will that work between us? Our lives move in such opposite directions, and the next few months will be even worse than the past week.

I don't even know when his hockey game is or if I can make it, but at this moment, I'll move mountains if it means making him happy because nothing else matters to me. No skating medal has ever made me this happy.

Reaching out to rest my hand on the side of his face, I look right into his wondering eyes and nod my head. "Yes. Jeremy Page, I will be your girlfriend."

Sweeping me up in a bear hug and swinging me around, he gently lowers me before pulling the necklace from the box and placing it around my neck. "You like it?" he asks as he places his hands on my shoulders.

"I love it, but you could have just asked me to go to the hockey game with you," I say as I place a soft kiss on his cheek.

"Yes, but this way, if you're wearing this, people will know that gorgeous blonde girl in the stands belongs to me, and you have no idea how happy that makes me right now," he says, pushing the flying blonde hairs out of my face. Making his way to the blanket, he starts packing everything back into the backpack before motioning for me to get back on his back. "Now, it's time to feed *my* girl, so let's go have our first dinner as a couple. Shall we?"

Laughing because I still can't believe this insanely hot weirdo is my *boyfriend* now, I say, "As long as there aren't any martinis involved at dinner, I'd love to celebrate our first night together."

JEREMY

I still can't believe she said yes. I thought for sure she would have hemmed and hawed over the question. I mean, I'm not complaining, but Emily is one of the most indecisive women I know. It took her eight years to realize she is worth fighting for and actually go on this date. It shocked the hell out of me when in less than a minute she accepted the idea of being my girlfriend.

It will be one of the most tested dating experiences I think I'll have to endure, ever. I'm still not convinced that something won't happen to screw this up. Starting next week, I have regular morning skates and training camp continues with the whole team. Once that's over, it's right into the exhibition games, and then the season officially kicks off. I'm not even sure where I'm going to find the added time for Emily, but if I can see that smile or hear that laugh through a phone call, I'll take whatever I can get. I just hope she thinks the same about me and wants us to work just as badly.

Our table isn't ready for dinner yet, so Emily and I sit outside at the bar overlooking the harbor. I've brought her to The Black Cow for dinner, one of Newburyport's finer dining establishments. The sun has just set below the water, and the boats are bobbing up and down against their moorings below us. Glancing over at Emily, I see her staring out at the water, watching the people come and go on their boats. The necklace I gave her twinkles on her neck in the fading light. She must sense me staring because her attention turns toward me. *That's right, I'm the crazy motherfucker under her spell.* God, she's beautiful, and she's mine.

A small chuckle slips from her lips as she stares up at me. "What?" she asks.

Trying to find the right words, but knowing I'll screw up whatever I say, I lean toward her, grab her chin and move my lips down to hers. I pull away slowly, moving my tongue over my lips and tasting her lip-gloss. "You taste like coconuts and smell like warm vanilla." It's a heady combination, causing a stirring of sorts in my stomach.

A slight moan escapes her as she rubs her lips together. "You keep that up, and we'll never make it through dinner," she says while trying not to laugh.

Emily turns away to look at the boats again while sipping on her sangria. She is not going anywhere near martinis tonight. Not that I didn't mind her little striptease the other night, but I really want her to remember tonight for the rest of her life. Tonight I want to get to know the real Emily Cameron, not the one the world knows from a three-minute clip they see on television before she performs during a competition. I've seen the YouTube videos with the stories they put out there about how her so-called loving parents have supported her throughout her career and how they always knew she was a hidden talent as a child. What the segment neglects to show is her mom yelling at her as a child at the rink, or how her parents have messed with her head so much that she hasn't been able to fully open up to anyone until recently.

I stand behind her as she sits on the bar stool, my hands massaging her shoulders. I hear the hostess call my name, and we both turn to make our way to the dining room. Emily grabs her bag and drink as I urge her in front of me while keeping my arm wrapped around her waist. We have a seat near the large windows that overlook the water. Small tea lights flicker on the tables, and fresh fall flowers adorn all the tables, adding to the nautical theme.

After we slip into the booth, the waitress hands us our menus, and I order a local microbrew, while Emily is content with water. Eyeing her suspiciously, she says she has a morning practice set up, so she can't risk having too many sangrias. I reach out and grab her hand in mine on top of the table, continuing to rub my fingers over her smooth knuckles. I want to ask her to skip her practice tomorrow, but I know she won't and can't. Plus, since I've already stolen her for Sunday with my family, I may be pushing my newly acquired boyfriend status. I just want to spend time with her because I know it won't always be like this.

The waitress comes back with our drinks, and we order dinner. I order the roasted statler chicken, while Emily sits there staring at the menu a little longer.

"You are not ordering a salad, just in case that's what is about to come out of your mouth," I say, stone-faced.

Laughing, she looks up from her menu at me and sassily says, "Oh, so you think you know me that well?" I nod back at her in agreement because that's all I've ever seen her eat besides the toast I made her last week. That's when she totally throws me a curveball. "I'll have the grilled salmon, hold the crème fraiche, and a side of jasmine rice, thank you." She turns her eyes back to me and winks, while handing the waitress our menus.

"Aren't you the little daredevil tonight? You're full of surprises." I lean back into my seat. "First, you don't even make me beg you to be my girlfriend, and now you order a full entrée for dinner. Any other surprises you have up your sleeve?"

Very flirtatiously, she pulls her bottom lip under her teeth and says, "Well, perhaps after this, you can search under my shirt to see what else I'm hiding." My eyes bug out, and my dick wakes up. *Calm down, killer. Just 'cuz you got a taste of her the other day does not mean it's a sure thing tonight.*

"Babe, remember. I'm following your lead. If you need me to do a full-body search, I'm good with that."

Dinner is served, and even though Emily doesn't eat much more than a few bites of her salmon, she is at least trying something new. I commend her for that. We talk as though we've known each other for years. Technically, we have, but this is the first time she's been willing to open up and give me a shot. I'm not sure what changed her mind, and I'm not sure that I freakin' care. She's here, and we're finally trying this relationship. For once, she is making her own decisions instead of someone else making them for her.

Emily talks about her skating some more. She mentions she placed fourth at last year's World Championships, but that wasn't good enough for her parents. Because of that, she'll be doing two international competitions this fall before the US Nationals hit Boston, which will ultimately allow her placement on the Olympic team in February should she medal. She says her parents have invested too much money and advertising into her career for her to not try her hardest. The more I hear about her parents, the more I hate them for not thinking of their own daughter as anything more than a money maker.

Outside of skating, Emily doesn't have that much going on in life. She briefly talks about her days at Boston University and how much she loves to travel. If she didn't have skating in her life from such an early age, she would have wanted to travel to Europe after high school to learn about its history and the beauty of the landscapes.

She really is an amazing woman once she finally lets down her guard. I ask her what she plans on doing once her skating career is over. That's when I think I lose her. She sinks back inside her shell, and the walls she finally begins to let down, well, they quickly go right back up.

I stand outside the bathroom waiting for Emily to freshen up before we leave. I'm not really sure where I went wrong or how asking about her future was a bad thing, but my funny, sassy, light-hearted girlfriend is now gone. Somehow, my screwed-up mouth made this night shit, and I've got to fix it fast before she walks away for good and back out of my life.

CHAPTER
Twelve

Emily

Staring at myself in the mirror, I see what I am. I'm nothing but a commodity for my parents to use for their own self-worth. I'm disgusted with myself for never putting up a fight, even once I was old enough to realize it. So, why did I freeze up when Jeremy asked me what I wanted to do with my life once my skating career is over? A part of me saw that everything I've worked for in my life so far is going to be gone soon, and after that, I've got nothing. What *do* I want to do? I have enough money saved, but that doesn't give me happiness, let alone a job. I have never considered my life or future. I've never once thought of *me*. I have a degree in geography from Boston University, but besides that, I'm qualified for nothing.

My reflection grows even more dejected than it was when I came into the bathroom. I'm almost certain Jeremy is wondering why the hell I'm still in here. Truth is, I'm not sure I can face him at the moment. My first official date, and I've ruined it already. He's probably out there wondering why the hell he ever asked me out. This might go down as being the shortest relationship ever on record. Throwing my compact and lip-gloss back into my bag, I glance up and see the shimmering diamonds around my neck. His words sound in the back of my head. "You're worth fighting for." I'm not so sure of that anymore, but I know it's time for me to face the music and head out of the ladies' room. *Put on your big girl panties, Emily. The one guy you have actual feelings for might just be ready to break your heart once you open that door.*

Taking a deep breath, I open the door and make my way out into the foyer. I see him sitting in the waiting area, his elbows on his knees holding his head in between his hands. He must have sensed my impending arrival because he raises his head and stares me in the eyes. I'm uncertain what I see in his eyes, but it isn't good. Feeling a tightness in my chest, I step even closer until I'm directly in front of him. Reaching out, he grabs my trembling hand and slides his fingers into mine. Okay, maybe things aren't as bad as I anticipated.

Walking out the front doors, we don't head in the direction of Jeremy's truck. Instead, we turn the opposite direction and head toward the boardwalk along the waterfront. Even after a few minutes, he still hasn't said anything to me. The only sounds I hear are the ropes stretching with the pull of lines holding the boats to the docks and the metal dinging on board that almost sounds like bells.

Jeremy stops at an open bench that overlooks the water. Sitting next to him, I look out at the water and the illuminated dock lights that line the harbor. Still, neither of us has said anything, and he pulls me close so my back rests against his chest. Wrapping his arm around my waist, he leans his chin on my shoulder so we both look out at the lights on the water.

"You know you can do anything you put your mind to, right? Just because you haven't had the chance yet to figure out your future, doesn't mean it can't be amazing. Dreams can come true. You just have to go after them and live them," he says, finally breaking the awful silence. Tears sting my eyes, and moisture begins to coat my cheeks. I'm not sure what I'm happier about, the fact he's not quitting on us just yet, or the fact that he believes I can accomplish anything I want in life.

Turning around so our knees are touching, I look at his face through the moonlight as I lower my hand to his thigh. "Jeremy, how did I ever get so lucky to find someone like you? My whole life my family has never once pushed me to believe I could be something else. You say the words, and I feel as though I'm going to be all right, that my life has purpose outside of what I know. How are you so sure of it?"

"Babe, life is one big trial and error. I'm not saying it's going to be easy, but it's just like skating. When you fall, you get the fuck back up and try again. Keep trying until you find what works. See what I mean?" I hear his confident words as he appears relaxed and runs his fingers along my back.

"I'm sorry I ruined our night," I say as I wipe a stray tear from my cheek. "It was going so well, and then I had to go and screw it up. I didn't ask you about your hockey…ehh…thing either." I've never actually talked about hockey with anyone. I mean, I've seen the guys at the rink and watched them in passing on the ice, but I'm not well informed about how the sport is played.

"Hockey 'thing'? You mean my job? We'll get to that in due time. Right now, I'm going to tell you straight up. Tonight's not ruined. We're learning more about each other. That's what dating is."

Relief. That's all I feel as a slow smile forms on my lips. "So, we're good? I thought you might have changed your mind about being my boyfriend. I can't say I would have blamed you. Why would anyone want to date me?" I say as I rest my head against his shoulder.

"Are you kidding? I didn't spend all these years wishing you'd somehow walk back into my life, only to let you go in less than a few hours. And, I'm kind of hoping to see what other ways I can make you moan like you did the other day," he says, winking my way.

My face must show either total shock or mortification. First, did he just admit that he's been waiting for me for years? And second, I can't believe he's bringing up our bedroom activities. I slap him on the arm, and he makes a wincing face as though I really hurt him.

"Keep it up, and I'll make you work harder the next time you want to hear me *moan*." I feel his lips against my neck seconds later. He licks along the sensitive spot just below my ear as he softly pushes my hair off my neck. The minute his mouth makes contact with my earlobe, my eyes roll into the back of my head, and a throaty moan leaves my mouth. He laughs softly by my ear, and I realize what he just did. *Bastard!*

"Well, if that's all it takes to get you to moan, I'll consider myself a lucky man," he says, his lips hovering over my ear. He stands and adjusts his pants before reaching out to take my hand.

"No fair." I stand with my hands on my hips, facing him. "You cheated. I wasn't ready for the sneak attack!"

He pulls my body into his, and I'm instantly weak in the knees. Grabbing my ass, he whispers into my ear, "I haven't even shown you how sneaky I can be yet." Gasping softly as my heartbeat races, I realize I'm actually eager to find out how sneaky he can be.

As Jeremy and I walk back to his truck, we talk about random insignificant information in the form of a game. He says it is like playing *Twenty Questions*, but with a twist. If I can't come up with an answer to one of his twenty questions, he gets a free pass to show me another one of his sneaky talents. I agree without any reservation. Who can't answer the questions in *Twenty Questions*? Thinking I have this in the bag, I tell him the rules go both ways, but if he can't answer one of my questions, I get to cancel out his sneaky clause. Game on! The questions start easy enough.

"Favorite color?"

"Easy. Green."

"Favorite television show?"

"No problem. *Friends*."

"Favorite band?"

"Hands down. The Civil Wars."

"What one item would you take with you if you were stranded on a deserted island?""That's tougher. Sunscreen."

Easy enough, right? That's what I think until he raises the ante on question twenty. "What song was on the radio when I dropped you off at your house after Margaritas?" he asks me. What the hell? How am I supposed to know the answer to that? Nothing comes to mind except remembering being completely mesmerized by his eyes. "Give up?" he asks. Like I have a choice.

I can guess, so I say, "Kelly Clarkson's 'Since You've Been Gone.'"

Shaking his head no, he reveals, " It was 'Lonely no More' by Rob Thomas."

"How was I supposed to remember that?" I raise my hands up in defeat before releasing a long breath.

"Well, I remembered it, and you were in the car with me, so therefore, fair question. I guess it's time for me to get sneaky," he says playfully.

While we drive back to my house, I try to think of nineteen questions to ask him before I lay on a trick question myself. I'm not going down without a fight. No way! I start with the simple ones.

"Favorite Color?"

"Blue."

"Favorite hockey team?"

"Monarchs." He winks after that one because I know he most likely wants to say the Bruins.

"Favorite sexual position?"

He hesitates, clearly not expecting me to ask that. "Letting the girl ride me."

I'm guessing he's done this before with other girls, but at least I know what he likes now. Next comes question twenty, just as we pull onto my street.

"I have a tattoo. What is it?" By the shocked look on his face, I'm guessing the past few times he's seen me partially naked, he hasn't noticed it. It's not large, but you can see it if you are truly looking for it. "I'm going out on a limb by saying the lack of an answer means you don't have a clue, and therefore, cannot answer the question."

Putting the truck in park outside of the garage, he turns to stare at me in the dark, only illuminated by the spotlight mounted on the garage. He shakes his head, and I can tell he's trying to replay all the places he hasn't seen me naked. "I can't answer the question, but when the hell did you get a tattoo, and *how* the hell have I not noticed it yet?" he says with some frustration behind his voice. I cannot contain the smile on my face because he's unable to answer the question.

I tease, "Guess this means I'm able to cancel the clause of the bet, unless…" I watch as his eyes widen. "…unless, of course, you want to come upstairs, and I show you where my tattoo is hiding."

The last sounds I hear from Jeremy as I push open the truck door to hop out are a low growl and the muttered words, "Woman, you are such a cock tease." We'll see how much of that statement is true when he realizes where my tattoo really is.

JEREMY

As Emily leads me into her place, I shut the door behind me. I tell myself I'll let her take the reins with what we do in the bedroom, but this woman has made my dick stand at attention since we left the boardwalk. How was I supposed to know she'd turn *Twenty Questions* into a sexual exploration of knowledge? Every fuckin' question she asked I pictured her doing exactly that to me, on me, and under me. Then, to take the cake, she has a tattoo?! Where the hell is it? Whenever I heard that as her last question, my dick went hard as a rock. I'm just glad it was dark in the truck, so she couldn't see. She sashayed out of the truck and realized she was most certainly a cock tease. That little minx has a naughty side, and I'm determined to find that hidden tattoo before the night is over. Hell yes. Call me a horny bastard. She started it, and every girl knows you don't start something you can't finish.

So, here we are now in a showdown in her place. I know she's waiting for me to pounce. Sorry, babe, two can play this game. I'm just not sure I'm going to win. The girl has twenty-two years of dedication to keeping men away. My resolve isn't that strong. I'm shocked she actually caved earlier this week at my house. I just have to use the right head to play my cards properly.

Slipping out of her blazer, she saunters over to the fridge to grab a bottled water. Then, she slowly discards her scarf as she leans over to begin removing her boots. Yeah, I know what she's trying to do, but I'm not breaking. I don't even care that when she bent over to unzip the boots she gave me a fantastic view of her rack nestled nicely in another lace bra. Seriously, does this girl own anything but lace bras? I'm not complaining, but holy fuck, it's killing me not to run over there and shove her against the wall to remove all her clothing.

Before I know it, she's standing right in front of me with her chest pushed into my stomach. A low growl releases in my throat, and she starts laughing. Pushing her hands into the back pockets of my jeans, she pulls out my phone and tosses it onto the kitchen table. She must have hit something on the screen because my music starts playing. Clearly, I didn't close out of something while we were dancing at the beach. Nickelback's "Shakin' Hands" blasts from the phone.

As I reach to turn it off, Emily pulls me back to her and toward her bed as she walks backward. "Keep it playing. I want to hear what kind of music you like to listen to. Plus, you've got a search mission to go on," she says with a devilish grin on her face as she pulls me closer to her bed.

Her legs hit her bed, and before I can tell my brain to ask before I act, my lips crash into hers, and I aggressively push my tongue into her mouth.

She moans as she's forcibly unbuttoning my shirt while pulling it out of my pants. After she pushes the shirt off my shoulders, I pull away from her just long enough to pull my arms out of the sleeves. Before my lips are back on hers, she's removed her tunic top and is standing there in that fantastic lace bra. Just like that, my dick is ready to burst through my pants, and she's reaching for my belt, pulling it back and pushing open my button and unzipping my fly.

Before I can register what's happening, she's pushing my pants to the floor and kneeling before me. She reaches up to run her fingers under the waist of my boxer briefs.

"Emily?" I question what she's trying to do. Not that I don't already have a general idea, but she shouldn't think this is all about me. Although, the look she's giving me from on her knees as her face is a mere inches away from my cock is telling me she wants to take control. *Not happening tonight, sweetheart. I've got a tattoo to find. Yeah, you thought I'd forgotten all about that.* I may have a lot of pucks hit my head, but when it comes to a challenge, my head is completely in the game.

Reaching down, I pull her up to her feet and toss her onto her bed. When her ass hits the bed, she bounces along with her fluffy comforter. Quickly kicking off my shoes and pushing my feet through the ends of my pants, I crawl up onto her bed and lean over her to look her into her eyes. Tucking her bottom lip under her teeth, she leans up on her elbows and shakes her blonde hair away, letting it fall slightly to touch the bed. Fuck me. Is she sure she's never done this before?

Infant Sorrow's "Inside of You" begins filling the air. Are you fuckin' kidding me right now? Emily starts laughing hysterically. Moving up to wrap her arms around my neck, she pulls me down to her. "I didn't take you for a Russell Brand kind of guy, but good to see you have a softer side."

Pushing my hardened cock into her thigh, I say matter-of-factly, "Does that feel soft to you?" Suddenly, Emily goes silent. Shit, there I go thinking with the wrong head again. I drop my head to her chest and let out a long breath.

She must sense something about my change in mood, because she pulls my head back up to look at her. "I thought you were on a mission to find my mysterious tattoo?" Just like that, my right head is back in the game.

"Tell me if anything I do is too much, too fast. Okay?" I say as I begin to move up to my knees on her bed. Nodding back at me, she gives me the green light.

Hmm. If I were a hidden tattoo, where would I be? It's got to be under her pants. It's the only place I haven't ventured a look yet. She's been in her underwear before, but I wasn't scoping something out like I am now.

Slowly and tantalizingly, I begin removing her black leggings until I pull her feet through the ends. Her eyes never leave mine. I see her visibly relax a little until I begin checking out her body for the hidden treasure. The only clothing remaining on her are her lace bra and pink lace thong. I know it's not anywhere near her breasts. I've had a close view of those already.

As if right on queue, TLC's "Red Light Special" starts playing on my phone. What the hell? I break out into a full-bellied laugh. "Seriously, I didn't plan on these songs popping up." I shake my head in between my laughing as she eyes me questioningly.

"If I didn't know any better, I'd say you purposely put those songs on there just to try to get me to submit to your advances."

"Trust me. I don't need music to seduce you, babe. I'm pretty sure you're the one who took off my clothes. Now, where the fuck is this tattoo?"

Emily reaches up to slide her hand beneath the top of her thong as if giving me a clue. I gently begin pushing my fingers into the sides of the lace, pulling it down. I watch her close her eyes for just a minute as I pull them over her feet and toss them onto the floor. She's pulled her knees tight together now; I know she's nervous as all hell. I may have had my hand on her heated wetness the other day, but this time, she's completely exposed to me. Placing my hands on each of her knees, I feel her relaxing under my massaging fingers. Within a few seconds, she opens her legs for me to see what she's hiding. Running across her pelvic bone directly above her neatly trimmed landing strip of hair are the scrolled letters "Dreams are your escape from reality." Holy shit! When did she get that? The only way I missed this the other day was because her yoga pants covered my hand. Well, that and my eyes were fixated on her breasts and lips.

Trailing my fingers across the lettering, I feel her body shudder under my touch. "You're beautiful, Emily. Are you still waiting to escape into your dreams?"

Her arm reaches up to rub the stubble on my cheek. Then, her fingers slink into my hair as she pulls me down to her. "I think some of my dreams are right in front of me," she says before licking her lips and bringing my own lips to hers. Pulling away slowly, I bring one of my hands to delicately rub her thigh and wrap her leg around my waist.

"Tell me what you want, Emily. I told you before. You're in control here." She turns her head, and I know she's scared to ask. Pulling her chin back to face me, I ease her mind by saying, "If this is too much, too fast, just tell me. It's just me, Em. Don't be scared to tell me what you're feeling."

Shaking her head, she replies, "It's not that this is too much. I'm just not sure what to do. I mean, we haven't talked about this yet, and it probably should have been one of my twenty questions, but I'd assume you've done this plenty of times, and I'm..."

Em! Stop!" I cut her off before she goes any further. Shit, that came out harsher than I wanted it. "Sorry, I didn't mean to snap at you. If you are asking how many girls I've been with, then the answer is five. None of them hold a candle to you, though. You are without a doubt the sexiest and most beautiful woman I've ever been with. Now, if we can focus your attention back to us, tell me what's going on in that head of yours."

I see a sliver of playfulness in her eyes again before she says, "Well, I've read books and seen pictures of things we can do that don't necessarily involve us having sex. I mean, it's not that I don't want to. God, I want to. I'm just not ready yet." So, she just basically gave me permission to do anything except have sex with her. Game on!

Pulling her into my arms, I roll her over so she's straddling me. I see her nervous smile as her hands rest on my abs, and I can feel her heat pooling against my boxers that are still keeping Fido contained. *So help me, if she removes those, there's no telling what he's capable of.*

Pushing up, I reach behind her, unclasping her bra and watching as it slides down her arms and onto the bed. Looking up into her eyes as I lie back down, my hands hold onto her hips as my thumbs rub over her tattoo again. Funny thing, those dreams. If she only knew how many of my dreams include her. I see her slickness on my boxers the longer I gently trace her tattoo. Her body shivers and moans as her head drops back and her fingers skate over my chest. Taking her by surprise, I start to shimmy my body between her legs. "Trust me?" I ask before my head goes to places unknown. Nodding with widened eyes, she gives me the go ahead, and I go in for the kill.

Once in position, I spread her a little more so her pussy sits right above my mouth. I grab her ass to hold her still. Something tells me the minute my tongue makes contact, she'll be moving her hips like Shakira. Keeping her positioned right above my head, I pull her forward a bit, running my tongue over the words inscribed on her body. A shuddering moan leaves her lips, and I know she fully trusts me as her body goes lax.

I start slow at her clit, and the minute my mouth is on her, all I hear is, "Holy shit, Jeremy!" She tries grinding against my mouth almost immediately, but I'm not having any of that just yet. I keep her still as I lick and suck her clit teasingly slow until she is close, and her moans become shortened gasps. Before I know it, I set her off with one more circular lick. I glide my tongue to her slit, gently letting it slide inside her to suck up her juices. Feeling her body start trembling again as she gasps my name and mixes a few *Oh's* and *God's*, I know it's time to let her crumble. I bring my mouth back to her clit and push two fingers inside her, looking for the spot.

Feeling all her muscles tighten around my fingers, I look her dead in the eyes as she tries to focus.

"Come for me, Emily. Come on, baby. I want to hear you scream." Seconds later with one last lick, I let her hips go wild, feeling her inner muscles throb around my fingers and her knees tighten around my head. Things get a little fuzzy with my lack of air, but I believe I hear her scream my name amidst the floodgates opening. Once I know she is fully sated, I roll her onto her back. As she looks up at me with glazed eyes, I realize I've done a good job. She reaches for me to kiss her, letting our tongues twist as she tastes herself on my lips. She slides one hand down my boxers and grabs my cock. Holy shit. That hand of hers is deadly. "Emily," I say through gritted teeth.

"I need to repay the favor," she replies with pleading eyes. As much as I'd love to see what her mouth could do to my cock, tonight is not the night. I'm not that much of an asshole, but she is offering, though.

I know she senses my hesitation, and before she can get her mind thinking, I suggest another idea. "I'll tell you what. Let's go take a quick shower, and we'll let your hand work its magic on me, and then I get to wash you from head to toe." After pulling her hand from my boxers, she sprints for the bathroom. Slowly making my way over to her, I notice the biggest shit-eating smile on her face. "What's that smile for?" I ask.

She giggles to herself as she places her palms on my chest once I'm in front of her. "I was just thinking that you are sooooo much better than Gigi!" she says straight-faced.

"Who the fuck is Gigi, and how is *she* better than me?" I scowl.

Another chuckle comes from Emily's mouth as she begins to slowly turn for the shower. "Oh....Gigi's just my vibrator." *What the double fuck?*

I drop to my knees, slapping my hands over my heart. "You've got a vibrator named Gigi? Any other sexual surprises you want to share with me?" She laughs as her naked ass walks away from me to turn on the shower, and my last thought before she disappears into the steam is I think I'm in love.

CHAPTER
Thirteen

Emily

Sunday morning has always been my time to be alone. Me and the ice. Nothing else matters. After my first official date with Jeremy on Friday and then an awful practice yesterday, I'm glad to have this hour-and-a-half to myself. Milton is making his final pass along the outside edge of the ice on the Zamboni as he drives by me. After tying the last knot of my laces, I pull down my leggings over my boot. I slowly make my way over to the ice, remove my blade guards, and step onto the even surface. I love the smoothness of the clean ice and the quietness of the rink without anyone judging me from the stands.

Skating my way over to the end of the rink, I stop to say good morning to Milton. "Hi, Milton. How have things been?"

Milton stops scooping the remaining slushy snow from the Zamboni and looks up at me. "Things are good around here. I see our local skater is a top contender for next year's Olympics. The article in the *Globe* last week really put you in the spotlight." Ugh! That article. Mother didn't even tell me about the questions. Great manager she is. All I was told was the *Globe* was stopping by for some pictures and to ask a few questions. What she neglected to inform me of was the fact that they emailed her the article questions, and she answered them for me.

Not wanting to be rude to Milton, I respond, "Yeah, they did a great job. Guess I'm really going to have something to prove when I hit the ice in January for Nationals. Fingers crossed, right?"

With a big grin on his face, Milton leans the shovel against the wall and turns to say, "Well, if I don't see you before January, best of luck to you, sweetie. We'll all be rootin' for ya' here, but I'm sure you'll do great."

"Thanks, Milton. It was nice talking to you," I say as I skate my warm-up laps around the rink. Feeling the need to do a quick run through of my programs before I work on jumps and spin, I crank up my iPhone and speakers. This year, I'm apparently into dark themes. I really don't know why; I just feel a sense of impending doom. The story of my life. A lyric-free version of "Breath of Life" from the *Snow White & the Huntsman* movie fills the rink. My mind is on autopilot. I'm just moving around the ice, each move calculated just right. Double axel…spiral into footwork…sit spin…crossover into back outside edge…turn…stroke…gain speed…turn…triple lutz, triple toe…all calculated. No room for error. I screw up the short program, and there's no coming back. My mother's voice in my head instructing me to be perfect plays over and over, and I just want it to go away.

I don't know what has changed in me. Normally, I am able to come out here day in and day out and handle all the pressures that go along with being a Cameron. I find myself sitting on the ice as my music continues onto my long program. The love theme from *Romeo & Juliet* rings through my ears as tears well in my eyes. What the hell is the matter with me? Sucking in a deep breath, I begin to stand when I hear my music suddenly stop.

"Anything I can help you with? I've got moves you won't believe!" I hear someone say from behind me. Turning around, my eyes shoot up to see Dave standing in the players' bench area.

Drying my eyes, I skate over to him. "What are you doing here?" I ask because there is no way anyone could know I would be skating here this morning.

He laughs to himself. "Well, when I checked the books to see a last minute ice block under the name 'Gideon Cross,' I found it a little odd since I've never seen that name before. I came to check it out and…well…here you are, 'Gideon.'" Ah, one of my many pseudo names I've started since last year. If I reserve anything under my actual name, cameras tend to show up around here.

I raise my arms. "You caught me. Are you going to have me arrested for using a false name?" I say, teasing him. Really, I'm just trying to keep his eyes focused on my face after the last time I saw him. I might be covered at the moment, but it's still awkward to know he's seen me naked from the waist up. Then again, I did see all his goods too, so perhaps, we're even now.

"Emily, Emily, Emily, I should have you arrested for what you did to Jeremy back in high school, but after my phone call with him yesterday, I'd say you've more than redeemed yourself in my book. I hear congratulations are in order. You are officially my best friend's girlfriend. That means we are certainly going to be getting to know each other better," Dave says with a wink and a soft punch to my shoulder.

"Oh, God. I don't know if I should be scared of that or not, but I can tell you I should probably get back to practice." Trying to make any excuse to avoid that conversation, I skate backward away from him, hoping he'll walk away.

"Yeah, you probably should. From what I saw, you kinda sucked," he says, laughing at me. "Are you gonna be at Sunday dinner this afternoon?" he asks.

"I should be, unless someone has me arrested," I mock back, trying to be sarcastic.

I reset my iPhone and get my long program ready to run through as I see Dave pushing the doors to the lobby open, shouting, "See ya later, Gideon!" Skating back to the middle of the ice without hesitation, I realize my momentary feeling of dread has been replaced with a joyous expression.

JEREMY

As I'm leaving the team's Sunday morning skate in Manchester, my phone chimes from my pocket. It's a text message from Dave. Narrowing my eyes, I scratch my chin, wondering why he's contacting me. I thought he was working at the rink this morning. He is planning on coming over later for dinner with the family since everyone, including Sue, is supposed to be there. There's something going on there with him and her, but I'm not about to ask. Pulling up his text, I have to look at it twice to make sure I am reading it correctly.

> *Your girl is here skating-Or she was. She's sitting in the middle of the ice crying right now. What do you want me to do?*

Emily never mentioned that she reserved ice time at the Forum for this morning. Why would she be crying? Everything with us was good yesterday. We both had practice, but talked last night, and she was excited about coming over to meet my parents this afternoon. I type a quick text back to Dave.

> *Didn't know she would be there. If she's crying cheer her the fuck up asshole & do NOT hit on my girlfriend!*

Laughing after I hit *Send*, I know he's going to try to flirt with her. It's just who Dave is. It's like trying to keep a moth from a flame, but he knows she's mine, so he'll cheer her up with his cockiness.

Before I know it, it's already three in the afternoon, and everyone should be arriving for dinner soon. Once I get home, I shoot Emily a text telling her to bring her swimsuit, since Dad spent hours cleaning out the hot tub for the *celebrity* coming to dinner. I haven't heard from Dave or her since this morning, so I assume everything worked itself out. Emily has a strong head on her shoulders. If she was crying, something was definitely going on. I plan on finding out what prompted her little meltdown after dinner today.

As I'm about to call Emily to see where she is, I hear footsteps coming up the stairs. Assuming it's Emily, I put away my phone. Dave throws open the door and storms in, causing the smile on my face to immediately disappear. "What, not happy to see me, asshole? You should be. I saved the day with your girl this morning," he says sternly before smacking my shoulder and heading to the fridge for a beer.

"I thought you were Emily coming in, that's all," I say, disappointed it isn't her.

"Dude, you didn't know she was here? I saw her and Sue heading into your parents' house before I came up here. Sue was basically dragging her in, but I think she was just trying to get away from me. That chick's been avoiding me since we slept together. I'm not sure how she couldn't *not* want another piece of this fine specimen." Dave glances down at himself before running his hands over his abs down to his crotch.

Shaking my head at him, I can't help but think he had to have been dropped as a baby. "Well, I know after what I saw here last week I don't ever want to see your junk again." Making my way to the door, I call Aspen to go over with us. "Let's go. I've got to save Emily before Mom and Dad get to her. I'm pretty sure Mom will have already made my wedding plans before dinner if I don't intercede."

Walking into my parents' house, I hear Mom in the kitchen giving orders to Dad about setting out the good china on the table. *Good china? We have good china? Is the Pope showing up for dinner?*

Moving further into the house with Dave on my tail, I smell Mom's famous meatballs simmering on the stove. My stomach growls, so I move to snatch a piece of Italian bread off the counter before she catches me. Too late. "Jeremy Page, that's for later!" Mom scolds while hitting me with her dishtowel. Dad and Dave stand in the doorway just watching the scene unfold.

With my mouth full of bread, I ask, "Where's everyone else?" Then, I hear the girls laughing hysterically, and I know they are downstairs in the family room. "Never mind. I know." Before I make a move out of the kitchen, Mom grabs my elbow and whispers into my ear, "She's absolutely wonderful, Jeremy. So sweet and polite. You screw this up, and I'll disown you. You hear me?" Nodding, I try to make my quick escape to the family room, but not before I hear my mother say from behind me, "Grandchildren, Jeremy. I'm not getting any younger." This is why I never dated regularly or brought girls back to the house.

I make my way down the basement stairs with Dave behind me. When I get to the bottom landing, my heart stops. Literally, it stops dead in its tracks. Dave nearly tumbles into me because I'm standing motionless. I mean, I am a defensive hockey player. I'm not going over easy. There, before my eyes, are Emily, Sue and Courtney all singing and dancing along to *Pitch Perfect*. Josh is sitting on the sofa shaking his head. The girls are swaying their hips, grinding, and singing along with the movie as all of them pretend to have a role. My eyes never leave Emily's hips.

Josh sees us and sits up. "Dude, this movie sucks!" That gives away our position, and the girls all turn to us. Courtney starts laughing, but keeps humming along to the music. Sue moves to sit opposite Josh on the sofa, but diverts her eyes toward Dave. Seriously, I know they slept together, but what the hell? They've been friends for years. Eventually, those two need to talk. Emily stalks over to me, still lip-synching along to the movie and fist pumping the air. Once in front of me, she wraps her arms around my neck and leans in to whisper into my ear, "Were you standing there long?"

Shaking my head no, I tell her, "Long enough to know your hips do magical things in and out of the bedroom." Hearing Dave choking behind me says I wasn't subtle with the delivery of my words, and by the blush on Emily's face, I know the whole room must have heard my response. Great, just great.

Before anyone can question my slip of the tongue, Dad appears at the top of the stairs to announce dinner is ready. Thank God! As everyone begins running for the dining room, I need a minute alone with Emily before heading into the lions' den. "Hey, is everything okay today? Dave said he saw you at the rink this morning, crying. Wanna talk about it?" I ask her.

"No, I'm good. I just had a moment, but it's all good now."

Reaching over to run my fingers across her cheek, I move my lips down to hover over hers before giving her a warm kiss. "All right, if you say you're good, then let's go up to the interrogation room. Are you ready for this? It's going to be worse than *Twenty Questions*, but I'm right here if you need saving," I say as I start walking toward the stairs.

Behind me, I hear her laughing before she says, "As long as they don't ask about sexual preferences, I think I can handle the paparazzi."

CHAPTER *fourteen*

Emily

Dinner is more pleasant than I imagined. His parents don't poke or pry any more than concerned parents would. Travis asks me to sign the *Globe* feature article for him and says he is framing it for his sports wall. Jeremy gives Travis a pensive look since he has never been asked to sign anything before. Travis then tells him, and I quote, "You're my fuckin' son. I can get an autograph whenever the hell I feel like it. This girl, she's not only destined for the fuckin' Olympics, but she's the first girl to get invited in to meet your mother and me. That my boy, makes this autograph worth a million bucks."

I feel bad not gorging myself like the rest of them do. Jeremy was right when he said she would try to get me to eat way too much food. I manage to appease him and eat a decent amount of pasta, salad, and half of a meatball. After eating all that and washing it down with a smooth Cabernet Sauvignon, my stomach is ready to burst.

Grace doesn't allow me to help with any of the cleanup. She says the boys handle the kitchen cleanup since she slaved over the cooking all morning. Jeremy kisses me on the forehead as he leaves to help clear out the dishes. I notice his mother wiping at the corner of her eyes as they disappear into the kitchen.

After dinner, I relax in the living room with the girls. Sue has been relatively quiet all night, which is unlike her. Courtney tells her mother about my skating ventures to Europe and how someday she hopes to have the chance to see it. Europe is a photographer's dream come true. I wish I could have had more of an opportunity to see its history and landscapes while I was there.

Taking me out of my train of thought, I hear Grace ask me a question. "Emily, I can't help but notice that necklace you are wearing. Is that a hockey stick?"

My heart swims with happiness as I think back on Friday night when Jeremy gave it to me. "Yes, Grace. Jeremy gave it to me when he asked me to be his girlfriend. I thought he was pro... well, I wasn't sure what he was doing. I mean, he was down on one knee and holding up the black box with the necklace in it. I didn't know what to think. When he opened the box, he asked me if I'd be his girlfriend and escort him to the Monarchs home opener." Grace and Courtney stand and run over to me, checking out the shimmering necklace around my neck.

"Travis!" Grace yells. "Travis, come in here. You have to see what Jeremy gave Emily."

Courtney chimes in by asking, "So, where did you go? What did you do after that?" Oh my gosh. You'd think I was the first girl he ever brought home. Apparently, this family doesn't have many steady relationships, or this wouldn't be considered big news.

I'm not about to burst their happy night, so I say, "Well, he asked me on the beach at Plum Island at sunset…" *Queue awws.* "…then he took me to dinner at The Black Cow, and we went for a walk along the boardwalk." I purposely omit that he proceeded to play *Twenty Questions* with me and gave me the best orgasm with his mouth since the dawn of time. *Yeah, that last part I'm keeping to myself.*

The guys pile into the living room, and Grace pulls Travis over to show him my necklace as Dave and Josh all cough what sounds like "pussy whipped" into their fists before taking their seats next to us girls. Dave moves over next to Sue and says something quietly into her ear. Turning her head as they stare into each other's eyes, she nods and they stand to leave the room and head downstairs. Weird. Oh, well. Josh eyes them leaving and I have to think whether he knows about them sleeping together and if that is why she is so quiet. I remember they dated in high school, so I guess it can be awkward, but then again, I'm not exactly a relationship expert.

Jeremy sits next to me, wrapping his arm around my shoulder. Leaning in, he whispers, "Did you bring your swimsuit?" I nod yes as I glance over at him. "I'm about to head back to the garage to change if you want to join me in the hot tub." He winks at me. "Not sure if anyone else is going in, but I am for sure."

I can't argue. Soaking in a hot tub sounds absolutely wonderful right now. The nights have been getting significantly cooler around here, and the relaxing air jets will do wonders for my tired muscles. Standing to leave, Jeremy grabs my hand and excuses us from the family conversation, saying we are going to change and use the hot tub.

I grab my suit from the car on the way back to his place and use the bathroom before I change. I pull my long hair up into a loose bun on top of my head before adjusting the straps on my bikini, making sure everything is contained where it should be. Slipping on my flip-flops, I make my way back into the living room where Jeremy is sitting on the sofa playing on his phone. Hearing my flip-flops, he turns his head to look my way, and his jaw instantly drops.

"What?" I ask as if I don't know what prompted his jaw to drop. I deliberately brought my Victoria's Secret string bikini with black and white stripes and turquoise blue ruffles outlining the top triangles and bottoms that hardly leave anything to the imagination.

"Emily, are you purposely trying to kill me? Oh my God! We've got to go now before I untie everything on you, and we never make it to the hot tub," he says as he pulls my hand toward the door.

Laughing under my breath, I follow his lead. I can't help but notice his perfect abs and chiseled arms right before me. He thinks he's having a hard time controlling his desires. I want to tell him it's a good thing we're heading into the hot tub, because I'm already wet just thinking of all the fun things I can do to his very lickable body.

JEREMY

I make it to the backyard without any issues controlling my libido. Fido stays down like a good dog. It isn't hard, no pun intended, considering the minute I round the corner from the garage I see the rest of the crew already in the hot tub. *Well, that kills any pool action with Emily.* I'm not surprised they are all in there, though; we typically do this on Sunday nights once the weather cools. It's even more fun when there's a fresh coating of snow on the ground, and we all make a mad dash for the hot steaming water while our feet are numb from standing in the snow. Dad sets up strings of twinkling white lights on the bushes surrounding the hot tub, and with the snow, it's actually really cool.

Dave shouts from inside the tub, "C'mon, you two love birds! Get your asses in here, and please, make sure everyone knows whose legs they're touching when in the water."

A muffled groan sounds from my throat. "Really, Dave?" I ask as if I expected anything less.

"Hey, I'm just saying if people start getting frisky in here, it's better to know beforehand, right?" Dave holds his hands up innocently as he takes a pull from his beer can. Courtney kicks Dave's shin and tells him to stop being gross. If he so much as tries to touch my little sister, I will cut off his hand. Although, Josh is the one having more trouble than me right now as he watches Dave snuggle into Sue's side. It also appears she might be in fact rubbing more than his leg under the water. Hey, I'm not going to judge. I'll probably be doing the same thing to Emily once we're in there. The bubbles and foam create a nice barrier to conceal actions, and the dark night sky is an added bonus.

Hopping in first, I make sure to sit next to Dave and put Emily beside Courtney. Dave gives me a stink eye as if wondering why the hell I'm sitting next to him.

Laughing, I say, "Oh, like hell I'm putting Emily next to you in here." Dave shrugs his shoulders and leans back to put his arm around Sue. Emily and Courtney must see the same thing as me, because not a minute later, they get a nodding smile from Sue, confirming what I can only assume is that they are a couple now. I eye Josh at the other corner of the tub, while Courtney and Emily whisper something to each other. Josh is running his hands through his hair, sighing in frustration, and then he leans back and shuts his eyes. I've never understood his thought process with Sue, but he thought she would have been better off without him after he started working for the Massachusetts State Police. When he broke up with her, I knew it hurt him more than her. He'll never admit it, but I know he still loves her. Love, it's a funny thing sometimes.

Everyone goes quiet suddenly, and Emily slides over while rubbing my leg. Slowly moving her hand higher, her fingers move like spider legs creeping under my board shorts. She finally makes contact with my cock. I shoot her a look, silently asking her what she thinks she's up to.

Leaning up to my ear, she softly nibbles at the bottom lobe, making my eyes roll into the back of my head. "It's just us at your place tonight, right?" she asks softly. Nodding yes, I pull my arm around her waist, feeling her heart rate accelerate, as her body is now flush against me. She grabs my cock, whispering, "I think I need to feel this inside me tonight."

She moves away from me slowly. Our eyes meet, and hers say everything. She's taking control, and she knows she wants this. I ask her silently with my eyes so no one else in the hot tub knows what's going on. She nods yes before sliding back to talk to Courtney. What just happened here? She tells me she's ready to have sex with me tonight, and now she's over talking to Courtney. Again I say, what a *cock-teasing vixen!*

I run my wet hands through my hair as I let out a bated breath, knowing she's making me wait. Reaching over to wrap my arm around her, I move closer toward her and kiss behind her shoulder. She continues her conversation with Courtney about sights around Paris, completely ignoring my advances. I take my opportunity for a sneak attack and slide my hand slowly from her waist under her bikini bottoms and over her sensitive area. She yelps, and her body goes rigid as she realizes now everyone knows what I just did. Smacking my chest, she jumps out of the hot tub and wraps a towel around her. Her face is bright red, and she takes off toward the garage after picking up her flip-flops.

"Good job, Jeremy," Dave says. "If I were you, I'd be making my way up to your place to apologize to your girl." Really? Dave is giving me relationship advice?

"Dave, you're my best friend, so don't take this the wrong way, but you're the last person I want relationship advice from. I'll handle my girlfriend my own way, got it?"

Tipping his beer can in the air toward me, I know he gets it. "Touché."

As Courtney heads across the tub to talk to Sue, Josh moves over to my side. His eyes fixate on Sue and Dave across from him before he turns his head toward me. "Sometimes we tend to overlook what's right in front of us. We let go of the only thing that allows us true happiness. When it's too late, you know you can't take it back. Don't make that mistake with Emily. If you care for her the way I think you do, never allow yourself to think she's better off with someone else," he quietly says. While staring at Josh, I want to ask him why he ever thought letting Sue go was the right decision at the time. Sometimes I think he thought at some point she'd come back to him, and now he knows she'll only be a friend.

I'm unsure of what to say or what to do to help ease his remorse; I just know I've got to go and talk to Emily. I've been sitting here in the hot tub listening to Josh for way too long. Pushing myself out of the hot tub, I quickly run the towel over my body, wiping off some of the dripping water and then slip into my sandals. Running up my stairs two at a time, I storm into my place, shutting the door behind me and making sure to lock it, just in case. I see my bedroom light on at the end of the hall, and I figure Emily must be changing. Shit. Why couldn't I just keep my hands to myself in the water?

"Em?" Nothing. *Sigh.* I start walking toward the light, and when I enter my room, the sight before me makes my heart jump into my throat. Standing there in front of my full-length floor mirror, looking at herself is Emily. She's wearing a matching black bra and thong with lace bows attached above her ass crack along with sky high black heels and black thigh high nylons. "Holy shit," I mutter, slowly entering the room. How long was I out there for?

"Like what you see?" she asks, finally turning her head in my direction as she slowly rolls up a black thigh high nylon on her leg that's perched on my storage trunk.

"Uh, Emily, what's going on? I thought you were upset back there in the hot tub." Then the realization hits me. "Wait. You did that on purpose?" I ask as I cross the room, now almost standing in front of her.

"I couldn't very well say I needed to go change into lingerie before having sex with you in front of everyone, now could I? You just moved things along faster when you decided to start touching me *all over*," she says as she takes my hand and rubs it over the front lace of her thong.

"Emily, first, I can't believe you're standing here, wearing that, looking all smokin' hot, and second, I need to know you're one hundred percent sure about doing this. There's no going back if we do this tonight. As much as it will kill me for you to change your mind right now, I'll understand," I tell her as I wrap my arms around her waist.

"Jeremy, I'm ready. I'm not sure when we'll have this chance again after tonight, and I know we're moving fast, but this feels right to me," she pleads. "You make me feel beautiful and open, and I've never felt this way before. I want my first time to be special, and I know in my heart it was always meant to be with you."

I slowly lift her in my arms, grabbing her exposed ass in my hands and carrying her over to my bed. Pulling down the top comforter, I lower her onto the sheets as her hair spreads out under her in soft curls. Her breasts push up in her lace bustier bra while her legs move together slowly in an up and down pattern.

"God, you're the most gorgeous woman I've ever known, Emily." I watch her breathing grow faster as I slowly remove her heels. "You're going to remember every second of this, and I'm going to make sure it is pleasurable for you as best as I can. I know it's going to hurt a little, but just trust me, okay? If something isn't right, let me know."

I grab the towel from the floor and place it under her on the bed. She doesn't say anything while I'm doing it; she just watches. I kiss my way up her legs until my hands are slowly caressing her bra. Agonizingly slow, I pull back the cups of her bra and begin placing light kisses around her breasts. She's already moaning in pleasure, as I see her clutch the sheets at her sides. I step back to remove my wet shorts as her eyes scan my entire naked body. She looks determined, but I notice worry in her eyes. *Don't worry, baby. It will fit.*

Placing my body just above hers on the bed, I kiss her slowly and lovingly. She's right; this feels right for us. It's as if all this time we were meant to find each other again, and this was supposed to happen. A tingling pain shoots its way through my chest, and I pull back slightly, shutting my eyes.

Emily reaches for my face and rubs my cheek. "Are you okay?" she asks. The minute I look into her eyes, I see it. I feel it. I haven't felt this since the day she walked away from me in high school. She's it for me. When I agreed to bring her home to meet Mom and Dad today, they knew it before me. It's the reason why Mom has been crying so much the past few days. Josh and Courtney saw it, too. I'm in love with this woman, and it's taken me this long to realize she's been holding my heart since I met her. God, I was so blind. "Jeremy? Is something wrong?" I hear Emily ask, and I'm roused from my thoughts.

Shaking my head no, I lean down and kiss her with so much love, she has to know how strong my feelings for her are. "Babe, are you sure you're ready?" I ask.

"Jeremy, please make love to me. I need to know what it feels like to have you inside me."

Reaching over her head to the nightstand, I open the drawer to pull out a condom. Emily grabs my hand on my way back, silently telling me no. Wait. What does she mean no? She can't be thinking straight.

"Emily?" I question.

"I'm on the pill. I have been since high school. I don't want anything between us when we do this. I know it's going to be messy, but I need to feel all of you. You're mine as much as I'm yours, right? No barriers, just us," she says, running her hand over my chest while her other hand covers the necklace.

How did I ever get so lucky to have her come back into my life at this time? Slowly lifting her back off the bed, I unhook her bra and toss it to the side. Then, my hands find her thong, and as I'm about to rip it off of her, she places her hand over mine. I slow my pace, gently discarding it next to her bra. We're both completely naked, and I know I can never let this woman go. *Ever.*

CHAPTER

fifteen

Emily

I'll never let him believe I'm scared to death right now. If he knew how much I've lost control, he would never have gone through with this. Truth is, I haven't told him I'm leaving the day after his first home game and won't be back for three weeks due to the first major skating competitions on the Grand Prix circuit. I'll be in Denver for Skate America until the last day of the event, and then I'll fly to Vancouver, British Columbia, for Skate Canada. I can't break his heart. I know I should have told him, but he would have never given me all of him if he knew the truth.

To tell him I want to feel all of him with nothing between us for my first time takes some coercing on my part. I'm really not sure what to expect during this whole sexual experience. I'm hoping he senses my fear enough to go slow at first. I only know I'm ready, and I know it's supposed to be with him.

He has brought out something unknown in me, and I can't tell if he's broken into my head or my heart. Either way, he's the reason for my happiness these past few weeks. If I'm completely honest with myself, I'd say my heart already belongs to him. Once we have sex, I'm sure without a doubt any walls will be shattered, and my heart and soul are all his. Is it love, maybe in time, or it may actually be what I'm feeling at this very moment.

Lowering himself down my stomach, he licks his tongue over my tattoo again. This time he traces the words with his tongue. He loves to do that. I don't know why. But, God, it feels incredible. The tingling sensation begins low in my stomach and moves further south as his mouth descends onto my clit. He slips one finger inside me, and I can feel the wetness pooling around his finger. Arching my back as a wave of pleasure shoots throughout my body, I grab onto his hair, hearing him chuckle around my clit. I explode as he speeds up the finger inside me. Riding the wave of ecstasy, my hips grind against his mouth fiercely until I'm completely out of breath.

Removing his finger from me and licking the juices from my folds, he kisses my nipples before planking himself above me. Looking me straight in the eyes he asks, "Are you ready?" I just nod and flutter my eyes as I look down at his cock sitting over my clit. He grabs his generous length and begins running it up and down my folds, coating it with the remnants of my orgasm. "This is going to pinch at first, but once I'm in, we'll move slow until you're comfortable. Just tell me what you're feeling," he says as he places his cock at my entrance and slowly guides it in.

A slight tight pressure fills my lower body, and Jeremy never loses eye contact with me. He pushes a little further, and I hear him groan in pleasure. A little more and there's a larger pinch, and I wince in pain as my face falls to the side. Biting my lower lip with my teeth, I squeeze my eyes shut to avoid him seeing just how much. Grabbing my chin, he pulls my face back to his. He looks for any sign of fear. *You're not getting it, Jeremy, not now. I'm tougher than that,* I reassure myself. I've dealt with worse things than a little pinching pain. In all honesty, I really thought the pain would have been significantly worse than it is.

Bringing my hips up a little, I feel Jeremy slide all the way in and then I feel it. All of him. "Holy shit, Em. You're so tight, and oh my God, you feel amazing around my cock. Can you feel it? Can you feel yourself throbbing around my cock? Holy fuck."

Breathlessly I find my voice. "Jeremy, oh my God, please. Deeper, please. Holy shit. Keep moving like that. Right there."
I feel Jeremy's body go rigid above me. "Emily, babe, I hate for this to be over so quickly, but there's no way I'm lasting inside you much longer, especially with you squeezing around my cock like that. Tell me where you want me to come."

"I need to feel you inside me. Please, harder, Jeremy. I'm so close to coming. Please." His pace quickens as he raises my arms above my head, and I feel his balls smack against my ass. His cock is still hitting the one spot that's making me see stars. Then, all the pressure in my core releases, my back arches and my eyes roll into my head as I'm screaming his name. "Jeremy! Oh. My. God. Jeremy!"

I feel him pause for one split second before hot fluid begins filling me with his release, and his eyes squeeze shut as he groans out something like, "Fuck, Emily." If my own orgasm wasn't still rushing through my body, I could have sworn I heard him say the words "I love you" in there, too.

Our erratic breathing returns to normal after a few minutes as he lifts his head off my neck and slowly places soft kisses all the way up to my ear before he looks me in the eyes. I run my fingers over his back and feel his tight muscles start to relax. Kissing me on the nose, he pulls back a bit. "Stay here, and I'll go grab a washcloth to clean you up." Sliding slowly out of me, he moves toward the door and down the hall. Sitting up on my elbows, I wait for him to return. Funny, I thought I would feel different. Right now, I feel bolder and more aggressive in a sexual nature.

Jeremy comes back holding a wet washcloth and wearing a pair of boxer briefs. He sits up on his knees in front of me, softly running the cloth over my swollen folds. I can see the remnants of my virginity as he wraps the towel under me with the washcloth before I hear him heading down the hall to toss them into the trashcan. I guess you can say I just threw my virginity in the trash. *Au Revoir!*

I may have fallen asleep shortly after that, because the next thing I know, Jeremy is running his hands up and down my side as he's lying beside me, whispering my name into my ear. Blinking my eyes open, I look over at him.

"Hey," he says.

"Hey, back at 'cha. Did I fall asleep?" I hoarsely ask while trying to clear my throat.

"You might have dozed off, but I'm content with you sleeping in my bed. How are you feeling?"

"Good, just a little sore, but nothing unbearable," I say, trying to adjust my body around to face him.

"Em, I don't want to sound insensitive, but how was it for you?" Jeremy asks while twisting a loose thread on his comforter.

Leaning over to prop my head up on my shoulder, I look into his worried eyes. "I can't even put into words how that felt. I just know we have got to do it again." Seeing something I haven't seen in his eyes makes my body come to full attention. I'm not sure if it's fear or sadness. "Hey, what's wrong?" I ask. "Do you not want to do it again with me? Was...was I bad?" Every fear imaginable is running through my mind. Was I that awful? Did he use me just to have sex with me? Was all of this a lie? Oh my God, I need to leave. Pulling myself straight from the bed, I gingerly run toward the doorway to grab my clothes and go. Jeremy's voice stops me in my tracks, and the words he says nearly level me.

"Emily, I've fallen in love with you." Silence. I turn and meet his eyes as he slowly makes his way over to me. He grabs my arms, his eyes pleading with me to say something. "Did you hear what I said, Emily? I love you, and I don't think I can let you go, ever." More silence. *Jesus, Emily. Say something,* I tell myself. The look in his eyes now is nothing compared to what they will be when I have to tell him about Denver and then Vancouver after that. "C'mon, Emily. Talk to me. Please tell me you feel the same. This...us...we're right for each other. I know it's fast and all, but after tonight, it's so clear to me. God, please say something," he begs.

Tell him you love him too, Emily. Tell him he's all your dreams come true. Tell him he broke through the walls to your heart.

Shaking my head, I say the one thing that will make everything we have in this moment, all nothing. "I'm leaving the day after your home opener Sunday. I'm sorry."

JEREMY

So, that's what this feeling is. It's my heart breaking all over again. She's fuckin' leaving me. I tell her I love her, and I'm fighting for her no matter how hard I know our relationship will be, and she's leaving after next Sunday's home opener. She has to feel something; she wouldn't have just given up her most prized possession to me if she didn't. Something's not right in all of this. I don't even realize I'm on my knees in front of her. Standing, I search her eyes for any sign that she's not really leaving me. There's nothing there to tell me otherwise.

Pacing in front of her now, not knowing what words to say, I catch a glimpse of her grabbing for her underwear on the floor. She's quickly putting them on, nearly toppling over as she frantically throws her legs into her thong. She makes it across my room to grab her folded clothes off the dresser. Where the hell does she think she's going? I just confessed I love her, and she's seriously going to leave me, right here and now. She couldn't even respond to my question. No, I just got the words "I'm leaving." Why wait until after my game next week if she doesn't feel what I feel for her? Shaking my head as I pull at my hair, I know I need answers. This is ridiculous, and none of it makes sense.

Finding my voice again as she's standing in the doorway with her back to me, I ask, "Tell me something, Emily. Was it worth it? Was it worth giving up your virginity to me, knowing damn well how I feel about you, only to leave in the end again?" I walk toward her, her back still turned to me. I lean down beside her ear, pushing some of her hair out of the way before I whisper, "Why won't you fight for this? What's holding you back from taking a chance? I thought you were stronger than this, Emily. I guess I was wrong." She flinches as I punch the wall with my fist before moving back to make my way around her because I can't deal with this right now.

I'm almost through the door when I feel her hand reach out and grab my arm, turning me back around to face her. Tears are rolling down her face. Her chest pulsates as the sobs wreak havoc on her body. She drops her clothes onto the floor as her other hand covers her mouth before she looks up at me. Her eyes are etched in pain as she shakes her head at me. I want to wrap her in my arms and comfort her, but I can't. My mind relives how I felt after high school with her. How's that phrase go? *Burn me once...*

Making my way to the kitchen, I grab a beer from the fridge. Twisting off the cap, I take a long pull from the cold bottle as I stare out the window overlooking the backyard, watching everyone still out there laughing and having fun. My parents are sitting around the fire pit on the loveseat holding hands, laughing as Dad says something to Mom. Running my hand through my hair, I wonder how the hell this night has gone to shit so fast.

Oh, that's right. I confessed my love to a girl who I allowed my heart to open to a second time.

Hearing movement behind me, I turn to see Emily standing there fully dressed. She tosses her bag from her shoulder to the floor. She's no longer crying. If anything, she looks pissed. Why is she pissed at me? Storming over to me, she grabs my beer from my hand and chugs the rest of it before placing it forcefully onto the counter. What the hell?

"You think I'm not taking chances? That I'm not fighting? I'm fighting everything in my body at the moment not to tell you to go fuck yourself." *Whoa! Where did she pull that from?* Before I can reach my arms out to calm her, she continues, "For saying that having sex with you was me saying goodbye. Would I have ever asked you to make *love* to me and not think for once I might actually have feelings? I fucking love you, Jeremy! Is that what you wanted to hear before you tried to make me feel like shit in there? It's not that I'm leaving you. I'm leaving for my skating competitions next Monday. I'll be gone for three weeks. The same friggin' three weeks you'll be on the road with the Monarchs. I'm scared shitless because I have no idea how to make this work until we get back. More than anything, I'm scared of losing you. It seems I already did since it appears you're not willing to fight for us either."

Making her way back to her bag, she picks it up and tosses it over her shoulder. As she walks toward the door to leave, I run over to her just as she has it partly opened, slamming it shut with my palm. I turn and face her head on. "Sit!" I yell.

Startled with the authority in my voice, Emily stammers back to the living room. "What are you going to do, Jeremy? Tell me that a month apart with hardly any contact after having one date and going out for a week is going to work? How?"

"Emily! Stop! Just stop making excuses that you think will justify you walking out that door. Were you honest just then when you said you loved me? Don't lie." Tears build up again in her eyes as she nods yes. "Then, why are you trying to run away? Why do you think it won't work with us before this even happens? Yeah, it's scary, and this is new for both of us, but we try. You. Me. Together, we fuckin' try because I love you, and you love me. Got it? We'll be working on our communication skills after this too, so this..." I point my finger between her and me, "...this doesn't happen again." I make my way to the bedroom with quick strides. Before walking in, I turn back to the living room and stare into Emily's eyes. "Are you coming?" I ask her. Slowly standing and walking toward me, she stammers, "Jeremy, I'm sorry I didn't tell you about leaving sooner, or that I didn't explain properly. I didn't know how you'd take it. Then, you told me you loved me, and I didn't know how to tell..." My lips crush hers at that instant, cutting her off from her thoughts. Breaking my fevered kiss, I hold her hand as I bring her back into my bedroom. "What are you doing?" she asks as she follows me.

"Now that you've finally admitted you love me, I'm going to spend the next several hours making sure you know just how much love I've got to give you."

Jeremy and I basically went from having our most intimate experience sexually to having a huge fight to make-up sex all in the same night. In the end, though, after several hours of touching, caressing, and more orgasms than I can remember, I can honestly say I've become well educated on the many levels of sexual positions, and now I'm ready to fall asleep in Jeremy's arms. He has begged me to stay the night with him, and as much as I want to wake up in the strong, tender arms of the man I've grown to love so much, I know I can't. We take a long shower, and I inform him that I have to get back home since I have practice in Boston early in the morning. Jeremy also has hockey practice early and then an exhibition game in Worcester on Monday afternoon against the Sharks.

This is how it is for the entire week. I train, he practices, and we hardly have time to talk on the phone, let alone actually see each other. I have to keep telling myself that despite all this distance, I have to try, if not for myself, for him. Easier said than done. I haven't even left for Denver yet, and already I have a sense of unease heading into Sunday's home opener.

Jeremy must keep in touch with Sue and Courtney because they have not left me alone for one minute of my free time. Since it's Friday afternoon, Jeremy is at his first game of the season. Courtney called earlier and said I was going with her to Sue's studio for a workout. After complaining and saying I was too busy, she saw right through me, and before I knew it, it was time to leave. I am going to learn how to climb a stripper pole. Can you see my mother's face? The look of horror if that image ever leaked the front page of the *Globe*? I can see the headline now, "Figure Skating Star Trades Ice Skates for Stripper Poles."

We have a lot of fun despite my initial reserve. Come to find out, pole fitness is actually really hard. Sue teaches me a few of the basic moves while Courtney is already well versed in working the pole. I know that sounds so crazy, right? Pole dancing for working out with clothes on? Imagine the concept! After about an hour in Sue's studio, my arms are shot, and I've done more fireman spins than I know what to do with. It turns out I actually have a knack for this, and the girls can't believe I am already doing death drops from the top of the pole in such a short time.

We sit in the studio floor for a couple of hours after that, just hanging out and having a few bottles of wine. Sue cranks Grace Potter over the speaker as we talk and laugh about everything. Without martinis involved, it turns out I can be social. Who would have thought?

Courtney and I manage to get Sue to talk about what is going on with her and Dave. As it turns out, Dave is a fairly decent guy. He may come off as a cocky jerk sometimes, but he really wants to do right by Sue. She wasn't sure if she was going to say yes when he asked her out after Sunday dinner, simply because it is Dave, and he is good friends with Josh. She doesn't want to flaunt her relationship with Dave in front of Josh, and I understand her reasoning. She also informs us that Dave was supposed to talk to Josh that night. I must have been otherwise occupied and missed that exchange.

It doesn't take long for the girls to figure out that I had sex with Jeremy. Courtney tells me Jeremy wasn't his typically brooding ass after practice on Monday, and when she cornered him, he caved. Then, of course, Dave found out and told Sue. How my life has gone from lonely solitude to being thrown into this pile of chaos, I'll never know. What I do know is I'm having fun just actually living life, laughing and finally experiencing things I've missed out on for so many years. It still sucks that it's not perfect, given the amount of training I still have to put in, but it's moving in a better direction.

It's Sunday morning, the day of Jeremy's home opener. I packed all my skating gear last night as I talked to him on speakerphone at my apartment. He asked me about my night out with the girls at Sue's studio. I told him he'd see the evidence of the brutal attack when he picked me up Sunday. I'm just glad I don't have to wear my skating costume before Thursday since I have bruises all over my calves and forearms. My mother would be livid. Plus, to others, it might appear I've been manhandled. Of course, I told Jeremy he would be handling me after the game in an entirely different way.

The weather has changed slightly this past week. Heading into October, the leaves are starting to change, and the nights remind us that summer is gone, and winter is just around the corner. Winter. To me, winter is the devil, sneaking his ugly face in here and turning my life upside down for about four months. It is the Grand Prix, Nationals, Worlds, endorsements, scores, cameras, fake smiles, and let's not forget, appearances. To say I hate winter is being nice, but at least I get paid.

128

Sitting outside on the balcony on my chaise lounge, I begin a new novel on my e-reader. After reading this story, I may try picking up a British accent and start calling Jeremy "My Lord." He still wonders how I became so well versed in my sexual nature. If he picked up my e-reader and read any of the books I have on it, he'd know easily.

A few minutes later, I hear his truck pulling into the driveway. I told him I could drive myself, but he said we'd be hanging out after the game at one of the pubs near the arena. Shutting off my e-reader, I stand and head over to the railing as I look down at him getting out of his truck. As he stands there with his hands in his pockets staring up at me, I feel as though I'm in a scene from a Shakespearean play.

The crackle of the pea stone under tires diverts our eyes to the black Lexus pulling around the driveway toward the exit. It keeps moving, never acknowledging either of us. "Anyone you know?" Jeremy asks, nodding his head in the direction of the Lexus.

"That's just Daddy. He must have needed to confirm my schedule with Mother for the next month. Can't have bad press for Daddy's company, now can we? Enough about my sperm donor, I'll be down in a minute."

Picking up my bag and jacket, I make my way out the garage door and meet Jeremy at the passenger side of the truck. Reaching around my waist, he pulls me into his body and gives me a soft kiss. Grabbing his flannel shirt, I pull him in closer, trying to intensify our kiss until he pulls back, saying, "I've missed you so much this week."

He takes my hand in his, leading me into the truck. Walking around to get in the driver's seat, he starts up the engine and Florida Georgia Line blasts through the speakers. *Really, country? Oh, Jeremy, no, no, no.* After turning down the speakers, he grabs something from the backseat. Leaning forward again, he hands me a gift bag. Well, not so much a gift bag as it is a plastic bag with the Monarchs logo on it. Giggling to myself, I unroll the bag on my lap and pull out a Manchester Monarchs jersey with his name and number on it.

"Thank you. Perhaps the necklace would have been enough, but add in the jersey, and the next thing I know, you're Tarzan and I'm Jane. Or, you're pissing circles around me, making sure you mark your territory." I laugh and look over at him as he gives me a narrowed eyed glare. "Not funny. You haven't met these guys. They will try to make a pass at you tonight if they don't know you're mine yet," he says deadpan.

"Fine, let me just take off my sweater." Lifting my sweater over my head, I reach over to grab the jersey to put it on as Jeremy's eyes burn holes in me. "What?" I ask, pushing stray hairs out of my face.

"These bruises on your arms. Are they from Sue's pole class?" he asks, running his fingers over them.

"Yeah, I told you they were bad. I'm just hoping they go away before Thursday." I think I'll need a lot of concealer if they don't.

Jeremy leans down, placing delicate kisses over the spots and then pulling back to put the truck in reverse. "Might be a good idea to keep the sweater on under the jersey. Just sayin'."

I let out a frustrated sigh. Guess I'll be sweating all afternoon now.

The drive to the arena only takes about a half hour. As we make our way into the players' entrance, a security guard checks our ID's. Jeremy says it's all right that I don't have a pass since I'm with him. Since it is still early, hardly any of the players are here yet, so Jeremy takes it upon himself to give me the grand tour. He shows me the family seats, which his parents and Courtney, will be sitting in later. Josh is working, so I have his ticket.

When it is time for Jeremy to start getting ready for the game against the Devils, he walks me up to the seats and tells me after the game to head down to the security desk, where we entered, and wait for him. He leans down to give me a subtle kiss, and I wish him luck, and in true cheesy Jeremy fashion, he replies, "I don't need luck; I've got you."

"Har-Har," I fake laugh.

As he takes off down the stairs toward the players' bench that leads to the locker room, I hear him say, "Love you, babe." My breathing hitches. We haven't seen each other or even mentioned the *love* confession from last week. Sitting down in my seat, I glance up and see Jeremy still standing there, waiting with his arms crossed.

"Love you, too," I say barely above a whisper. He knows I said it, and he also knows as he walks into the tunnel that it will take more time for me to be comfortable enough to say it in public.

JEREMY

Standing on the ice as "The National Anthem" is about to get underway, I glance up to see my family and Emily engaged in conversation. Courtney is being her usual animated self and flailing her arms about. She's weird. I'll never deny that, but it suits her. I'm just uncertain how she's blood-related. Mom is seated next to Emily, and I can't tell what they are talking about, but Mom is giving her a long hug and running her hands over her back. Perhaps Emily just told them she'd be leaving tomorrow for three weeks. Almost a whole fuckin' month. I thought I would be okay with this. I mean, I really didn't have a choice either. I'll be on the road with the Monarchs until a few days before she gets home. The situation sucks; there's no denying any of it. I just hope both of us are strong enough to make this work.

The final words of "The National Anthem" are sung, and as I make my way toward the bench, I get a nudge in my side from Dylan. "Hey, who's the hot piece of ass with your sister up there?" And, here we go. It's a good thing I play hockey. If I didn't already have on my gloves and wasn't making my way to center ice for the puck drop, I'd check him into the boards and make sure he knows Emily is hands off. So, instead I have to keep my top from blowing off right now.

"That's my girlfriend, Emily. Hands off. She's not available," I scowl as I lean over onto my stick next to the Devils player.

"Dude, she's Grade-A meat. After you're done riding that, send her my way, and I'll show her just how good it can be," he says dead serious, staring into my eyes. Dylan is a man-whore, and normally I couldn't care less what sloppy seconds he gets, but my blood is boiling at the moment. I'm also pretty sure it's against the rules and player conduct to check your own teammate. Guess I'm going to find out soon enough.

The puck drops, and everyone starts racing after it, except me. I have another agenda. The puck sails toward the Devils end of the ice, but I only notice Dylan. Gaining speed, I see him trying to free the puck with his skate against the board, and that's when I check him in the back. His face hits the glass hard, and he's lying on his back instantly. I hear whistles in the background. Looking down at Dylan, I kneel and stare him dead in the eyes. "You'll be smart to know Emily is mine and isn't going anywhere near you. You so much as breathe in her direction, ever, I'll have no problem checking you into the glass again. Understood?" Dylan rapidly blinks his eyes and nods in agreement as I rise to my feet and make my way to the players' bench, hearing Coach yell something at me, but I'm not paying attention. I'm only looking in one place. Emily stares at me with her hands over her mouth as if she's praying. Giving her a quick nod and smile, I wink and she sits in her seat, knowing it's all good and normal. I see Dad talking to her, as Mom rubs her back again. She's in good hands for now. After I'm done making sure all the guys on the team know she's off limits, it will be my hands she's in.

At the end of the period, we are winning 2-0. While we make our way back to the locker room, Dylan finds me in the group. "Dude, I'm sorry about before. I swear, had I'd known that girl was a keepa' I wouldn't have said anything." We exchange fist bumps, silently accepting our momentary truce as I make my way over to my locker. For some reason, the words above my locker mean more to me now than they ever have before. "Embrace Your Future." Emily has always been a part of my past and my present, and I'll be damned if she's not going to be there in my future.

Coach walks in as we all are seated on the bench, and although we may be winning, he still looks mad. As he is giving an animated pep talk about things we need to improve for the next period, it doesn't register with me that everyone is staring at me. I must have been lost in my own head.

"What?" I glance around, thinking I missed something.

At the other end of the bench, I hear Dylan clear his throat. "Don't mind him, Coach. His girlfriend is in the stands today." There's a group groan and a few coughed "pussy whipped" thrown in there for good measure. Coach laughs, realizing that explains a lot as he walks back to the white board to start drawing more plays.

As two more periods pass, I manage to keep my focus on the game. We win 4-1. After the final buzzer goes off, I see Emily walk out with my parents. Courtney must have left early; she sometimes works weekend afternoons at a small bakery to help pay some of her bills. She loves photography, but I'm pretty sure she can take up being a pastry chef any day of the week. She's that good.

I quickly shower and get my gear packed up and ready to load onto the bus in a couple of days for the road trip. Once I'm certain I'm not forgetting anything, I make my way out to my truck. When I come around the corner to the exit, I have to take a second look. Emily is standing there laughing and carrying on a conversation with Dylan and Bryce. *What the fuck?*

Quickening my pace, I am at her side almost instantly wrapping my arm around her waist and nuzzling my lips near her ear. "Don't make me remind you who you belong to, babe," I whisper. I feel her hand come up and touch my chest to almost push me away, but I pull her in front of me, so her back is to my front. Eyeing both the guys, I say, "If you two dicks are finished making a play for my girl, we can start heading over to Murph's for a drink, and you can pick up whatever is *free* over there." Dylan and Bryce laugh and turn to walk out the door. Emily and I are behind them walking hand in hand. "Did you have fun at the game?" I ask her.

"For my first hockey game, it was fun. Your dad helped explain a lot of the play-by-play that didn't make sense to me, but I think I understand the basics now. Your dad wasn't happy when you checked that guy up there into the boards. Wasn't he on your team?"

"Just marking my territory, babe. It won't happen again, unless one of those idiots forgets you're mine." I nod toward Dylan and Bryce, and Emily laughs.

We have been at Murph's for about a half hour, listening to the live band they hired. Killer Buzz Float must have been in another town on tour and stopped by. Typically, Murph's doesn't have bands play on Sunday nights, but Killer Buzz Float is huge. I mean, like off the charts. The lead singer Letty has some serious chops, but what appears to have grabbed the guys' attention is the hot raven-haired chick working the stripper pole on stage. I think I saw somewhere that she is with that Rax guy in the band.

I send Dave a quick text about Killer Buzz Float being at Murph's and rockin' the bar. He isn't pissed that he couldn't make it up for the game; he's pissed that he's missing Eve work the pole. Standing at the bar and grabbing a couple more drinks while Emily is in the restroom, I turn back toward the stage and that's when I see her. Fuck! Her eyes immediately meet mine, and I know there's no escape route now. Once she's right in front of me in her pleather skirt and halter top with fake tits hanging out, I want to run.

"Hey, love. I haven't seen you around here since last season. Care to make another go of it? I could use another good fucking against the wall." Seriously, how drunk was I that night I thought Avery was attractive? Leaning in and placing her hands on my chest as I take a pull from my beer, she says, "Maybe this time I'll let you suck the Patron out of my pussy instead of off my tits." Choking on my beer as I try to ignore her, I see Emily standing right beside me. Fuck! There is no denying she heard every word of that. Well, this just went to hell in a hand basket. Still trying to recover from choking on my beer, I attempt to get Emily's attention to explain the whole thing. Too late. Avery already catches her staring between the two of us. "You got a starin' problem, bitch?"

Oh, shit.

"Avery, enough!" I yell as my nostrils flare. Dylan and Bryce hear me from the other side of the bar and must notice Avery standing with Emily and me. They begin walking over toward us just as Emily saddles up to my side and looks at me. "Em, please let me explain."

She holds up a hand to me as if telling me to just shut it. "Just marking my territory!" she fumes at me. Aww, fuck. She turns toward Avery just as the guys are standing by my side, watching as this all goes down. Her hands are on her hips as she tries to take on Avery. "Listen, skank. I'm pretty sure you've had your go with every dick in this bar, but this dick..." *Oomph. And those are my balls she's got in a vice grip right now. Ease up a little, Emily.* "...this dick is mine, and the only wall you'll be against is that one when my fist connects with your face if you come near him again."

Dylan and Bryce look at Emily in amazement; their mouths hang open, probably because nobody assumes she has that in her from the looks of her. Seconds later, Avery takes a step forward to get in Emily's face, and I grab Emily by the waist, pulling her into me as Dylan gets in front of Avery to drag her back toward the doors where Killer Buzz Float is still playing. Good, maybe Avery will hit on Shades. I'm positive Letty will cause a death by a lubed dildo if Avery gets close enough. Scratch that. Letty may be the one to suck the Patron from her pussy.

Turning my attention back to Emily, I see her breathing settle and shoulders relax. I know she's never had to confront anyone like that before. I'm proud of her for standing up for once, even if it was against Avery. I know I should have avoided Murph's, but Manchester is only so big, and we have a limited number of hangouts after games. I move my body so I am facing Emily. The look I get in return is not what I expect or want. Trying to resolve her anger, I say, "Emily, you have to understand, Avery and I were never anything. It was a drunken night last season and I can't..."

"Stop, Jeremy. Just stop! I spent the entire time in the ladies' room having to listen to her tell some other girls how she was going to be coming all over your dick until the sun comes up again since...oh. What. Were. Her. Words. Oh! Yes! Since she apparently made sure you came twice while sucking your cock deep enough to swallow every ounce of come you shot down her throat. Oh! And that's not the best part. Apparently, she had the pleasure of the infamous Page Patron body shots you licked off her tits before you made her have the best orgasm of her life. Now, did I miss anything, or was that pretty much everything you *don't* remember?"

Holy fuck. Seriously, I don't remember any of that night except waking up and getting the hell out of there. Avery may be lying to make herself sound good, but the Page Patron body shot is a regular occurrence at Murph's, so that part may be true.

I glance back at Emily after rubbing my hands over my face. Her eyes are glassy now. Shit. I did this, and I have no idea how to fix it. I reach out to bring her into me, but she throws her hands up and backs away. "Take me home, now. I just want to go home."

Moments later, she's heading toward the door and crossing the street as I am trying to keep up with her. Her Chucks allow her to make headway. Once I catch up, I reach to grab for her elbow, and she pulls it hard back against her. "Emily, please. You have to know I'd take that night back if I could. She's slept with every guy on the team. It's what she does. She fucks 'em and dumps 'em."

"Seriously, Jeremy! Your excuse before was you were too drunk, and then it's 'she's slept with every guy on the team,' so gee, I guess it was your turn for a ride on the Avery roller coaster. Shit, I've got to take a urine test before my competition this week. Should I be worried now about finding some STD in my system? I can't even believe this is happening." She reaches my truck, holding her hand on the door handle, waiting for me to unlock it for her.

"What do you want me to say, Emily? It was nothing but meaningless sex with her! You can't hold my poor judgment from months ago against me. It was the worst mistake of my life. I know that now since I've experienced love firsthand with you."

Once I hit the button on the fob, she gets in, not waiting for me to help. Standing in front of my truck with my palms firmly on the hood, I wonder how the hell I am going to make this right. I'm not losing her, but she's leaving tomorrow morning, and that only leaves me the next hour to think of a way out of this hole I've dug for myself. Picking my head up, I glance at Emily through the front window. She's crying hard now and swiping tears away at a rapid pace. Pushing myself off the hood, I release all my frustration as my fist pounds against my truck, leaving a dent as I look to the evening sky and scream. *Fuck!*

CHAPTER
seventeen

Emily

I'm sitting at Logan Airport waiting to board my plane to Denver for the first competition of the Grand Prix. We'll be staying at my Uncle Richard's downtown loft for the duration of the trip. Uncle Richard is Mother's younger brother, my only living relative, and when I say "relative," I mean person who hasn't made contact with his only niece since I was maybe three, but shares my blood. You've got to love my family. I'm kidding, of course. Even better, I've got to board this airborne jail cell for four hours sitting next to mommy dearest. Just. Kill. Me. Now! She's the last person I want to deal with after the way things ended with Jeremy last night.

The entire ride home consisted of me crying, Jeremy pleading with me to talk to him, me not talking to him, me storming out of the truck, running up my stairs, and slamming the door in his face. I know I'm partially at fault. I'll own that one. I should have talked to him before our hiatus, and I'm almost positive I'll drive myself crazy worrying about where we are in this relationship. Jeremy stayed at my door for maybe ten minutes, trying to get me to open it for him. I couldn't do it. When he finally pleaded with me for the last time, I told him I needed time to think about our relationship and perhaps our time apart would help settle my wayward thoughts. I fell asleep listening to his truck back out of the driveway and seeing his headlights illuminate the almost limp bouquet of flowers sitting on my kitchen table.

Maybe those dead flowers I threw in the trash before leaving this morning were a sign that whatever we had is dead now, too.

After hearing the gate attendant announce that First Class is now boarding, I hear my mother snobbishly say, "It's about time." I shake my head at her inability to actually act civilized. She's pissed because we had to wait until people with disabilities and young children boarded. *Seriously, Mother, get your nose out of the air; you'll give yourself a nosebleed.* She walks right by me, slightly throwing me off balance. Handing the attendant my boarding pass, I follow her down the long hall walking away from one set of problems and toward another. I let out a deep breath as I find my row and take my seat. I reach into my purse to turn off my phone, but not before glancing at the screen. Twenty missed calls. Thirty missed text messages.

Seven voicemails. The screen shows the first few text messages before I even open them. Two are from Jeremy, pleading for me to call him. Another one is from Courtney, asking if she can do anything to help because she heard Jeremy and her dad talking in the house last night. The last text is from Sue, asking me to call her ASAP because she needs my help with something. Sue is the only one who didn't ask anything about Jeremy, so I quickly respond to her before shutting off my phone.

> *On my way to Denver and then Vancouver for the Grand Prix.*
> *Won't be back 'til the end of Oct. I'll call you once I get to Denver.*
> *Hope everything is ok.*

I place my phone back into my purse and put it under the seat in front of me and fasten my seatbelt. Within a few minutes, we are airborne, and I'm shoving my earbuds into my ears and pulling out my e-reader to find something to stop the lump forming in my throat. What to read next? I narrow my options down to two. The first one involves a woman with a troubled past and secrets, courage, and love. The other is about a hot football player who comes to Boston not looking for love, but finding it nonetheless. Both of them sound like they will bring me to tears almost instantly, given my current relationship status. If I were on Facebook, my status would read *who the hell knows.*

As the flight attendants make their rounds for drinks and snacks, I simply ask for a coffee and water since it's only nine in the morning. Mother turns to place her order. "I'll have a vodka orange juice very little ice, just a splash of juice. I want the top shelf vodka, not the cheap stuff." She turns and catches me staring at her. "What?" she asks.

"Really, Mother, it's a little early to be getting drunk. Plus, you wouldn't want to tarnish that Cameron image. Appearances are everything, or so I've been told," I respond tersely while folding my arms across my chest. *Whoa. Where did that come from?*

Obviously agitated at my condescending tone, she leans over, pulling out my earbud cord. "I'll have you know your father has invested a lot of money into your Grand Prix endorsements. Perhaps you should consider your tone before speaking to your mother that way. You wouldn't want your father to cut that funding, now would you?" Yes, actually I would, but I don't say that. It's what comes next that has heat pulsing through my veins. "Your father caught a glimpse of that lower-class boy in the driveway yesterday. I might have mentioned how rude he was to me the last time we had an encounter at the house. Needless to say, he wasn't happy. You should focus more on winning the Grand Prix and then the Nationals, instead of associating with trash."

My neck shoots around, and I stare at her with narrowed eyes. How dare she call herself a *mother* and then insult Jeremy's status in society and threaten to make up a story to Daddy about him. How? I know how. She's the insensitive spoiled bitch who gave birth to a child just because it was another business deal for Daddy. Well, I've just about had enough in my lifetime.

As we begin our descent into Denver International, the Rocky Mountains are covered in white, and the airport's tented roof blends in with the blanket of new snow. Denver may be my chance at a new beginning. All I know is I'm going to focus the rest of the time away on the Grand Prix, and when I get home, I'm focusing on my future. The future I know needs to have all the people who have shown me more love in the last month than my so-called managers have my entire life. I need to find my way off this stairway to hell, even if I die trying.

The first thing I need to do is make a phone call. Waiting at the baggage claim as Mother argues with the limo driver that was sent for us, I pull out my phone and wait for it to power up. It dings a few more times, notifying me of more incoming messages. I ignore them all, until I find the person I should have contacted in the first place and press *Call.*

Ring.

Ring.

Come on. Please pick up.

Ring.

JEREMY

I'm pretty sure life can't get much worse than it is right now. How one drunken mistake long before Emily came back into my life can be the reason I'm feeling the way I am, I'll never know. I've begged and pleaded with her voicemail all night and didn't make any progress. Even talking to Dad last night about my ultimate screw up and what I could do to fix the mess I'm in didn't help. The moral of the story is don't get sloppy drunk and screw the bar whores, and at no point in time, do you bring your current girlfriend to said bar where said bar whore makes her rounds. *Got it, Dad. Thanks for the pep talk!*

I'm sitting on the bus heading out with the Monarchs on the first major road trip of the season. Trying to catch some sleep, I listen to my iPod and shut my eyes. I didn't get any sleep last night since I spent most of the night getting my gear packed, and I ended up wasting nearly six hours salvaging my relationship with Emily. Clearly, she's still not speaking to me. Courtney tried to get in touch with her this morning, too. She wouldn't respond to her either. Covering my eyes with my arm, I lay my body over the seats, resting my head on my bunched-up jacket. I'll pay for this later, but right now, I just want to stop reliving the last twenty-four hours.

Moisture pools in the corners of my eyes, and I'm glad my arm is covering my face. Crying over my failed relationship will do nothing for my image with this team. It's bad enough I cross checked my own teammate during the game yesterday over her. Coach will surely bench me for being a pussy if he sees this.

About two hours later, we're pulling into Portland, Maine. Each of us is given our hotel room assignments and the practice schedule before being released for the night. Early morning skate means none of us would be hitting up the town for an all night binger, not that I would anyway. This isn't college anymore. This is my job, and we are supposed to keep a level of professionalism when playing for the American Hockey League.

Swiping my keycard in the door to my room, I drag all my gear behind me before tossing it in the corner. Three weeks on the road means a lot of luggage, but after doing this enough times, it becomes routine. I pull my phone from my back pocket to see a text from Courtney from a few hours ago.

Never heard back from E. I really thought she'd text me back. Sorry J. Good luck in your game 2morrow.

Well, that about sums it up. If Emily won't talk to Courtney, I've clearly lost my chance at redemption. Deciding a hot shower might help, I strip off my clothes and head to the bathroom. Stepping into the standard-sized tub that is definitely not meant for anyone over 5'5", I lean my hands against the wall and drop my head in the scalding heat. After a while, the water begins to cool off, so I turn it off and wrap a towel around myself while I brush my teeth.

Stepping out of the bathroom, I search through my luggage to find my sweatpants to throw on and pull the blankets down on the bed. Plugging in my phone to the charger, I see I have no missed calls. I decide to take a nap before heading out to dinner later with the team. It's only one in the afternoon here, but I had hardly any sleep last night, and I'll need to catch up if I'm going to play well during the game tomorrow night.

My phone begins vibrating on the nightstand just as I'm about to fall asleep. Ring. Ring. Ring. Rolling over quickly, I unplug it, not glancing at the screen. *Emily.* Shit! "Emily?! Em?! Is that you, babe? Please say something."

"Sorry, sweetie. It's Mom." God, I love my mom, but I would much rather hear Emily's voice right now.

"Hi, Mom. Is everything okay?" I ask in a flat tone as I lie back on the bed.

"Everything's fine here. Your father is still at work, but wanted me to tell you he says hello, and he'll take good care of Aspen. The main reason I'm calling is to see how you're doing. Anything you want to talk to me about?" I knew Dad couldn't keep the situation with Emily quiet for long. She would have eventually figured out something was wrong. Dad's poker face sucks. "When did Dad spill the beans?" I ask her.

"Your father didn't say anything to me, which I will be confronting him about later when he gets home," she says accusingly.

"Well, if Dad didn't tell you, how did you find out about Emily and me?" I wonder out loud. There couldn't be anyone else who knew.

"Emily called here earlier. Jeremy, she told me about yesterday. Sweetie, she's confused and clearly upset over what happened, but she loves you. Just give her some time to focus on her skating for now. When the two of you get home, then you can see where her feelings are."

Emily called my mom? Of all the people to call her, Emily would have been the last person I would have suspected. "Not to sound mean, Mom, but why did she call you?"

"Jeremy, you're a smart man, but when it comes to women, you have absolutely no idea how we operate, do you? Emily called Courtney's phone and asked for the house number. When I got home a little while ago, she called from Denver. She said she didn't know who else to call, and she couldn't talk to her own mother about this, so she hoped I'd be able to offer her some guidance. After she told me everything, I was a little disappointed, but I'll never judge what you choose to do in your life."

I suddenly feel as though I've lost all control over my emotions, and hot tears trickle down my face. "How do I fix this, Mom? I love her, and she won't even talk to me. I can't lose her again, and I feel as though I already have." Not knowing what the next three weeks will bring us, I'm not sure how I will focus on hockey and not her.

"If you love her like I know you do, you'll know that a woman's heart is a fragile thing. Your father didn't win my heart overnight. He's mended it plenty of times over the last thirty years, and he'll tell you love isn't easy. Do you remember what I taught you kids about what to do if you break something?"

"Own up to it, fix it, and do everything we can to make sure it never happens again."

"She'll come around, but you have to allow her time to take it all in. She's never been in a relationship before. Everything is new for her, and she doesn't know how to cope with the emotions she experienced yesterday, and Jeremy, you can thank me later."

"Thank you for what, Mom?"

"For getting Emily to agree to attend the annual Jeremy Page Halloween-Birthday Bash."

She didn't. She couldn't. She insists on having this even now. One of the drawbacks of being born on Halloween is my mom always has a reason to invite people over for a costume party. "Mom, what did you do?"

"All I did was have a long talk with your girlfriend to assure her what she was feeling was completely normal. Once she gets back, I told her I'd be here to talk whenever she needed me. Trust me. She'll come around, just concentrate on hockey for now. She'll call if she wants to. If not, you'll see her on your birthday. Love you, Jeremy."

"Love you too, Mom, and thanks for talking to Emily. I'll fix this when I get home. Tell everyone I said hi. Bye."

I feel at ease after talking to Mom. At least I know my relationship with Emily isn't a complete loss at the moment. If Mom thinks it's best if I allow Emily time to figure out everything, then I'll give her the space. I won't like it, but I'll do it. The first thing in making things right will require me to find the team doctor. Grabbing a T-shirt and my sneakers, I make my way to his room at the end of the long hall. As I knock on the door, the team physician opens it to see me standing there.

"Jeremy? What can I do for you?" he asks.

"I need to get some tests run. Can you help?"

CHAPTER eighteen

Emily

I spent much of yesterday afternoon unpacking at the loft in downtown Denver. My mother took off shortly after we arrived, and I haven't seen her since. That's fine with me. I needed the time alone in order to call Jeremy's mother, Grace. When I talked to Courtney earlier, she didn't let on that she knew what had happened yesterday, but something in her tone told me she had an idea.

When I finally reached Grace, she assured me everything I had been feeling was normal. She suggested I use my time away from Jeremy to think about what I wanted for myself before thinking of him. She knew he'd been relentlessly trying to reach me, and she said his actions with Avery were inexcusable last season, but he's a man after all, and I need to learn how to control my emotions if I'm ever going to handle a relationship with a guy like him.

I took everything she said to heart. I was glad she decided to talk to me and help me understand what I was going through. My own mother would never have even given me the time of day, let alone advice.

Today, I'm sitting at a high top table, enjoying my morning coffee along the 16th Street Mall in downtown. My coaches are scheduled to arrive later today for an afternoon practice at the Pepsi Center. For now, I'm just trying to sort through some emails and social media updates I've missed over the past few weeks. My earbuds pump music through my head, keeping my thoughts focused on the task at hand and not on Jeremy. Although, listening to Adele's *21* album may not be in my best interest. Realizing I still need to call Sue back, I begin dialing her number when a text message shows on my screen.

> *I talked to my mom and I'm giving you time to think, as hard as that might be. I just wanted to say good luck in your competitions and don't forget to think about your Halloween costume. Love U-J*

Placing my coffee down onto the table, my concentration shifts to the trolleys traveling up and down the street. I know I should text Jeremy back, but Grace was adamant about allowing myself the time to see if after a few weeks I still felt the same way I did two days ago. I'm more confused now than I was then because I'm scared of losing him more than anything.

I call Sue to see what she needed me for, but I'm sent straight to voicemail. That's odd. She must have a dance class or something this morning. Her voicemail picks up, and as I'm telling her I'll try to call her back later after my practice, a headline from the *Denver Post* catches my eye on my tablet. It reads "Figure Skating Sweetheart Emily Cameron: Quest for Olympic Gold." Well, I know where my mother has been since we arrived. She couldn't resist making me front page news, adding to my already shitty week. *Well, guess what, Mother? Emily Beth Cameron has arrived, and she's done taking shit!*

Packing up my shoulder bag, I make my way back to the loft as fast as my UGGS will let me. Ten minutes later, I'm grabbing my skate bag and security pass and riding the elevator down to the street. Alicia Keys is fueling my fire over the speakers. I glance up at the surrounding mirrors and see a new Emily staring back at me. My mother wants a "Quest for Gold." She'll fucking get one!

As I hail a cab outside the building, I tell the driver to take me to the Pepsi Center. Pulling out my phone, I shoot Courtney a quick text.

> *Tell your mom I said thank you for the advice. It's already being put to good use. I'll be in touch.*

Then, as my fingers hover over the screen, I see Jeremy's last text again. I really have to try figuring out things on my own, but I still feel a pang of guilt for how I left things. Before I know it, my fingers are sliding over the screen as I hit *Reply.*

> *Thank you for the support. I've been thinking about "us" too. I'll talk to you when I get home. <3 U - E*

I manage to run about four miles before my scheduled practice with the other top five skaters. Once my coaches arrive, Mother conveniently shows up, wearing her fur coat and Chanel sunglasses to stand watch along the sidelines. Warming up, I skate about four very quick weaved laps around the ice, deliberately making eye contact with her every time I pass.

I hear my name called to the officials' booth, and I know what's coming. Official entry information, music selection, and drug testing. Jeremy crosses my mind. *Get your head in the game, Cameron!* Worry about him later. Well, that is unless the test is positive, but until then, focus on sticking it to that conniving witch sitting about fifty feet away right now.

Taking the urine cup to the ladies' room while being escorted by an official is always a pleasure. We're figure skaters. Do they really think we want to test positive on a piss test? I know there's a ton of money involved in these competitions, but test positive once, and your career is done. I'm just hoping that my test doesn't come back with anything questionable this time either. I have sex with one guy, and I have to deal with this impending question. I finish producing my sample and hand it to the official as I exit the bathroom and make my way back onto the ice.

Everyone has one final run through on their short programs, and when my name is called, I make my way toward center ice and wait for the drums to echo through the arena and Florence's haunting "Oh oh oh oh" to filter through the speakers. Digging my blade in underneath me, I skate with a vengeance. Every arm thrust matches every drumbeat. Every string section my body is tucked tight in a varying degree of spins. Turning, crossing over back toward my next jump sequence, I pass Mother as she watches every movement. I know she's calculating every point, each deduction. Glaring at her as I pass, anger fuels my desire to bury her once and for all. Setting up for one last triple and landing it perfectly, I skate into my final move, a flying camel into a back sit spin and ending with an abrupt stop from my backward tucked scratch spin.

I'm breathing heavily as my breath fogs the air in front of me. I'm satisfied with my practice skate and so are my coaches, who don't say anything other than simple suggestions for cleaning up a couple edges.

Suzy calls me over. "Everything okay out there? You don't seem to be acting your normal self today. That skate had an edge behind it that I haven't seen from you before."

Staring back at my mother, who is currently on her phone talking, I tell Suzy, "Consider this my season of vengeance."

JEREMY

Days pass, and I've heard nothing from Emily. I didn't think I would, but after I sent her my text on Tuesday, I thought I'd get something. I watched her perform her short program from Thursday night on my tablet. It's funny. Other than that one time when I first saw her at the rink when I was thirteen, that was the only other time I've watched her skate. The video feed wasn't exactly the clearest, but she was absolutely gorgeous, wearing an all black skating dress with shimmering feathers and a fitted high neck. I knew the song she skated to was from a movie, and I saw the fire in her eyes as she sat in what they called the "kiss and cry" area. She was breathing heavily as she stared up at the scores. She skated perfectly from what I could tell, but she would know better than me. Then, her scores appeared on the screen. Overall total points, 72.30, placing her in first place going into Saturday's long program. That's my girl.

Sara Shirley

After another lengthy bus ride and an early morning flight, we're now pulling into St. Johns, Newfoundland. Welcome to Canada. Border crossing is always a treat. With so much gear and so many people on the buses, it takes forever to get up here. Fortunately, this is the only team we play against that's located in Canada, and we'll spend an entire weekend here. So far, this season has been going well. The team is really progressing nicely, and it will only be a matter of time before things begin to shake up. When the LA Kings start their regular season, it becomes a constant to have players from the Monarchs called up to fill in. Since I started with the Monarchs a couple of seasons ago, it's been mostly offensive players and goalies that are called up. As a defense player, there hasn't been much interest in us unless one of the Kings players is out for an extended period of time. Hopefully, one day that call will finally come in for me. To finally skate on NHL ice, even if it's for a short period of time before I'm sent back home.

After bringing my hoodie up over my head as I exit the bus when we arrive at the hotel, I put my iPod into my pocket as "Wait for Me" fills my ears and snowflakes stick to my sweatshirt. With a new season creeping in, I can only assume this is my fresh start. A fresh start to what, though? I can't right the wrongs of my past. I can't go back to high school and change the fact that I never went after Emily when I needed to. Possibly all these things happened for a reason. We might never be the people we are now had the years we weren't together happened. What's that phrase? *Distance makes the heart grow fonder.* When I think about our first kiss a month ago and how far we've come since then and now our time apart, I wonder if Emily is feeling the same way. It's only been a week and already it feels like it's been a month.

I push my hoodie off my head as I make my way into the hotel room, glancing at the clock to see that it's a little after midnight. It's too late to call home, but I send Josh and Courtney a text that I arrived at the next destination and to tell Mom and Dad I'll call them after the next game. I may be an adult, but I've never stopped letting my family know where I am. My dad has continued to play an integral part in my hockey career, and I love getting his input after he reads or hears about my games. They are all my biggest fans, and I love them to death. I know; I'm a big sap.

I send Dave a text as well because I haven't been in touch with him since last Sunday. Once hockey season starts, the Forum gets busy for him, and my schedule is just as hectic.

Just checkin' in. How's everything at home? Anything new goin' on?

146

As I grab my shower bag and sweats from my suitcase to take a shower, my phone alerts me of a new text.

> *Dude, wish you were here. @ Promiscuous and some girl called*
> *Mystic just gave the world's best lap dance. Like jizz in my pants*
> *good.*

I chuckle at the thought because leave it to Dave to compare a lap dance to bursting a nut. Shooting him a response to let him know I'll take his word for it, I don't want to tell him I'm really not in any shape to be heading to the club after seeing how things went down with Avery. I can't even imagine how Emily would handle knowing about my nights with Dave at Promiscuous. The things that happen in their VIP booths stay in the VIP booths, not that I did anything incriminating in there. Let's just say that on one of my more recent birthday celebrations, Dave might have been willing to spend the extra money to have two girls provide more visuals than normally required. Just sayin'. I never said I was a saint; I just wasn't an asshole.

Emily

Taking gold at Skate America seemed almost unreal, and yet, here I am on my way to the next Grand Prix event in Vancouver, BC. Scoring a combined total of 212.02 overall, set me up to be a front-runner for Skate Canada. As long as I place in the top six of each of the events in which I'm scheduled to compete, I'll be in good standing for the US Nationals in January.

Suzy asked me during a practice session before my long program what I wanted to do after this season ended. She swore no matter what I told her she wouldn't tell a soul. Well, I sure as hell hope not. You don't get paid nearly fifty thousand a year to tell everyone my business. Giving her the benefit of the doubt, I explained that after this season was over, so was I. I needed time to get away and just learn to be me. I had to find a way out before it killed me all together. I didn't know what I'd do or where I'd go, but it was going to happen, and I knew it would be the beginning of the end between my parents and me.

How was I planning to inform them of my plans? My parents might be the most manipulative and uncaring people I know, but they are smart and not in a good way. I'd need to beat them at their own game. A chess game seems easy compared to this challenge, and I know nothing about chess.

Then, of course, there is my unresolved relationship with Jeremy. It's been two weeks since I've spoken to him. Just before we left Denver, I talked with Courtney. Grace told me to try to not have any contact with him while I was away, but she never said I couldn't talk to Courtney. Courtney confessed she had overheard her father and Jeremy talking in the kitchen the night he dropped me off. She had mentioned he'd sent her a few text messages, but she only knew that he spoke to her parents and was still upset over the way we left things. She didn't have any information on how he was other than the Monarchs had won all the games they had played so far, and Jeremy had scored three goals and was in a fight that required him to get a few stitches on his eyebrow during one game. Before hanging up, I asked if she had talked to Sue since she hadn't called me back, even after my voicemail. Apparently, she's avoiding everyone, because even Courtney said she's only talked to her a couple of times in two weeks, and for Sue, that's abnormal. There's something going on there, and we both said it couldn't have anything to do with the fact that she's dating Dave now. They've been friends for years, so this has to be completely out of the ordinary. Courtney said she'd try to get to the bottom of it while I focus on my competitions.

I wanted to ask her so many times to relay a message to Jeremy if she talked to him, but I not only needed to prove to Grace I could listen to her advice, but also myself. I need to prove to myself I have the strength within my body to do it. Each day I wake up, I'm one day closer to reaching my goal, not anyone else's goals. Mine. When I make it back to Boston in another week, I can say I did it. I can win gold and handle my relationship situation on my own. That's all me and nobody else had their hands in there helping.

Our flight from Denver to Vancouver is uneventful, thank goodness. I find myself finishing another book on my e-reader that sounded interesting. This one involves a small Southern island girl who meets a famous actor who's hiding out from the media; a relationship forms between them, and she experiences her first love, but his past catches up with him and things begin to unravel. Something tells me I can relate to this girl on so many levels.

Stepping outside of the airport I discover that October in the Pacific Northwest is extremely raw and rainy. The limo driver takes us on the short drive to the Fairmont Hotel Vancouver. Since we don't have any relatives living in this city, we are forced to stay in a hotel for almost a week. At least my mother has decided to give me my own suite. I can't handle having her in the same room with me for that long. A long lunch with her can be difficult; a week is pushing the limits of my sanity.

As the limo pulls up in front of the hotel, I notice some commotion outside. Evidently, it's the paparazzi since cameras are perched on tripods and flashbulbs are going off every few seconds. They can't be here for me, unless my mother is responsible for this nonsense, and if she is, I will most likely throw a tantrum right here on the sidewalk. The driver comes over to open the door for us, and I step out. As I wait for my small bag from the trunk, cameras start going off even more and people yell louder. I pull my earbuds from my ears as "Black Sheep" by Gin Wigmore can no longer be heard over the screaming. Looking up, I can't see anything but spots when I shut my eyes. I hear peoples shouting something, but it's definitely not my name. Turning quickly to avoid more blinding, I run right into a tall, muscular man in a suit, knocking my shoulder bag to the ground and spilling out some of the contents.

"I'm so sorry," I say to the man, not yet making eye contact as I drop down to retrieve my stuff off the ground.

"Here, let me help you with that," he says in a very suave Irish accent.

Peering up from my crouched position, I see the face attached to the voice and stand quickly. "Oh my God! Oh my God! You're. You're. Shit!" *Nice, Emily. Find the words, dipshit.* He hands me a couple of my belongings and asks, "Name's Jamie, and you are?"

He's asking who you are. Speak! "Oh-uh, I'm Emily. Sorry for running into you. The camera flashes blinded me for a second. At least I know they aren't here for me. They're stalking you," I say as cool as I can without acting too nervous. Seriously, I skate in front of thousands, and I'm nervous about this.

I hear my mother say from the revolving door, "Emily, we have a schedule."

"I've got to get going. It was nice meeting you," I say, trying in every way possible not to mentally undress him right now.

"Thanks, it was nice to meet you, too. Take care, Emily," he replies before stepping into the back of a black tinted sedan.

I can't wait to tell Courtney and Sue what just happened. A sudden feeling of pleasure overwhelms me just thinking of finally having friends with whom I can share my experiences. I'll never know how or why it happened the way that it did, but to just have them now means the world to me.

Stepping into the lobby of the hotel, I see my mother at the registration desk, finishing our check-in. She eyes the concierge to ensure that our luggage arrives to the proper rooms. Once she notices me, she strides over to hand me my room key.

"Emily, I entrust you are aware of your training schedule the next few days before the short program Thursday? I emailed you all the details and times in case you should forget." I want to tell her that I'd like for her to forget to run my life for just one day.

My hands curl into fists, and my back goes rigid as I respond with as much sarcasm as I can muster, "Yes, Mother. I will try not to cause too much trouble while I'm cooped up in my room."

Leaning over toward me, she says, "Emily, dear, it would behoove you to speak nicer to your mother. I don't care for your tone of voice."

"Really, Mother? What 'tone' would that be? Sarcasm? Contempt? Because if you're talking about bitchiness, just take a good look in the mirror."

I never saw it coming. The sting to my cheek was the telltale sign of her hand connecting with my face. She just slapped me in the lobby of the hotel, and people are staring in our direction.

"The next time you speak to me that way, I will inform your father of your recent behavior," she says quietly with a look of superiority.

"Perhaps Daddy would also like to know his *wife* just publicly abused America's top contender for a gold medal at the Olympics. Considering the number of cameras out on the front sidewalk and the glass doors, you can almost be certain one of them just caught your little act." I begin walking away confidently, but not before turning back to her. "Maybe, as my manager, you ought to go out there and give a statement on my behalf. You know, before they run video of your slap to my face on the six o'clock news."

Halfway to the elevators, I realize I need to confirm my ride to the rink with the concierge. Making my way back toward the counter, I notice my mother standing outside on the phone. Hiding behind a column, I force myself to listen in on her conversation. "Charles, cameras caught me slapping her across the face. How do you want me to handle this? Yes. Well, I can't see any other way to play the story. If you think it would be best, I will turn the story into tomorrow's newest headline. You know I can handle it. I've been dealing with your infidelity for years. This will be no different. She'll never know anything. She may be rebelling, but I've still got her under my thumb." After hearing enough of my parents' repulsive plans, I need to get away, quick.

I never look back. I walk with purpose to the elevator and press the button for my floor. Once I enter my suite, my legs give out below me as I sink to the floor and cry. I will not let them ruin me. I'm twenty-two years old. I need to do this. They can't control me all my life. They can't. Screaming at the top of my lungs, I gather my strength and move into the room. I need to talk to someone. I want to call Jeremy so badly right now, to hear him tell me to fight for what I want. I know I can't do that. Unlocking my phone, I pull up the number of the next best thing and hit *Call*.

I hear the line pickup on the other end. "Hello."

"Grace, it's Emily. Do you have time to talk?" I sob between the words.

"Sweetie, what's wrong? Are you crying? What happened? Tell me what's going on; I'm here to listen if you need me."

Proceeding to explain the events that ultimately led to where I am today, I give Grace all the details. She remembers vaguely how my mother was and still is. Apparently, she witnessed one of her infamous yelling sprees at the Forum when I was a kid. She said she thought it was the same day Jeremy accidentally ran into me. God, that was so long ago. So many years have passed, and nothing has changed with her controlling my life. If anything, it's become worse. When I tell her my mother slapped me across the face and has recently threatened my father's business power over my head, she is shocked. She can't understand how parents can be that insensitive and cruel to their own flesh and blood.

"Grace, what do I do? I feel as though I'm stuck in quicksand and can't get out." I wipe the tears from my cheeks as I sit at the desk, tapping a pen to the hotel notepad with my hand.

"Emily, I know we have only just met, but knowing you trust me enough to tell me this, tells me how much you need friends on your side. I don't mean that in a bad way, dear. I only mean that I believe you have the strength in you to make the right choices with our help. You're just a little lost, and we're here to help if you need us, all of us."

"Have you talked to Jeremy?" I know I have to ask, but I'm uncertain of her reaction.

"I have. I've also told him the same thing I've told you. Take the time apart to see what your hearts want. He's hanging in there, too. I can tell he misses you desperately, and he's upset. He's talked to his father much more than me the past few nights, but he'll be home on Sunday. I'll talk to him more then."

"Grace, I know you told me not to be in touch with him, but can you please tell him I will talk to him when I get home on Monday, and that I'm fighting the best I can right now?"

"I'll give him your message when I hear from him. You should also know when he called last week, he mentioned he watched your skating programs, as did we, and we couldn't be more proud of you winning gold. I believe Jeremy said he saw a fire in your eyes, and he knew you'd take gold."

"I miss him so much. Is it weird to tell you that?"

"It's not weird; you're just not accustomed to expressing your feelings. It will all come in time. That's why having this opportunity to figure yourself out is so gratifying. I am already noticing how much more open you have become."

"How can you tell?" I ask her as I try to remember times where she could have seen me like this.

"Sweetie, instead of trying to handle the burden of your mother's behavior, you called someone. When you realized your error with Jeremy, you reached out for guidance, and you asked Courtney to check in on Sue to see if she was okay. All those things show me you're willing to help others just as much as you're trying to help yourself."

"I'm really trying, Grace. I just don't know if it's hard enough."

"You'll be fine. Focus on this week's competition, and when you get back, we'll celebrate Jeremy's birthday along with your wins."

"Wins? How do you know I'll win this weekend? I haven't even skated the short program yet."

"We all know you'll win because you're going to get yourself up, realize you're strong and determined, and when you step on that ice, the end result will be the one thing your heart wants the most."

Jeremy. He's my gold.

"Thank you for talking to me, and tell everyone thank you for the support. I'll see you next week, fingers crossed."

"You'll see me. Don't worry. Well, unless I'm dressed up as Casper. Goodnight, Emily," she says with soft laughter in her voice. "Goodnight, Grace."

JEREMY

I'm back on the bus again, but this time, I'm finally heading home from Scranton, Pennsylvania. Thank fuck! I need my own bed, shower, and most of all, Emily. I know. Everyone is sick of me saying it. I was called a pussy when Dylan and Bryce tried to get me to go out for dinner Saturday night, but turned them down to watch Emily on TV. When I talked to Josh last night, he literally groaned over the phone when I mentioned her name for the millionth time. Everyone is over having Sunday dinner when I call on the way home after the game. Mom can't stop talking about watching Emily on TV Saturday night, and I hear Courtney say something in the background about not mentioning anything about a front-page picture. I'm not sure what she is talking about, and when I ask Mom about it, she becomes really evasive. When she tells me she'll explain when I get home Monday morning, I have to find out immediately.

After hanging up the phone with her, I pull out my tablet to see what picture she could be talking about. It has to involve Emily somehow. I pull up *Google* and type "Emily Cameron" to see if anything comes up. Scrolling through, I don't see much other than a couple of articles here and there about her recent competitions and interviews. Then, I click on *Images* and see what they were talking about. I enlarge the image, and it fills the entire screen. I pull up the article to read the headline, "Fifty Shades Star & Ice Princess: Secret Romance Revealed?"

Staring at my tablet in disbelief, I slip and say, "Are you fuckin' kidding me?" Dylan and Bryce lean over the top of the seats to see what is pissing me off. Both of them say there is no way it could be real because Emily doesn't seem like the type.

As I read the article, it reveals that Emily was dropped off at a hotel and quickly turned into the arms of the up-and-coming actor. A statement from Victoria Cameron is included, declaring she neither confirms nor denies her daughter's relationship with the actor. When asked how Victoria felt about her daughter being involved with a married man and ultimately trying to break up the Dornan family, she stated that her daughter is old enough to make her own decisions, and should she get involved with a married man, then she has to be an adult and face the outcomes.

I almost throw the tablet across the bus until Bryce takes it from my hands. Running my hands through my hair in agitation, I know I have to get off the bus and fast. It will be another few hours before we pull into Manchester, and I can get home. Even then, Emily won't be back until Monday night. Mom knows when Emily is due to come home, but won't tell me until I'm settled. I send Courtney a text after I see the picture and article. She assures me it is purely coincidental, and Emily called Mom right after the incident to talk to her about something else, but that isn't her story to tell.

I want to call Emily and ask her how her hands ended up on this guy's chest on the cover of a tabloid magazine, but I think better of the idea. She's finally coming home after three weeks, and she totally kicked ass at both competitions. Her scores from Skate Canada were even higher than Skate America. With two gold medals under her belt, she's proving to be a tough one to beat this year. I want to wrap my arms around her and tell her how proud I am of her, but we've got to sit down and have a heart-to-heart at some point about where we are after the Avery Invasion and now her cover story.

It's almost one in the morning by the time we pull into the parking lot in Manchester, New Hampshire. I'm exhausted and ready to get home. I finally managed to get about two hours of sleep on the bus, so I'm ready for the commute home. As we stand in the parking lot waiting for all the bags to be unloaded from the bus, Coach calls a brief huddle before we're released. He tells us it's been a long few weeks and to not report to morning skate until Wednesday. He follows with a quick congratulations on coming off the road trip with a record of 6-2, and he's happy with how the team is progressing this season. Quick and painless. Thank God because it's cold as all hell outside and blowing hot air onto my hands isn't helping anymore.

Once I find my bag, I'm back at my truck almost instantly. I wait for it to warm up before heading toward Route 93. On the highway, I see nothing but stars in the sky, immediately thinking of Emily and the first morning I drove here almost two months ago. I haven't heard her voice since she told me she needed time to figure things out with us. Mom says she's talked to her and for me not to worry. I'm relieved that my mom seems to be playing the mediator role in all of this. She cares for Emily; if she didn't, she would have already told me to move on.

Checking the clock, it's almost two now. If she's still in Vancouver, it's early enough that she might be up. I can't help but wonder what's she's doing at the moment. Fuck it! Plugging my phone into the charger, I turn on the Bluetooth and say "Emily." A dial tone echoes through the cabin.

On the fourth ring, I'm ready to leave a voicemail until I hear a soft, groggy voice come over the speaker.

"Hello."

"Hi, it's me," I say just above a whisper.

"Jeremy?"

"Should I not have called? I thought it was still early in Vancouver, and I really couldn't wait to talk to you," I quickly shoot out while squeezing the steering wheel nervously.

"I'm not in Vancouver. I'm at home. I decided to leave Sunday morning instead."

"So, I just woke you up is what you're saying? I'm already scoring major points here."

"Jeremy, what is so important that you need to call me at two in the morning?" I hear her yawning on her end.

"I miss you and your voice. I can't take not talking to you one more day. The minute I got in my truck to drive home I figured that my mom couldn't yell at me for calling since technically I'm home. Plus, I need to apologize for everything. I know you never read my texts or listened to my voicemails from that night, so I'll tell you now. After all this time apart, I still fuckin' love you. I just hope you find it in your heart to love me back."

"Can you come over?" she pleads.

"Absolutely."

"What I have to say I need to say to your face."

I wonder what she needs to talk to me about face-to-face at this time of night. "I'm not sure I like the sound of that, but if you want me to come over, I'll be there as fast as I can." How can I ever deny her what she wants despite the growing uneasiness in my stomach?

"I'll open the garage door. Just pull in the open stall and come upstairs."

"Okay, I'll see you in about twenty minutes."

"See you soon."

Emily

After taking home the gold at Skate Canada, I had mentally had enough. I changed my flight and hopped on a red-eye home. Mother wasn't happy when I called her from the airport and said I was leaving. Once the picture of Jamie Dornan and me hit the tabloids, I somehow thought my mother could be involved after our hotel incident. I was right. I never thought she'd stoop that low when it came to slandering the Cameron name. It turned out the tabloid picture boosted people's interest in me, therefore, helping sales. It figures my parents would consider using me in a scandal for their own benefit. The cameras held firm outside the hotel until the story blew over, but I only focused on winning the competition and getting home.

Pulling myself out of bed, I head downstairs to open the garage stall for Jeremy. As much as I know I should wait to talk to him, it's been three weeks, and I need to see him and touch him. Grace wanted me to figure out where my head and heart were during our time apart. In more ways than none, I think I knew where my heart was before I even left. It was my head that needed to get figured out.

About ten minutes later, I hear the truck pulling into the stall and the garage door closing. A nervous feeling spreads over my body as I make my way around the kitchen trying to make myself a cup of chamomile tea. His footsteps up the stairs are fast and loud, and the soft knock on the door tells me it's time to face the music. I turn the knob slowly, opening the door to see his forlorn face staring back at me.

"Hi, come on in," I mutter as I turn, walking back toward the stove where the teakettle is beginning to whistle. Grabbing a mug from the cabinet, I look back at him and hold it up, silently asking if he wants one as well. He shakes his head no as he sits on the sofa. Pouring the steaming water over the teabag, I wait for it to finish steeping before joining opposite him on the sofa.

We sit silently for what seems like forever. My nails tapping the side of my mug is the only sound in the room. Why is this so difficult? It should be simple to talk to the person you love. This feels as though everything we worked toward before we left is all gone, like we're strangers again. I take a quick sip of my hot tea before placing it onto the coffee table in front of me. Jeremy still doesn't saying anything; he just sits with his head down and his hands folded over his knees. Is this it? Is this really goodbye? *Please say something, anything.* I fight back the tears that begin to cloud my vision before covering my mouth with my hand. Jeremy glances in my direction, noticing the change in my expression and comes over to my side. As I shake my head, he pulls me into his chest as a few tears slide down my face.

"I'm so sorry. I never should have left things the way I did. Had I just talked to you this whole thing could have been avoided," I say between sobs.

Running his hands over my back, he shushes me. "Emily, you have no idea how hard it was to know what I did in my past caused you that much pain. I never wanted that to happen. You have to believe that before you, I really wasn't seeing what was worth going after. I would go out after games with the guys, and on occasion, some of the girls took advantage and hooked up with us. The night I was with Avery was the one and only night that went to that level, and that was my fault entirely. Had I not drunk as much as I did, none of the last few weeks would have happened. Can you forgive me for this?"

I can't allow him to think he's completely at fault here. Swallowing back the lump in my throat, I respond, "Jeremy, I understand how it happened, but I can't condone how I reacted the rest of the night. I didn't want to think I was as insignificant as the next. The past few weeks needed to happen for us. I needed the time apart to figure out where my true feelings stood and sort out a lot of other things in my head."

"And did you?" he asks, clearing his throat.

I nod my head silently against his chest before pulling away to look into his brown eyes. "If it wasn't for your mom, I might not have understood everything going on in my head, but I managed to separate the good and the bad. I know what I need now and where I need to get to in my life. You. Jeremy, you were never a question in my head. You had my heart before I left. It was the family drama and skating that needed to get sorted out. I love you for who you are and what you made me see. Can you forgive me?"

Staring into my eyes, he reaches for my face and brings his head down to mine. "Babe, I missed you so damn much it hurt not knowing how you felt and what you were going through. Mom just kept telling me to focus on my own life and to let you figure out things. I can't take back the last few weeks, but I can make the future better. I promise. I love you, and I'll spend forever showing you how much better it can be for us."

Tears pool in my eyes again as I rub my thumb over his stitches just above his eye before asking the big questions, "So, does this mean we're okay? We're still together?"

"Was there ever any doubt? You've had me all along, Emily, unless, of course, you're still having an affair with that actor?" he playfully hints, but his eyes tell me he may actually think the story is true.

"I was hoping you wouldn't have seen that. Really, it wasn't anything. I turned around too quickly and bumped into him. The cameras caught it at just the right angle to make it look like we were embracing. Do you believe me?"

"So, I don't have to use any of my hockey fighting moves to get him to back off? Damn! I was so hoping to have to fight for you." He winks at me. "Well, then I guess there's only one other way to make sure you don't run off again, but it's going to involve less clothes than you have on right now," he suggests as his lips hover just above my neck. My breathing grows rapid because I need him just as much.

Breathlessly, I mouth his name before standing up, grabbing his hand and guiding him back to my bed. "Make love to me again, Jeremy."

I slowly remove my tank top and pajama bottoms. He reaches to pull me close to him, and I make quick work of removing his hoodie and the T-shirt underneath. Then, his lips fall on mine as if the past three weeks never happened. After he pulls back suddenly, I wonder if he's having second thoughts as my hands hover over his belt straps.

"Emily, before we do this, I need to tell you something. While I was on the road, I went to the team doctor and had him run an STD test. The results came back last week, and I'm clean. I didn't want you worrying." Before he can say anything more, I pull him on top of me and watch him make quick work of his pants and boxers. He slowly rolls me on top of him as he kisses me passionately; our tongues join together in a battle. Jeremy grazes my legs and ass with the tips of his fingers as chills of anticipation spread across my body. Feeling his hardness growing under my stomach, I reach down between us to begin stroking him. Throwing his head back, a groan escapes his lips. "Oh my God, Em. I missed you so much. That feels so good."

Knowing I'm entering a whole new territory, I start placing kisses along his pecks and begin slowly making my way south. As I linger just above his trimmed happy trail, he smirks as if he's asking what I'm planning on doing. *Lie back and relax because I'm taking control right now.* Sitting back on my calves in between his legs, I lower my head to the tip of his cock, still stroking it slowly. I open my mouth and let my tongue circle the tip before sliding all the way down his length to the base of his shaft.

I watch as his chest rises and falls quickly, and his eyes never leave mine. He says nothing, so I assume I must be doing this right and begin massaging his balls in my other hand. I slowly slide my mouth up his length, wrapping my lips around his tip and tasting the warm smooth fluid already flowing from his cock. Continuing my torturous motions, I slip the tip of my tongue between the entrance of his cock before sliding my hollowed mouth down until he's hitting the back of my throat. Jeremy's hips thrust up as his hand finds its way to the back of my head. Pushing down just slightly until I'm almost gagging and tears prickle my eyes, I look up at him as he watches me go down on him and becomes completely at my mercy. It's a feeling I've never felt before, knowing I'm the one making him feel his pleasure.

Then, as much as I don't want to go there, the mental image of Avery in this same position flashes across my mind. I stop all movement along his cock, and Jeremy notices my mood change. "Don't think about whatever is going through your mind. We're here now, and you're my future. Good?" Nodding in understanding, I remove my mouth from his cock and move to straddle him.

Knowing his favorite sexual position from *Twenty Questions* comes in handy when I have control in bed. Hovering my already slick entrance above his cock, I slide my folds along his length, arousing my own pleasure points in the process. Moans escape me before I lean behind me to pull his cock up to my entrance, looking into his eyes as if silently asking for help on what to do. Jeremy moves his hand over mine on his shaft assisting silently, never breaking eye contact and gliding himself in slowly as I lower myself until he's all the way inside me. He's already placed right at the point, where with just the slightest angle movement, I'll be spiraling out of control. It's been too long for the both of us, and I'm not sure I can ever do without this physical connection ever again.

Resting my hands on his stomach, I look into his eyes while his hands grab onto my waist, moving me just enough to make me feel him inside me even more. I throw my head back in pleasure, letting my nails dig into his skin lightly.

"Emily, I need to feel you come around me. I've missed the feeling of being inside you." His hand slides over and starts massaging the wetness between my legs over my pulsing bud. My mind races, and I try to move my body with his as he tenderly strokes me. I begin to tremble above him, and I know my release is close. Looking down into his eyes, I see his emotions pouring out of him. "Come on, baby. Come. If you don't, I'll be forced to take back control and show you what I'm capable of making you feel." *Holy Shit!* Moving my hips faster along his cock, my breath shortens right before I feel him thrust his hips up to hit the spot, sending my orgasm out of control. I can't move anymore; I just feel the pulsing and throbbing between my legs and around his cock. He moves his hips up even more, and I'm screaming his name before he pulls me close and rolls me on my back, staring down at me while he wraps my legs around his waist.

"Hold on, babe. I'm not going to be gentle." His pace speeds up as he rises slightly, and I watch as his cock slides in and out before he's stilled and groaning through clenched teeth. "Holy fuck. Oh. My. God. Emily." Before I know what's happening, with one last hard thrust, he sends another wave of pleasure through me, and I'm clutching the sheets at my side, screaming his name.

Completely sated and exhausted, Jeremy glances around the bed to look for something. "Tissues?" Shit. "In the bathroom." He pulls out slowly before running to the bathroom, coming back with a wet washcloth to wipe away the remnants of our late night pleasure fest. Sitting up, I go to grab my pajamas, but Jeremy stops me to kiss me like he never has before. "I love you, Emily."

I know you do.

"Stay with me?" I ask as I feel the warmth spread through my body again. Giving me one more kiss on the lips, he silently nods yes before making his way over to his pants to grab his phone. After typing out a text, I can only assume to his sister, he comes back to bed with me. "I had to tell Courtney I'm home, but won't be at the house until later. She'll figure it out."

Feeling him curl behind me and wrapping his arms around my stomach, he places a lingering kiss on my bare shoulder as I lay a hand on his. "I love you," I whisper as I turn my head just slightly before flicking off the bedside lamp. The only light in the room now is the moonlight casting shadows about.

"Babe, I almost forgot to tell you. Congrats on the gold medals. I was so proud of you when I watched. We all were."

Happy tears slip onto my pillow. Where has he been all my life? A family I just met has helped me in leaps and bounds over the past two months more than anyone in my twenty-two years. I have friends that are supportive and caring and a boyfriend who has shown me how much love is truly worth fighting for. Having all that means more than the two gold medals currently glistening on my kitchen table in the moonlight. I finally fall into a peaceful sleep that I haven't had in so long, looking forward to what I'll wake up to in the morning.

JEREMY

The morning sun has just started to peek its way through Emily's French doors. The night's early frost is melting against the sun's rays, as it didn't hold a chance against the blaze, therefore, allowing more sunlight to enter the room. Emily is snuggled tightly into my side, trying to keep warm. Staring around the room and afraid to move since she is still asleep, my eyes train toward the glare from her kitchen table. Her two gold medals sit glistening.

Slowly moving out of the bed, I make sure I don't wake Sleeping Beauty next to me. When I know I'm safe, I quietly head to her bathroom to take a piss after throwing on my boxer briefs. Having morning wood and post-sex pee is never an easy task, just ask any guy. After tossing some water onto my face to freshen up and brushing my teeth, I know I'm in need of coffee, soon. As quietly as I can, I walk toward the kitchen, stopping to check out the medals on the way.

As I hold one of them up to get a closer look, some papers on her table catch my eye. Some appear to be documents from the United States Figure Skating Association, but sticking out from underneath her other medal, is one of the checks from her winnings. Are you fuckin' shitting me?! She took home eighteen thousand dollars for one event. I skate for eight months out of a year, and I make just more than double that. I'm in the wrong friggin' business.

Placing her medal back onto the table so she won't notice I've been looking, I head to the fridge to grab something to drink. Opening the door, I peer inside. Seriously? Water and condiments? Okay, water it is. My stomach is growling; I know I need to find something to eat. It's either that, or I'll get moody as all hell. Twisting off the cap of the water bottle, I take a long pull from the bottle while I quietly start opening cabinets looking for anything to eat.

Searching cabinet after cabinet, the only thing I find that's edible is peanut butter puffs cereal and shake-n-pour pancake mix. Noticing the one-cup coffee machine on the counter, I turn it on and wait for it to warm up. So much for being quiet. Turning toward Emily, I notice her stirring and her hair falling over her face, but she doesn't wake up. After a couple of minutes, I find the mugs and coffee pods. I manage to get the cup of coffee brewed and already begin to feel alert after a couple of sips.

It's always when you're trying to be quiet, that you're the loudest. When I start pulling the frying pan from her lower cabinet that is buried under about a million other pans, all the pans on top begin tumbling on each other. Shit! She'll be awake now. That's when I hear soft laughter from behind me.

"Do you think you can be any louder? Some of us are trying to sleep over here," she says, clearing her throat.

"Listen, woman. You have nothing to eat here other than coffee and pancakes, so I'm slightly limited on choices."

Stretching her arms above her head, Emily slowly throws her legs over the bed and makes her way to me. She walks toward the door and pushes a button on what appears to be an intercom on the wall. A few seconds later, an older woman's voice comes over the speaker. "Good morning, Emily. Welcome home."

She pushes another button to speak back. "Good morning, Louisa. It appears I don't have any food supplies here. Would you mind making some breakfast and bringing it over?" She has a maid? As if knowing what I'm thinking, she turns to me. "She's my mother's maid, not mine." Well, that's about right. Louisa buzzes back inquiring as to what Emily wants for breakfast. Looking at me for an answer, I'm acting dumfounded before Emily says, "Today, Jeremy. I'm not getting any younger here." Staring at her, unsure of what I can even ask for, she tells me, "Whatever you want." Seriously, it's weird. I won't even ask my own mother to make me breakfast.

"I don't know. Eggs, bacon, toast and *real* creamer."

"You and that damn creamer! Are you sure you don't want pancakes, too? I mean, it would be a shame not to have to lick all that maple syrup off of you afterwards, but it's totally up to you." She playfully winks back at me before pressing the *Talk* button.

"Pancakes it is. Make sure she sends over extra syrup," I demand, rubbing my hands together in excitement. Emily places our order, and we have about twenty minutes to wait.

Making her way over to grab a coffee mug of her own, she notices her USFSA documents on the table. Seizing them forcefully, she shoves them into the kitchen drawer and slams it shut. Looking at me before pushing the button for her coffee to brew, she says, "Just a bunch of crap Daddy wants me to do every year for tours that will allow him a chance to advertise his company. Right now, I couldn't care less if I speak to either him or my mother."

"Something happen while you were away?" I question her even though I have an idea from talking to Mom something went down.

"I know we are supposed to be working on communicating more, but for now, I just want to enjoy being back here with you. Once I'm ready, I'll tell you. I Promise."

All I can do is take her word. I want to push her to open up to me and trust that I will be able to help, or at least try to help. If she doesn't tell me, the only thing I can do is assume, and I don't like where my mind wanders when I do that. A knock at the door removes me from my thoughts. Emily walks over to open it, while I go to put on my pants that are still on the floor from last night.

Once I'm slightly more clothed, Emily lets in an older, attractive woman carrying a tray with two plates covered with a silver topper. While she catches up with, Louisa, I think her name is, I take it upon myself to grab my phone and call my parent' house. Just out of earshot, I think I hear Emily tell Louisa that there was a falling out between her and her mother in Vancouver. After the photo in the tabloid, she needed to get home early. Why couldn't she have just told me that? I'm about to listen more when I hear the phone pick up on the other end. Josh answers and says he saw the note from Courtney on the table when he woke up this morning. He stayed over Sunday to help Dad get the house ready for this weekend's Halloween-Birthday party.

As much as I hate the annual party, it is still a fun time. Extended family and friends all come over and Dad usually has a party tent set up in the yard with tables and chairs. Courtney makes the desserts, and Mom spends all day throwing every item of food she can think of into crockpots and onto serving trays. Josh handles the beer selection and typically finds the craft beer of my choice for the keg. My dad says we still celebrate it every year because it reminds him of all the people we have in our lives that make us happy.

Josh hangs up, saying he has things to do, that we all can't skip out helping to play hockey and get laid. He seriously needs to find a girlfriend. I sit here, remembering some of the parties we used to have as kids and some of the costumes we've had over the years. I must have been lost in thought for a while, because when I look up, Louisa is gone and Emily is fussing around the kitchen looking for something.

"Anything I can help you with?" I question as I make my way over behind her, wrapping my arms around her waist as she leans into the fridge.

Jumping back in surprise until she realizes it's me, she answers, "Don't do that! You scared the shit out of me." She places her hand over her heart before turning back to the fridge. "What are you looking for?" I rub the scruff on my chin as I stare from behind her.

"I need blueberries. I can't have pancakes without them." Jumping up and down, clapping her hands, she shouts, "Ah ha! See. I knew they were in here." She pulls out the bag to show me.

"That's a six-pound bag of blueberries. How many pancakes do you plan on eating?"

"These don't just go on pancakes, silly. I put this shit on everything!" She rolls her eyes at me and laughs as she grabs a spoon to sprinkle them over her plate. I'm pretty sure I've lost sight of the pancakes that used to be on the plate seconds before.

"Babe, that's a bit much. Don't you think?"

"I'll have you know, there's never such a thing as too many blueberries. Now, do you want some or not?" She places her hands on her hips, and a cocky grin spreads across her face. Waving my hand toward the plate, I gesture for her to start piling that healthy shit onto my breakfast. I want butter and lots of it, none of this antioxidant, good for you shit. Fuck that! I'm going out of this world eating all the things that are not good for me.

Emily had already made plans with Sue and Courtney to go shopping for their Halloween costumes. I'm a last-minute costume selection kind of guy. In other words, if I can't find it in my house, I'm not wearing it. I think I was a hockey player for four Halloween parties in a row.

Emily is in a rush to get me out of her place since we've finished eating, and I'm a little curious as to why. I know the girls won't be upset if she is a little late, but as we are both driving our cars out of the driveway, I spot the black sedan pulling in with her mother in the backseat. Well, that explains it. I'm pretty sure after what I overhead Emily telling Louisa about what happened, she would be avoiding her parents for a while. She still hasn't gone into detail about the severity of what actually went down, but in time, she'll open up to me.

CHAPTER
Twenty-one

Emily

I really do have plans to meet the girls for costume shopping. Jeremy keeps fishing for more information about what transpired between my mother and me. I want to tell him, I really do, but I can't, not while I know she'll be pulling into the driveway any minute. I need to rush him out of here, and he knows I'm doing just that.

"The longer we stay at the house the more chance I won't get the best costume for Saturday," I tell him.

His gives his typical guy response. "You don't need a costume since naked requires no clothes at all."

"Your parents won't be impressed if I show up naked at their house," I say, pushing on his chest and heading toward my car.

Once we are both driving in opposite directions and I see my mother's hired ride pulling into the driveway, I know I am right for not telling Jeremy about her and my father's devious plan as well as her slap across my face. Had he known, he would have turned his truck around, and I would have been involved in some kind of smack down or murder cover-up story. *No, officer, the last I saw of her she was still in Vancouver.*

I see Courtney and Sue parked at the strip mall parking lot and pull in next to them. Sue still doesn't appear her normal bubbly self as she stands there solemnly. I asked Courtney a few days ago if she found out anything about her. She said she couldn't get any information out of her. It's so bizarre.

While I'm getting out of my car, Courtney comes running over, squealing and hugging me tightly. "It's so good to see you! We've missed your gold medal winning ass around here!" she shouts. "Wait a minute." Courtney pauses while pulling away and staring at me from arms' length away. Shock overtakes her face. "You made up with Jeremy. Didn't you? You did! So, you guys are good now? I mean, I heard about what happened at Murph's, and we all wanted to kill him, but you know, he's family and all. When Mom found out, even Dad went and hid in the basement, because she was furious, and Mom never gets mad."

Reaching out to grab her arms, I stare her in the eyes as she looks at me with raised eyebrows. "Breathe, Court." I chuckle, trying to calm her nervous chatter. "Jeremy and I are good. He came over last night, and yes, we *made up*." My face radiates from the blush I'm sure that has just spread across my cheeks.

As I make my way over to Sue, I hear Courtney say, "Eww, I don't want to know. Way too much information!"

Stopping mid-stride, I turn toward her, laughing. "You're the one who just asked me if we made up. All I did was confirm it." I make my way to Sue, who's still standing by her car, and I start playing with my necklace, hesitant of how to approach her since I'm not sure what's really going on. Standing there in front of her with Courtney close on my heels, I gaze into her solemn eyes and push my shoulders back. "Okay, that's it! What's going on with you? I've never seen you like this, and you're not your usual crazy ass self. Spill the beans. Did you break up with Dave already?"

Just when I think I'm showing my firm resolve with her, she begins crying. I look over at Courtney, who is staring at me and shrugging her shoulders as if we are both thinking the same thing. *Why the hell is she crying?* She must have broken up with Dave, but I'm going to wait until she is the one to tell us.

Lifting her head in our direction with tears and mascara streaming down her face, Sue looks between Courtney and me as we stare, but says nothing. Her hands fly to cover her mouth as her tears continue flowing heavier. As Courtney and I move to her side, she opens her mouth, and the words she says need clarification. Either that or we didn't hear her correctly.

"What did you say?" I question again just to be sure I heard her correctly.

"I'm pregnant," she sobs.

Of all the things it could be, I never would have thought that. A heavy feeling settles in my stomach. Courtney is gently rubbing Sue's back as I look around the area. Noticing a small coffee shop, I urge Sue and Courtney in that direction. I'd rather have this conversation in a comfortable place than in the middle of a strip mall parking lot.

Relaxing on a well-worn sofa while Courtney grabs drinks, I sit, rubbing Sue's back and trying to calm her crying. I simply wait for Courtney to return and help back me up since I don't know what to ask or what to do. Within a minute or two, we're all sitting and sipping our chai teas. Surprisingly, Sue is the one who breaks the silence.

"Well, you guys must think I've seriously got issues. I'm really sorry, guys. It's just it's the first I've actually said it out loud. I haven't even called my parents to tell them. They live in Florida, so they can't do much. You're the first to know, and guessing from your expressions, you've probably got a good idea who could have done this to me." She pauses to take a sip of her tea. I have an idea of who that person is, and if it's him, she's going to need a whole lot more support to get through this. Sue continues after placing her tea onto the coffee table, "It's Dave. I mean, clearly it's him since he's the only one I've slept with in two months. To answer the next question, how? Well, here's the kicker. Turns out the night we all went to Eavesdrop, and he brought me back to Jeremy's, well, that drunk idiot forgot to put on a condom. I'm one to talk since I'm no better than him. It's just as much my fault as his, but it happened, and I've got to be an adult about it now. I'm scared to death, though. How am I supposed to do this?"

Taking a deep breath to calm myself before gently reaching for Sue's hand, I say, "I know this is probably cliché by saying this, but it will all work itself out. Dave will be a good father. You'll make a wonderful mother, and we'll all be here to help you. You won't be alone in any of this. Right, Courtney?" I look at her for some kind of confirmation of my statement.

"Sue, you know my mom loves you. You're like my sister. We'll help you no matter what, but you know Josh is going to kill Dave. You know that, right?"

Sue softly shakes her head. "I'm not telling Josh. No way, he's going to go ape shit!"

"This might come as an obvious question, but when were you planning on telling Dave he is going to be a father?" I ask as Sue's shoulders fall in defeat.

"That's where I might need you guys to help me."

At an eager attempt to change the topic of that conversation, Courtney stands quickly, "So, what you're saying is I should choose a costume that involves weapons and restraints." After her awkward attempt at deflecting the question, Sue finally cracks a smile for the first time since I saw her today.

"I know I'm going to screw this up big time, but I'm happier knowing I've got you guys supporting me, and just to clarify, I will not be your on-call designated driver for the next seven months. Not. Happening!" She stands, throwing her hobo bag over her shoulder and looking Courtney and me.

Yeah, Sue's going to be just fine, and that baby will see more love in its lifetime than I've ever known from my family. Everyone seems to be back to normal and smiling as we make our way out of the coffee shop toward the costume shop. Walking alongside each other, Courtney turns to Sue. "So, should we get you a bun in the oven costume for Saturday and see how long it takes for everyone to get it?"

Sue stops dead in her tracks, clapping her hands. "That's an incredible idea! The guys will never figure it out."

JEREMY

Once Wednesday rolled around this week, time with Emily became almost nonexistent. After her two major wins in the Grand Prix, she was focused entirely on the last remaining Grand Prix event. She'll be leaving again in two weeks to head to Paris for the Trophée Eric Bompard. Should she win, she'll have qualified for the Grand Prix final and in good standing going into the Nationals. To say I'm extremely proud of her is an understatement.

My own schedule is no less trying. I had an away game last night, but it was close enough to Manchester that we took the bus back after the game. Emily was here at the house with Sue and Courtney helping Mom cook and set up decorations. They were in the kitchen talking about something before I left in the afternoon for the game, and when I walked in, they went silent. Eyeing them suspiciously, I had to wonder what was being said before I stepped in. It's not as though the party is a surprise. Either way it still struck me as odd.

I knew everyone would be setting up until almost midnight, so I called Emily before she left to come over and asked her to bring an overnight bag. She willingly accepted, saying when I got back, she needed to tell me something that she's wanted to tell me all week. I could only assume the immediate silence in the kitchen had something to do with that. Man, was I ever wrong on that thought.

When I finally pulled in after the game last night around midnight, Emily was already lying in my bed, wearing some kind of lace top and matching lace boy shorts. She was watching her *Friends* reruns, laughing until she saw me walk into the bedroom. Turning off the TV, she asked how the game was and circled around her true reason for needing to talk to me.

Once I threw my pants onto the storage chest and climbed into bed with her, she sat up and tucked her legs under her. When she started her story, saying, "Well, you already know about the tabloid picture and story fabricated by my mother, but there's more to it than that," I knew I was going to need a drink before hearing any more.

After two shots of Patron and a handful of fists hitting the wall, I heard the entire story. She admitted everything, from her mother's threats on the plane, the slap to her face, to her parents setting up the fake tabloid story. Livid didn't even begin to describe the level of anger I felt at that moment. I'm a hockey player; I hit people on a pretty consistent basis. She told me she didn't want to tell me earlier at her place because she was afraid I'd go off, and if I did anything in the presence of her parents, there was no telling what they would do. Basically, they had the ability to take away my career in

170

the blink of an eye. I asked her if that's what she was talking with my mom about in the kitchen when I walked in earlier, but she said it was something totally different.

A scratching paw to the side of my bed is how I ring in my Saturday morning. Not technically my official birthday, but it will still be celebrated tonight. When I roll over, a pair of big, pleading eyes stare back at me. Aspen, noticing I am awake, becomes even more anxious and wants to go out even more. Throwing my legs over the edge of the bed, reaching down to grab my boxers and pulling on a pair of lounge pants I tossed over the storage chest at the foot of the bed last night after getting home from my hockey game, I crawl back onto the bed.

"Babe, I've got to let Aspen out. Do you want anything from the kitchen?" Placing a soft kiss against her bare shoulder, she moans softly before shaking her head. "All right, I'll be right back."

Today is a new day, but the thoughts of Emily's family still wreak havoc in my mind. I wasn't here to help while all of this was going on. That alone tears me up inside. It should have been me helping her, but at least my mom was the one talking her through her issues. The fact Mom never mentioned any of it to me is going to be addressed when I see her later this morning.

After opening the door at the bottom of my back stairs to let out Aspen into the yard, I turn back up the stairs to head back to bed to be with the most beautiful woman ever. I stop at the freezer to pull out an ice pack. Placing the ice pack on top of my right hand knuckles, I already know they will be swollen and hurt like hell in my hockey glove during tomorrow's game, but I'd rather hit a wall than someone else. Well, that's only partially true. I'm pretty confident I'll end up hitting someone in Sunday's game. At least there's a way for me to take out some of my frustration over all this.

Once I pull back the covers and get into bed, Emily immediately pulls them back close to her. "What do you think you're doing? I need some blankets, too," I joke before pulling her close to my chest.

"It's good now. I have a heating blanket in here to snuggle against," she teases as she snuggles into me and kisses my bare chest. Gently removing the ice pack, she asks, "How's the hand?"

"Feels like it hit a steel wall." I throw my arm over my face.

Tantalizing slow kisses begin sweeping over my knuckles as Emily suggestively says, "Well, it didn't seem to have any issues last night when you decided to play hide and seek." Peeking out of the corner of my arm,

I see her sliding out of bed to her bag on my bureau. "What are you doing over there?"

"Well, since neither of us is around for your actual birthday, I figured I'd give you your gift today."

"I told you not to get me anything, unless you are planning on telling me what your costume is for tonight, then I might make an exception." I wink at her.

"Sorry, *babe*, you're going to have to wait just like everyone else. You'll have to deal with the standard wrapped present," she says, handing me a small box with a ribbon on top.

Sitting up in bed, as she sits next to me, I see her running her hands over the sheets. Why is she nervous? Grabbing her hand, I lean over and kiss her on the forehead. "Hey, you know I love you, right? Don't be nervous." I try to give her some solace before she nods back at me as I slowly start unwrapping the box. I hear it click open and push the top lid up. My eyes widen in amazement. This is too much. Why would she spend this kind of money?

"Do you like them?" she asks while wringing her fingers together. I'm still in awe of the fact she just gave me a set of sterling silver cufflinks engraved with the Monarchs logo and embossed on the crown logo are three small diamond studs.

"Babe, they are awesome. I don't even know how you did this or when, but you had to have spent a fortune. Are you sure you trust me not to lose these?"

"Well, no, I don't trust you wearing them, but you'll need them if you are going to attend this." She hands me an envelope.

"Seriously, Em, this is too much already. What's this?" I open the envelope, seeing five tickets for a suite at the TD Garden in Boston for the US Figure Skating Nationals in January. My mouth hangs wide open. I'm in complete shock.

Moving closer to me while looking me in the eyes, she says, "If I win gold at the US Nationals, I want you and your family there celebrating with me. I owe all of you so much already that I don't think I can stand there on that ice without all of you, and I know you won't be able to make it to the Olympics in February. But, Nationals is really a big deal for me. Plus, that means you're stuck with me at least until January. Think you can handle a long- term relationship?"

"I think I'm up for that challenge."

"Happy Birthday, Jeremy."

CHAPTER
Twenty-two

Emily

I'd never been so nervous in my life as I was while giving Jeremy those tickets. I didn't know what he would think. I don't know if what we have will last a few months or forever. I mean, I'm hoping it isn't going to end anytime soon, but life happens and people change. Jeremy and I haven't discussed our future together. It's been moving at such a fast pace as it is, and we've actually spent more time apart than together. Who knows what will happen when we actually have the time to spend together? We could end up hating each other. To give him the tickets to attend my pinnacle event with his family that's two months away, that's like saying, "Hey, hope you don't mind, but I pretty much just guaranteed you a steady girlfriend." From what I know, Jeremy doesn't do steady girlfriends, unless you count his college girlfriend, but apparently Grace never met her. I need to stop worrying so much. I have a party to get ready for.

Jeremy assumed all of us were talking about him in the kitchen yesterday. Truth is, Sue had just told Grace about the baby. We weren't sure how much Jeremy had heard about our conversation, but it didn't seem as though her cover was blown. After he left, Grace had taken it upon herself to help with Sue's costume design. Apparently, she is quite the crafty type.

Grace wasn't surprised at Sue's confession. She said she noticed her *change* almost instantly after Courtney and I mentioned something was off. Of course, Grace had Sue in tears again when she openly admitted that she would be happy to support Sue any way she needed it. Sue was a part of the Page family whether she knew it or not. Who was this incredible woman? She's become the Mother Theresa to two crazy chicks in the last month.

The guys are in the backyard finalizing everything for the party that is set to begin in a few hours. I still have no idea what Jeremy is dressing up as. All of us girls are in Courtney's bedroom doing hair and makeup before putting on our costumes. Grace said she'll be up later after she is done making sure all the food is holding steady in the kitchen.

Courtney wasn't kidding the other day when she said she was going to dress up with weapons. Her hair is the easiest to handle. All I need to do is braid her hair down the side, and she will handle the rest. After that, all she is left with is putting on her boots, gold pin, blazer and adding her bow and arrow over her back and *voila!* instant Katniss Everdeen. Sue is a little more of a process. We have to tease her hair after shoving a handmade cardboard box over her shoulders. It hangs just right, and the oven knobs and door Grace drew are incredible. We just have to attach some rolls to the stomach section of her shirt, and she's instantly a bun in the oven. I'm not hopeful any of the boys will figure this out, but you never know, they could surprise all of us.

Then, there is my costume. It's more for Jeremy's entertainment, or more his torment, than anything. I've overly applied my makeup and let my hair drop in heavily defined curls with a black satin ribbon tied in a bow on top. My old skating costume with a blue tulle skirt and puff sleeves has been nicely shortened, and Grace has attached a white apron that falls to maybe thigh high. Finishing the costume are my bright blue platform heels and white thigh highs with a big black bow on the front where it meets my thighs. My little bunny rabbit will complete the transformation into the sexified Alice from *Alice in Wonderland*. Jeremy will die a thousand deaths before this night is over.

All of us are sitting around laughing and talking about absolute nonsense, when a little girl no more than three comes barreling into the room wearing a princess costume. "Cotwey! Cotwey!" She adorably attempts saying Courtney's name.

A woman's voice comes up the stairs from behind her. "Maggie, where do you think you're going?" After introductions, I learn that this is Maggie, Courtney's cousin Jim's, little girl and his wife Kristen. Kristen is clearly interested in finally meeting the one and only girl Jeremy has ever brought home to meet the parents. Evidently, I am all Grace talks about to everyone in the family these days.

Grace comes up shortly after to give the thumbs up on the costumes and also to secure the buns to Sue's oven. As bad as it is, we can't stop laughing, and Sue can't either. I think after realizing she will have so much support, she is finally becoming comfortable with the idea of pregnancy. It's Dave she's worried about. Courtney keeps the light atmosphere by snapping a few selfies of all of us together smiling, hugging and being supportive of each other. I don't want to be anywhere else right now.

JEREMY

While the girls are busy inside for the afternoon, Josh, Dave, and I spend a good portion of the time setting up tables and decorations. Everything is coming together just before family and friends are set to arrive. The sun is setting, allowing the lights under the tent to twinkle with the soft cool breeze. Josh is busy arranging hay bales and filling the dunk-for-apples bucket with water. Dave is spray painting a makeshift yard

Twister game on the grass. My cousin Jim is just arriving with his wife Kristen and daughter Maggie. I'm not sure who we hear first, Maggie yelling all our names as best a three-year-old can, or Jim wheeling in the keg of Otter Creek Oktoberfest shouting, "'Sup Kids!"

Jim is around my age, and being my dad's brother's only kid, we are more like brothers than cousins. Kristen walks over with Maggie on her hip. The big mop of curly red hair and foam bow and arrow aren't easy to figure out, but Kristen had mentioned to Mom a while ago that Maggie was coming dressed as Merida from *Brave*. Maggie bounces around, as Kristen listens to something she whispers into her ear.

"Miss Maggie would like to know where Courtney might be hiding. She wants to show her the costume."

Pointing toward the house, I tell them, "Apparently, all the girls are inside. We've been told not to go in. Something about the costumes being a surprise."

Maggie gets down from Kristen's arms and runs her little legs through the back door with Kristen quick on her heels. Jim is still setting up the keg as Dave sits on a nearby hay bale telling him about his most recent excursion to Promiscuous.

Walking over to join in on this conversation, I ask, "Correct me if I'm wrong, but aren't you going out with Sue now?" I know Dave wouldn't cheat, but at the same time, I can't think Sue would be completely okay with him going there without one of us to confirm his faithfulness. Standing slowly, he makes his way over to what is now a small circle since Josh has made his way into our conversation. I can't confirm or deny, but I'm pretty sure Josh isn't thrilled about the Dave-Sue dating situation.

Grabbing at my shoulder, Dave says, "Sue's a big girl. She knew exactly what I was and did before she decided to get involved with this fine piece of male." Shaking my head at his clear love for himself, I make my way back toward my place to start getting dressed for this shindig. Jim has the keg ready just as I'm about to walk through my back door. "You want one?" he yells.

"Yeah, just have Josh bring it up. I've got to get dressed," I tell him before shutting the door behind me.

As I'm almost dressed in my nerd costume, Josh walks in wearing his own costume and carrying two red Solo cups. All it takes is one look, and I am laughing hysterically. I swear, he can't have it any more spot on. The bathrobe, the dress shoes without pants, the winter hat with earflaps and the shitter hose. He is the epitome of Cousin Eddie from *National Lampoon's Christmas Vacation*.

"That's the best costume I've seen in years!"

Josh hands me my cup and looks me over. "What the hell are you supposed to be?" I hardly put any thought into the costumes, but this year I did actually go out to buy the pocket protector, bowtie, black thick-framed glasses and suspenders. It should be totally obvious what I am dressed as.

"Dude, I'm a nerd."

He looks me up and down. "Really? Kind of thought you were that guy from *Family Matters*, but it's decent."

As he starts walking back toward the living room, we hear the door slam open and Jim and Dave storm in boisterously. What the hell? My head angles around the corner, and I have to do a double take. Jim's costume is straightforward. He's dressed as a cowboy, but Dave's costume just set the bar. Josh and I are at a loss for words, standing there staring at this genius of a costume. It's almost as though Justin Timberlake is standing in my living room. Dave already has the shaggy hair and scruffy beard, but the black sunglasses, gold chain, black blazer and wrapped gift box held up by his belt is seriously the best "Dick in a Box" costume I've ever seen.

Dave begins singing the song from the *Saturday Night Live* skit, and that's all it takes for us to just start laughing so hard tears come to our eyes. Dad walks in from the stairway a few seconds later wearing his Hugh Hefner costume and shakes his head in disbelief. He's always been amazed at our ability to make each other laugh.

"Everyone is starting to arrive, and you're going to want to see the girls. Even your mom dressed up as Daisy Buchanan from *The Great Gatsby*," he comments. Before heading downstairs, Dad eyes Dave's costume and shakes his head.

"All right, boys, let's do this," Jim says, rubbing his hands together before pulling out four shot glasses and my bottle of Patron from the counter. Dave finally replaced the bottle he consumed nearly two months ago, as a birthday gift. He pours the four shots, all of us raising them in the air. "To Jeremy, Happy Birthday. Here's hoping you continue to live your dreams and follow your heart. Cheers!" Jim toasts, winking at me before we all tip our heads back and slam the glass onto the counter. Damn, that shit's smooth.

We continue to laugh about random shit all the way to the backyard, which is now swarming with about thirty or so people. Everyone came over to wish me a Happy Birthday as they normally do. Most of the crowd is family, friends, and neighbors that have known us for years. Glancing around for Emily, I don't spot her yet, but I do see Courtney and Mom leaving the house. Mom is carrying her infamous spiked hot apple cider, and Courtney is bringing out the cupcake tower. She really has talent. Making my way over to Courtney as she's arranging the cupcakes on the table, I look at each one and wonder how much time she spent on these for me. "Thanks, Court. I know these must have taken a really long time."

"Anytime, plus, it is your birthday, and I get to practice all at the same time. You know I love this shit." I know she does, but I still appreciate it just the same.

Scratching my temple, I ask, "What exactly are you supposed to be?"

She narrows her eyes at me before stating with confidence, "I'm Katniss Everdeen, winner of *The Hunger Games*, and don't you forget it."

Laughing at her attempt to get into character, I'm just about to ask her where Emily is when I catch a blonde moving out of the corner of my eye. Looking up, I only see her back from afar, and then she turns with some of Mom's cider in her hand, and my heart stops while my dick twitches. Holy shit. No, no, no, she cannot be wearing that in public.

I hear Courtney snickering next to me, nudging me in the side, "Em's looking pretty naughty tonight, huh?" She walks away back inside the house as I bump my way through people to get to Emily.

Once I'm almost next to her, I clear my throat. As she turns to face me, I realize she's dressed as naughty Alice. I'm so fucked. "Em, seriously, what are you wearing? Aren't you cold? I mean, you really should have a sweater or something. You don't want to be sick before the next competition." *Way to go, dude. You just rambled off a million reasons for her to dress like a nun in less than five seconds. Next time try to be subtler.* I rub my fingers over my temple as a feeling of dread overwhelms my entire body. Guys will be looking at her, and I know I can't slap a tag on her that reads, "Belongs to the birthday boy—hands off." Well, I could. I just don't think she'll go for it. Smiling at me, she chugs back the cup of cider. I wonder if Mom told her she puts about a bottle and a half of rum in that. "Em, you may want to go easy on that cider."

Pulling it back from her lips, she glances at the crockpot, then back at me, and shrugs her shoulders. "Why? What's the matter with it? I've already had three cups. It's yummy." Okay, it's time to get some food and water into her stomach.

"Em, let me just say the last time you had something like that you puked at the sight of my dick, and I'm really hoping that tonight isn't a repeat, 'cuz that costume is making me want to do some really naughty things to you."

"Oh my God! The cider is spiked?! Are you serious? No wonder I find this nerdy getup all sexy hot and want to straddle you right now." *She what?*

"Seriously?"

Walking away toward the fire pit Dad's building in the backyard, she turns to me, saying, "Nah, it's cute, but the glasses really have to go. And, I knew the cider was spiked. That's why I've only had this cup. I had you going, though. Didn't I?"

Speeding up my step to chase her, I say, "You better run, 'cuz if I catch you, there's no telling what I'll do to you."

Laughing and out of breath, Emily and I find a spot around the fire pit. I wrap my arms around her waist as she snuggles into my side. The rest of our usual group finds us by the fire and decide to join us for a while. Emily's competitions appear to be the hot topic of conversation. I remain seemingly quiet during the whole thing, since I just found out what her parents did, and the swollen knuckles on my right hand remind me not to go there.

The ringing of the cowbell tells us that the games are about to begin. It's something my parents always do. We all pair up and whoever wins the most games gets to take home a separate platter of Mom's meatballs and a bottle of wine. The prizes aren't usually why everyone plays. The adults have more fun just playing the games.

Courtney jumps from her hay bale and runs to grab Emily's hands. "You're my partner this year. Jeremy doesn't get to win again. He wins every year because he cheats."

Emily takes off in a sad attempt to run in her heels while the guys and I walk over to the games just to watch this year. First game up, bobbing for apples.

While I'm talking to Dave about some random hockey play, his eyes go wide, and he spits his beer from his mouth. "I need a minute. It's just not right." What the hell? I watch him walk away before turning in the direction he was just looking, and then I see what caused him to turn away.

There's my girlfriend in her naughty *Alice in Wonderland* costume on her knees, blindfolded with her hands bound behind her back. She's bobbing her head, and a million different thoughts race through my mind. Just the main one is enough for me to run my hands through my hair and start pacing the yard because the wrong head is working at the moment. Adjusting my dick in my overly tight dork pants, I see Dave laughing at me because he knows exactly what I'm thinking.

Then, the winner is announced. Well, of course, it's Emily. I knew that girl could suck. I know I shouldn't go there; I need to think of hockey and get my mind out of the gutter. As if this night isn't already strange, Dad appears from the house with Sue on his arm. How am I just now noticing she hasn't been around? Apparently, neither has Dave, but he tends to bounce from person to person at parties. I notice Sue's costume, and I stand there, trying to figure it out. Dad gives her a kiss on the cheek before turning back toward the house. Emily and Courtney join her moments later, and they begin making their way to me while Dave and Josh stay near the keg.

Sue is still looking down when Dave comes over to her. "Hey, where have you been? You've missed most of the party." Shoving food into his mouth, he hands Sue his cup of cider, silently asking her if she wants any. When she shakes her head no, he pulls back his arm and shrugs his shoulders. "So, what exactly are you supposed to be? That oven chick from the *Beauty and the Beast* cartoon? What's her name?" *You idiot, Dave. That was a guy who played that role.*Something's not adding up. Looking closer at the girls' expressions and the costume, I'm still unsure. When Dave hands Sue his plate with the pulled pork sliders, her face goes green and the plate drops, along with an apron, as she runs to the house. I bend over to pick up the plate and apron. Courtney is running with her, but I grab Emily's arm before she can go anywhere.

"What's going on?" I demand before unfolding the apron to reveal the iron-on letters spelling out "Bun Maker." Was she supposed to be a baker? Emily fiddles with her necklace nervously. She leans in to whisper into my ear. "What?!" I yell, jerking my head back.

"Jeremy! Don't say anything," Emily stresses before running off for the house. Like hell that's happening.

I turn to Dave, who continues to pour himself a drink and piles more food onto his plate. He looks up at me, shrugging his shoulders. "What? What'd I do?" he asks with a mouthful of food.

Sensing my anger, Josh comes over to my side. "What's going on?" he asks.

"Let's go! Everyone in the house. Family meeting in the basement. That includes Dave!" I shout.

Because everything always has such incredible timing in my life, just as we are about to head to the house, Mom comes out with a cake, singing "Happy Birthday." Just. Fuckin'. Great.

CHAPTER
Twenty-three

Emily

All of us are sitting around Sue in the bathroom. Obviously, she has found her first food aversion, pulled pork. We hear a commotion in the kitchen, and given this is the only bathroom in the house, I assume someone needs to use it. A slight knock on the door alerts us that someone is trying to get us out of here.

Courtney cracks the door since she is closest to it, and Travis sticks his head in, looking at Sue with sadness in his eyes. "Jeremy's called a family meeting downstairs. That includes Sue and Emily." The door closes, and we look around until Sue begins to stand and freshen her breath with mouthwash. I should break the news to them now that Jeremy knows.

"I might have just told Jeremy about the baby," I confess. "He knew something was up outside and questioned me."

Sue spits her mouthwash into the sink. "Well, *clearly*, Dave didn't get the costume, so let's just get this over with. It's now or never."

Leaving the bathroom, we see a few people gathered outside waiting to get in. "We've all got your back," Courtney assures Sue before we head toward the family room. As we walk down the stairs, it feels as though we are entering the legendary "kiss and cry" box. It is either going to go well, or really, really bad.

Everyone is gathered on the sofas; their eyes meet ours when they hear us enter the room. Jeremy immediately finds mine as I go to him. After giving him a soft hug, I stand in front of him as he rubs my back, sensing the tenseness in my body.

Grace joins us moments later since Travis is staying upstairs with the partygoers. Turning around to join Sue's side again, I move next to Courtney while Grace pulls us all together. "No matter what the outcome, we are all here to help. It's time to face your fears, dear."

Sue nods back silently, sighing before making her way toward the center of the room. "Dave," she says, getting his attention, "do you have any idea what my costume is?"

Looking her over, his eyes narrow, and his mouth forms a thin line. "I'm guessing it's not that character from the cartoon. Unless you are an oven, I have no idea."

Sue, drawing her breath and sighing, asks, "And what is in the oven?"

He glances at her stomach in complete confusion. "Bread?"

She throws her hands up as if this is a total lost cause before she announces the truth. "I've got a bun in the oven, Dave. Do you get it now?" He shakes his head, not understanding. Jeremy begins pacing at the other end of the room. "Dude, really?"

Grace makes her way over to Sue's side just as she looks at Dave. "I'm pregnant, Dave." Pulling the box over her head, she makes her way over to him. Josh stands and leaves the room almost instantly. I knew there was something there years ago, and obviously, he still holds some feelings for her after all this time apart. Jeremy sits alone on the ottoman while Courtney stands with me, watching this all unfold. Grace silently takes off toward Josh, and then there are five.

We all realize when it finally sinks in with Dave. He shoots up from his seat with anger blazing his face. "You're what?! I'm not sure I heard that correctly. It sounded as though you said you're pregnant. How is that even possible? I've used protection every time we've been together." There's a moment where the light bulb finally goes off. "Oh, shit. *That* night."

Sue stands with her arms wrapped around her stomach, saying, "Yeah, *that* night." Dave begins pacing the room so fast that my head and Courtney's look like we're watching a tennis match. After five minutes of silently going back and forth, I have a cramp starting to form in my neck.

Jeremy makes his way toward Courtney and me, trying to get us to head upstairs and give them some privacy. Dave continues pacing a hole in the rug, and from the looks of it, Sue is ready to run up the stairs and curl into a ball.

Somehow by the time the three of us make it halfway up the staircase, Sue finds her inner strength. I knew she had it in her. She yells, "Would you stop pacing?! Just tell me we're going to be all right. Tell me you're not going to bail on me now that I'm having a baby. I'm scared shitless, but it would help to know I'm not doing this alone. Talk to me!"

Dave stops abruptly, clearly not expecting Sue's outburst. He comes over and grabs her hands in his. "I have no idea how to be a father. You know me. I'm the most immature pig there is, but somehow, someone's drunken night is going to make a man out of me after all." Leaning around Sue, he gives me a wink before turning back and kissing her forehead.

They continue talking. Well, Dave talks, and Sue cries. Her hormones are already running rampant. Once we know the situation is under control, we excuse ourselves to head back to the yard for the *Twister* tournament because Sue and Dave really need time alone.

As we walk back into the yard, we notice everyone going about their ways as if nothing happened. I see Josh at the fire pit, wearing a glum expression. Leaning over, Jeremy tells me he will be back in a bit; he needs to talk to Josh alone for a second. I push him away as I make my way to the table with the delicious looking fruit arrangement. I'm pretty sure someone will notice if I take the whole thing, but picking pieces off one by one is a little less obvious.

A few minutes later, I hear Courtney yell my name. "Get over here, Emily! I need my partner for *Twister*." I know of the game, but I have never played. How hard can it be? Courtney draws the team we are going up against and spins the wheel, while I pose on the colored circles. I remove my heels and make my way over to the circles. *Left foot yellow. Right foot blue. Right hand green.* That one is a little harder since I have Jim to work around now. *Left hand blue.* Yay! I did it.

"Are you trying to kill me, woman?" I hear from behind me.

Glancing upside down between my legs, I see Jeremy standing behind me. "What did I do?" I mumble as my hair covers my face in this position. Oh, shit! Shooting straight up, I turn to face him. I couldn't care less about the game right now. My *Twister* position and the fact my skirt is covering no less than just my underwear is why Jeremy is steaming at the moment. Just as I grab my heels from the ground, I'm lifted into the air and carried toward his apartment.

He's moving quickly, and there's no time to think before he's pushing open his door and setting me onto the floor. Aspen comes running down the hall thinking it's playtime. "Aspen, bed," Jeremy says sternly. What's with him? I know it's been a long night, but why is he upset now?

"Jeremy, what's going on? Are you pissed at me for some reason?"

Grabbing a bottle of Magic Hat beer from his fridge, he pops off the top with his bottle opener before taking a long pull. "Emily, I have had just about all the self-control I can handle with you tonight. You're lucky you're not already naked in my bed. Do you even realize all the sexual positions you were in? Then, add that costume to it, seriously, my mind can only run so many scenarios before I act out at least one of them," he says before making his way over to me.

I'm not sure if he wants me to apologize or not, but before I can ask him, he's pulling my hand down the hall toward his room. "Don't we need to get back to the party?" I question as I stop in his room.

Slowly making his way to me, he throws his plastic glasses onto his bureau and shoves his suspenders off his shoulders before snaking his arm around my waist. "No one is going to miss us down there. Trust me." His lips linger over my ear as his breathing quickens. I run my hands up his shirt before deliberately taking my time unbuttoning it. Jeremy's lips run along my neck until he pulls back and looks me in the eyes. "Babe, I've had so many naughty thoughts tonight about what I can do to you, but I'm not sure what you're comfortable with. I don't want to scare you away. I kind of like having you around."

"Naughty, huh? Care to elaborate?" I ask, slowly placing kisses all around his chest and abs.

He releases a hissed breath as his arousal shows in his extremely tight pants. "All in due time, but given the events of the evening, I'd really just like to make love to you and have your extremely gorgeous and sexy body naked in my bed, if that's okay with you?"

Turning my back, while lifting my curled hair, I say over my shoulder, "Once you unzip this dress, you can do whatever you want with me. Drink me. Eat me. Spank me. Fuck me. I don't care, just so long as you end up in me."

JEREMY

After our anatomy lesson in my bed, Emily drifts off to sleep. When she gave me the go ahead for spanking, I'm pretty sure my dick said, "Fuck you! I'm taking over from here," since my mind literally stopped working. I have absolutely no coherent thoughts about what went on the past hour. I recall Emily screaming my name no less than four times, thank you very much. I know there was spanking, and I think my dick was in her mouth, while her hands were tied behind her back. Once I shot my load into her mouth, I watched tears form in her eyes as she swallowed every drop, and everything else after that took a backseat. Don't get me wrong. I love standard sex with Emily, but she took this to a whole new level. It still blows my mind to think she was a virgin only two months ago. Where the hell did she learn that shit?

As Emily stirs in the bed next to me, I mute the TV I turned on a little while ago because I couldn't sleep and had no interest in the rest of the party. Josh agreed to pick up my half of the cleanup duties after I talked to him. When he saw Emily's ass end in the air during *Twister*, he told me to get the fuck over there and handle that shit. I'd say I *handled* it quite well.

My mind has been bouncing back and forth between Sue's pregnancy news and Josh's confession that he is the biggest fucking idiot in the world. He thought he was doing what was best for her all those years ago by not dragging her through his career choice. When Sue announced she was pregnant with Dave's baby, he knew he missed his chance and it was time for him to move on. He said if you let something go for too long, you end up missing your only shot at happiness. Right now, I know my happiness is next to me, snoring no less, but I love her and refuse to let her go again.

Rolling over and running my hand under the sheet covering her naked body, I snake way around her waist. That is all it takes to wake her up. She moans as she pushes her ass into me, while pulling her arm back to run her hand over my neck. I take the opportunity to gently kiss her head.

"I love you," I whisper as I rest my chin on the top of her head. I need to tell her just how much. I know we'll be heading toward more time apart over the next couple of months, and I need to make sure we don't have another separation like last time. "Babe? You know how much I love you, right?"

She nods and rolls onto her other side to face me. "Jeremy, what's going on?" she asks, confused where the conversation is going. I'm not even sure where this is going, but this is about to get serious, and I don't know why I'm about to do this. But, here goes nothing.

"Where do you see yourself in the next five years? I mean, what do you see for your future? Outside of the figure skating career and everything, what do you want?"

"Why would you ask that? You know I've never given it much thought. I'm just starting to live my life and figuring out things for myself. Five years down the road, it's still fuzzy for me. Where do you see yourself?"

What I'm about to say should just about ruin the night, but it needs to be said. If neither of us is on the same page, this will end in catastrophe. Sighing, I respond, "In five years, if I'm not still skating for the AHL, I'm probably going to be married, and hopefully, have at least one child already. I need to figure out how to manage a decent salary if I'm not skating, so that's another item for my list, but I want a family of my own. I know that without any doubt. I need you to know, this thing between you and me, I want it long-term."

"Jeremy, there has never been any doubt in my mind that we care deeply for each other, but how can you be so sure about me, about *us*, long-term?"

Reaching up to caress her face in my hand, I run my thumb over her cheek. "You make me happier than I've ever known. You have no problem being yourself around my family. Your smile is so infectious, that every time I see it disappear, I think of nothing other than finding a way to bring it back. I know this, right here, right now. I know I want to wake up to you next to me. Not just tomorrow, not just five years from now, but fifty years from now, I still want to see your smile and hear your laugh. I want to see how beautiful you'll look carrying our baby and proving just how loving and supportive you are as a mom. I know it's scary to think about all of that when you've never had the opportunity before. I'm not even saying you need to decide right now if that's the future you want. I need you to know that I'm seriously in love with you. If and when you finally see what your future holds for you, I hope to God I'm in that picture."

I kiss her as warm salty tears fall over her lips as she chokes back sobs. No words are exchanged between us as I roll her back so I'm looking down into her eyes and she is staring back at me. The only sound we hear in the room is music reverberating from the backyard. The slow ballad "All of

Me" flows through the room. Both of us are following our hearts. She may not be able to see what her future holds for her, but right here, right now, we're happy and in love. Wrapping her legs around my waist, I kiss her like she's my last breath. Slowly, I push my erection inside her, feeling her walls collapse around me with each thrust. Her back arches off the bed, and her hands grip the sheets at her side as I still just before coming inside her, moaning her name as my racing heart settles. While I look back into her eyes, it's her words that take my breath away.

"You're my everything. You're my yesterday, today, and my tomorrow. No matter where we are five years from now, you're a part of my heart, Jeremy Page."

We both fall asleep in each other's arm shortly after that, leaving us to our dreams.

CHAPTER
Twenty-four

Emily

Training. That's all I've done since I left Jeremy's the morning after his party. Since he's asked me where I see myself in five years, I can't stop wondering what that life looks like. However, my time to think about that is at a minimum. I have other things on my agenda, like my season of vengeance. I've avoided my mother almost completely, except for a few emails and text messages regarding my schedule. I'm training everyday during the week in Boston, and it doesn't give me a lot of time to spend with Jeremy on weekends, since he usually has games. When you add in his promotional events during the week, he has even less time than I do.

In two days, I'll be on a plane heading to Paris for the final competition in my Grand Prix circuit. I was supposed to see Jeremy before I left, but he's currently filling in for another teammate delivering pizzas for one of the team sponsors. So, for now, I'm spending the night with Courtney and Sue watching *Sons of Anarchy* episodes from the past few weeks. That Charlie Hunnam is one gorgeous bad boy whose bike I'd gladly ride on the back of. I'm pretty sure I caught Sue licking the TV screen at one point. Her hormones are all over the place with the pregnancy. She might be laughing right now, but a half hour ago we needed Grace's assistance while she had a crying fit. Courtney and I had no idea what was going on. I'm glad she has her first appointment with her doctor in the morning.

After Grace helped us console Sue, she went back upstairs to make dinner for us. She said she'd make it healthy for not only me, but also for Babykins. Grace caught Sue pigging out on hot dogs, sour cream and onion chips, and orange juice the other day. Safe to say, she was not thrilled with the cravings. I've witnessed Sue's food consumption and nearly threw up.

A short time later, we are all upstairs in the dining room eating grilled chicken with a pineapple-mango salsa and Caribbean rice. Nothing is over the top in this house. Simple works for everyone, and I love everything about it.

Jeremy finally returns and finds us in the kitchen helping clean up as Grace and Travis go on to bed. I am standing over the sink, scrubbing the area down when I feel his hands wrap around my waist behind me. "I've missed you this week," he says against the back of my neck.

"I've missed you, too," I say, turning in his arms before placing a more than affectionate kiss on his lips. Courtney looks our way, catching us in the middle of Jeremy fondling places he probably shouldn't be in his parents' house.

"Oh my God! Would you two go do that in your own place? I mean, hello, family here!" Courtney mutters as she walks toward the bathroom. Both of us laugh, and once the kitchen is clean enough, we head back to the garage apartment.

Once at Jeremy's place, I grab a water bottle from the fridge and head to sit on the sofa. He pulls my legs over his thighs as he sits next to me. "I probably won't see you again before you leave for Paris, so I want to make sure that this time apart will not be spent like the last." He eyes me with a flat look.

"Well, unless you have another one of your harems visiting tonight, I think we ought to be good." I laugh at my attempt to lighten the mood.

"Not funny," he cautions with a stern face.

"Sorry," I say as I play with my hair nervously.

Jeremy and I go over our schedules for the next week. He has practice and two more home games over the weekend. As usual, I have routine practices once I arrive in Paris, followed by my short and long program. We determine it will be best not to contact each other outside of a quick email or text. Focus is key this week. I need this win to secure myself the top-ranking position in US Figure Skating.

His Monarchs season is going really well. From what he tells me, they have the most points in the Eastern League, and Jeremy has been named the AHL defensive player of the week this week. I'm really trying to learn his sport the best I can. I am picking up a few things here and there, but when your main focus is participating in the Olympics, there are a lot of things that get lost in the shuffle.

We say our goodbyes as if we are not going to see each other for a very long time. "It's only five days, Emily. By the time you're in Paris, you'll already be ready to head home. When you return, we'll have a few of my games left before Christmas break, and then we can spend as much time as possible together before Nationals. Sound good?"

I had almost forgotten amidst the training, family, and baby drama that I am expected to attend the annual Cameron holiday party in a few weeks. It typically includes my parents' business associates, which ultimately means that their *investment* needs to make an appearance. I know Jeremy still has some major issues surrounding my parents' trustworthiness, but I can't *not* ask him to go with me.

"Hey, um, before I forget." I slide my hands over his waist as I stand in the doorway. "My parents' annual holiday party is on December 14th. As much as I'd like to avoid going, I really don't have a choice. I know you don't have a game that night, so it would be nice to have someone there who's on my side for once. You don't have to, though. I know how you feel about my parents."

"Emily, if you want me there, I'll be there. I'll put aside my issues for the night and keep my comments to myself," he stresses. "I know how difficult it is for you to deal with the pressure you are currently under with the Nationals in Boston and Olympics coming up. If I can help ease the tension for just one night, then I've done my job as your boyfriend." He leans in to give me a kiss on the forehead. "Now, go to Paris and kick some Parisian ass for me. We'll be here when you get back." He points to his crotch area.

Playing the dense card, I reply, "We? Aww, you mean you and Aspen are going to miss me? That's soooo cute!" I then make my way toward the stairs to head out.

"That smart mouth of yours is going to get you in trouble, Miss Cameron."

Turning, I see him leaning on the doorframe at the top of the stairs. "I can only hope my mouth gets into something, Mr. Page. I love you."

He lets out a full-bellied laugh at my dirty response. "Love you too, babe. I'll see you in a few days."

When I open the door to my car, snowflakes begin to fall, a sure sign that winter is approaching. Pretty soon everything will be blanketed in white. Once in my car, I start it, allowing it to warm up a bit before driving off. My phone dings in my purse, alerting me of a text message. A smile forms on my face as I read it's from Jeremy.

We miss you already. "Hands Down" <3 U –J

I open *Spotify* to listen to the song before leaving. While the music is playing over my speakers, I look up to Jeremy's living room windows to see him staring back at me. Blowing steam onto his windowpane, he draws a heart in the fogged glass with his finger. Then, because he's not cheesy enough, he leans his entire chest onto the glass with his arms out to the side yelling, "Don't go, Emily!" Aspen hops up in excitement behind him, not knowing what to make of it all. Laughing so hard with tears clouding my eyes, I send him a text.

See you in five days. Until then "I Touch Myself" <3 U –E

As I'm pulling out of the driveway, I notice Jeremy checking my text on his phone. His mouth drops open, and he shakes his head in disbelief. He types something on his phone, and within seconds, my phone signals me of another text.

You are an evil woman. It's a good thing I love you.<3 U —J

JEREMY

I'm really not sure why I told Emily that sending a random email here and there for the next five days was going to cut it. I've received maybe two emails from her so far. One saying she made it to Paris and that her mother is still alive, unfortunately, and the other telling me she won gold, barely. I might have sent her at least two emails a day. To my defense, it is the beginning of the week, and all I have going on are morning skates until Thursday when our usual weekend games take place.

Josh has a couple of days off and stops in to see how things are going at the house. I know he is fishing for information on Sue. I tell him everything around the house is hunky dory. Basically, I end up telling him everything except what is going on with Sue. This only pisses him off and forces him to ask the question about her and the baby.

I explain to him that she had gone to the doctor recently, and everything checked out fine. Dave showed me their first ultrasound picture when he was here after the appointment. Something tells me he is already a proud papa. I never thought he could take on something so grown up, but maybe he just needed the right girl to steer him in the right direction.

I've lasted the entire five days without Emily, and she is due to return from her Paris trip late tonight, but I won't see her until tomorrow. Mom wants to make sure I ask her over for Thanksgiving dinner when I see her. It is always a huge affair at my parents' house to have dinner, watch football, and then turn on the outside holiday lights. If Josh isn't working that day, he'll make sure we end up watching *National Lampoon's Christmas Vacation*. No matter how many times we watch that movie or know exactly what's going to be said, we still laugh hysterically.

Josh and I help get out all the Christmas decorations from storage in the garage. Dad is busy tinkering with his snow blower as I pull the last of the lights from the closet. Putting the box down, I make my way over to him. "Need any help with that?"

He pulls out his Phillips head from his pocket and starts tightening the panels. "Nah, she's just about set to go. Just need to add some oil and tighten her up. You know what they say about a fuckin' tight blower?" he jokes as he nudges my side with his elbow.

I laugh at my old man's sick mind. "No, Dad, what do they say about a fuckin' tight blower?"

"Well, Son, if you don't have a tight blower, she's gonna leak all over the place. Need to make sure all those hoses are secured properly." Dad laughs as he walks back around to his tool table. I really never, ever want to imagine my saint of a mom doing anything of that nature with my dad. It's just so wrong, but Dad has been this way all my life. He's sick, but he's a funny shit. "Is Emily coming over for dinner on Thursday?" he asks.

Turning back to grab the box of lights and zipping up my hoodie as the temperature continues to drop, I answer, "I'll ask her tomorrow after she gets back. Her flight doesn't come in until almost midnight tonight."

I think Dad has really started thinking of Emily as family. Sue is practically a daughter to him since her parents moved away years ago. She became a fixture at the Page house once she dated Josh and became Courtney's best friend. Emily seems to have fit into that role in just three short months. It's no wonder I was immediately drawn to her that first day; she has such a contagious beauty about her that you can't help but fall in love with her.

As I begin walking out of the garage with the decorations, I hear Dad say behind me, "Son, she's a little firecracker, that one. She might be new to the Page house, and no matter what happens between you two, she's always welcome here."

"Thanks, Dad."

CHAPTER
Twenty-five

Emily

Paris was certainly an uneventful trip. It was dull compared to the trip to Denver and Vancouver last month. My mother kept to my side for the majority of the event. After spending so much time with Jeremy's family, who are so understanding and allow breathing room, her continued annoying persistence got on my last nerve. It didn't take much to set me off. However, after my last trip with her and the tabloid story, which no doubt earned my parents a few dollars, I had my guard up just in case.

Other than a few emails here and there, Jeremy and I kept our word not to be a distraction to each other during the week away. The Trophée Eric Bompard normally attracts more international skaters than the last two because it's held in Paris. This allowed me to get a feel for the competition. These are the girls I'll be competing against should I be selected by the International Skating Union to represent the USA at the Olympics and the World Championships. From the sneak attack I just endured from a fifteen-year-old Russian girl, I have my work cut out for me. I still took home gold, though. Don't get me wrong; she was a threat without any doubt, but I had my eyes set on winning, and that was it. My scores weren't as high as the other two competitions, which pissed me off, but it was still enough for me to earn the top spot. My mother couldn't find much to fault at Skate Canada since she was too busy working the front-page story with Daddy. When she saw my lower combined average in Paris, I heard all about it. She claimed I was spending too much time with "bad influences," which ultimately caused my lack of focus on skating. I blatantly laughed in her face, caught her completely off guard. Then, she proceeded to call my behavior childish and unwelcome, to which my response was, "So was your front-page tabloid picture and attempt to sell me out to save your own ass?"

That was the last time I spoke to her or Daddy. I spent Thanksgiving at the Page house, where I ate far too much food, but I managed to get two days off from training since Suzy had returned home to be with her parents for the holiday. I woke up from a deep sleep to Jeremy's alarm going off at six this morning. He had to attend a morning skate and then head out to lunch with Dave.

While sitting in the back seat of Grace's Honda Pilot with Sue while Courtney sits in the front passenger seat, I am experiencing my first time Black Friday shopping. So far, I'm not going to lie. It sucks. I mean, I get the hype of the whole thing, but I prefer to just shop online and avoid the madness of everyone trying to find the big *sale*. I've never had to really buy for anyone. Growing up at the Cameron house, I'd only ever get skating gear or something impersonal like a gift card to the salon. I never bought anything for my parents except for a bottle of wine, which I'm sure was opened and consumed before I made it back to my apartment. Holidays were never warm and inviting. Sure, my parents held their annual holiday party, but that was all for show. Sorry, *appearances*. There were never warm hugs and shared memories. Not like when I walked into the Pages' house yesterday before dinner, where I was greeted by numerous hugs, laughter, and family stories.

Once we finally get back to the house and unload the overabundance of bags piled in the trunk, I make my way to Jeremy's apartment. I send him a quick text, letting him know I'm home and I'll see him when he gets back, but not to rush his lunch with Dave.

I rest on the sofa, brushing out Aspen's fur and watching one of the *Hallmark Channel's* holiday movies in my yoga pants and one of Jeremy's hoodies. I have a strange feeling running through my body at how I had texted Jeremy that I'm home and yet he never asked what home. Did he assume I meant here? Should I be here? It's only been three months, but it feels as though me being in his place waiting for him is right.

I must have dozed off on the sofa, because when I wake up, I have a blanket covering me and the sun is just starting to set. The TV has a Bruins game just finishing up, and I hear the shower running. Jeremy must have come home and didn't wake me.

Stretching out my arms as I stand, Aspen stirs on his dog bed next to the sofa. "You want a cookie, boy?" Walking towards the glass jar on the kitchen counter, I pull out a biscuit and toss it as he jumps up to catch it mid-air. "Good boy," I say, rubbing his head before heading toward the bathroom.

Closing the door quietly, I remove my clothes swiftly before opening the steam-covered glass door. Jeremy turns when he hears the glass shut behind me. "Hey, babe, sleep well?" he asks before pulling me against his wet body and giving me a long passionate kiss.

"Not really, you weren't there next to me. Why didn't you wake me?"

"You looked so peaceful. I couldn't do it. Plus, I'd have to wake you up soon anyway. We're heading out to pick up the Christmas tree before dinner. Mom wants you to come over to help bake cookies with Courtney and Sue, while Josh and I help Dad get the tree."

Who is this family, and how did I ever get this lucky to have them come into my life? Wrapping my arms around his waist as the water streams down his back, I glance up into his eyes. "Nothing would make this day any more perfect."

"You sure about that, babe? There are a few other things I could do to make this day better." Winking at me mischievously, he kneels down in front of me, spreading my legs before he makes good on making my day just that much more perfect.

JEREMY

Why the hell I'm standing here dressed in a chimp suit with my hair slicked back, I'll never know. Pushing in the other cufflink Emily gave me for my birthday, I realize why. I love her and would do anything to make her happy, even if that means dressing in this fancy suit and tie for her parents' holiday party. I'm fairly certain my bruised nose from the puck that deflected off the ice during practice the other day will piss her parents off to no end. Fine by me, if I have to behave myself all night, just the thought of my face embarrassing them in front of their clients will please me.

About a half hour later, I'm pulling into Emily's garage. The party isn't to start for another hour, so catering trucks and valet attendants at the front gate are all that are in the driveway. I have to tell the asshole to check the guest list since he isn't going to let me through easily. Apparently, guys that look like me are not the typical Cameron party types. Shocking!

I knock on Emily's door before hearing her tell me to come on in. I see movement in her bathroom as I make my way to her. Before I get halfway there, she steps out, and I stop mid-step. As she's adjusting her necklace, she sees me and smiles from ear to ear.

"Hey, look at you. You look handsome all dressed up," she says as she stalks over to me. "Emily. You. My God. You literally are just the most exquisite beauty I've ever seen." She shyly slaps my arm before walking over to grab her heels from beside the bed.

Her floor-length black sequined strapless gown shows off all her incredible curves. Her long blonde hair is pulled to the side in a messy braid, and her makeup does nothing to hide just how gorgeous she is, and although I know for a fact it doesn't fit with her attire, she's still wearing the necklace I gave her almost four months ago. I love her for always being true to herself. She could have easily removed my necklace and worn something more refined, but she didn't.

Stepping into her heels, she peers up at me, as I stand there with my hands in my front pockets, admiring everything I have in front of me. She is my everything. She is my forever. Slowly making my way over to her, I stand in front of her while she gazes at me, shaking her head slightly unsure of my intentions.

"What?" she asks. "Jeremy, what is it?" Trepidation clouds her eyes.

"You know I love you with all my heart?" Reaching up to slide my fingers under the chain of her necklace, I continue, "You have made me so happy these last few months, and I know I should wait for Christmas to give you this, but I can't." Slowly sliding my hand from my pocket, I hold the little black box in my palm before turning it to her, waiting for the sound of the click before pulling it open to her curious eyes.

"Jeremy, it's gorgeous," she says, running her fingers over the stones. After removing it from the box, I take the infinity shaped diamond bracelet into my fingers. She covers her hand over her other necklace. "But, I don't want to take this one off."

"Babe, you can wear this again after tonight, but on special occasions, like tonight when you look amazing, I want you to wear this." Pouting, but nodding in approval, she removes my hockey pendant and places it onto her bureau. "One other thing, Mom wants a picture. Dad thought hell froze over when he saw the suit before I left. So, I told them I'd send them a picture when I got here." I pull my phone from my pocket, holding it at arms' length to take a picture of the two of us with cheesy grins on our faces, and then send it off to my parents' email.

"Ready?" she asks.

"As I'll ever be, any advice before we head in there?"

"Yeah, avoid my parents at all costs. If you get separated from me at any time, just find Louisa in the kitchen or a quiet room and wait for me to find you. There are a lot of Daddy's clients here who invest a lot of money, so even I'm afraid to talk to half of them."

"Seriously, should I have taken Special Forces training before coming here tonight? You did say 'party', correct?" I ask as I rub my hand over the back of my neck.

"You'll do fine. Just don't body check or punch anyone," Emily jokes.

"Hey! See, you are picking up some of my hockey terms. I'm impressed."

A few moments later, we walk into the foyer of her parents' house. Everything looks warm and inviting, including the twenty-foot Christmas tree, which is most likely showcasing empty boxes wrapped with pretty bows underneath. They even have tags on them that read "Emily," "Victoria," and "Charles." How sweet. People stir about, some chatting quietly while others carry silver platters of hors d'oeuvres. A string quartet is playing Christmas songs at the base of the long staircase. Everything seems as though a loving family carries on under this roof. Well, looks can be deceiving.

Emily squeezes my arm, breaking my concentration on the rest of the house. Glancing down at her, I notice she isn't staring at me, but rather straight ahead. I turn my head in that direction to see what's caught her attention. "Showtime," I say softly.

Coming straight for us are the two people I was warned to stay away from. My stance goes rigid, and Emily notices immediately as she tilts her head toward me, whispering, "Stay calm, please."

As soon as I nod in agreement, her mom is standing less than a foot in front of her. "Emily, dear." Victoria leans in to air kiss both sides of Emily's cheeks. "You look…well, you look decent. I'm not so sure what is going on with your hair, but you really should have had it properly done up. I see you brought your *friend* again. How lovely." Victoria turns to speak to me, leaning in to speak quieter. "If you think for one minute about trying to steal anything, I'll have the police called immediately."

"Mother! Don't be rude," Emily scolds just above a whisper.

"Babe, it's fine. I realize I'm not exactly what the front page of the tabloids would consider newsworthy, but I'm pretty sure she could spin it to somehow play into the favor of the Cameron family. Isn't that right, Mrs. Cameron?" I flash a cold smile at her.

Moments later, Emily's father, Charles returns to Victoria's side, eyeing me suspiciously as he escorts her toward a back room. I breathe a sigh of relief that they are gone for now. Emily turns to look at me once they are out of earshot. "I need a drink. Follow me." I follow her toward a back kitchen area where I notice Louisa pulling trays from the oven. "Hi, Louisa. Merry Christmas," Emily greets her.

"Merry Christmas, sweetie. What are you doing back here?" Louisa asks as she scoops mini quiches onto a serving platter.

"Just looking for something to drink," Emily states as she opens the fridge door, swiping a Hibernation Ale beer and a bottle of Chardonnay. Handing me the beer, she takes the bottle opener from the side of the fridge for me to pop off the cap. Once she opens the bottle of wine, she opens a cabinet and brings out a wine glass and pint glass. Handing me the pint glass, I pour my beer into it. She does the same for her wine before taking a long sip that results in the whole glass emptying out. Damn.

"Emily, please tell me you are going to eat something before the night is over, because if you plan on drinking like that for the next few hours, I'm going to have my hands full."

She smiles deviously at me as she pours another glass of wine. "Don't worry about me. In an hour, half of these people won't even know we exist."

We make our way back into the foyer, and the party appears to be in full swing. People are dancing to the festive music, and everyone seems jovial. A few people stop to talk to Emily about the National Championship coming up in a few weeks, and should she win gold, they make plans to sponsor her before she heads to the Olympics in February. It still comes as a shock to me that my girlfriend could be an Olympian in another month. How would that not be a dream come true for her? I totally understand her parents putting the pressure on her to win, win, win, but a part of her has to have some desire to go to the Olympics for herself.

Emily breaks my train of thought when she motions to me that she's heading to the restroom. Walking down the hallway from where we just came, I admire photos of Emily skating as a little girl. Plainly, these are here simply for bragging rights or a selling tactic.

Someone moves up next to me. Turning, I come face-to-face with Emily's father. "Sir. Lovely party you have here tonight."

"Son, if you would, please come into my office. I'd like to have a word with you in private."

"Certainly," I say, following his lead, but not knowing what he could possibly want to talk to me about.

Moving to stand behind his desk, he reaches into his desk drawer, removing a leather bound folder. "Listen, Son. I don't know what you want with my daughter, but I can tell you whatever it is, you won't get it from her. Her mind needs to focus one hundred percent on her skating career. Since you've come into the picture, she's been flippant with her mother and distracted to points where she blows off training. I hope you understand what I'm asking of you here. If you cannot leave her alone willingly, I think there are other ways we can work out a deal." He slowly reaches for a pen in his drawer and opens the folder to reveal a checkbook. Seriously, he's going to try to buy me off in order to get rid of me. "So, how much will it take for you to leave my daughter alone? 40? 50? 75? Name your price."

"Mr. Cameron, I understand you think I'm a worthless piece of trash, but I've loved Emily for a very long time. She's the most genuine, loving, forgiving woman I've ever met. She doesn't judge people for their status or self-worth. When you threw her to the tabloids to cover your family scandal, she came to my family for help. Not you or your wife. My family was willing to help and listen. No amount of money will ever constitute leaving her, so you might as well put your checkbook away, asshole," I say as I try to calm my clenched hands and not start a yelling or punching match.

198

"Well, you really give me no other choice. If you won't leave her willingly or take the money I offer you, perhaps a quick phone call to the local police regarding a few missing pieces of jewelry and other items might make you think differently. Maybe a little jail time will push you in the other direction."

"Daddy! Enough!" Emily yells as she storms into the room. "You think buying him off or threatening him is the answer to your problems? If you had *any* interest in me as a daughter instead of a business deal, you would know that getting rid of him is not the answer, but you just proved you really don't think of me as a daughter. So, let me make this easy on you in a business deal type of transaction you will understand. After this season, I'm fuckin' done. No more skating for *you* or your company. If I skate, it will be under my terms." Turning to me, she grabs my hand and looks into my eyes to show me she's fighting.

"Emily Beth Cameron, you will do no such thing. You have sponsors and commitments," Charles states as she is about to leave with me, but stops as her body goes rigid.

Looking back at him, Emily stresses, "No, *you* have sponsors and commitments. I have a life to try to live. Take this as my two months' notice." She struts out of his office with me right behind her, nearly knocking into her mother on the way out.

"Emily Beth! Where do you think you're going in such a rush?" her mother demands.

Releasing my hand, she eyes her mother scornfully. "Perhaps you can ask your husband, as it seems I'm nothing more than a negotiable deal to you people. Oh, and Mother, you're fired!"

Rushing after Emily through the front door, I see her grabbing the bottom of her dress, allowing her extra room to walk on the paved driveway. Once I catch up to her, I look her in the eyes as I stand in front of her. "Feels good to finally fight for something, doesn't it?" She's shivering, wrapping her arms around her bare shoulders, so I wrap my coat around her and pull her into my arms. Tears start falling over her cheeks. "Come on, Em. Let's get you inside."

She sits in her kitchen silently while I make her some warm tea. I wonder where she's going to go from here.

"Jeremy?" Her quiet voice is barely heard as I place the steaming tea in front of her.

"Yeah, babe?"

She takes a small sip before speaking, "Can I stay at your place? I need to get away from here for a while."

"Emily, stay for a while. Stay forever if you want. I love you, and if you are there waking up next to me every day for the next five days or five years, I won't care. Just so long as you're in my life."

We pack everything she needs, and I fill her car and my truck with suitcases, skating bags, and important papers. Twenty-two years of her life, and all of it fits in a few suitcases and boxes. As we are leaving, I realize I needed to pick up one more item before Christmas. I just hope the store will still have the right one.

Emily

I've been staying with Jeremy for almost four weeks now. Christmas and New Year's were completely unexpected. There were gifts galore on Christmas morning as Jeremy's family and I sat around the tree buried in wrapping paper. Perhaps that was because Jeremy tried to rewrap me and say I was the best Christmas present ever. Grace framed the picture of us from the party and placed it over their fireplace mantle. That night was the start of me finding my new identity, and I felt free of all the pressures I'd been forced to endure for so long.

I've never laughed as hard as I did New Year's Eve after Jeremy returned home from his game. I had an afternoon practice, so I couldn't make his game, but the entire gang came over to our place for the night. It still feels weird to call it *our* place. Once Jeremy was home, all of us set up the Wii for non-stop games and fun. Even at almost four months pregnant, Sue still beat us in the dance off. Katy Perry has nothing on that girl. Josh and Jeremy went against each other in a *Guitar Hero* round, and Courtney and Dave broke out the beer pong table. Courtney accused Dave of cheating. Dave told Courtney to read the house rules clearly stated on the board. Her response was that she couldn't read anything because someone had drawn dicks and tits all over it. It was technically true. When I first saw the pong table, I wasn't sure where to look. There was bickering between the two, and finally Courtney conceded. At the end of the night, all the guys crashed on the sofas from drinking too much beer. We girls had a sleepover in the guest bedroom where we drank apple juice and painted each other's nails. I couldn't remember a time before this where I had ever been so happy.

It is the morning of the US Nationals. I am currently in first place heading into tonight's long program. Jeremy is trying his best to calm me down, but nothing is working. I know my parents will most likely show up, trying to make my life hell again. My mother has tried to contact me a couple of times, but I've emailed her back to explain her services are no longer required, and if she wants to schedule an appointment with me, she should contact my new manager, Grace Page.

Surprisingly, once I had all my contacts and documents in order, I found a few of my endorsements weren't clients of my father. Grace helped me organize most of it, and I still have a decent backing heading into today's long program.

Unfortunately, Grace and Travis aren't making it to the long program tonight. A major Nor'Easter is scheduled to hit Boston at some point tonight, dumping nearly a foot of snow with blowing wind causing some blizzard conditions. Given the uncertainty of the exact timing of the storm, they've opted to watch from home. Jeremy will drive his truck in with the rest of the crew. Josh can't make it either; he was already ordered into work for storm coverage in Boston. Once I have my car packed and ready to go, everyone meets me outside to wish me luck since I won't see them until after the skate.

"I want you to know that no matter what happens tonight, we are all proud of you. I've watched you grow in the past few months, and right now, I see a woman who is able to hold her own and be whoever she wants to be," Grace says as she pulls me into an embrace unlike anything I've ever known and then wipes a stray tear from the corner of her eye. Travis gives me a kiss on the cheek and wishes me luck before heading inside with Grace.

Before stepping into the car, Jeremy shields me in his arms since the winter is unseasonably frigid. At around fifteen degrees, today has been one of the warmer days we've seen. I'm bundled in my beanie hat, infinity scarf, puffy winter coat, and mittens as Jeremy leans down, giving me a warm kiss. "When you go out there tonight, just skate for you. Don't skate for anyone else. Win or lose, you're still coming out on top. You've still won since you fought against the odds and beat them. I love you. Now, get out of here and go get ready to kick some ass."

"Jeremy, remember when you said, 'Don't wait too long to start living your dreams. Someday they might actually come true'?"

"Vaguely." He gives me a cocky smirk because he knows I realize he's kidding.

"Even if I don't win tonight, you should know that it was you who made my dreams come true. You made my reality something worth living. I no longer need to escape into my dreams. My dreams and my reality are all in you. I'm so glad you never gave up on me."

He leans down to give me one last kiss. "Emily, you've always been my weakness. Something happened that day back in high school. I never knew what it was, until now. Now, I know it was you taking my heart. How could I give up fighting for the one person who held that captive?"

202

"Don't you dare make me cry before I leave," I say, sniffling back tears that threaten to spill and smacking him on the chest with my mittens.

"Fine, then after you win tonight, we'll all go out for a celebratory drink. You know, before the media stakes itself outside of the house looking for interviews with the newest member of the US Olympic team."

"No pressure at all." I laugh as I turn to open my car door, sliding down into the seat and looking up at Jeremy as he leans over me with his hands on the hood of the car.

He smiles before coming down to kiss my cheek. "You'll come out a winner. You know why? You still get me at the end of the day."

"Someone doesn't love himself too much," I say, rolling my eyes while starting up the engine and turning down the speaker volume.

Jeremy laughs as he shuts the car door. He hits his palm on the roof a couple of times before walking off backwards, still facing me. "Give 'em hell, Barbie!" he shouts as he walks back inside the garage.

The drive into Boston is quiet and almost traffic-free. You'd never know a major skating event is taking place around the city. I park my car in front of the Garden in a spot typically reserved for the professional athletes. *Was that what I had become?* I am about to embark upon what may be the biggest night of my life, and I am focused on the parking spot. What the hell? I seriously needed to focus.

Once I am in the dressing room changing into my practice clothes, I pop in my earbuds and start dancing in the room to The Civil Wars as a text from Courtney comes through on my phone.

Good luck, girl! We love you!

Below the words is a picture of Jeremy, Sue, Dave, Courtney and Grace holding signs that read, "Go Emily! Sochi Bound, and Reach for Gold, Emily!" Tears blur my vision, but I laugh as I send a response telling them I love them, too. I have a true support team coming to root me on for the first time ever, and that warms my heart to no end.

I finish lacing up my skates and make my way toward the ice. Suzy and a few other coaches are already standing together talking. One thing about the figure skating world is we are all somehow interconnected. Some coaches have multiple skaters competing against each other. Fortunately for me, Suzy only coaches me, but she'll be recruiting a new student once I'm done. It will be sad to say goodbye, but I know she'll do just fine.

Suzy sees me glide onto the ice and comes over to the boards to give me a pep talk. "Are you ready for this? It's only you tonight. There's no one else forcing you to go out there and win. You still want it?" she asks, knowing exactly what went down between my parents and me.

"Yeah, whether they are here forcing me to do this or not, I've still worked too hard to give up now. This is for me and only me now," I say, exuding a sense of determination. I bang my fists against the top of the boards before turning to warm up my legs with the other skaters in my final group tonight.

Hours pass, and I hear groups of skaters come and go on the ice. The crowd echoes down through the tunnel, scores announce over the speakers, and news cameras follow our every move. Wearing my warm-up suit and sneakers, I slowly jog up and down the halls, trying to stay calm and keep my legs loose. Being in the lead heading into tonight's skate means I will skate last. Friggin' last, because *that* doesn't allow my head to wander and get worked up all night!

I emerge from the tunnel as the Zamboni clears the ice after the first group of skaters finish. I take in the crowd and see all the signs and banners everywhere. I find the suite that contains my very own fan club. A few minutes pass before they realize I'm down there. I hear little girls in the crowd scream my name, and I walk over to their smiling faces along the railings. All of them say they are my biggest fans and wish me luck. Some ask for autographs. Once I wave goodbye to all the girls, I turn around to see the camera is pinned on me, broadcasting on the jumbo screen above the ice. I smile and wave back at the camera while the crowd begins cheering.

This is what it should feel like to be doing what you love to do. People in the crowd, who only know you by name and face, cheering you on, and complete strangers supporting you in a moment when you need it most. I look up at Jeremy and see him gazing back at me with the biggest smile. I know he can't see me that well from up there, so I put my hand over my hockey necklace and wave at him. He'll understand what I can only say silently.

I am due to take the ice in a half hour. Suzy has my hair styled by her salon team in cascading curls and held back with a scrolling sequined band. I am wearing a Vera Wang dress that features soft beige tones and sheer fabrics with a tapestry of beadwork that extends from my right hip and up over my left shoulder. It is soft and exquisitely designed without being a distraction from the music.

After warm up with the final group of girls, I go backstage and wait alone while listening to music. The entire warm-up time I don't look at Jeremy; instead, I keep my mind focused on everything I need to do to ensure I bring home gold and secure my spot on the Olympic team. I am finally doing this for me.

Suzy comes back about ten minutes later. Pulling out my earbuds, I remove my warm-up pants and make sure my skates are laced up tight. I can't remember anything else from that moment until the minute I'm standing next to the ice. I vaguely recall Suzy talking to me, but none of it registers. I've never been this nervous in my life. *Breathe, Emily. Just breathe and find Jeremy.* Looking up into the stands, I see him sitting with his face in his hands. Dave is telling him something, but I can't tell what they're saying. Jeremy turns to Dave, and it appears he's yelling at him for some reason. Courtney walks over to the two of them and says something, but points down to where I'm standing. Jeremy stands quickly and looks right at me with a forced smile. What the hell is going on?

I don't have time to process any of what just transpired, because the previous skater's scores are being posted, and I'm set to take the ice. Suzy gives me a hug, and after removing my blade guards, my feet take the ice. I'm circling the end of the ice as Suzy gives me some last words of advice, saying, "Make it all worth it and leave your heart on the ice."

After my name is announced, the crowd cheers as I move to my starting position in the center of the ice. Silence fills the arena. My heart is beating through my chest and pounding through my ears. I let out one slow, final, deep breath before I hear the music begin. Everything fades away around me. The audience isn't there anymore. I hear the violin. I feel her pain. I become Juliet. I float across the ice, moving from jumps to spins, and in this moment, it's only me. It's me fighting for what I love. There aren't any stipulations from my mother. This time my free skate is mine and mine alone. The crescendo in the music takes on a new meaning as I come to terms with the fact that I do love this. Skating is my life, even without my parents' involvement. Entering into my final spin and then gradually ending my program on my knees, I hold my hands over my heart and cry. I cry for everything I've done up to this point in my career. I stand in front of my home crowd, knowing this is the culmination of my skating. Taking a final bow before heading toward Suzy, I glance up to see my support group all cheering.

As I make my way back to the end of the ice, Suzy stands there with tears in her eyes before hugging me like never before. I sit there, waiting for the scores to be posted on the board with my knees shaking with excitement. I'm breathing heavily, and Suzy is rubbing my back. She leans in and asks, "How did that feel?"

I shake my head in disbelief as I try to process the last five minutes. "That was probably the most amazing experience I could have ever wanted right here and now."

The wait on the scores seems longer than anything I've ever experienced. The little girls finish picking up the stuffed animals and flowers that are thrown onto the ice and begin handing me a few of them. The crowd starts clapping as we all wait for the number. The announcer says over the speaker, "And the scores for Emily Cameron." I see them light up on the board, and I'm immediately in shock. I gasp, and my hand flies to my mouth as I see the number 213.05. The announcer continues to relay to the crowd, "A personal best and also the highest score ever posted by an American Ladies Figure Skater." Oh my God! Rising to my feet, I wave to the crowd. Before I can find Jeremy, the news cameras have rushed me, and I'm forced to do interviews before the medals ceremony.

JEREMY

We sit in the suite at the Garden, watching random skaters perform. Food is brought in, and we are having a great time waiting for Emily's group to take the ice. Today is her day. I know she will rise to the occasion without a doubt. My girl will go home with that coveted gold medal at the end of the night. Everything is finally working itself out.

Then, I receive a phone call that changes everything.

I have to move into a closed-off area in order to hear what is being said to me. I actually have to ask the person on the other end of the line to repeat himself because I have to make sure I'm hearing him correctly. This couldn't be happening at a worse time.

A thought runs through my mind, but there isn't any way for Emily's parents to be involved in this. I keep telling myself that as I sit in the seat holding my head. I hear little girls screaming, but nothing is calculating. Of course, they *could* be involved in this. It's the only way this could have happened this fast, or I just have some of the worst luck in the world.

Dave comes over when he notices my change in mood. Grabbing my shoulder, he asks what is wrong. I shake my head and play with the cufflinks Emily bought me on my dress shirt. Courtney and Sue start cheering.

I turn to Dave, saying, "This can't even fuckin' be happening right now."

"What? What's happening? Who were you on the phone with?" Dave asks.

"The Monarchs coach called..." I stop mid-sentence as Courtney taps my shoulder to point at something at ice level. Looking in that direction, I see Emily standing there looking back at me as she signs autographs for a group of young girls. I try to smile back at her, but how can I, knowing what I will have to tell her later. I throw on the biggest fake smile I can muster. There's no way I can tell her this news tonight. Then, I see her touch her necklace on the jumbo screen, and I know she's telling me she's thinking of me.

I head back into the suite once I know Emily has gone back into the tunnel. I grab a beer from the ice bucket and chug it back, trying to take away some of the pain I know is in my heart. Everyone else follows behind me, trying to figure out what is going on. "All right, that's it. Spill the beans, asshole. What did the Monarchs coach want?" Dave demands.

Standing there in the middle of the room, rubbing my hands over my face, I let out a long breath as I say the words that will ultimately kill my relationship with Emily. "I've just been called up to the LA Kings. I leave in two days."

The rest of the afternoon is a blur. I remember everyone asking me questions about what will happen once I leave. I don't have any of those answers. I know I should be absolutely ecstatic about having my dream of playing for the NHL come true, but that dream was before I had Emily in my life. Dave tells me not to say anything tonight, which means I'll have to tell her tomorrow that I'm leaving the next day. No matter what I do or how I say it, I am still leaving on a plane in two days away from Emily, again.

I call home during one of the breaks, thinking my parents might offer some advice. Mom answers and asks about Emily and how it is going. Before I can respond, I tell her to put Dad on the other cordless phone in the house. After I share the news about getting the call up to the Kings, I hear them shouting in excitement at first. Then, I hear Mom say with such torment in her voice, "Oh, Jeremy. Does Emily know?"

Mom tries to talk through every possible scenario she can to make this as pain-free as possible with Emily. None of them end with her coming with me to LA for the duration of the season. I have to let them go on the phone because Emily's group is about to take the ice. They say they are happy for me and wish me all the luck in handling the news with Emily.

About fifteen minutes later, I see Emily emerge from the tunnel as Courtney points her out. I have been going back and forth with Dave on how to break the news to her. Once I see her take the ice, all arguments stop. She has a new dress for the long program, and I haven't seen it yet. She told me before she left this morning that it is a custom-made Vera Yang or something like that. I had no idea what she meant, but the dress is stunning on her. She looks nervous for the first time since I've met her. Sitting here, I'm speechless. I can barely breathe as I feel each and every one of her nerves with her. Her coach gives her one last word of advice and then she makes her way toward center ice as her name is announced.

The music starts, and she moves gracefully with each new pitch of the violin that echoes through the arena. I am in a trance as I watch her move effortlessly through each move. Tears sting my eyes as she transforms fluidly into the character she represents. Are we the star-crossed lovers never meant to spend eternity together? Emily comes out of her final spin before gliding across the ice, holding her hand to her heart. All of us stand and yell as she takes her bows on the ice. How am I ever going to leave her in two days?

CHAPTER
Twenty-seven

Emily

I stand on the podium accepting my gold medal proudly as my friends stand at ice level. After "The National Anthem" is played, I skate over to everyone as they give me big bear hugs over the boards. Jeremy gives me a kiss, and I can tell something is off, but can't place it.

They all plan to meet at The Greatest Bar for a drink before heading home. I tell them I'll meet them out at the front parking lot once I am done changing and packing my car. As I shut my trunk, I begin walking toward the front gate. Snow is falling at a steady pace, but nothing a person from New England can't handle. Jeremy is standing there all bundled up with his winter cap and winter coat. His stance straightens when he sees me getting closer.

"So, how does it feel to be the United States Figure Skating Champion?" he asks after placing a kiss on my cheek.

"I don't know. No different than I felt before I won," I say as we walk hand in hand toward the bar.

When we enter The Greatest Bar, I am shocked at how packed it is. There is a private party on the third floor, so everyone is packed on the first two floors. The gigantic screen over the bar on the first floor can be seen all the way up to the second floor balcony seating area. Dave, Sue, and Courtney are on the second floor sitting in a section with comfy sofa seats, trying to talk over the loud music and array of conversations going on around them. When they see Jeremy and me approach, they get up except for Sue who stays seated sipping her club soda with her hand on her little baby bump. I make my way to sit next to her, giving her a soft hug.

"You feeling ok?" I ask her with a concerned eye.

"Yeah, just tired. It's been a long day, and this one keeps pushing on my bladder, which doesn't help when there is only one bathroom on the floor," Sue says, stifling back a yawn. "If you want, I'll take you home, and these guys can stay a little longer. I'm pretty exhausted, too. One drink and we'll get out of here."

She nods and turns to Dave to tell him she is leaving with me after my drink. "You sure?" Dave asks me.

"Yeah, it's fine. I'm beat as it is. Plus, with the snow, it's going to be a slow drive home anyway."

Courtney comes over to hand me my drink. "So, you won't believe this douche bag over there." She points over her shoulder at this tall, ruggedly good-looking guy who's standing with a skinny attractive brunette and another guy who makes my mouth water just thinking about what he's hiding underneath his clothes. The guy catches me looking in his direction as his eyes lock with mine. Unfortunately, it is the douche bag that Courtney was pointing at that makes his way toward us. Shit. Dave gets up to head downstairs with Jeremy to grab another drink since the waitress is taking too long for their own drinks, and Jeremy leans down to say he'll be right back. After waving him off to let him know I'll be fine, he makes his way through the crowd and out of sight.

Still sipping my drink, I warn Courtney that her D-Bag is making his way toward her again. *God what is in this thing? It's yummy*, I think as I look down at my drink.

Courtney shouts over the music, seeing me looking at the cocktail in my hands. "They're called Pink Panthers. Aren't they fabulous?" She moves her hips to the music while sipping through her straw as the guy comes up behind her.

"Hey, ladies. How are you all doin' tonight? Name's Luke. You girls from around here or out of town?"

Courtney turns to him. "Listen, buddy. You already grabbed my ass once tonight, so you can take your wandering hand elsewhere." Courtney waves at him to scoot.

"Damn, girl, you are a feisty one. Are you that crazy in bed, too? 'Cuz I know I already made you scream once tonight, what's one more time?" Oh, shit. If there's one thing I know, you don't mess with a Page. Luke never sees the knee to his groin until he is hunched over the seat next to where Courtney is standing. I notice the other two people Luke is with scurry toward us.

The girl comes over first and eyes the three of us before saying, "Oh my God! Was he trying to hit on all of you? Luke! Didn't hitting on Piper teach you anything?" The hot guy behind her grabs Luke and takes him elsewhere.

The girl sits next to Courtney. "I'm so sorry about him. He tends to be an ass sometimes, but he really is a good guy. He's just having a rough couple of months, but that was one hell of a crotch shot you gave him. It totally made my night. I better go check on them. Again, I'm so sorry." The girl waves as she takes off to find the guys.

Sue starts to get antsy next to me. I can see she's uncomfortable, and I know I need to get her home. Leaning toward Courtney to grab her attention, I say, "Hey, let's find the guys. I'm going to take Sue home." She nods as she looks at Sue.

"Are you ready to get out of here?" I ask Sue.

"Yeah, this kid is really starting to be a pain in my ass tonight. I think Itty Bitty in here must not have liked something I ate," she says as she rubs her belly.

"What did you eat?" I ask, internally cringing of all the various possibilities.

"Nothing out of the ordinary. Hot dogs, nachos, pretzel, sausage, and chicken fingers."

"In one afternoon?" I exclaim. "Oh my God! No wonder Itty Bitty isn't happy."

While we make our way through the second floor crowd to the staircase, I peer over the balcony to see Dave and Jeremy at the bar on the first floor. It also appears an attractive girl is making herself comfortable against Jeremy as she's running her hands over his chest and laughing at something. Jeremy doesn't look pleased at all about having her there with him. What the hell? Who is this broad?

"What the fuck is she doing here?" I hear Courtney shout as her stare shoots in the same direction as mine.

"You know her?" I ask.

"Know her? Yeah, that's Becca. Jeremy's ex-girlfriend from college. The bitch whore who told him since he wasn't getting into the NHL, she was kicking him to the curb. After her, he didn't date again until you. She was a real trip, that one," Courtney says with contempt in her voice. At the same time, Sue's hand hits Courtney's shoulder.

"Ouch! Oh!" Courtney says to Sue as my eyes catch some kind of silent message between the two.

"What's going on?" I ask.

Sue grabs my arm and pulls me in the direction of the exit. "Nothing, Courtney will go tell the guys we're leaving, but I really need to get moving 'cuz my bladder can only take so much these days."

"Uh, okay, you sure we shouldn't go take care of that situation with Jeremy's ex?" I ask, wondering why I'm still standing here and not staking my claim next to him.

"Nah, trust me. He hates everything about her. He's probably doing everything in his power to not knock her teeth out right now. I'll call Dave once we get to the car," Sue says as she continues to rub her hands over her belly.

I assume she knows what she's talking about. She has known Jeremy longer than me, but something isn't sitting right in my stomach. Trekking through the couple of inches of snow already on the ground, we finally make it to my car. Sue gets in while it warms up, and I brush the snow off the windows. I get back into the car, shutting the door quickly and trying to warm my frozen fingers on the heat vents. She is playing with her phone when I get into the car. "I tried calling Dave, but he didn't answer. It's probably too loud in the bar. So, I sent him a text telling him you were taking me home."

"All right, is everything else going okay tonight? Something seems off with Jeremy tonight. Did he say anything to you?" I ask as I put my car in drive and pull out of the parking lot. "No, Jeremy had a phone call earlier, but other than that, I haven't heard anything," Sue says as she diverts her attention out the window. I don't push any further since I know she's already not feeling well.

Within minutes, we are on 93 North heading home. The highway is coated with a thin layer of snow, but drivable. My wipers are on full speed, trying to keep up with the falling snow. It also doesn't help that I am only driving about forty-five in a sixty-five speed limit zone. Traffic is light considering. About a mile outside of the city, I see a few taillights in front of me. Everything is blurry with the blowing snow.

A moment later, Sue winces and holds her stomach. "Are you okay?" I ask, trying to look at her and the road at the same time.

Out of nowhere, I see taillights approach quickly, and Sue shouts, "Emily, look out!" My arm reaches out to hold back Sue, preparing for the hit. Headlights are coming in my direction. I try hitting the brakes, but with the snow, I skid rather than stop. There is a loud crunch and screeching metal as I feel my head lurch forward, hitting the steering wheel. My right arm bucks back with shattering pain before I see a bright light and then darkness.

JEREMY

I've had just about enough of Becca the minute I hear her say, "Jeremy, is that you?" in her evil, but nice voice. When I kicked her out of my dorm all those years ago that was the last time I ever wanted to speak to her. After about ten minutes of her barking in my ear, she starts running her hand over my chest as she says, "Have you heard who I'm dating these days? I mean, he's kind of a big deal. Do you know who Matt Bartkowski is?" Yeah, I know he plays for the Boston Bruins, and I'm not even going to tell her about my most recent news about the LA Kings. My main concern is getting back upstairs to the girl I love more than life itself, the same girl I'm about to leave in a couple days.

Since I can't help myself, I have to get the last jab at Becca, just because she's Becca. Looking her dead in the eyes, I grab her hand, pulling it off of me forcefully. "Key word there Becca is you're still dating him. Not married like you thought you would be to secure your future. What happened over the past few years, huh? Couldn't get another sucker to fall for your bullshit after me? Turn around and walk back the way you came in because I'm not about to have another conversation with you."

I grab my drink and walk away with Dave, who is rubbing my shoulders and laughing when I see Courtney moving toward us, staring daggers straight at me. "What the hell was Becca doing with you?" she scolds before slapping my arm.

"Nothing, she was trying to rub in the fact she's dating a Bruin, and I told her to go back where she came from. Wait. How did you know Becca was down here?"

"Seriously, Jeremy? The second floor looks over the entire bar. It would be pretty hard not to see she had her paws all over you," Courtney scoffs.

Shit. If Courtney saw Becca, Emily saw her from up there, too. "Did Emily see her?" I question, grabbing her shoulders.

"Well, yeah, but she wasn't pissed or anything. She left with Sue about thirty minutes ago. I would have told you sooner, but some douche bag, who grabbed my ass, tried to apologize on my way over here," Courtney says as if it isn't a big deal.

Dave pulls his phone from his pocket, checking a message on his screen. "Dude, she's telling the truth. Sue texted me. She said Emily was driving her home 'cuz she wasn't feeling well. I'll try calling her, but we should probably get going anyway."

"Yeah, let me just finish this, and we'll head out." I suck back my beer and lay the empty bottle onto the bar.

Dave comes back with the phone to his ear, shaking his head. "No answer from Sue. I'll keep trying, but she could have the radio up in the car."

"All right, let's get out of here. Let's get Courtney and head home," I say. Dave nods and shoves his phone back into his pocket.

Leaving the bar, we walk about a half block to the parking lot, and I start the truck. All of us are brushing the snow off our clothes when my phone starts ringing. The name "Josh" comes across the screen. Why the hell is he calling me? Maybe he's just wondering how Emily did in the Nationals, or he's heard from Mom about the Kings. Sliding my thumb over the screen, I bring the phone up to my ear.

"Hey, Josh. What's up? Did Mom tell you to call me?"

"Jeremy, I don't know how to tell you this. There was an accident on 93 about twenty minutes ago. I was first on scene with the ambulance. It's Emily and Sue. I'm at the ER with them now. It's not good. How fast can you get to Mass General?"

My life flashes before my eyes, and my phone drops from my hand. Courtney grabs it, and I hear her talking to Josh as I begin to make my way across the city to the hospital as fast as I can. Courtney is in the backseat, trying her best to get information from Josh, but finally has to give the phone to Dave who keeps rubbing his temples with his fingers. When he hangs up, he says nothing, just punches my dashboard with his fist. I don't even care that he's left a dent. All I care about is getting to Emily.

Within fifteen minutes, I am across town running into the ER with Courtney and Dave. Josh is waiting for us, but he hasn't been able to get much information from the doctors about either of the girls since he's not family. Emily's parents were notified earlier and arrived before us.

Apparently, a tractor-trailer jackknifed on 93, causing a pile up of cars about a mile outside the city. As the drivers began rear-ending each other, some of the cars in front of Emily's Audi locked up their brakes, causing her to slam into them before she had a chance to stop.

Dave is concerned for Sue and the baby, and Josh tells him, given he's the father of the baby, he might be able to get more information from the nurses. He walks over at the front desk, trying to find out anything he can. Courtney and I sit in the ER, attempting to process it all. How could this have happened? Was she pissed at me and just took off? Holy shit. I've still got to leave in two days. The Kings will never allow an extension.

"Fuck!" I shout as everyone in the waiting room turns and stares at me.

Josh sits next to me. "I'll see what information I can get from the doctors, but I can tell you when I got there, her car was not in good shape, man. There was a lot of blood. I was with her when they loaded her into the ambulance. She didn't say anything, but when I held her hand, I told her I'd get you to her as fast as I could, and she responded by squeezing me back. At this point, you have to stay positive."

"Positive? Are you fuckin' kidding me? I've literally had one of the worst nights of my life so far. First, I get a call from the Monarchs saying I've been traded to the Kings. You'd think that would be good news, but no. I'm leaving in two days, and I can't even find a way to tell the woman I love on the night she wins the National Championships that both of our dreams have come true. It's going to hurt us even more in the end. Now, she's lying back there with God only knows what injuries, and when she may or may not make it through all of this, I might not be here to tell her I'm not coming back for who knows how long. How the fuck do I stay positive? Please enlighten me, Josh, because right now I just don't see it."

"I'm sorry, Jeremy. I really am. If I could make this better, I would and you know that, but I can't. I'll call Mom and Dad to tell them what happened. I'll be back in a little bit. Okay?" Josh puts his hand on my shoulder, trying to comfort me as he makes his way through the ER doors.

Courtney is still crying, and Dave is still at the front desk when I look up, obviously distraught as he talks to the nurse at the desk. Scooting over to Courtney, I wrap my arm around her shoulder and kiss her head, trying to calm her down. All I want to do right now is walk through those doors to see Emily and check on Sue and the baby.

About an hour passes, and my phone has been ringing nonstop since we've arrived at the hospital. I know it's Mom, but I can't deal with her right now. The ER doors open, and I see Emily's parents walking through the entrance. They say nothing, and no emotion is shown. I stare at them from one end of the room to the exit. How the hell can they even call themselves family? After they pass, Josh comes through the doors toward me.

"What's going on?" I stand quickly, trying to remain calm.

"Well, here's what I know. Your girl has a good head on her shoulders. Did you know she named Mom in charge of all her medical decisions and financials? I guess she had the right frame of mind to get all her documents changed over just after she moved into your place and made Mom her manager. Maybe if you answered your phone, you'd know that. When I talked to Mom, she was emailing the proxy to me and talking to Emily's doctors on the phone. She told them in the event that she couldn't be here to make the medical decisions for Emily to let you in to monitor her status until she can get here. So, if you want to see her..."

Making my way to the doors, I realize I can't leave the others. "What about Courtney and Dave?"

"Sue's out of ICU and being transferred to a regular room right now. They will both be allowed up there momentarily, and before you ask, yes, the baby is fine. If it weren't for Emily holding her back in the car before the accident, it might be a different story. Emily threw her arm in front of Sue before they hit. It ended up hurting Emily more, but Sue only had minor injuries."

I look at Josh, fearing the answer to my next question. "What do you mean 'ended up hurting Emily more'?"

Josh tells me that Emily is in Room 262 and not to lose it when I walk in. Before I go through the doors, he calls my name. He reaches into his uniform jacket and pulls out Emily's gold medal. "I didn't want to leave this in her car. The rest of her personal belongings should be in her room. Everything else will need to be sorted through at the tow company."

I fear the worst, but nothing could have prepared me for what I see when I round the corner into her room. She has an oxygen mask over her face, and machines are beeping. Her right arm is in a cast up to her elbow. Her right leg is raised, and her foot is in a boot fixture of sorts. Moving to stand by her bed, I run my finger over the cuts on her cheek, letting my head fall to my chest as tears stream down my face. "I'm so sorry, Em. I'm so sorry." She doesn't respond to my touch or to my voice. "Please, babe, wake up for me. I need to see your big blue eyes. I know I'm selfish. Call me an ass. Just wake up and tell me to shut the fuck up 'cuz you're okay. Please, babe. I love you so much."

Sinking into the chair next to her bed, I continue to hold her unresponsive hand. A nurse comes into the room after about ten minutes to check on her. She explains Emily suffered a minor concussion. She should respond within a few days; however, her fractured ankle and both broken right forearm bones will take longer to heal. I lay my head on her bed with the reality of what that means flashing through my mind. No Olympic dream come true.

Everything that she has worked her ass off for the past four months has been taken away in a few hours. She'll never be able to handle the fact that the same night her dream was taken from her, mine had come true. She'll probably resent me when she finds out. What if I'm not the one who tells her when she finally wakes up? There isn't one positive outcome in any of this. For every positive, there's a negative. Right now, the only positive is the fact that Emily and Sue are both alive.

About two hours later, a hand on my shoulder wakes me from my sleep. "Emily?"

"No, sweetie. It's Mom."

I look up into her somber eyes, realizing she knows I am hurting and tormented by tonight's events. Standing up, I step into her open arms. "Tell me she's going to be okay. Tell me she won't hate me when I tell her I have to leave her after all of this."

Rubbing her hands over my back, she sobs with me. "I wish I could tell you everything will be all right, but I'm not sure right now. You just have to stay positive and hope for the best."

CHAPTER
twenty-eight

Emily

My head hurts as I hear beeping and voices around me. I can't move.
Why does my arm hurt so badly? I feel someone brushing hair away from my
forehead. *Where the hell am I, and why can't I open my eyes? Why can't I see
anything? What the hell happened?*

I remember driving my car with Sue in the passenger seat. It was
snowing. I heard her wincing in pain and my hand flew up to hold her back
because… Oh my God! The brake lights and the headlights of another car
headed right for us… Sue and the baby… Oh my God! Am I dead? Is Sue
okay?

"Sue!" I scream.

More voices around me become louder, and I feel hands on my
shoulders. "Emily, can you hear me? Babe, open your eyes."

Jeremy?

"Sweetie, can you hear me? It's Grace, dear. I need you to open your
eyes. Can you open your eyes?"

Grace?

I hear unfamiliar voices and then flashes of white light scroll from left
to right and then back again. The cars and the lights flash again through my
mind, along with the crunching of the metal as it hits my car. Suddenly, I
can't breathe, and I'm gasping for air as my body surges forward, and my
eyes fly open. Screaming and trying to catch my breath, I'm unaware of
everyone around me. A nurse gently lowers me back onto the bed, and I see
Grace, Jeremy, Travis and Courtney all standing along the back wall while
the nurse still tends to a few IV's stuck in my arm. Glancing at my other
arm, I see a cast covering my forearm, and my foot is in a boot. The
realization has set in that Sue may be hurt as well, and if my arm and foot
are in casts, my Olympic dreams are over. Tears spill down my face as I
begin sobbing.

Grace is at my side almost instantly as the nurse moves out of the way.
"Shh, dear. We're here. Everything is going to be fine now. You're awake."
She gently strokes my hair as I turn to face her.

"Sue?" I quietly ask, hoping for the best possible answer. "She's fine.
Dave's upstairs with her now. She should be released in a few hours. They

needed to keep her overnight to monitor the baby, but they are both fine, thanks to your quick thinking in the car."

"She's fine. The baby's fine, too? How did I help them?" I ask curiously.

"When you saw the car coming toward you, you must have thought to protect her more than yourself." Grace nods down to my cast. "Sue said she remembered feeling a pain in her stomach, and you looked her way. When she warned you about the oncoming car, you pushed your right arm out to keep her back against the seat before the car hit, and well, you can see what the result was."

Grace turns toward Travis and Courtney, telling them they should go upstairs to see Sue before they head out. Before she leaves, she gives Jeremy a saddened look as she pats him on the shoulder.

Once the door is shut, Jeremy walks to my bed. "Hey, babe. I can't tell you how happy I am to see your big blue eyes again. I was so scared I had lost you when Josh called to tell me about the accident. The last twelve hours have been awful, but you kind of already know that don't you. Sorry." Jeremy starts pacing around the room before making any further eye contact with me. Is he mad at me for some reason?

"Jeremy, what's going on? Why are you acting so strange right now?"

"Emily, God, this fuckin' sucks. I probably should have told you this last night before you left, but it was your night, and I couldn't ruin it. Then, the accident happened and what I have to tell you may hurt you more than that."

"You're scaring me. What do you need to tell me?" I ask nervously as my eyes search for answers on his face.

"Emily, the Monarchs called me during your competition last night. One of the LA Kings players is injured. They've called me up to play for them. Basically, I've been traded."

"What does that mean? I understand the traded part, but what does it entail?"

"Well, it means I no longer play for the Monarchs. I'll be in LA playing hockey for the NHL instead."

"Oh." This explains why he was acting strange last night.

"That's not the worst part. I have to leave for LA tomorrow morning."

I blink my eyes rapidly, trying to process all the information I've just been given and hoping I misunderstood something, but I know I haven't. Jeremy's telling me he's heading to LA to play for the NHL tomorrow morning. There has been no mention of him coming home. No mention of me included in that statement. He is setting off to finally live out his lifelong dream. Where does that leave me? Can we handle months upon months apart? My skating career is ultimately over. I don't even have any idea what

I'm going to do once I recover from these injuries. Then, there is the big question. Where does that leave us?

"Jeremy, tell me something. If you leave and fulfill your goals or get traded to another team, where does that leave me in the equation?"

"Babe, this changes nothing with us. I still love you, but I don't have a choice. I have to go. It's part of my contract. You could always come out to Los Angeles if the doctor says it's all right," he says without any doubt, but it does change everything with us. A part of me wants to tell him to stay with me, but I know I can't. I have no right after just four months. I know what I need to do for myself.

"Jeremy, I need you to go. Maybe this time away will allow me to really figure out what I have in my life outside of skating."

"You have me, Emily."

"It's not enough, and it's not fair of me to ask you to stay with me," I aggressively say as my hands wrap around my head that has begun to hurt again.

"Do you think I want to go and leave tomorrow? You think I want to leave you here, knowing I won't be able to help you through this? I know how hard three weeks away from you was. I don't even want to think about how long this might last."

"You don't think I know what I'm going to have to go through without you? I haven't even given any thought yet about what my injuries will include for rehab. I can't even walk right now! Nothing about this is easy," I say, as the throbbing in my head grows stronger.

"Emily, I've fought for you. I've loved you. Fuck, I still love you, and I won't stop loving you. You're going to throw that away because you think you have nothing? Look around you, Em. If you have nothing, then what is my family to you? What are Sue and Dave to you? You want us to end because you're scared of not knowing what you might find if you break down the fuckin' walls around you? That's not fair, Em. That's called taking the easy way out."

"Jeremy, I can't let you resent me for holding you back in life. I won't. I don't know where we'll be at the end of all of this. I just know that whether it's together or apart, I need to do this for myself. When you get back, we'll see where we are."

He comes over to sit on the edge of my bed, taking my hand in his. "Emily, I love you. I've loved you since, God, I don't even know when. I'm lost without you. You have to know you are the only thing that makes me happy."

Tears sting my eyes because I know I make him happy, but I'm not his true happiness. "No, Jeremy. I'm not the only thing that makes you happy. Hockey makes you happy, which is why you need to go and do this without me. I'm so sorry."

He gets up from the bed, placing a soft kiss on my forehead before he turns toward the door. "If that's how you see it, I'll leave and let you decide when you're ready for me to be a part of your life again. Understand this, though." He points his finger between him and me. "What we have is not over. You're mine just as much as I'm yours, remember?" Before he exits the room, he turns back to me. "Do me a favor while I'm gone, Em. Please stay at *our* place until I get back. At least that will give me a reason to come home in a couple of months during the break." I nod yes to make him happy, even though I have no idea what I plan on doing after this. As he's walking out the door, I hear him softly whisper, "I love you."

He's gone, and I'm alone in my life all over again, but this time, I'll be able to find my own direction in life to see where it takes me. I'll have to fight for myself, and I'm scared to death.

Moments later, the door opens again, and I quickly turn my head. "Jer…"

"Hi, Emily, I'm Dr. Cranston. I see you have had quite a night. I'm sorry to hear about your injuries, but I'm here to help you understand the rehab process."

Coming in behind Dr. Cranston is Grace, who appears to have also had a very long night. Her eyes are puffy, and she looks tired. Running her hand softly over my hair, she says, "Sweetie, I promise he'll be brief, and I know you're tired, but try to listen to him."

My head is throbbing, and I want to go to sleep. I've had enough agony for one day, but I may as well take another blow while I'm already down.

"What about the Olympics and skating again?" I ask timidly.

"I'm sorry, Emily. I just don't see that in the cards, at least not this year."

There's only one other person who can help me now besides me. "Dr. Cranston, considering my current frame of mind, would you mind bringing Grace up to speed on everything? I'm not feeling very well."

JEREMY

I have to leave. If I don't leave the hospital now, I never will. I would break my contract right now and stay with her; I love her that much. But, Emily is right. If I don't do this, if I don't at least see what it is like to play in the NHL, a part of me will always wonder. What if? What if I stay with Emily in the hospital and tell her I'm willing to fight for her tooth and nail just because I want forever with her? No matter how many times I replay that conversation over in my head, not one scenario has a happy ending.

When I get back to the apartment to pack my things and get everything in order, I see all the ways Emily has become a part of my life. Her clothes in the closet. Her vanilla body wash in the bathroom. Her infinity bracelet on my nightstand from when I took it off as she fell asleep in my arms after making love. That stupid fat-free creamer in my fridge. She has made me laugh more times than I can think of since the end of the summer.

When I finish zipping up the last of my suitcases, I find the little black box with her ring I bought before Christmas. I never found the right time, or I always chickened out. Now, I may never have the right time after our time apart. I grab a storage box labeled "youth hockey stuff" in my closet and place the ring inside it. I haven't opened that storage box since I was thirteen, but the hockey stick I went back to the ice for that day, still sits in my closet.

Today is my first game with the Kings. Already I know that after practicing with these guys, I'm in another league altogether. They are bigger, tougher, and the stakes are set much higher. I miss my rink back home in Manchester. I'd grown so accustomed to my lifestyle there the past three years that this feels foreign to me.

While I sit on the bench with the players and watch their speed and hits, everything seems unreal to me. In a matter of seconds, I'll be on the ice in front of a sold-out crowd. I will officially be an NHL player. Why are my only thoughts of the woman who isn't here to watch me play my first game?

"Page, you're up!" Coach blows the whistle and yells, distracting me from my thoughts of Emily.

Pulling one leg over the boards, I wait for the line change. When my guy is on the bench, I swing my other leg over, and this is my moment. Everyone speeds past me as I move quickly with the stick in front of me. The puck goes sliding in the opposite direction. Skating after it, I try to avoid having it anywhere near the Kings goal. Once I reach the puck next to the boards, I glance up quickly, but it's not fast enough. A six-foot-three powerhouse is headed right for me. Before I have a chance to think about what to do or where to skate, his shoulder connects with my face, and the back of my head slams hard into the glass.

I shake my head to regain my vision, and once the puck becomes visible, the whistle blows again. Two players are fighting now at center ice. I've had my fair share of fights, but they weren't to this extreme. This feels as though it's all for show. People are cheering. Players are talking to each other. At what point did these guys stop playing for the love of the game, and instead, start playing for the paycheck?

Three hours later, my NHL debut is over, and I'm back at my hotel the Kings set me up in. We have a morning skate tomorrow morning and will board the jet to Denver to play the Avalanche in two days. There won't be a bus trip with these guys as I've been used to in the past with the Monarchs. This is a completely different lifestyle. Most of the guys on the team are nice enough, but there won't be any post-game drinks at the local pub. Too many players on the team are superstars in LA.

As I get ready to shave, I splash some warm water on my face before slathering shaving cream and getting rid of the three days of scruff. I wash and dry my face before changing into my sweats. As I sit on the bed, I scroll through my phone to see if I've missed any calls. I've probably checked at least fifty times today to see if Emily has called, and still nothing.

It's already eleven here and way too late to call Mom and Dad, so I decide to send Courtney a text instead.

> *Just checking in. First game went okay. How's Emily? Miss all you guys already. –J*

I pull back the covers on the bed and crawl under. Taking out my tablet, I check the news from home. The top headline doesn't surprise me at all, "Boston Olympic Favorite Involved in Accident: Withdraws from Games." After clicking on the link, I read as the article describes in detail the severity of the accident and the press release about her withdrawal due to her injuries. Another headline catches my eye as I scroll down, "Charles Cameron of Cameron and Dean, LLC Selling Company, Files for Divorce." Well, that didn't take very long. I wonder if Emily has heard the good news? I toss the tablet off to the side of the bed, suddenly feeling exhausted from everything that's happened this week.

I'm just about to turn off the lights when my phone vibrates on the nightstand. Removing it from the charger, I see it's Courtney calling. What is she still doing up at this hour?

"Hey, Court. What are you still doing up?" I hear her yawning on her end of the line and the sound of a door shutting in the background.

"I'm keeping an eye on Emily. Mom and Dad have the days and evenings for now. I took the night until Josh has a day off."

"What do you mean 'keeping an eye on Emily'?" I ask, scratching my head.

"The hospital released her just as the news broke the story about the Olympics, and she didn't take it well. Plus, she's on pain meds for the injuries, and well, she's still trying to cope with you leaving."

If I could hit something, I would. "Court, what was I supposed to do? You know I didn't have a choice, and it's not as though she asked me to stay. I wish she wasn't going through all of that, and I know it's rough on you guys, too. If I could be there to help I would, but it's not what Emily wants," I say as I hear the sounds of the coffee machine brewing over the phone.

"She's not the same, Jeremy. I mean, yeah, it's Emily, but she's closed herself off completely. She doesn't speak. She won't even sleep in your bed. She's in the guest room. Sue came over today, and Emily just cried when she mentioned your name. None of us know what to do. You are the only one who can see through her when she needs help. Mom says to give her time, but she's never been this bad. Tell me what to do, Jeremy. I'm afraid she might not come out of this."

How can I tell Courtney how to get through to Emily? I didn't exactly have much luck during my last conversation with her. It might be different if I was there to help firsthand, but I have no idea when I will be back home.

Pinching the bridge of my nose as I feel my head start pounding, I respond, "Court, I wish I could tell you how to help her, but Emily needs to figure out what she wants to do in her life. She needs to learn to fight on her own again. If she gets worse, call me. I've got to get going. I have an early practice, and then I'm off to Denver for the next game. Tell Mom, Dad, and Joshthat I miss them. I'll send Dave and Sue a text tomorrow to see how things are going there. Take care of Emily as best you can. I still love her and miss her. It just has to be this way for a while. I'll talk to you soon, Court."

After hanging up, my thoughts drift to Emily. I have to control every urge I have to pick up my phone to text her. God, I miss her. As I roll over, the last thing I think of before falling asleep is my happiness is missing, and I can only hope it's still there when I finally get home.

We arrive in Denver the following afternoon. When we make it to the arena for the game against the Avalanche, I realize this is the same rink in which Emily won her competition. I know I said I'd give her time, but after the three weeks we spent away from each other a few months ago, I can't possibly not hear her voice or let her know I'm thinking of her. I pull my phone from my pocket.

> *I know you said to give you time. Tough. I'll call u soon. Here's a song for you.*

> *"Peace" by O.A.R. Love U-J*

Pushing the phone back into my pocket, I grab my gear and follow the rest of the team into the locker room. I'm just about finished throwing my pads over my shoulders when my phone alerts me of an incoming text.

Sara Shirley

"Arms" I'm so sorry for what I said at the hospital. I was angry and in shock. I miss you. Luv U 2-E

Pulling out my headphones, I listen to her song, hearing the meaning of every word. *Don't worry, babe, I'm coming home to you. Just give me time.*

CHAPTER
Twenty-nine

Emily

It's been six weeks since the accident. Six weeks since everything was taken from me. I've been to rehab for my injuries and spoken to therapists. I feel as though I'm being suffocated in every direction I'm headed. Everyone thinks I'm made of glass, so they are walking on eggshells around me. Topping it off, I'm watching as the Olympic Games are going on without me.

Since the accident, I've had numerous nightmares during my sleep. The therapists say that in talking my way through the pain and what's bothering me, the nightmares will subside. On occasion, Sue joins me in therapy to tell her side of the story, how none of it could have been prevented, and how I did everything I could in the situation. She also mentions that I'm the one who saved her little girl.

Yes, she and Dave are having a baby girl. They found out shortly after the accident. Her bump continues to grow every time she stops by. I try to be happy for her when she's around, but I'm still no further into finding out where my life is headed once my injuries have healed.

The concussion symptoms have gone away completely now, and all I have are a few minor headaches here and there. The doctors removed the cast on my arm a couple of days ago, and I've started rehabbing slowly. Unfortunately, my ankle is still in a brace for support. They say that will take the longest to heal, but I tend to disagree. My heart is one thing that's still just as broken as it was six weeks ago.

No one has mentioned anything to me about Jeremy. His name seems to be some kind of taboo subject around me. I saw a few weeks ago the Bruins played the Kings in LA. Travis was watching the game in his living room when I heard Jeremy's name filter across the speakers. When he noticed me staring at the screen and only blinking, he tried to change the subject by switching to another channel. It was too late. I saw him there on the screen as he was living his dream.

They know he's been in touch with me, and they know I miss him like crazy. When he can, he texts, or on a rare occasion, he calls to say hi and tries to cheer me up. He seems to be in a new city every time I talk to him. Nothing has brought him to the East Coast yet to visit. With having all the time in the world right now, I'm easily bored and waiting for any kind of new entertainment.

Some days I find myself carrying on a conversation with Aspen. He sits and listens for hours, and I know he misses Jeremy just as much as I do. The two of us are our own support group. My heart breaks when he hears someone coming up the back stairs. He thinks it's Jeremy, and his tail wags a mile a minute until the door opens, only sending him back to his bed and looking at me with those big sad eyes.

Today is a new day, though. Courtney is taking me with her to her cooking class she signed up for. The damn girl won't stop feeding me. She claims she has to practice for her class. She brings Grace and Sue over to use us as test subjects, and since I can't exactly workout at the moment, I've put on more weight than I care to. Grace says the added weight looks good on me, but I disagree. Sue has no problem pulling up the rear when it comes to eating all the food. Grace has tried to use a scare tactic with her by saying the more she eats, the bigger the watermelon she'll have to push out of her vagina. Sue's decided to take her chances.

I'm standing with my crutches under my arms in Courtney's cooking class, assisting her with the ratatouille she's preparing. I've been slicing vegetables for what seems like forever. This week they are learning the basics of French foods. I'm mid-slice when someone asks her a question that sends my head into a whirlwind. *Wait. What?*

"He said he'd be back sometime before the end of the week. He didn't say exactly when, just said they called him back down," Courtney responds to the girl. I stare at the vegetables in front of me, motionless. A hand on my shoulder startles me from my thoughts. "Emily, are you all right?" Courtney asks as she goes to grab the array of vegetables neatly placed in the baking dish.

My head turns toward her voice, and my face twists in confusion. "Jeremy's coming home?" I ask.

Brushing a stray hair from my face, she pushes it behind my ear since my hands are covered in random vegetable juices. "Yeah, sweetie. He called a couple of days ago. He didn't want us to tell you because he thought you might freak out. The Kings released him, so he'll be back playing for the Monarchs by next week."

"Why didn't anyone say something to me?" I ask as if I didn't already know the answer. Jeremy knew I'd start freaking out. Stepping over to the sink, I wash and dry my hands. He's coming home, and I've managed to do absolutely nothing as to figuring out my future since he left. He'll see right through my lies if I tell him otherwise. My mind starts processing a million different things, but it always comes back to one thing. My one true happiness outside of Jeremy. Skating.

"Court? I need to go somewhere in the morning. Do you think you can give me a lift?" I ask her since I still can't drive with the brace, and I haven't replaced my car.

Grabbing my phone from my pocket, I pull up the number of someone I know who can help me. I'm just surprised I hadn't thought of this sooner. Listening to the phone ring, I hear her pick up. "Hey, it's Emily. I need a favor, and I'm hoping you're the right person to help me. Can you meet with me tomorrow?"

It's time for me to get my life back on track.

JEREMY

As the Kings management tells me I'm being reassigned back to the Monarchs, it is literally the best news I've heard in weeks. It's not that I'm not playing as well as the other athletes. It's just part of being affiliated with the AHL. The Kings decide who gets called up and sent back to the AHL all season long.

The last six weeks have been worth the experience; however, it's not for me. I'm used to weekend games and being home almost every night with the Monarchs. I miss my family. I miss Emily. Playing for the NHL is no longer my dream. My dreams are sitting at my apartment waiting for me.

I told my parents to keep my homecoming news from Emily. I want it to be a surprise, but some of my family friends are Monarchs season ticket holders, and it is likely my assignment will be posted all over the web. When I talked to Courtney before my flight, she said Emily *might* have an idea that I'm coming home. I'm surprised Emily didn't try to call me when she found out. We've at least been talking during our time apart, but the distance is still doing a number on the both of us. We talk about her progress and how she's getting better, or she asks me about my games. We still have yet to discuss what was said at the hospital or the reason she's been seeing a therapist for her depression. I know I'm partially to blame for that, but that's a conversation I'm not having over the phone.

Once my flight lands at Logan, I make my way down to the baggage claim area. I retrieve all my bags and head for the automatic doors to look for Courtney. The minute my face hits the cold winter New England air, I know I'm home. Spotting Courtney's car, I walk over and shove my hockey bags into the already popped trunk. Once I'm inside the car, she pulls me over the center console and gives me one of the biggest hugs ever.

"Don't you ever leave for that long again! You hear me," she threatens as she puts the car in drive to head home. Home. I can't get there fast enough.

We pull into the driveway as the sun is just setting below the horizon. The sky is a fiery orange-red, and the snow banks appear to have grown since I was here last. Courtney turns off the car, and we both look up to the windows over the garage. The lights are on, and I hear Aspen barking.

"She's mobile again, but slow. Go get her. I'll hold off Mom and Dad as long as I can."

"Thanks, Court!" I yell as I storm from the car, leaving my bags behind and bounding up the stairs two at a time until I reach the door. Taking a long breath, I open the door slowly and shut it quietly behind me. Aspen comes barreling down the hall until he jumps on me with his front paws resting on my forearms. Putting him down and rubbing behind his ears, I ask him, "Where is she, big guy? Em?"

"Oh sure, Aspen, you big showoff. You've got four good legs against my one," Emily teases from down the hall. There's the smart mouth I've missed so much. As I'm about to start running down the hall to see her, she hobbles around the corner and greets me with the biggest grin on her face.

"Surprised to see me?" I saunter toward her.

"If I said yes, would you believe me?" she asks as she meets me halfway.

She's finally standing in front of me, and I can reach out and touch her again. Her hair is longer, and her curves are more defined than when I left, but she's still the most beautiful creature I've ever laid eyes on. Both of my hands reach out and cup the side of her face as I bring my forehead down to hers and close my eyes.

"Babe, I've missed you so damn much," I say. Opening my eyes, I see her eyelashes are coated in tears, but her smile and laughter crack through the light sobs.

Reaching her arms up, she wraps them around my neck. "I've missed you too, Jeremy, but do you think we can sit? This standing thing isn't the easiest thing in the world."

"Oh, sorry, of course," I say as I bend down and pick her up under her legs and butt, carrying her out to the living room.

"Easy with the arm," she says as she pulls it in protectively. "Even Aspen isn't as rough as you."

I make my way to the sofa with her in my arms, never losing eye contact with her. "I'll be gentle."

"You can put me down now. I'm surprised you didn't throw out your back trying to carry me just now," she insinuates.

"Em, you look as gorgeous as always, and if you don't stop trying to crack jokes to try to hide being nervous, I'll give you a reason to be nervous." I wink at her. "Now, can you please shut up for five minutes, so I can kiss you?"

Giving me a huge devilish grin, she closes her eyes, shaking her hair out behind her shoulders and then sticking up her chin. She thinks she's going to fool me. I'll make this the best second "first" kiss ever.

Sitting on my coffee table in front of her, I angle her legs in between mine. I'm careful not to hit her walking boot before pulling her chin toward me with my finger. I kiss her cheeks, her eyes, her nose, and then my lips barely touch hers before I stand to lean over her. Placing both of my hands on the back of the sofa, I coax her to fall back. My lips find hers, and the past six weeks have disappeared just like that. Her mouth opens for me as my right hand holds the back of her head to keep her lips that much closer to mine. Emily's left hand grips my shirt, pulling me closer to her as she moans in her throat.

Before I know it, my door flies open and Dave bustles into the living room. Breaking my kiss from Emily, I stare up at him. "Seriously? Knock much?"

Then, the parade of people follows behind him. Mom's bringing in a cake, and Dad has Sue by the arm as she holds her rounded belly. Courtney steps in last. "I told you I'd hold them off as long as I could. Time's up."

Laughing, I lean down to Emily and whisper into her ear, "We're not done yet. I'm just getting started."

"I've got all night." She points toward her boot. "I'm not exactly going anywhere." Kissing her on the cheek, I say, "I'm glad to hear it. We've got some catching up to do." Everyone groans around me, and Dave says, "Get a room." That's when I realize it is good to finally be home. I've missed all this madness.

The night wears on as all of us catch up on stories from the last six weeks. Dad wants to hear all about the NHL lifestyle, what Los Angeles is like, and if I met any movie stars while I was out there. Sue talks about names that Dave wants for their baby girl. I have to laugh at some of the ones he comes up with. Sue says he wants Minnie, as in Minnie Mouse.

Everyone is laughing, and it is as though I never left, except I did, and I still need to fix my relationship with Emily. When I say I'm actually happy to see the snow, I notice Emily shudder next to me. She's clearly still going through a difficult period after the accident, but I'm here now, and I plan on getting her to talk to me about it.

Once everyone leaves the apartment, I see Emily yawning on the sofa. It has been a long day for both of us. I gently pick her up and carry her to the bedroom, gently placing her on the bed. Removing my shirt and jeans, I stand there in my boxer briefs. When I look over at her, she still hasn't changed out of her clothes. Eyeing her curiously, I ask, "Em, what's up? Do you not want to go to bed?"

Glancing away shyly, she fiddles with her hands before quietly saying, "I don't know why, but I'm nervous. Is that weird, considering after just one date I already had my hands down your pants? Now, almost six months later, I'm nervous. What's wrong with me, Jeremy?" Tears begin welling in her eyes before she admits her true fear. "I hate how we left things at the hospital, and when we'd talk on the phone, it seemed as though you were so distant and that we were forcing a conversation neither of us wanted to have. I ended up having to see a therapist because my moods were so screwed up, and they wanted me to talk about how I was *feeling* or what made me so depressed. I hated every minute of it. Now, you're here, and I'm even more confused because we've not talked about us as a couple yet, and I'm still living here."

I have to stop her rambling. It's true; she has changed. This is not the seductive little minx full of surprises. This Emily is not the same one I left before the accident. Somehow I knew I would find her buried deep within her soul, but for now, I need to comfort her and take care of her. Making my way around to her side of the bed, I sit next to her, turning my body to face her. "Emily, listen to me. You and me, we'll work out our shit. Will it be today or tomorrow? Maybe not. Who knows? All I know is I love you, and if I have to spend every night telling you how sorry I am for hurting you and leaving you when I did, then I'll do it. As long as I have you in my life, I'm complete."

CHAPTER
Thirty

Emily

I can feel the late February sun coming through the windows warming my face, but that isn't what wakes me. The warm arm wrapped around my waist, pulling me against him as his fingers slide under my waistband of my flannel pajama bottoms. That's what wakes me up. I've missed having him in bed with me.

Once everyone finally left Jeremy's mini welcome home party last night, I was wiped out and could barely keep my eyes open. I really can't wait for the doctor to finally remove this boot, so I can start rehabbing the ankle completely. It never required surgery, but given the results from the x-ray, they wanted to make sure it was aligned correctly before taking the chance of removing the boot. I've come to terms with the fact that foot won't be going inside a skate boot anytime soon, and I'm fine with it for now. I need to talk to Jeremy some more about my plans and see where he's at and where our future is together. There is still a lot to be said, even after our talk in bed last night.

During one of our talks on the phone, he said he understood how traumatized I was that night at the hospital and how we both said things we probably didn't mean. Although I knew I needed to figure out things in my life, I also knew that didn't mean I had to throw away my relationship with him. His simple text messages would always make me smile, even when I knew there wasn't much he could have done during my recovery, and I always had my girls by my side to make my days just a little better, too.

Six months ago, if someone had told me this was where my life would be now, I probably wouldn't have believed them. I would have never predicted in a million years that my parents would be getting divorced, selling the house and Daddy's company, and removing themselves from my life. Nor would I have believed that I'd gain a new family of seven, well, eight if you include Aspen, who shows me more love in one day than I have ever experienced in twenty-two years of my life. Sometimes, I need to pinch myself just to believe this is my reality and that I'm not in a dream anymore.

I'm removed from my thoughts when I hear Jeremy groan behind me. "Woman, shut those blinds. It's way too early to be getting up, especially when I don't have a morning skate today."

Smacking him on the arm, I say, "I would, but someone thought it would be funny to confine me to the bed, so he threw my walking boot across the room last night. If you would be so kind as to fetch it, I really have to pee."

Throwing back the covers, Jeremy pads over to the boot and brings it back to me. "Need any help?" He yawns through his question.

"Nah, I've become a pro at this," I say as I place the boot on and wobble to the bathroom, but not before turning up the heat on the thermostat in the hall. Looking out the front window, I notice a few inches of snow fell again last night. Shivering and wrapping my arms around my body, I feel a cold chill run up my spine as thoughts of the accident enter my mind again. Squeezing my eyes shut to ward off the memories, I feel unexpected hands come around my waist, and I startle.

"Jesus, Emily. It's me, babe," Jeremy says as he runs his hands over my arms, and I rub my face with my hands.

"I'm fine, really. It's just a flashback. We do have to talk today, though. Do you mind starting the coffee for me? I don't know what's in the fridge for food. Courtney usually gets whatever, but I'm trying not to eat any of it. My ba-dunka-dunk could shed a few inches."

"Babe, did you really just say the word 'ba-dunka-dunk'?" he questions as he moves about in the kitchen.

"Might I remind you that you did leave me with Dave to cover 'Emily Watch Third Shift' on certain days?" I playfully tease as I head to the bathroom.

When I come back into the kitchen, Jeremy already has the coffee brewing and is standing in front of the open fridge staring inside. He pulls a carton from the shelf as I sit at the kitchen table and watch. Aspen paws over to rest his head on my leg. The fridge door shuts, and Jeremy stands there perplexed.

"Babe, I don't even want to know, but this carton does say *EggBeaters* on it, so I'm going to assume there is some kind of egg in it. However, why is it liquid?" he asks as he heats up the skillet and begins cooking us something to eat.

Once he's finished making the healthier version of eggs and toast, he brings the coffee over to me and sits at the table. After a few sips of coffee and a couple of bites of toast, I feel as though I can tell him where I am with everything. Placing my mug gently onto the table, I stare up into his eyes. He leans back with his arm resting over the back of the chair while bringing his foot up to rest on his knee. "Tell me what you need to tell me, Emily," he says, resting his coffee mug on the table.

I take a deep breath before saying what I need to tell him. "After the accident and after you left, I wasn't in a good place. I couldn't process what had just happened. One minute I had the world in my hands. I was finally going to the Olympics. I was finally doing something for me, and I owed it all to you. You made me realize something you love was worth fighting for. That night on the ice in Boston, it finally hit me that I really did love skating. It took standing up to my parents to figure that out." Jeremy brings his chair closer to mine, reaching out to grab my hands in his. I continue my confession, "Then, in a flash it was all gone. I didn't have the Olympics. I didn't have skating, and my own parents left me once they saw I wasn't able to make them all the money and notoriety I used to. What hurt the most was that I didn't have you after that night either. It was *all* gone. I can't blame you for leaving. You had to do it, and I had to tell myself it was the right decision not to ask you to stay with me. It took a long time for me to see what I needed to do and where I wanted to go in life. I called Suzy one day, and I met with some of the board members at the Boston Skating Club last week. Once I finally get this boot off, I'll be one of the newest members of the children's skating program at the club. I'll be teaching a few days a week and will be able to provide private lessons once all the paperwork is in order." I look up at him to see if I can tell what he's thinking or feeling about everything I just told him.

"Babe, I'm so happy for you! I couldn't be more proud that you finally worked out everything, and you're going to be doing what you love. Being away from you made me realize how much all of this," he throws out his hand, pointing around the room before continuing, "means to me and how much I missed everyone. The NHL career, it's not what I want for my future. I love making my average salary with the Monarchs. I want to be with my family and friends. I don't need the big life to be happy. I may have back in college, but that all changed over time. It became a definite the minute you walked back into my life. We've spent more time apart than together, and once I get back to the Monarchs, I'm going to make sure I'm here for good. If that can't happen, then I'll find something else to do. All I know is I'm not leaving you ever again. I love you more than any career. It's you and me and Aspen for good now. Do you think you can handle that?" Jeremy asks as he starts to stand.

Holding back happy tears, I nod and tell him, "I think I can handle you."

Grabbing me out of my seat and into his arms, he begins walking toward the bedroom. He gives me a kiss on my cheek before his naughty side comes out to play. "Good, because I've got something that you can handle right now, and it's in desperate need of being inside you." He winks at me as he places me onto the bed.

I sigh at him as though I'm uninterested. "Oh, I suppose. Besides, Gigi's batteries are completely worn out."

"You 'suppose'? Dear God, I really have been gone way too long, especially if Gigi isn't fully charged. I need to fix this right now." He laughs as he strips off his boxers and takes off my clothes slowly until we are both naked. I watch as he tries to make up for the last six weeks. My heart is finally whole again, and I'm the happiest I've been in a long time.

Jeremy places kisses along my neck, and I'm instantly aroused. Gigi has superpowers, but nothing compares to actually having Jeremy work his magic. His hand slinks its way between my legs until his thumb circles my throbbing bud and two fingers push inside me. I gasp in pleasure as he sucks on my nipples, arousing all my desires. My hands clutch his shaggy hair, and I pull his mouth to mine. His hands are now feverishly running themselves over my waist and legs as I try to catch my breath in between kisses.

"Emily, I need to be inside you soon, or this is going to get real interesting."

Reaching my hand around his cock, I pull him toward my entrance. "Jeremy, if you don't stick your cock in me soon, I'm going to take over control of this situation."

"There's my little minx. Glad to see she came out to play this morning." He gives me a devilish grin before he pushes himself deep inside me. Whatever nervousness I felt last night was just tossed out the window. Jeremy slowly moves in and out as I lift my hips. I feel him throbbing inside me as we stare into each other's eyes. Feeling bold again, I reach down and begin pleasing myself as Jeremy watches with his cock still buried in me. "Babe, that's so hot," he says before he speeds up his pace. My finger continues to speed up as well, until I'm on the edge of coming.

"I'm close," I say as I look into his eyes and then with one last hard thrust, we're both coming and everything we thought we lost in six weeks has all come back to us in this moment.

Pulling his head back from my chest, he looks me in the eyes, saying, "I love you so much, Emily."

"I love you too, Jeremy." I smile back at him.

JEREMY

A few weeks have passed since I've returned home, and things with Emily have been wonderful. She and I are closer than ever before. However, due to some scheduling issues with the Monarchs games, we have to celebrate Emily's birthday at the end of March, instead of her actual birthday on St. Patrick's Day. Mom says it's fate that brought us together because how could two people actually be together and have holiday birthdays is just unheard of.

Emily has been able to remove the boot on her foot and is rehabbing it every day. The doctor says she might be able to put it in a skate boot by

June. She just isn't going to be landing any triples anytime soon. When the doctor told her that news, you'd think he'd just handed her the moon. She was absolutely ecstatic. It's funny how her feelings about skating changed once she realized the pressure of winning and competing was no longer on her shoulders.

She still can't drive a car, but that doesn't matter. Today, I'm taking her out for her belated birthday, and she has absolutely no idea what I have planned. We drive around the city until we arrive at our destination. Looking at me with a raised eyebrow, she asks, "Jeremy, what are we doing here?"

I smile as I hop out of the truck and head around to help her out since she still can't chance putting too much weight on her ankle.

Walking into the building, I make my way over to the front desk where a woman with three lip piercings and two arm-sleeved tattoos stops to talk to us. "Can I help you guys?" she asks.

"Yeah, I need to see about getting a tattoo today," I answer, turning to wink at Emily as her mouth hangs wide open in shock. The woman hands me some paperwork to fill out, and I hand it back to her after explaining what I want to have done.

"Jeremy, what are you doing? You know you don't have to do this," Emily says as if she is going to talk me out of this.

I face her and grab both of her hands in mine. "Babe, I told you. It's you and me, always. And, what kind of man can go around knowing his girlfriend has her crotch tattooed, and not have one himself?"

"It's your body, but what do I know?" She chuckles.

Almost two hours later, after sitting through the monotonous buzzing sound of the tattoo gun, my tattoo for Emily is complete. I stand to put on my shirt as Emily gently traces her fingers over the words sketched above my left pectoral for her to see whenever we're together. "Live your dreams. Follow your heart." She'll always know it's for her, and she knows I'm permanent now.

Little does she know I've got another surprise up my sleeve, but this one the whole family can enjoy together. After we leave the tattoo parlor, we meet everyone for lunch at a small Irish pub just outside of Tewksbury. Everyone is seated at the round booth at the back of the restaurant already waiting for us.

Before she can push herself up off the seat, Emily rushes over to give Sue a hug. Dave won't let her go out as much as she wants to now, and it's been a few weeks since we've seen her. Her latest doctor appointment showed she might be on bed rest earlier than she expected. That news made my gift to Emily all the trickier, but Dave and Sue were totally behind it either way.

Emily gives Josh and Courtney hugs as well before sitting next to my parents. We haven't seen Josh in a while. He says he's been working a lot; however, there's something different about him when I talk to him on the phone. It's almost as if the night of the accident something changed in him. Mom even asked me if I noticed a few weeks ago. If she couldn't get any information out of him, I sure as hell wasn't going to succeed.

After we order our meals and drinks, everyone begins giving Emily her birthday gifts. When the gifts are piled onto the table in front of her, it looks as if she is going to cry. I still tend to forget this whole *family* situation is relatively new to her and she never had the amount of love and support until recently.

In the beginning, I thought for sure Mom and Dad's gift was going to upstage mine. When Emily opens the jewelry box and sees a silver charm bracelet, she is lost for words. It has a hockey and figure skater pendant and two round sterling silver discs with our initials and birthstones. Pulling it from the box, she hands it to me as she reaches her arm out for me to put it on immediately.

When she thinks she is done opening gifts, she begins squishing the wrapping paper together. The whole table is silent as they wait for me to give her the last gift. Removing the envelope from my back pocket, I slide it over in front of her on the table. Eyeing me suspiciously, she slowly opens it, pulling out the documents. Her hand flies up to cover her mouth before she turns to me. "Jeremy, this is too much, really, and what about Sue and Dave? The baby is due any week."

Sue leans over toward Emily. "Sweetie, we're okay with it. Jeremy already asked before he made the decision, and this little girl isn't coming anytime soon. You'll be good to go. You deserve it after everything you've been through."

Mom wraps her arm around Emily's shoulder. "We've all pitched in to go down. It's been a very long time since we've gone anywhere as a family, and to be honest, I've always wanted to visit Savannah."

Emily is still thumbing through the papers. "Jeremy, what about the Calder Cup? You can't leave during the end of the season."

Grabbing her hand to stop her from fidgeting nervously, I reply, "Emily, it's all set. It's all worked around the hockey games and practice. It's time to have fun and relax in life. We're finally back to a good place, and I want all of us to enjoy this time together. What do you say?" When I see her glance up at Mom and then smile back at me, I know I've sold her.

Emily thumbs through the papers one last time while biting her nail. Placing the documents onto the table, she stands to walk over to my side. "I guess we're going to Savannah in May." Everyone starts clapping and sighing in relief as I stand to give Emily a kiss.

"Get a room," Dave groans.

"Happy Birthday, Emily!" we all chant.

She runs her hands over my chin. "The trip and the tattoo are an added bonus. I was happy just having you in my life. Thank you."

CHAPTER
thirty-one

Emily

April blows by in a flash of the eye. I have just about finished my rehab for my arm and my ankle. The doctors have said I can basically continue my daily therapy at home. I'm also happy to be able to drive again. The initial movement has been awkward, but they say it will be a strange feeling until the muscles and tendons strengthen back to normal. I miss my Audi, but I'm the new owner of a fabulous white Ford Escape with four-wheel drive.

Jeremy's Monarchs season has finished, and the Calder Cup Playoffs are set to begin after we return from Savannah. The team led in points in the Eastern Conference this year, and they are the favorite to win the East. Jeremy alone had a great season, scoring fifteen points and ten penalty minutes. I still don't know what half of these terms mean, but between Travis and him, I should learn quickly during the Calder Cup. Jeremy's contract will be up at the end of the postseason, and he hasn't said if he'll be returning to the Monarchs. He did say he's keeping his options open in case another opportunity arises.

After everything Jeremy and I have gone through since we started dating last summer, we are surprisingly in a very good place now. The final two therapy sessions I attended for my post-accident depression, Jeremy came with me. The doctor was extremely optimistic about Jeremy's interest in helping me channel my thoughts to a better place and ensuring that the two of us would continue to talk through our issues.

Everything is moving in a better direction. I still can't put on my skates, but I have been able to assist on the coaching staff at Boston Skating Club, allowing me to earn my own paycheck each week. I haven't heard from my parents, not that I'm upset over that. However, one of Daddy's lawyers did call me before the sale of the company went through. I guess there was some misappropriation of funds between my father and my old sponsors, and I was owed nearly two hundred thousand dollars in past wages. *Well, thank you, Daddy!*

Jeremy has rented a beach cottage just outside of Savannah for the long weekend. As all of us pack into the SUV to drive there, I can't help but roll down the windows and let the warm breeze flow around me. The winter in Boston was absolutely brutal this year. Seventy degrees is delightful and refreshing.

As we approach the island, colorful houses appear at every corner. We finally find our cottage and pull into the driveway. It is a small two-level house with crazy knickknacks all over the outside, and for some strange reason, all the cottages here have a shower outside of the house. It's cute and quirky. Jeremy carries my bags through the house after we find the hide-a-key. Courtney is busy taking pictures of everything outside, and Josh is standing in the front screen porch on his phone talking to someone.

Grace comes in with the few bags of drinks and food we picked up on the way in. Travis helps put everything away with her as I admire the interior design. There are white walls, white furniture, and colorful beach décor everywhere I look. A large wooden spiral staircase leads up to a second floor where Jeremy has gone.

I see him unpacking as I make it to the top of the stairs. When he sees me, he throws everything that is in his hands into the dresser. As he makes his way over to me, he grabs me and tosses me onto the bed before leaning over me to kiss my neck and massage my breasts. I laugh at his boldness since his family is downstairs, and the room does not have a door.

"So, what do you want to do tonight?" he asks as he pulls one of my breasts from my bra cup.

"Trying to think and stay focused while you do that is almost impossible." I laugh as I roll my head back in pleasure before releasing a moan. Slapping my hand over my mouth, I remember we are not alone. "Shit, do you think your parents heard that?"

"Em. I don't think they care," Jeremy says as he slowly starts pulling off my capris.

"Yeah, but I do. I can't have them thinking we're having sex up here." I am unsuccessful in my persuasion, considering Jeremy has now removed my pants completely. I throw my hand over my head in embarrassment. "We are so going to get caught. I know it." There go my lace panties onto the floor. "Jeremy!" I try to yell just above a whisper. Jeremy stands taking off his shirt and removing his shorts. I make a move to retrieve my underwear, but he's having none of it. Still standing over me, he moves quickly and has me pinned in an instant. He pulls my shirt over my head and removes my bra in the process. "This is *so* not a good idea," I say as my fingers trace the words etched over his heart.

"Babe, there are a lot of things that are not a good idea, but having sex with you is not one of them."

He slowly enters me, since he already knows how ready I am after his breast massage. "Hmmm, Jeremy, I don't know if I can be quiet."

"When you're close, tell me."

"Jeremy," I say, tapping him on the shoulder.

"Already, Em? Damn, I'm good! Either that or my dick has super powers today." He thrusts harder and faster, and the minute he sees my breathing go ragged, his lips crush mine, and I scream into his mouth, muffling the intense orgasm shooting through my body. Jeremy isn't far behind once my orgasm hits. Lying there after our afternoon quickie in true Jeremy fashion, he asks, "So, did you think about what you want to do tonight? It appears you've already done me."

He's impossible, and yet I can't help but laugh at him because I wouldn't want him any other way.

JEREMY

Last night Emily decided we would have dinner and drinks at a rooftop lounge in downtown historic Savannah. All six of us sat on cushioned chairs and watched as the sun set along the river. People walked along the waterfront below us, some hand in hand and others with children in tow. The trolley bell dinged as it rolled past all the buildings. I was enjoying my first SweetWater beer while Emily was sipping on her Sangria. When I looked at her, she was grinning from ear to ear as Courtney told her something amusing. Josh chatted with Dad about work, and his plans for retirement in the next year. That was the other reason for this trip. Mom and Dad are looking for potential places to come visit during the winter months. Mom has admitted they could never leave for good. She said she'd miss all six of her babies. I love my mom to death, and the idea that she includes Sue, Dave, and Emily in her "babies" group makes my decision all the more gratifying. Everyone was happy around me, and I knew in my heart I was doing the right thing.

Today, the early morning sun is shining over the water, and it's warm enough to walk the beach barefoot and wear summer clothes. Mom and Dad are relaxing on the porch at the cottage. Josh and Courtney decide to head out and do some sea kayaking with a local tour guide, and Emily and I decide to walk along the beach. She wants to search for those baby turtle nests she saw in a movie once. I have no idea what movie she is talking about, but she muttered something about it being filmed just down the road from here.

As I'm walking barefoot with Emily along the soft, almost white, sandy beaches, she notices a wooden swinging seat. The sand crunches under her feet as she heads away from me to sit. Grabbing my phone, I snap a photo of her with the tall lighthouse behind her. Laughing, she kicks her feet out in front of her. There's no more pain in her life. She's knocked down every barrier, and she's finally able to just live her life as she wants.

I walk over to sit next to her on the swing and hear the wood creak under my added weight. This swing has seen its fair share of hurricanes and high tides. I lean back to rest one arm behind Emily on the swing as she watches the shrimp boats float on the water. A few dolphins poke their noses out of the water in the distance, and she gasps with excitement.

"Oh my gosh, Jeremy! Did you see the dolphins? We absolutely have to do one of those tours tomorrow."

"We'll see, babe," I tell her without trying to make her think it's not going to happen.

"What do you mean 'we'll see'? Why can't we go? Did you have something else planned?" She looks me in the eyes, hoping to find some kind of answer. I tell myself it's now or never. Stop being a wimp and just do it.

Rising from the swing, feeling my toes sink in the sand, I turn toward Emily and begin the speech of a lifetime. I lower myself onto one knee in front of her. I grab the box from my pocket, the box she almost caught me with until I made sure to distract her with an afternoon sex session. The minute I hold the box out in front of me, Emily's hands cover her mouth. I see my parents standing off behind her. My father has his arm over my mom's shoulders, and I can tell she is crying. Josh and Courtney are off to the side where Emily can't see them. Per my request, their kayak tour *conveniently* took them in this direction. Courtney has her camera out capturing the moment for eternity.

Gazing up into her big, beautiful blue eyes, I take a deep breath and say, "Emily, the day we met something changed in me. When I accidentally ran into a blonde figure skater and knocked her on her ass, she had spunk and a hardness about her that I couldn't resist. You may have been the one on the floor, but you knocked me off my feet that day. Then, you stole my heart a little bit more in high school with your shyness and gentle ability to work your way into my soul. Your laughter and spirit always lingered within my mind. It wasn't until you completely came back into my life that I realized I could never let you go. You had to be mine, forever. You made me realize life was more than just hockey. Life was about dreaming large and setting out to conquer your fears. Every day you made me want to dream bigger. Until one day I realized you, Emily Beth Cameron, were my biggest dream of all. Once I reached you, I knew I couldn't go any higher. You are my life, my love, my happiness every single day. I will not spend another day of my life without you by my side fighting for us." Tears roll down the sides of her cheeks as I open the black box with the carat and a half cushion cut diamond ring I bought last year. Pulling it from the box, I hold her hand out to me. "Emily Beth Cameron, will you make me the happiest man alive and say yes to becoming my wife? Will you marry me?"

CHAPTER
Thirty-Two

Emily

Yesterday, while sitting on that swing, I never expected Jeremy to propose. A million thoughts ran through my mind. Was this too fast? Was I ready? What happens if he gets sent away again to another team? Can I handle the pressure of a long-distance relationship?

For every negative, there was a positive. We loved each other, and I loved his family as much as they loved me. We had seen each other at our worst, and yet, still made each other happy. He's been the only one to see who I really am and made me fight for what I really wanted out of life.

I heard noises behind me on the beach and turned to see the Page family in the distance watching. They all knew he was planning to propose. Apparently, it was the reason for the trip in the first place. I realized I hadn't answered Jeremy at that point. He was still kneeling in front of me in the sand as waves crashed and seagulls squawked in the distance. I stood and pulled him up with me. The look on his face was that of absolute fear. I leaned in and softly explained my answer into his ear.

Here I am just over a full day later, staring out the window, wondering if I made the right decision. A part of me keeps telling myself I'm crazy for doing this, but as Travis walks in, I know in my heart this is right. It will all work out in life.

Looking at me with tenderness in his eyes, he asks, "Are you ready?"

"As ready as I'll ever be," I say, grabbing my belongings on the table before walking through the door Travis is holding open for me.

Turning the corner, I see the arched wooden beams and the scrolled bronze chandeliers along the ceiling. My eyes lower to see Jeremy at the end of the aisle, dressed in a tan suit adjusting the cufflinks on his shirt. Courtney is taking pictures, Josh has his phone pointed in my direction, and Grace is smiling as she wipes tears from the corners of her eyes.

Travis grabs my elbow, and we begin walking down the aisle closer to Jeremy. Once I'm in front of him, I turn to hand Grace my flowers before turning back to take Jeremy's hands in mine. I can tell he's nervous as his finger starts twisting my ring on my finger. He leans down to my ear, saying, "There isn't a single doubt in my mind that this is right. You're the most beautiful woman, and I'm the luckiest man in the world today, because today, you become my wife. I love you, babe. Always and forever."

I smile as I wipe a stray tear from the corner of my eye. Courtney stops taking pictures to come up behind me and adjust the train on my simple wedding dress. Today, I become Mrs. Emily Page. I'll have a husband, mother, father, sister, and brother added to my family. I know eloping is the right decision. Everyone I could ever want at my wedding is here now, including Sue and Dave, who are watching from Josh's phone at home.

When I whispered to Jeremy yesterday on the beach the simple word "yes," he lifted me and spun me around before slipping the ring onto my finger. Once I was safely back on the ground, he said he had one more request to make this weekend complete, and I'd do anything to make him happy.

He asked, "Marry me tomorrow at sunset." My mouth dropped to the ground as he waited for an answer. Before I could spew a million questions as to how that was even possible, he said everything was already taken care of. His parents had taken care of booking the tiny island chapel and the flowers. All I needed to do was go to the courthouse, find a dress, and show up.

I found my dress this morning at a little boutique in Savannah, and I showed up, with just enough time for Courtney to handle my hair and makeup and Grace to get the flowers. She always had a strange way of knowing things. I can't remember ever telling her what Jeremy had given me for flowers on our first date, but when she walked into the bridal suite earlier with the same flowers, I was speechless.

I stand here now as Jeremy and I exchange the rings he picked out himself, repeating the vows the minister is reading to us with our eyes locked. Engraved on the inside of my ring is "Always Fighting for You."

Once the minister gives Jeremy permission to kiss me, our lips meet for the first time as husband and wife, I know my dreams are no longer my escape from reality. My dreams are my reality. Breaking our kiss, Jeremy's forehead leans on mine. Since we're not having a reception, Courtney insists we have a first dance. Only one song seems fitting as we dance in the middle of the chapel lost in our own world. Cascada's voice echoes through the tiny chapel as I sway within Jeremy's arms.

When the song ends, he lifts me in his arms as I wrap my arms around his neck, giving him a soft kiss on his lips. He places me back on the ground, taking my hands in his. "You ready to get out of here, Mrs. Page?"

I look back into his eyes with a heart full of love and happiness. "I've never been more ready, Mr. Page."

EPILOGUE

JEREMY

Christmas

2015

Everyone is sitting around the living room after Christmas dinner at our house. The fireplace is crackling and a fresh dusting of snow is falling outside. Emily and I took on the holiday dinners once we bought our own house just after we were married. She used the money from her father's company sale to pay for the small cape-style home about two miles from my parents' house. She said she couldn't think of a better way to use the money. We had saved up enough from our skating careers to live comfortably for a while. We owe a lot of that luxury to our parents who never charged us rent a day in our lives.

Dave and Sue moved into our old garage apartment, and Mom and Dad welcomed them with open arms. Mom is able to baby-sit Brittany while Dave and Sue work in the afternoons. I have no doubt that little ragamuffin with curly brown hair, hitting Aspen over the head with a red Solo cup, belongs to Dave. Sue has her hands full with not only her, but also Dave. It's as though she has two kids. Mom hounds them on a regular basis about getting married, and he usually has a panic attack. Someday, he'll finally see his full potential as a dad and a husband. Today is just not that day.

Courtney is currently home from her internship abroad. She finally made it to Paris and spent six months there working on becoming a freelance photographer. Mom has missed her around the house this past semester. With Court being away, her little sous-chef wasn't around to help create new dishes with her. Emily and Sue tried to fill that void the best they could, but both of them didn't have a lot of extra time. Now that Courtney is home, she's testing out the photography scene in Boston and working full-time at the bakery. She's learned a few new culinary skills with the French cuisine.

Mom enjoys days like these when the entire family is together, and she can sit back and relax with all of us. She's relaxed now from too much turkey and presents that she's passed out on the other end of the sofa. Not even Brittany's high-pitched squeals can wake her.

Josh is sitting at the dining room table talking to Dad about some kind of legal documents he had to file the other day for the State Police. I watch as he glances up past me toward the girls. A ghost of a smile forms at the corners of his mouth. He's finally found happiness after years of regret. It might have taken him a while, but it's right there in front of him. It's as if the night of the accident something finally clicked, and he was able to let go of the past.

Mom and Dad have retired completely. They spend about a month or two in Savannah during the winter and summer months. Dad's retirement package from the chemical company allowed them to buy a small one-bedroom condo on the ocean. They like it, but they miss all of us when they are gone.

Emily stops talking to the girls and catches me staring at her from the sofa. She slowly gets up and walks over to me. She's still as beautiful as the day I married her; in fact, she's become more so since then. Slowly sitting next to me, I reach my arms out as she hands me my little boy who's fast asleep dressed in his baby Santa suit. Ben is a little over three months old and missed being born on the day I asked Emily out by a few days.

She runs her fingers over his fuzzy hair as she looks up at me. "Best Christmas ever?"

"Well, considering last Christmas you told me you were pregnant, and this Christmas you've given me this little guy, I'd have to say yes." I lean down to kiss her on the lips as she smiles softly. I pull away, trying not to wake Ben. "I'm going to put him in the crib," I say lightly as I stand with Ben on my shoulder as his little arms dangle against me.

I turn on the baby monitor next to the crib. Watching my son take little breaths as he sleeps, I can't help but think my decision to leave the AHL after the Calder Cup win last year was the best decision I ever made. I never stopped playing hockey. I just stopped playing competitively. Turns out the Monarchs had some connections with a local youth hockey league and they were in search of a Manager, and given the Monarchs were already working closely with them, I was a shoo-in for the position. I love teaching the kids all the skills I learned growing up, and the best part of it all is I still get to come home every night to my wife and son.

Emily was finally able to lace up her skates again after many months of rehab. She coached the girls at the Boston Skating Club for about six months. Once she found out she was pregnant, she knew she had to make another huge decision in her life. She decided to step away from the lengthy drive to the Boston club. With a number of fantastic references, she managed to find coaching positions at the Forum.

Once her parents' divorce was finalized, Emily never heard from them again. Her father was pulled into some legal battle over the sale of his company. Emily's mother is apparently now living in Denver with Emily's uncle from what she's heard through the rumor mill on the news.

I hear her step into the room quietly and feel her arms wrap around my waist behind me. I pull her so she's in front of me as we watch Ben in his crib. Sliding her blonde hair to the side, I place gentle kisses along her neck, saying, "Babe, how is it possible to love you more every day I'm with you?"

"Probably, the same way my two favorite men fill my heart with more joy and love than I ever thought possible," she says as she turns to look into my eyes.

"Em? Are you living your dreams?" I whisper into her ear as I hold her tighter.

Nodding back with a warm smile and placing her hand over my heart, she replies, "The same way you're following your heart."

Walking back toward our family and friends, we know we were meant to run into each other that fateful day at the rink as kids. Had we never met, neither of us would have broken down the barriers in our lives in order to find what our one true love was.

Each other.

The End

CONTINUE READING
FOR A SCENE FROM

HIDDEN
Barriers

THE NEXT INSTALLMENT OF
THE *Barriers* SERIES

PROLOGUE

JOſH

January 2014

The pained sound in my brother Jeremy's voice as I told him about Emily's car accident earlier, I never want to hear again. I run through the halls of Mass General Hospital trying to remain calm as I attempt to find out any information about Sue and Emily. It's not easy when you have your family in the waiting room of the ER thinking the worst, and nobody will give you an ounce of help, even when you are in uniform.

My feet can't keep up with my racing heart until I walk into one of the two hospital rooms I need to be in. My heart breaks again as she's lying there in Dave's arms; their hands are clutching her rounded belly. The life I should have had. The family and future I threw away when I thought I was doing the right thing for her.

Sue is happy with Dave, and the baby will bond them forever. She'll never be mine again. *Why is it so fuckin' real now?* I've lost count of the number of times I've asked that question since they got together months ago.

Turning away from the room, I wander the halls, trying to keep myself from losing it. I slam my hands against the swinging door toward the waiting room, except it stops midway, and I hear a woman's voice on the other side spouting profanities left and right.

I push the door ajar, slower this time, peeking around to see a petite brunette staring back at me. She's holding her shoulder as her eyes shoot daggers up at me. When my eyes meet hers, I extend my hand, offering her some help getting up. She swats it away and rises to her feet on her own.

Her shoulder is in a sling, finger in a brace, and her nose is black and blue. This should raise red flags for me. I'm a cop. I should see these things as questionable, especially for a girl. I still haven't said a word to her. I'm mesmerized by the beauty behind her injuries. My gaze drops from her face, and I slowly take all of her in.

Her clothes pique my curiosity. She's wearing every color imaginable, pink and black stripped knee-high socks over fishnet stockings and boy shorts under what can only be described as an adult version of a Girl Scout mini-dress. What is up with this outfit? Does she not realize it's winter outside? Although it is kinda hot in a freaky way.

She speaks before I do, "Trying to lengthen my hospital stay? I'd really like to get the hell out of here, and not see what other injuries I can add to my list tonight." *Fuckin' A. Who is this girl?* Better yet, how does a girl with more attitude than size end up with injuries like this?

Giving me an annoyed look, she tries to push by me with her one good arm. "Do you mind? I can't get by if you're blocking the exit. I've got places to go, so move it or lose it."

As I move off to the side and let her pass, my head turns to watch her walk toward another section of the hospital. Catching the back of her shirt, I notice the writing. *Cosmonaughties.*

What the hell is a Cosmonaughtie? And why the hell am I still speechless?

Sam

I've been running away from my past for nearly three years. I'm not saying I had it bad growing up, quite the opposite, actually. I grew up in Connecticut about an hour from New York City. You can call my family upper middle class, but that's not what I've been running from. No, I'm the one who made a piss-poor decision when I chose the last guy I dated.

I've finally started over. I've found my footing here in Massachusetts. I have a group of roommates who I call my sisters. They will fight for me and back me up no matter what. They don't go by the names "Decker in the Jaw", "Juicy Lucy", and "Rose from the Dead" just for fun. Those are their fighting names. Their alter egos, so to speak.

I go by the name "Sammy Sweet Cheeks." You'll understand later.

Why is it when the phone call came in a few days ago, letting me know my one fear in the world could threaten to find me again, did I wonder if my girls would be enough to keep me safe. Fight all they want, this was a different beast to go up against.

He tried to kill me once. He most certainly will try again. This has been my fear for so long.

Being in the hospital brings back some painful memories. Memories I don't care to have cross my mind anymore. Memories of what he did to me on that dreadful night so many years ago. Running my hands over my neck, I recall gasping for what almost was my last breath as he choked the life out of me with just one hand.

You stupid fuckin' bitch! I hope you enjoy the feeling of my hands wrapped around your neck because it's the last thing you're ever going to feel as I kill you slowly.

Fingers snapping in front of my face bring me out of my horrid memory. My eyes shoot open, and I gasp in horror and suddenly feel nauseous. I quickly take in my surroundings, noticing Kim standing next to me. Stretching out to run her hands over my shoulders, she says, "Hey, are you all right? You look a little peaked. Another flashback?"

"Yeah, I think it's just because I'm here, and you know how much I hate hospitals," I answer, even though I can't tell her that my flashbacks have become more frequent since I found out about *his* recent parole.

All my roommates know about my past. After I moved into the C-Naughtie house two years ago, I had one night where my nightmare had me screaming bloody murder, and all my girls had to help calm me down. A few shots of Jack Daniels and I spilled all my dark secrets. The one night *he* sent me to the hospital with barely a pulse and an even longer list of broken bones and a shattered life.

Forcing myself to the here and now, I convince Kim that I'm fine and ready to just get the hell out of there. As we're walking toward the exit, I realize I left my messenger bag in the ER room. "Shit, I forgot my bag in the exam room. I'll be right back."

Kim sighs and looks at her phone before turning back to me. "Hurry your ass up. We've missed half of the after party because of your daredevil move tonight."

"I'll be five minutes. Keep your panties on."

"I can't make any promises."

I walk back to the room I was admitted to for my separated shoulder and jammed finger. I laugh to myself when I think about what happened earlier. The doctors didn't believe me when I told them how I really got my injuries. Apparently being five-feet-four and skinny as a rail doesn't allow people to believe I have the ability to bout with the rest of them. *That's right, I said bout.* Once I handed them my trading card as proof, I silenced them immediately. *Yeah, assholes.* I'm a mother fuckin' roller derby girl, and I'll kick your ass any day of the week.

What's even better is when people ask me how I support myself on that salary, and I tell them I do it for free. That's when I really throw them for a loop and tell them I'm the manager of a wine bar, and roller derby is just something I do for fun. It's an added bonus that I get to let out pent-up anger against other girls and get away with it.

The looks I get never cease to amaze me. Actually, all of us derby girls are the same. Derby is our passion. We practice some weekend mornings and weekday evenings. The actual season only consists of five bouts. All of us have careers outside of the roller derby. Kim is a dispatcher for a police department. Rose is a college English professor, and Lucy is a cosmetologist. She comes in handy when we need our bruises and black eyes covered. Through thick and thin we are family, bruises and all.

Making my way quickly down the hall after grabbing my bag, I check my phone to see who won tonight's bout that I had to leave. Not paying attention to where I am walking, I slam right into a hard wall of muscle. Pain shoots up my already bad arm, and I wince as my bag drops to the ground. His hands come up and grab my elbow, and my eyes shoot up to his. Him again.

"Hey," he says as he picks up my bag from the floor, wrapping it over my shoulder again. "We really have to stop meeting like this."

I finally take in all of him. It's hard not to considering how close we are. How did I miss that he was in uniform before? Clearly, I had an aching to be arrested or handcuffed. Either way, I wouldn't have minded at all. This officer is seriously hot. It's too bad I'm not in the market for picking up men anymore. I don't mean I'm into picking up women either. After my last relationship, I vowed I'd never be that victim again. Someday I may feel differently, but the memories are still too vivid in my mind. Maybe officers don't beat the shit out of their girlfriends. Guess, I'll never know.

He extends his hand out to me. "Josh Page, and you are?"

"Just leaving. Adios!" I say as I sway past him, waving my hand in the air without turning around.

"Hey! What's a Cosmonaughtie?" I hear him ask from behind me, stopping me from taking another step.

Turning around to face him again, I place my hand on my hip. "You've never heard of us? Seriously?"

"Obviously not. That's why I'm curious, because it's snowing like crazy out, and you're wearing that outfit so I had to ask."

Reaching into my bag, I pull out my trading card and derby flyer as I walk over to him. I hand them to him before saying, "You wanna know what a Cosmonaughtie is? You're gonna have to come see for yourself. Don't say I didn't warn you." I wink before turning to head back to Kim, who's hopefully still waiting for me.

"See you later, Sweet Cheeks!" I hear him say just loud enough for me to hear behind me.

Still walking away from him, never looking back I say, "Catch you later, Officer Page."

SONGS THAT INSPIRED
FROZEN *Barriers*

Love Theme (From Romeo and Juliet) - André Rieu

Just a Girl - No Doubt

I Won't Give Up - Jason Mraz

Just a Kiss - Lady Antebellum

Sail - Awolnation

You Found Me - The Fray

Eavesdrop- The Civil Wars

Promiscuous- Nelly Furtado, Timbaland

House of the Rising Sun- The White Buffalo with The Forest Rangers

I Gotta Feeling - The Black Eyed Peas

Falling Slowly - Glen Hansard, Marketa Irglova

Lonely No More - Rob Thomas

Since U Been Gone- Kelly Clarkson

Inside of You - Infant Sorrow

Red Light Special- TLC

Breath of Life- Florence + The Machine

Bellas Finals: Pitch Perfect Soundtrack - The Barden Bellas

Put the Gun Down- ZZ Ward

Paris (Ooh La La)- Grace Potter & the Nocturnals

A Thousand Years- Christina Perri

Whistle- Flo Rida

All of Me- John Legend

Girl on Fire-Inferno Version - Alicia Keys, Nicki Minaj

Wait for Me- Kings of Leon

I Touch Myself- Divinyls

Peace- O.A.R.

Sara Shirley

Stay - Sara Bareilles

I Never Told You- Colbie Caillat

Arms - Christina Perri

Everytime We Touch-Yanou's Candlelight Mix- Cascada

Shakin' hands-Nickelback

Cruise-Florida Georgia Line

Black Sheep-Gin Wigmore

Hands Down-Dashboard Confessional

ABOUT THE AUTHOR

Sara Shirley

A romance novel addict finds herself staying up well past her bedtime to see how the next story is going to end. Sara spends her days living on a vineyard in wine country with her husband and cat. Her family hailed from Italy where her ancestors lived in the mountains Rocca di Cambio. A former Broadway star and champion skier whose career was cut short because of her passion for being a wine sommelier. It was on her way west where she met her husband, the President of a very influential MC in California. You can find her riding off through the vineyards on the back of a Harley almost every night.

Her passion for books has been viewed as borderline obsessive. But, when all you have is time and a bottle of wine awaiting you as the sun sets off the veranda, writing became second nature.

In Vino Veritas

ACKNOWLEDGMENTS

Ok. I'm keeping this short and sweet.

Frozen Barriers would have never happened if it wasn't for my husband. RP you told me to write my own story. You created a monster for two months of my life. In the end I hope I've made you proud that I finally put the words to paper. It wasn't easy and I know we sacrificed even more time away from each other through it all. Just because I had the earbuds in never meant I didn't know you were there.

To my family, who I never once told I was writing this story. Here it is. I'm going to run and hide now.

Sue & Dave - yeah....you guys helped provide so much added material to this story. Here's to another summer of late nights and fun filled days!

To all my girls who helped me day in and day out beta reading, proofing, editing,   pimping, making teasers (Ellen), and kicking my ass when something didn't work and you wanted more.

Kristina Amit, Stacia Newbill, Tracey Murphy, Antoinette Candela - You girls are the best! Thank you for all your help. From early morning Facebook chats to late night sessions, you were always there for me. Without all of your help I never would have been pushed to finish that next chapter. Thank you for my daily smiles.

Tracey- For adding to my Nick Bateman pic folder everyday. He was such a great face (& body) to put to Jeremy. I'm going to miss not looking at him while writing the next book. I'm still going to take his shirts every day, regardless.

Paige- What can I say? You took my story and rolled with it for two weeks straight. You tweaked and nixed where it was needed and I cannot thank you enough for all your dedication. I can't wait to team up again for Hidden Barriers.

To those who know my real identity, thank you for all the support. For those who don't and to all the new friends and fans that Jeremy and Emily will reach out to once it's released- I hope you enjoy their story as much as I enjoyed telling it.

So, until I write again don't forget to drop me a note on Facebook. I'm always willing to chat with you.

Made in the USA
Middletown, DE
04 April 2015